# "YOU SUFFER ROMANTIC DELUSIONS ABOUT ME, EDEN.
## I assure you, I am not the angel I was named after."

His gaze roamed over her ribbon-bound hair to the renegade wisps curling softly in the hollow of her throat and trailing across her breasts. His lashes fanned lower. He didn't want her to see his long-constrained hunger, the primal need that would have had him drag her into his arms and feast upon that delectable bounty.

"You're only saying that," she said softly. "You want me to think less of you."

Her insight was unnerving, almost as unnerving as the realization that the child who'd once bathed his wounds had grown into a woman who could see clear to the bottom of his soul.

But Michael had never cowered before a worthy opponent, and he wasn't about to start now. He stepped closer. Then closer still. He halted only when his thighs were bare inches from her skirts, when his shoulders towered above hers and she was forced to crane her neck back to meet his gaze.

"I'm not afraid of you, Michael."

"You should be, Eden," he said huskily. "Very, very afraid . . ."

## Other **AVON ROMANCES**

ALWAYS AND FOREVER *by Beverly Jenkins*
MUCH ADO ABOUT LOVE *by Malia Martin*
MUSTANG ANNIE *by Rachelle Morgan*
NEVER KISS A DUKE *by Eileen Putman*
NEVER A LADY *by Marlene Suson*
WITH THIS RING: MEET ME AT MIDNIGHT
*by Suzanne Enoch*
WOLF SHADOW'S PROMISE *by Karen Kay*

*Coming Soon*

HIS FORBIDDEN TOUCH *by Linda O'Brien*
A WANTED WOMAN *by Rebecca Wade*

*And Don't Miss These*
**ROMANTIC TREASURES**
*from Avon Books*

AFTER THE KISS *by Karen Kay*
THE HUSBAND LIST *by Victoria Alexander*
NO MARRIAGE OF CONVENIENCE *by Elizabeth Boyle*

# Adrienne deWolfe

# Always Her Hero

**AVON BOOKS**
*An Imprint of HarperCollins Publishers*

This is a work of fiction. Names, characters, places, and incidents are products of the author's imagination or are used fictitiously and are not to be construed as real. Any resemblance to actual events, locales, organizations, or persons, living or dead, is entirely coincidental.

AVON BOOKS
*An Imprint of* HarperCollins*Publishers*
10 East 53rd Street
New York, New York 10022-5299

Copyright © 2000 by Adrienne M. Sobolak
ISBN: 0-380-80528-6
www.avonromance.com

First Avon Books paperback printing: October 2000

Avon Trademark Reg. U.S. Pat. Off. and in Other Countries, Marca Registrada, Hecho en U.S.A.
HarperCollins® is a trademark of HarperCollins Publishers Inc.

Printed in the U.S.A.

WCD   10   9   8   7   6   5   4   3   2   1

*To Lori*
*Happy Millennium Birthday, Sis!*

# Acknowledgments

Special thanks to Myrna Ward, RN, without whom I'd still be puzzling over some ponderous medical tome instead of completing this book.

And, as always, my undying gratitude to Paula d'Etcheverry for her keen eye and inspired suggestions.

# Prologue

*Autumn 1878*
*The Pine Mountains, Tennessee*

There were many ways to die.

Some men writhed in torment, fighting the inevitable with their last, rattling breath. Others succumbed quickly, cleanly, never knowing whose bullet had killed them.

But for Michael Jones, death was a lingering numbness, a curse that had dulled all pain, all pleasure, all *interest* he used to take in life.

"You sure showed Hoss, didn't ya, Mick?" crowed the toothless bootlicker dogging his heels as he slammed out the swinging doors of the Jade Rose Saloon. "You sure showed him you weren't no lily-livered preacher's brat."

Stalking away from the wreckage and the wagering his brawl had caused, Michael didn't bother to respond. What he'd shown Hoss tonight, actually, was that he was a mean-tempered sonofabitch with two ham-sized fists and a chip the size of Blue Thunder Mountain on his shoulder. But he didn't expect this stranger, this sewer weasel who scavenged off the other riffraff of Whiskey Bend, to understand. It didn't take courage to bring a man to his knees. It only took brute force.

"I never did see a chair get smashed up in so many pieces," the weasel yapped, scrambling to keep pace through the mud and garbage as they circled behind the saloon and entered the alley. "Did you hear the way them soiled doves was cooing when you knocked Hoss on his ass? I bet you'll get all yer humpin' fer free from now on at the Rose. Womenfolk like rough guys, don't they, Mick?"

Michael touched his tongue to his smashed lip. It hurt like hell. So did his ribs, thanks to Hoss's head butting. His right eye was swelling shut, and his knuckles were raw and bloody. Any woman who'd want him in this condition was either desperate or scared witless. Neither kind appealed to him.

Still, it had felt good, damned good, swinging his fists at the migrant logger who'd recognized him and had threatened to carry the tale back to Blue Thunder Valley. Michael wished he could say he was ashamed of busting the chops of a drunkard with a grade-school education. But ever since God had forced him to bury Gabriel two years ago, he'd welcomed opportunities to break the Commandments. What better reason for him to ride secretly to Whiskey Bend every chance he got? He couldn't disgrace himself openly without losing the respect of the kid sister who so misguidedly looked up to him, but he could stain his soul black enough to disgust the King of Heaven.

Pissing off God: That was the one pastime capable of sparking zeal yet in Michael. That, and snatching souls from the Angel of Death.

Thunder growled, low and ominous. Puddles glimmered in the crackling arcs of light that chased four-footed vermin from their feasts into their holes. The weasel stepped around a rotting dump of fruit rinds and darted him an uncomfortable look.

"You sure don't talk much, Mick. Say, you want to head on over to Rooster's? I hear he's got a new bawd. Ain't been humped but once or twice."

Michael's lip curled. Two weeks ago, while Rooster had snored off a drinking spree, Michael had spent most of the afternoon at the brothel, quietly administering to the fourteen- and fifteen-year-old orphans who'd been torn, beaten, or exposed to syphilis. The little fools had sold themselves for room and "romance," and there wasn't a damned thing Michael could do for them legally except tend their ills and pray they survived the terms of their contracts.

No, he had no desire to visit Rooster's. In his present state of mind, he'd probably kill the bastard.

He continued purposefully past the reddish glare of clapboard gaming houses, his ears closed to the whistles of scantily clad females and the calls of the hawkers trying to lure his purse inside their doors. The weasel's trot faltered.

"Where ya goin', Mick?"

"To hell."

This rejoinder didn't have the desired effect. Rather than slink off to the gutter that had spawned him, the weasel laughed, a raucous, brassy noise that sounded more donkeylike than human.

"That's a good one, Mick. 'To hell.'" Slapping his knee, the old man chortled again. "Ain't you figured out yet yer already here?"

*Blue Thunder is hell*, Michael thought acidly. *Whiskey Bend is merely purgatory.*

The weasel must have realized Michael's long, brisk stride was leaving him behind. He hurried to catch up.

"You reckon there's any booze where yer goin'?" the old man wheedled, darting a speculative glance at Michael's trouser pockets. "I sure could use a swig of rot-gut. Fer my rheumatism."

"Kill yourself on someone else's handout, old man. You won't get a nickel from me."

The weasel puffed up in indignation. "Here now. Is that any way to talk to yer friend?"

"If I'd wanted a friend, I wouldn't be in Whiskey Bend."

Michael's growl caused the weasel to slink sideways out of reach, but the old man still jogged close enough for Michael to smell the stench of urine and unwashed flannel.

"You sure are a strange one, Mick. You hardly touched that sipping whiskey you plunked down that gold piece fer. An' you didn't hump a single one of Rose's girls. Jest what are you after, anyway?"

*Retribution.*

But again, Michael didn't waste his breath. The weasel wouldn't care that Gabriel Jones had gasped tenaciously night after night, fighting for the right to the miserable life he'd been granted. He wouldn't care that Michael's medical education had proven futile against the lung plague that had been sent to murder his twelve-year-old brother.

Carefree youth, innocence, nobility of spirit—these were alien concepts in Whiskey Bend.

"Gimme them reins, you little whore!"

The bellow had cracked like a whip on the wind.

"What's the matter, Mick?" The weasel seemed surprised that Michael had stopped walking to search the shadows. The old man glanced toward the nearest shanty, a low-class crib with a scrawny woman-child preening in the window. "You seen some tits you wanna sample?" he asked hopefully.

Lightning streaked overhead. Against the backdrop of the livery, Michael finally spied the source of the threat: a man with a knife loomed over a young woman and her skittering horse.

The weasel must have seen them too. He retreated so fast, his spine collided with Michael's chest. "Holy shit! It's Black Bart!"

*Black Bart be damned*, Michael thought. A criminal whose legend had been spawned by butchering unarmed hillbillies and raping their widows, the guerilla was rumored nowadays to stalk stagecoach routes through the Pine Mountains. Michael didn't doubt the bastard was dangerous—if, in fact, this shriveled shell of a man was Bart. But as far as Michael was concerned, bushwhackers were cowards.

He shoved the weasel out of his way and headed toward the girl.

"What're ya doin', Mick?" The weasel dashed in front of him again, his arms waving like a windmill. "You can't tangle with Bart. He ain't no nancy-boy like Hoss!"

"Give me your gun."

"I ain't got one!"

"Then get the hell out of here."

The weasel whimpered, obviously torn between the impending sport and his contemptible life. "They'll scrape you off the street!"

*That would certainly solve my other problems.*

Michael pitched the old man toward safety then slipped into shadow. He could barely hear the weasel's retreat above the din of neighing, panting, and cursing by the livery.

"Bart," he snapped, his voice grating like steel, "get your own damned horse, or I'll blow your head off."

The outlaw started and whirled. It took only a heartbeat for the renegade to locate his challenger, but Michael had already tucked his duster back, just close enough to his belt to appear threatening. He hoped the lightning wouldn't expose his ruse. The deadliest thing he wore strapped to his hip was a flask of rotgut.

Meanwhile, Bart was wheezing, trying to discern Michael's black hair, black eye, and black broadcloth from the utter gloom of the oncoming storm.

"Yeah?" Bart gripped his knife more tightly in his shaking fist. Lighted by the lantern hanging over the livery's door, his face, which had been grizzled by nearly sixty years of depravation, revealed every nuance of suspicion, bravado, and fear. The lantern also lighted Bart's holster. It was stained with fresh blood.

"Who the hell are you?" Bart rasped.

"Someone you don't want to cross."

The outlaw darted an uneasy look around them. Michael recognized the signs of blood loss: pallor, tremors, desperation. Bart held his heavily bandaged gun hand close to his chest. He swayed a couple of times. But before Michael could let himself be moved by Bart's plight, he glanced at the girl cowering behind the teeth-baring, hoof-pawing brute she'd been defending—or had the gelding been defending her?

"There ain't no law in Whiskey Bend," Bart snarled, his timbre less menacing than plaintive.

"That's right. So don't think some badge will stop me from blowing you to kingdom come."

Bart's bushy brows locked. Michael guessed the outlaw was thinking twice about argument.

"The hell you say. I got a right to a horse when I wants one. I got a right to respect! I'm a war hero, goddammit." Bart spat at Michael's boots. "Me and my Sharps was blowing holes through them Yankee bastards while puny-assed upstarts like yerself were still wetting yer dia—"

"You want the slug in your brain or gut?" Michael cut in. "Because I'm not particular."

Bart bared his teeth, more mongrel than wolf. "If I weren't in such a hurry, I'd carve you up for crow bait."

*I'll consider myself blessed—for once.*

Bart half-turned to the girl. "And when I come back, I'm gonna give you what-fer, you uppity little—"

"Time's wasting," Michael interrupted.

Bart sputtered something unintelligible, cast another anxious look down the street, and retreated, his blade still held at a menacing angle. When he reached his bandaged hand behind the watering trough, he cursed, his face screwing up with pain.

The girl took a hesitant step forward, as if she meant to help.

"Stay back, whore!" He brandished his knife again. She froze, and he heaved a clinking flour sack into view. "Don't try an' follow me neither, smart-ass," he panted at Michael. " 'Cause you'll get what these others got when they came to steal my loot." He gestured at the dried blood smeared over the canvas. Then, hobbling as fast as his bowing knees would let him, he made his escape into the drizzle.

Michael expelled his breath. The ruse had worked.

"You all right?" he demanded of the girl as he lumbered out of the shadows. She gasped, retreating a step.

In that moment, he came to understand just exactly what he must resemble: the monster out of Mary Shelley's *Frankenstein*.

"Y-yes." She nodded hastily.

"Good. Then go someplace where it's warm."

Battered and bloody, he trudged past her, avoiding her eyes. He didn't want her thanks. He didn't want her adulation. All he wanted was some private place to nurse his wounds and wait out the storm. He figured he could share Brutus's stall if a vacant one wasn't available.

Michael rounded the corner of the livery. No longer pumping with adrenaline, he shivered as the rain sluiced beneath his collar. The cold tore inside his nose and throat. At this rate, his wounds would freeze closed without the need for bandaging. His lips twisting at such a macabre thought, he yanked on the ring that slid back the livery door.

Light. Michael squinted. The lanterns swung, flooding his mind with memories. He could almost see Gabriel kneeling in his pajamas, rumpled but exuberant, piling the straw closer to a laboring mare. He remembered how the boy had clasped his hands and prayed; how he'd laughed with delight when the colt had sprung forth; how he'd gravely considered a name. Brutus was the moniker Gabriel had finally chosen, because he'd hoped the spindly-legged foal would grow into it.

And Brutus had, villain that he was.

Michael's throat worked painfully. Must every new experience torment him with old memories? During the last two years, more visions had besieged him than he'd been able to drown with liquor: Gabriel, catching snowflakes on his tongue; Gabriel, chasing butterflies through the daisies; Gabriel, doing bellyfloppers in the swimming hole. Two years ago on this very day, Gabriel had painted him a placard to hang outside his future office.

" 'Michael Jones, M.D. The Best Doctor Brother in the World,' " Gabriel had proudly read the birthday gift aloud. "But don't let it go to your head," he'd teased, whacking Michael with a pillow.

Remembering childish laughter and airborne goose-down on that sunny October morning, Michael dashed away tears. He valued Gabriel's gift more than he did his own life, but he didn't deserve it. He didn't even deserve the sentiment behind it. How could he possibly bring himself to hang that sign anywhere, much less over the door of a medical office?

Shaking more now from grief than cold, Michael limped inside the livery and rolled the door closed. A blast of heat assailed him, and his numb flesh began to sting. Horse sweat and manure assailed his senses, along with a nervous chorus of whinnies. One of those nickers belonged to Brutus. The gelding was stabled near the back.

Stumbling over a pitchfork, Michael headed for the rear. That's when he heard the livery door roll open again. His damsel in distress appeared, tiptoeing her horse into a stall. Venturing into the center aisle again, she halted, twisting her pinafore as she gawked at him.

*Damnation.* Did she think he'd come here for a tumble?

Thunder rattled the eaves. Michael gritted his teeth, dropping onto a fresh mound of straw. Its wisps drifted down around him, winking in the lamplight, and he sneezed. The resulting pain doubled him over, and he cursed, wondering how many of his ribs were broken.

"Mister?"

Her voice was a breath, a sigh, and far too husky for her own good. He rolled to his side and drew his knees to his chest, pretending not to hear.

An uncertain scrabbling followed. A horse stomped; another nickered.

"Mister?" she whispered again, more insistently this time.

He cracked open a swollen eye. On a line with his chin, he glimpsed dusty boot toes, a touch of lace, and the thrice-turned hem of a faded green skirt.

"Go away."

The skirt moved closer. "Um . . . are you hurt?"

"No."

"You're bleeding."

"Doesn't matter," he snapped.

Those contrary skirts billowed about twelve inches from his nose. "You don't look so good."

"Yeah, well, I had a rough day."

"Were you in a fight?"

"More like a massacre," he muttered. Hoss was lucky he still had any teeth.

"Pardon?"

He forced his eyes back open. She was kneeling beside him now. "Why are you still here?"

His growl didn't have the desired effect. She leaned over him, a gleaming strand of auburn curling over the swell of her bodice.

"It's raining. I can't leave till the storm's over." She sounded apologetic. "Besides, you saved me and Valentine."

*Christ.* Now he had a babe in bloomers batting eyes at him, thinking he was some kind of hero.

"I always stable Valentine during storms," she prattled on. "He's afraid of thunder."

"Well, I'm not. Go away."

Her palm, smelling faintly of leather, hovered, trembled, then resolutely touched his brow. He wondered if she was ornery or just hard of hearing.

"I sure wish Talking Raven was here," she murmured, reaching next for his ribcage. "She always knows what to do."

He flinched, grabbing her wrist. "What the hell are you doing?"

She blinked at him. *Green eyes*, he noted fleetingly. *Curious and innocent.*

"Seeing what hurts."

"You don't listen so good."

"Oh. Did you already tell me?"

"Look." He struggled to sit again. "I'm a bad man. An evil man. And if you don't get away from me, you're going to regret it."

"Papa says there's no such thing as evil men. Just frightened ones."

Michael narrowed his eyes at this addlepated logic. "Where is your father?"

"Back at the wagon by now. Probably."

"Probably?"

She nodded, and something dusky dimmed her gaze. "The hotel wouldn't let Talking Raven have a room."

Michael ran a hand through his hair, found a tender spot, and winced. His head hurt. Every blasted inch of his body hurt. And her insistence that ravens talked wasn't making the least bit of sense—but maybe his rising fever was to blame.

She sat back on her heels, coming to some decision. "Wait here."

Suspiciously, he watched her rise and turn. Russet ringlets cascaded down her sleek little spine; hair ribbons bounced against her shoulders. She had enough patches on her skirt to quilt a blanket; still, she didn't have the manner of a cracker. And her accent wasn't southern white trash, either. He wondered fleetingly where she came from. Not this Tennessee border town, that was certain.

"I'm back."

He started. Had he dozed? She was standing above him again, streams of golden light radiating from her hair and shoulders. He blinked at this angelic vision, and she smiled, looking sweeter, purer, wiser than she had before. The clatter of a bucket at his side shattered the illusion. He heard a snap; something woolly and musty fluttered over his head. The next thing he knew, she was kneeling, tucking a horse blanket around him.

"You don't want to catch your death of cold," she explained.

He might have laughed if he weren't so certain the pain wouldn't be worth the attempt. He didn't give a damn about his own health. Living didn't have much appeal to a man who was a failure.

To the best of his ability, he screwed his features into a frightening expression. "I told you to go away."

"You didn't mean it." She dipped the hem of her apron in the bucket of water.

"The hell I didn't."

"Talking Raven told me sick people always say things they don't mean."

"Ow!" He jerked away as she dabbed at the gash above his eyebrow.

"It wouldn't hurt," she retorted matter-of-factly, "if you'd stop fussing."

"God almighty. When was the last time you had a spanking?"

A dimple creased her cheek. "You won't hurt me. What's your name, mister?"

"None of your damned business. This isn't a church social. Do you have any idea what your father's going to do when he finds out you've been holed up in a stable with a man? A bad man?"

Her hands hesitated in midwring. He thought he'd finally put the fear of God in her until she shrugged, twisting the apron free of sullied water.

"You're not so bad." She darted him a sideways glance. "Aside from your manners, I mean."

Michael groaned, dropping his head back against the stall's wall. Just what he needed: a smart-aleck nursemaid too naive to know her peril.

Still, he mused in growing resignation, to sit in fresh straw and suffer the ministrations of a pretty little redhaired maid wasn't the worst torment he'd ever endured. She was neat, in spite of her poverty, and she smelled clean, which was more than he could say about the whore whose fingernails had gouged his back the night before.

Cynicism carved his lips into a half-smile. Brawling, whoring, drinking, lying—in only twenty-four months, he'd made up for twenty-one years of misplaced faith. Now he knew why his father's "flock" repeatedly broke God's Commandments. Sinning was a hell of a lot more fun than squirming on a hard pew.

Oblivious to his corrupt nature, though, his Good Samaritan rocked back on her heels and frowned at her handiwork. "Your face is all swollen."

He watched her through heavy-lidded eyes. Her face was beautiful. Endearing in its worry. Transcendent in its compassion. Too bad she was such an innocent angel of mercy, even though she appeared about seventeen.

"Who did this to you?"

Her question reminded him forcefully of the iron-fisted bully he'd become that night. "What difference does it make?"

She seemed surprised. "Don't you want to tell a tinstar?"

"What for?"

"He'll arrest them."

"Not if I deserved it."

Her brows knitted. "But . . . you didn't, did you?"

He averted his gaze. "Someone died because of me."

"Oh."

A long silence stretched between them. She busied herself with her apron. "Is that why you aren't wearing any guns?"

"Why would you ask that?"

"Well, I figured you must have shot someone, and since you feel so bad about it, you went ahead and gave up gunfighting."

His lips quirked. She really was naive.

"Gunfighters don't think that way."

"They don't?"

"No. They just go ahead and kill someone else when they want to feel better. They don't have a conscience."

She grew grave as she considered this viewpoint.

"Well, you have a conscience. Otherwise, you wouldn't feel so bad."

"I suppose."

"So you're not as evil as you think."

He arched a brow. "Are you calling me a liar?"

She blushed, red cheeks against red hair. He found it charming.

"Well . . . no. I mean, even if you are, it's none of my business."

"That's what I've been trying to tell you."

Her heart-shaped face grew even redder, if that was possible. "You don't have to be so surly. I'm just trying to help. Papa's a doctor and—"

"The rain stopped," he interrupted sharply, having no desire to explain himself to a doctor. Especially a competent one.

She cocked her head, listening. The droning on the tin roof had dwindled to an occasional plop. The thunder was a mere whisper compared to its former cannonading.

"The storm's over," he insisted more gruffly. "You can leave now."

Anxious eyes, darkly fringed and greener than spring, delved into his. "I can't leave you alone."

"I'll survive. Unfortunately."

"That's a terrible thing to say."

"Which part?"

She opened her mouth, hesitated, then pressed her lips together. "You're just trying to make me mad."

"Nope. I'm trying to make you leave."

She wrinkled her nose, crowding freckles together. "So you can die?"

Her question hit his gut like a sledgehammer. As little appeal as living held, dying, apparently, held less.

*Craven*, he scorned himself. *Gabriel had more courage in his big toe than you do in all your two hundred pounds. My God, he crossed the threshold of death all alone! He did it bravely, while you dozed at his bedside.*

Michael began to quake, remembering that horrible discovery and the scene his reverend father had made.

"Laggard!" Jedidiah Jones had railed, his forefinger trembling. "I send you to school to make your brother well, and what do you do? You snore through his death throes!"

Michael choked. Squeezing his eyes closed, he clutched his chest, trying to force back the waves of grief that wrenched him from bone to soul. *Damn the plague.* He'd tried so hard to find consumption's cure. Awake before dawn, burning candles long into the night, he'd studied feverishly, finishing his university courses in record time so he could spend the last few months with Gabriel.

But none of his new-fangled prescriptions, none of his research findings or fancy instrumentation had even eased Gabriel's pain. Weeping uncontrollably over the emaciated little corpse in his arms, Michael had been forced to surrender his kid brother to the undertaker.

*I'm sorry, Gabriel. It should have been me, not you. It should have been me!*

"I'm sorry, mister," the girl murmured, her breath warm and sweet against his cheek.

Soft fingers laced through his, holding his hand over his crumbling heart. He blinked, and his angel swam above him, a vision of autumn-colored hair and golden lamplight shining through his tears. When she brushed a curl from his forehead, he flinched. He didn't deserve tenderness.

"I didn't mean any offense," she whispered, contrite. "Papa says I shouldn't always say the first thing that pops into my head."

Michael sniffed, dragging his last shreds of dignity like a suit of armor around him.

"Your father's right," he growled, pushing her away.

Shaking his head at the assistance she offered, he reached for the stall wall, hauling himself up, hand over hand. When he straightened, his knees wobbled, and his head spun. She reached for his arm, but again he shook her off, self-loathing roiling through his innards.

"Bring me Brutus, and I'll take you to your father."

"Brutus?" she repeated uncertainly.

"The bay gelding. Last stall on the right."

"Oh. That's okay, mister. We can walk. I mean, I can walk. The wagon's not far, just a block or two—"

"You're not walking anywhere by yourself in this neighborhood. And especially not at night."

She bit her bottom lip. "Oh."

Thanking God when she demurred for once, he clung to the top slat of the stall, his head bowed, his teeth gritted against the pain of each breath. "The saddle's . . . with the bridle . . . on the post," he gasped.

"Found them!" she called.

He shook his head, fighting the creep of fever. It occurred to him she might have trouble with Brutus. He was just thinking he should work his way to the rear of the livery when he heard approaching clip-clops. To his amazement, his two-year-old terror walked eagerly after her, wicked brown eyes trained on the pockets of her pinafore. She patted the gelding's nose, slipped him a carrot slice, and smiled shyly at Michael.

"All ready."

*So she has a way with four-legged beasts too?*

He heaved himself into the saddle. The floor shifted disconcertingly beneath him; still, he managed to hold on to his blanket and right himself without diving headfirst across the pommel.

"Open the door," he rasped.

She hurried to obey, the essence of cooperation—until he lowered his hand for her.

"Um . . ." Doubtful eyes swept up his boots, rested fleetingly on his hips, then bypassed the grip on his reins to lock squarely with his. "You sure you aren't going to fall off?"

"You ask too many questions."

She blushed again. Hiking her skirts, she grabbed his hand, her fingers all but disappearing in his fist. When he hoisted her before him, he marveled that anyone so full of spunk could feel so weightless.

Woozy with fever, he nevertheless felt a resurgence of clarity as the tang of a rain-washed autumn slapped his senses. He braced himself against the wind, doing his best not to be distracted by the silken curls that floated like a cloud, caressing his throat and chin.

"That way," she said, pointing to a vacant lot at the top of the street.

Dimly, he saw the outline of a wagon, reminiscent of a house on wheels, as the moon steered through the thunderheads. He nodded, wrapping an arm around a waist no wider than his thigh, and spurred Brutus past the clapboard gaming houses of Whiskey Bend's tenderloin district. Shattering glass and raucous laughter mingled with the plinking of off-key pianos; the stench of offal floated past him on the wind. But honeysuckle, too, was carried on that breeze, wafting from the angel in his arms. He hated the fact that his baser nature could be stirred by anything as sweet and trusting as that woman-child. The sooner he got rid of her, the sooner he could find a hole to crawl into.

An interminable five minutes later, he reined in before the crate that served as the wagon's doorstep. He had the fleeting impression of bold black lettering on the wall, a calligraphic scrawl across chipping blue paint. An Irish name, Mallory, was splashed above "Medical Doctor" on the door. Two windows were set into the compact quarters. A lamp burned in both, but he couldn't see beyond the pristine muslin to the furnishings inside.

"Looks like your father's been waiting for you," he said gruffly.

He swept her off the saddle, and she clung to his forearm, kicking up her petticoats until her toes touched the crate.

"You could at least come in," she said in disgruntled tones, tossing the hair out of her eyes.

"This isn't a courting call."

She shot him an exasperated look. "I didn't mean it like . . . Hey! Mister!"

He was already turning Brutus back toward the saloon district.

"You can't ride off. You need help!"

"Forget it. Forget me," he added bitterly under his breath.

He cantered for an alley and reined in. Peering around the corner, he squinted back through wisps of fog. He wanted to be certain she'd gotten safely inside.

Lamplight flooded the crate, illuminating the girl and her father. Her gestures were animated, her features anxious, as she communicated to a wiry, fortyish man, blocking the doorway. Michael caught a glimpse of thinning auburn hair, spectacles, and a stethoscope before Mallory stepped aside, urging the girl before him into the wagon. Then Michael watched the physician's head turn. Mallory seemed to be searching the mist and shadows, looking for some sign of the patient she'd described.

His chest flooding with shame, Michael ducked behind the wall, afraid the sawbones would spy him. He didn't want to contaminate souls worthier than his.

He turned Brutus north to Blue Thunder Valley in Kentucky.

For a prodigal son under Preacher Jones's care, there was no hell like home.

# Chapter 1

❦

**H**unger. Biting, clawing at his gut, it reminded him of the mountain lions Pa used to skin.

Collie shivered in the rising wind, squinting as dust and pebbles smacked his face. He couldn't remember the last time he'd eaten. Nothing stayed inside him very long, and everything burned its way out. It scared him, and he wanted it to stop. His belt was already double cinched.

Thunder rolled, and Collie sucked a forefinger. The taste of dirt was comforting as he huddled with the pill bugs and the worms. Every now and then, the planks on the porch above him would bounce, and he'd wriggle further under the stage depot, pressing himself into his trench until the boots strode by. He hated towns. Hated townspeople—except for Sera, of course. But most of all, he hated hunger. That's why he'd forced himself to come back to Blue Thunder, to hunt for slops and see what baked goods he could steal. Lately he'd been getting dizzy whenever he tried to strike a squirrel

21

with his peashooter. And the rabbits had all gotten smart, too smart to be snared.

But Pa must have been watching out for him from above. 'Cause not twenty paces from Collie's hiding place, a big black cat sat in a cage beside some trunks the whip was tossing off the five-o'clock stage.

Saliva moistened Collie's mouth. He stared hard and thought of grabbing that critter and filling his belly till it hurt in a satisfying way. The trouble was, a mustard-colored skirt kept swishing by. And a biddy with a crab-apple face had planted herself square in front of Collie's hiding place. He could see the cat between the biddy's legs, since she wore dungarees, but he couldn't get to the cat. Not without bowling the biddy over and slowing himself down.

Thoughtfully, he fingered his bowie knife. Scowling, he shoved it back in its sheath. Too risky. The whip could jump down and collar him. 'Sides, he didn't want to hurt nobody, just to frighten them off. If only the womenfolk would go away! He didn't want nobody to see him, especially Mustard Skirt. She looked like the kind who'd start flapping her jaw, asking where his ma was. Or his pa.

But Collie was fourteen. He didn't need no ma or pa, even though some folks, especially the female kind, thought he did. Good Samaritans, he'd heard them call themselves. Collie wasn't exactly sure what Samaritans were, although he was pretty clear they wanted to ruin his life. They always insisted he get a haircut and bathe, learn the three Rs, and live in an orphanage. But Pa used to say orphanages were worse than jails. And since Pa had come out of the last jail in a pine box, orphanages scared the daylights out of Collie.

A tremor shook his bones.

The cat growled deep in its throat. Collie narrowed his eyes. Dang if the varmint weren't staring straight at him. It bristled, as if it sensed his intentions. He licked his lips and bared his teeth.

Suddenly, a shadow dropped out of the sky. Mustard Skirt shouted a warning; a trunk struck the cage, and the bars crumpled, flinging the door wide. The cat shot out of its prison as if its tail were on fire. It made a beeline for the elm at the far end of the yard, and Collie swore foully under his breath.

Now how was he supposed to catch himself a meal?

"Dang cat. I never did see much use for 'em."

Eden Mallory winced at her great-aunt's denunciation of felines. For nearly ten minutes, the woman had done nothing but grumble while Eden tried to coax Anastasia out of the tree. After everything she'd been through in the past eight weeks, the last thing Eden needed was a cantankerous old woman whose coonskin cap and corncob pipe probably explained why Claudia Ann Collier was the last of her bloodline.

Eden clamped a hand over her bonnet to keep the lid on her frustration. The fact that she was also trying to keep the rising wind from snatching the straw from her head was a secondary consideration at this point. All her hopes, all her fears, hinged on the outcome of this first meeting with her only living relative. Eden wanted—no, she *needed*—to lead an inconspicuous life, to hide herself away in a nice, secure home without wheels. Claudia had agreed, albeit grudgingly, to let Eden and her cat live with her in Blue Thunder, and Eden was more grateful than she could say. She just hoped Anastasia's tree-climbing escapade wouldn't ruin their introduction.

Of course, if the weather had been balmy, Eden mused uneasily, she might have felt more confident. Whenever lightning cracked from the heavens, something bad happened—like her mother's riding accident. And Talking Raven's miscarriage. Eden wasn't normally superstitious, but lightning seemed to be an omen in her life. However, she had little hope of convincing her ornery kinswoman that doom flashed in the clouds.

"Anastasia isn't used to cages," Eden said, trying another tactic. "Considering I dragged her halfway across the continent, I daresay Stazzie has every right to be irritable."

Aunt Claudia snorted. "I ain't ever met a puss that needs an excuse to be irritable. Mark my words, missy, that mouser of yours ain't coming down."

"But the storm! Stazzie could be struck by lightning."

"Fried to a crisp," Aunt Claudia agreed, striking a match.

Gritting her teeth, Eden waved away tobacco smoke. Over the years, Papa had chuckled about his mother's spinster sister and her "peculiar" charm. However, he had somehow neglected to mention that Claudia had the manners of a street arab.

Meanwhile, the other object of Eden's frustration clung stubbornly to one of the elm's highest boughs, despite the way her perch was being pommeled by the wind. Eden could feel rather than see the accusation in those topaz eyes, because from the street level, Anastasia looked like a big black dandelion seed ruffling with each gust.

*Oh, Stazzie, quit being such a pill. Kentucky's not going to be as bad as Colorado—I hope.*

She glared back at her pet. The cat had an uncanny way of knowing things long before they happened. For instance, she'd refused to enter the medicine wagon for seven whole days before drunken miners had come to ransack it. And Stazzie hadn't left Eden's side, not even for a second, on the day Papa had died.

If Anastasia hadn't been Eden's single best friend, comforting her so faithfully through those horrible days in Silverton, Eden might have thrown up her hands and let the mulish feline get what she deserved: a thorough soaking.

The whip strolled over to Anastasia's tree. He was a barrel of a man in straining suspenders, and he made no attempt to conceal the tobacco chaw that made him look like a chipmunk with a toothache. "The kitty ain't come down yet, eh?"

"No," Eden answered, hard-pressed to hide her annoyance.

"You got any ideas?" Claudia asked him.

The whip shrugged, spewing a stream of tobacco juice at the elm. "Reckon you could chop the tree down."

"Use your dang head, Angus," Claudia growled. "That tree'll fall on the roof of my store. I got enough trouble with leaks as it is."

"Thunderation, Aunt Claudia. You can afford another roof. Hell, you can afford a whole 'nother store. Why don't you hire yourself a handyman who knows what he's doing? All that booklearning makes Doc Jones too high and mighty for hammerin' and sawin'. 'Sides, you got more money than God."

"I got money 'cause I don't squander it on hired hands." She drilled him with a ferocious stare. "As for Michael, we got an agreement. He's a fine carpenter once he gets around to it. And he's gonna get around to it, if I have my say about it. And I always do. So shut up, Angus."

Angus turned beet red, sputtering an excuse and hurrying back to his team. Eden couldn't blame him. Still, remembering how easily he'd heaved the traveling trunks she could barely drag, Eden marveled at the way her seventy-five-year-old aunt had glared the man down. Apparently, "Aunt" Claudia, as everyone called her, was someone to be reckoned with in this town.

The thought of Claudia's age made Eden squirm. She didn't want to think her last surviving kinswoman might be heaven-bound soon. She'd watched helplessly at the age of twelve as Mama had died from complications following a riding accident, and then eleven years later as Talking Raven's miscarriage had ended her life and Eden's last hope for a brother or sister. But her failure to save Papa eight weeks ago from pneumonia had been the final defeat. She'd been forced to the bitter conclusion that her calling to heal people made her more of a menace than a savior.

The people of Silverton had largely agreed. In fact, some of the more mean-spirited townsfolk had claimed that she and Papa had done nothing but bilk people. Once that rumor had spread, a veritable army of derelicts had started appearing at the wagon, demanding the wages that, they'd claimed, Papa owed them because they'd "pretended" to be cured during his medicine show.

Eden had been stunned by the accusations and the threats that accompanied them. Papa had been the most honest man she'd ever known. She'd never doubted the power of his remedies before, because from Texas to Montana, she'd watched his patients improve.

Of course, during their western travels, Eden had

learned there were *other* medicine show pitchmen, shysters who secretly paid actors to endorse their cures. But no one had ever dared say such things about Dr. Andrew Mallory. Not in her presence, anyway.

Tears prickled Eden's eyelids. Could she really have been so wrong about her father?

Eden felt a nudge against her hip. Grateful for the distraction, she glanced down and saw that a curly-haired boy of about ten years had joined them by the tree. She had a heartbeat to notice his expensive linen shirt, freshly soiled, and the eye-poppingly huge toad he gripped between his muddy fists. Then his brown eyes rose to hers.

"How much money does God have?"

She blinked. "I beg your pardon?"

"Mr. Angus said Aunt Claudia's got more money than God. How much money is that?"

Bracing her gnarled hands on her knees, Claudia grinned at the boy. "More money than your pa ever did, Jamie Harragan."

Jamie gazed at her thoughtfully, the toad giving an occasional kick to protest its imprisonment. "Then maybe you could pay God to bring Pa back."

Claudia cocked a bushy eyebrow. "Why would I want to do that?"

" 'Cause I miss 'im."

Claudia's blustery façade softened. "Jamie Harragan, you can't go bribing God."

"How come? Pa said anyone could be bribed."

"God ain't just anyone, Jamie Harragan," Claudia retorted, then muttered under her breath, "Dang, if I don't give that mother of yours a piece of my mind, letting a boy go on thinking such things." She fixed him with a keen, appraising stare. "Say, where'd you find that hoppy toad?"

He brightened, jerking his head in the direction of the general store. "Under your porch."

"He's a big 'un."

Jamie grinned, stretching his freckles from ear to ear. "I'm gonna call him Charlie."

He raised his pet for her inspection, and Eden hid a smile to see how solemnly her aunt made a fuss over the none-too-happy toad.

After a couple of nods and admiring whistles, Claudia dropped her arm around Jamie's shoulders and pointed up at the elm. "Lookie there, Jamie. We got a stuck cat. You know how to get one of those dang critters out of a tree?"

Jamie cocked his head, as if considering. "I got my peashooter in my back pocket."

Eden glanced warily at the Y-shaped stick and leather thong that jutted from the boy's broadcloth breeches. "I don't think slinging stones at Stazzie is a good idea."

Claudia drew the boy closer. "That there's my niece," she said in a conspiratorial whisper. "She's kind of particular about the whys and wherefores, on account of it's her cat."

Jamie nodded sagely.

"Well, I wouldn't hurt the cat, ma'am," he said politely. "I'd just spook her a bit, maybe hit some twigs up above her."

"Jamie's got a fine aim," Claudia said, patting the boy's shoulder. "If he says he's gonna hit a twig, he'll hit a twig. Isn't that right, Angus?" she bellowed at the whip.

"Sure," Angus shouted back gamely. "As peashootin' goes, Jamie's the best."

Claudia narrowed her eyes at him. "Not better'n me."

Eden cleared her throat. "I'm sure Jamie is more than proficient with his slingshot," she intervened, "but Stazzie can be quite unpredictable, and I don't want her to—"

"That storm's about to hit, missy," Claudia interrupted with a wag of her pipe stem. "You want your cat outta that tree, or don't you?"

"Yes, of course I do, but—"

A female voice sliced through her protest, shrill enough to cut through thunder.

"Jamie Harragan! What have you done to your trousers?"

The boy started, hurrying to hide Charlie behind his back. A youngish, smartly dressed woman in honey-colored taffeta sailed toward them. With her petticoats fluttering like froth, she looked like a battleship in full steam.

"Young man, you are filthy. Positively *filthy!* And you've torn out the knees in your trousers! How dare you go crawling around in the dirt, when I expressly told you to sit on our wagon and keep clean? Do you have any idea how much our tailor charges to repair your britches?"

Claudia stepped briskly to intercept the woman. "Bonnie Harragan, a boy's got better things to do than sit on a wagon, waiting for his mother to make up her mind over some silly new gewgaw."

"But—"

"Boys get dirty. That's the difference between boys and dolls. If you don't like mud on Jamie's fancy pants, buy him dungarees."

Eden bit her lip, fully expecting the younger woman to march up and knock Aunt Claudia on her impudent rear end. Instead, Bonnie halted, drawing a ragged breath. Something canny and disquietingly artificial flickered in her eyes. She bowed her head.

"Why, you're right, of course," she demurred. "It's just that Jamie can be so willful at times, and he really has to start learning his social graces if he's ever to follow in the footsteps of our beloved Mr. Lincoln and become the next Kentucky-born president."

Claudia muttered something about the apple not falling far from the tree.

"Hello, Mr. McGee," Bonnie called sweetly to Angus.

"Miss Bonnie," he grunted, tipping his dusty slouch hat.

Her cool gray eyes next turned to Eden. Eden felt her face heat as Bonnie's appraising stare swept from her fraying straw hat, past her modest, yellow muslin, to her scuffed and muddy traveling boots. Bonnie's lip curled faintly.

"Aunt Claudia," she cooed, dismissing Eden with a shoulder, "whatever are you doing out here in all this lightning? Getting spooked by thunder can't be good for your heart." She linked her arm through Claudia's. "Jamie, we can't allow Auntie to strain her heart, now can we?"

"I ain't plannin' on kickin' the bucket today," Claudia snapped, "so you can stop panderin' fer the fortune yer uncle left me. Eden, this here's Bonnie."

Bonnie turned fire-engine red.

"Pleased to know you," Eden said mildly.

Bonnie gave her a stiff nod, recovering her dignity and her chilly demeanor. "So you're Eden, Aunt Claudia's great-niece. Really, my dear, you've been the talk of the town. No one even knew you existed until you wired Aunt Claudia out of the blue. Strange how you should show up *now*, of all times."

Claudia snorted. Eden darted her aunt an uneasy glance. What had Bonnie meant by that last dig? Was Claudia's heart condition worse than she pretended?

Meanwhile, thunder rumbled, making the ground tremble. Eden hugged her fluttering hat tighter. The elm's canopy was lashing back and forth so crazily that leaves were starting to rip free. Anastasia, bless her mutinous soul, clung as tenaciously to her limb as a flea does to a dog.

"Jamie, come along," Bonnie ordered, holding out her hand.

The boy glanced anxiously over his shoulder, and Bonnie's eyes narrowed.

"What's that you're hiding behind your back?"

"Nothing," Jamie lied.

Clearly suspicious, Bonnie started forward when another clap of thunder made them all jump. Jamie dropped his toad. Bonnie spied the tumbling creature and emitted a strangled gasp.

"Warts!" Alarmed, she grabbed Jamie's wrists and turned over his hands. "Jamie Harragan, you are going to have—"

Her words broke off in midsentence, and she made a tiny mew. Her gaze was no longer fastened on Jamie. Instead, it was riveted behind the boy, on the yard beside the depot. A tall man in a well-tailored suitcoat was leading a bay gelding out of the farrier's shop. The blacksmith himself trailed in the gentleman's wake, but Bonnie hardly seemed to notice the stout and soiled smith. Instead, she stared at the gentleman, whose lean waist and narrow hips were accentuated by the dark fabric of his impeccable suit. When the gentleman stooped, running his hands over his horse's rear legs, Bonnie's eyes slitted, and her features took on a predatory expression, one much like Stazzie wore when she was anticipating the epicurean delights of a mouse.

Suddenly, Jamie was free. He collided with Eden, chirped an apology, then sprinted after his toad, which had made a beeline for the rhododendron bushes near Stazzie's tree.

Claudia chuckled, a low, throaty sound that hinted as much at mischief as amusement. "That there's Michael," she said, giving Eden a wink.

Her curiosity piqued, Eden glanced back toward the farrier's yard. Michael had stripped off his coat and now stood rolling up his sleeves. Eden had a moment to notice that the cut and color of the outer garment had been deceiving: the stark contrast of his white shirt against the silky black of his vest proved he was much broader across his chest and shoulders than she'd first imagined. Then he turned his back. When he squatted, exposing taut buttocks to examine his gelding's hocks, Bonnie breathed a dreamy little sigh.

The sound Eden made was more exasperated.

She supposed the man was attractive enough, with his form-fitting breeches and Olympian shoulders, but really. Her cat was about to be electrocuted!

"Aunt Claudia?"

No answer.

"Aunt Claudia," she insisted again, raising her voice above the rattle of an oncoming wagon. "Do you know where I can get a saucer of milk? I want to try to lure Stazzie down."

Claudia didn't answer. Apparently she was too busy gawking at Michael.

Before Eden could repeat her question, lightning spat,

arching earthward in an eerie blue display. It struck the grounding rod on the roof of the general store. A premonition scuttled down Eden's spine. She watched the horse spook in its harness. The wagon veered off course.

Suddenly Jamie dashed out from the bushes in pursuit of his toad.

*Dear God.*

It all happened so quickly. The driver cursed; the horse reared; Bonnie screamed a warning. Flailing hooves cleaved the air, and Jamie, his eyes almost as wide as his mouth, staggered backward. It was too late. The wagon overturned; flour spewed, and apples bounced around the cowering child beneath the wheels.

Eden was running before Jamie loosed his first howl. She didn't stop to consider how conspicuous she was being; she didn't consider her own danger. Her heart was in command, and she threw her weight on the leads. Just as she had dozens of times, when Valentine had spooked in his own harness, she dragged the horse back to earth before it could pull the vehicle over Jamie's legs.

The crisis was over as soon as it began. The driver gained control, the horse wheezed into stillness, and Eden ducked under the reins. Miraculously, a wooden crate had kept the wagon from crushing Jamie's head.

"Jamie, honey," she panted, wading past splintered barrels, dripping egg yolks, and seeping pickle juice. "Jamie, are you hurt?"

"Charlie!" he wailed, scrambling beneath his would-be tomb. She heard a frantic scratching as he dug through the wreckage.

"Move aside, young woman," a gruff voice commanded, "I'm a doctor."

Eden gasped as two strong hands grabbed her waist

and deposited her in a heap beside a box of nightcrawlers. Michael didn't seem to notice her exposed unmentionables, though. Like a man possessed, he braced his shoulder against the wagon. Hands as wide as her face grasped the bed, and he grunted, hiking the wood an incredible foot in the air.

"Jamie," he panted, "can you crawl free?"

"No! I won't leave Charlie . . ."

At this point, a crowd was gathering. Angus rushed to Michael's aid. He heaved his bulk under the wagon's other end. The driver, working frantically, unbuckled his horse from its twisted harness, all the while barking threats at the spectators not to steal his grub.

Jamie, meanwhile, sobbed brokenly beside a bloody patch of bone.

"Oh, Jamie," Eden murmured, "Charlie's in heaven now. You have to let him go."

With the help of a few more spectators, Michael and Angus managed to right the wagon. Eden, knowing firsthand the ravages of grief, didn't think twice about crawling beneath the bed to comfort Jamie. To her surprise, neither did Blue Thunder's well-tailored doctor. His neck nearly disappeared into his shoulders as he squeezed his mountain-sized frame between the wheels.

"It's all right, son." Michael didn't seem to notice or care that his linen sleeve had been shredded on a nail. "Are you hurt?"

The boy shook his head. "Charlie," he whimpered again.

Michael frowned, glancing toward the scarlet smear that had once been Jamie's pet.

"His toad," Eden explained quietly.

Midnight blue eyes delved into hers. Intense and strangely haunted, they struck a chord so deep within her that she was nearly bowled over by the intimacy. She'd seen those eyes before. Somewhere along the road, in the endless parade of seekers who'd begged miracles from Talking Raven's herbs, she'd met this Michael Jones. Her brow furrowed as she tried to remember.

"Come here, son." A curious blend of mountain growl and southern drawl, Michael's voice mimicked the storm's lowest rumble of thunder. It wasn't the sort of thing that inspired comfort in a patient, and yet Jamie, consumed with misery, crawled into Michael's arms. Eden's throat constricted as she watched the man embrace the child.

"It's not fair, I know," Michael murmured, "but sometimes we lose the ones we love."

His hands, surprisingly gentle for their size, probed Jamie's limbs and picked splinters out of tousled curls. When the boy buried his face in that paternal shoulder, Eden's own grief welled uncomfortably close to the surface.

"Dad blast it," snapped a voice beyond their haven. "I said make way. Give the boy some air, fer cryin' out loud."

A gnomelike face bobbed behind an army of elbows. Eden blinked rapidly, becoming aware of a legion of legs and skirts circling the wagon. They parted reluctantly as Claudia used her cap to beat a path to the wagon.

She ducked her head into view, wisps of her gun metal-gray hair sticking straight out with static. "Jamie? You okay, boy?"

"I'll need to examine him more closely," Michael said. "He's too upset to talk."

Claudia harrumphed. "Seems to me he's got just

cause." She spun around, planting a gnarled fist on her hips. "Berthold Gunther," she hollered at the grousing driver, "will you shut up about your dang canned peaches already? I got a whole store full; ain't nobody gonna steal your paltry fifty cents' worth. Show a little blamed compassion for the boy. You could've killed him."

"Ain't my fault the brat ran out under my Barney's nose," Gunther flung back. He was a grizzled, unkempt, stork of a man with little left in the way of hair or teeth. "And I paid you a sight more'n fifty cents fer those peaches, Claudia Ann Collier. You ain't running no charity in that store of your'n, and neither am I!"

The crowd's rumble of disapproval was all but drowned out by Claudia's expletives. As she waded back into the fray, yelling at the bystanders to be about their business, Eden chanced a glance at Michael, who rested his chin on Jamie's curls. He rocked the boy, crooning soft assurances, but Eden caught those inky-blue eyes sweeping down her traveling outfit. Suddenly she wished she were a bit less egg-splattered and a great deal more fashionable. Michael didn't dismiss her with the disdain that Bonnie had, though. Indeed, as his gaze lingered on the unruly red tendrils the wind had liberated from her chignon, her insides heated, as if a match had been struck at her core. She was just deciding whether she liked the sensation, when something dusky, like remorse, clouded his features. Ducking his head, he focused on Jamie. She felt unaccountably deflated.

Fortunately, Claudia returned to distract them. "Either of you two got smelling salts? Much as I hate the idea of the earache it'll cause, I reckon someone's gotta bring Bonnie out of her swoon."

"Oh. Um . . . yes," Eden stammered, still disconcerted by her disappointment. Did Michael remember her, too? If he'd been part of the crowd during one of Papa's medicine shows, chances were he *would* recall her more clearly than she recalled him. *Of all the rotten luck.* She'd never set foot in Blue Thunder Valley in all her twenty-five years. Where had Michael seen her? And in what context?

Somehow she managed to regain the use of her wits and her cramped legs. Stumbling back through the wreckage, she grabbed a satchel from her luggage and fell on her knees beside Bonnie. Thanking God when she found a steady pulse and no head injuries, Eden screwed open the bottle of salts, only to have steely fingers snatch it out of her hand.

Michael grimaced at the odor.

"Spirits of Hartshorn," she assured him hastily. "With lavender. I didn't find any bruises, but she could have a concussion—"

"Move aside. Please."

Eden winced. The platitude had done little to soften the iron in his tone. Much like her father, Michael considered himself the medical authority. Swallowing the little pride her succession of failures had left her, she pulled her skirts out of his way. She had to remind herself she'd given up the medicine-show life and moved to Blue Thunder to put her past behind her.

She noticed Jamie, standing fretfully in the circle of Aunt Claudia's arms, her coonskin askew on his head.

"Is Mama dead?" he whispered, a tear rolling to his chin.

"No, honey," Eden said quickly. "Your mama fainted, that's all. She was frightened when she saw you fall under the wagon. Look."

Bonnie was already groaning.

"Your mama's going to be just fine."

Bonnie's glassy eyes flickered open. "M-Michael?"

In the accompanying flash of light, his features looked chiseled, dissected by leafy shadows that slanted across the hard, square plane of his jaw. In that moment, he resembled a brooding thunder god more than the shining knight of some schoolgirl's fantasy.

"You fainted, Mrs. Harragan." Immune to the straining bodice at his knee, he probed Bonnie's head with deft, professional movements. "There's nothing to fear. Jamie's not hurt. Do you think you can sit?"

Bonnie frowned, raising a shaking hand to the hair he had mussed. "J-Jamie?"

The boy ran to her side.

"Jamie," she gasped, propping herself on an elbow, "that was a stupid, *stupid* thing for you to do. You could have been killed. Not to mention how you almost killed me!"

The boy hung his head. Claudia shook hers.

"Bonnie Harragan, are you hurt or aren't you?" she snapped.

"Well, I . . ." She hesitated, glanced at Michael, then groaned, oozing back to earth. "I'm not sure. I feel so . . . dizzy."

Claudia rolled her eyes. "Give her another whiff of smelling salts, Michael. Or better yet, let me do it. You see to Jamie. He's the one with the real hurt."

Bonnie scowled. "Michael said Jamie was all right."

"Jamie's grieving," Eden interceded.

"Well, that's silly. As my son can see, Michael has matters well in hand. In a couple of days, with proper medical care, I'm sure I'm going to be—"

"Not *you*," Claudia retorted. "His hoppy toad. And a

fine hoppy toad it was, too. The kind any boy would be proud to own." She draped her arm over Jamie's quivering shoulders. "I reckon any toad as fine as Charlie must have a strapping brood somewhere. How 'bout you and me taking another look-see under my porch?"

Bonnie grew distinctly paler. "Auntie, don't you dare! You know I don't allow pets."

"Bonnie Harragan, you ain't allergic to any dang toads."

"I am too! Besides, they breed warts."

Michael chuckled. A resonant rumble to rival the deepest strains of a cello, it caught Eden's attention as nothing else about the man had. She was rewarded to glimpse straight white teeth and the heart-stealing flash of dimples.

He climbed to his feet. "Mrs. Harragan," he said, offering her a hand, "if that were true about toads, then we'd have an epidemic among the boys in this town."

Bonnie blushed, wobbling as Michael gripped her elbow. When Jamie ran forward, burying his face in her stomach, she sighed, hugging him closer. Regret flickered across her features as Michael stepped discreetly to the side.

Claudia harrumphed in approval. "Well, Michael," she said briskly, "I reckon I needn't fuss with introductions now. Still, this here's my niece, Eden. Andy Mallory's girl."

Michael, who'd been rolling down his cuffs, paused a moment to gaze fully into her face. "Eden," he repeated, as if tasting the word for nuances of flavor.

The warmth rekindled in his eyes, and she drew a shaky breath. Suddenly she was aware of how close and sweltering the air had become. She liked to think the storm was to blame, until he released her from his gaze.

"Miss Mallory." He nodded. "Whatever possessed you to charge a rearing horse? You could have been seriously injured."

"Uh . . . I suppose I didn't stop to think," she stammered. "About myself, I mean."

"Hmm." He seemed to concentrate on buttoning his cuffs, but she sensed he was still watching her behind that veil of inky lashes. "A bit foolhardy, wouldn't you say?"

Eden's cheeks heated.

"I was the closest," she answered simply.

A single brow shot up, held.

"You would put the Good Samaritan to shame, Miss Mallory."

His smile, as fleeting as it was, struck her strangely. Perhaps it was a trick of the lightning, but she could have sworn she'd seen something cloud the indigo depths of his eyes.

"Any splinters? Cuts? Sprains?" he quizzed her crisply.

She swallowed, shaking her head.

"Pain of any kind?"

"Nothing I can't treat myself, thank you."

"Indeed?"

She wanted to kick herself for that slip of the tongue. Before she could stammer some explanation, however, Berthold Gunther started cursing at the top of his lungs. Eden spied a scrawny youth with matted blond hair running in a near crouch away from the wagon. His arms were laden with canned goods; an apple spilled out of his trouser pockets. Gunther, who'd been scouring the gutters to salvage his precious groceries, went apoplectic.

"Hey! *Hey,* you plaguey white trash bastard! That ain't your'n! Bring it back!"

Claudia pressed her lips together, watching Gunther drop his sack of grain and give chase.

"Collie's back," she grunted.

Michael's expression darkened as the young thief dashed on bared feet down an alley. "Looks that way." Regret edged his tone.

Bonnie sniffed. "That awful, *awful* boy."

She tightened her arms around Jamie, who stood now with his spine pressed to her waist. When Jamie tilted his head back to observe his mother's disapproval, Eden's heart twisted. She could almost see Jamie filing the experience away, learning contempt rather than compassion.

Michael broke the mood. Brusque and businesslike once more, he turned to Bonnie. "Mrs. Harragan, I suggest you bring Jamie to my office for a more thorough examination."

"Of course, Michael. Right away. And . . . well, I hope you won't mind taking a look at me, too," she cooed, probing her crown for emphasis. "My head does hurt."

Michael's jaw twitched at this none too subtle ploy. Nodding his farewell to Claudia, he swept his arm forward, motioning Bonnie and Jamie before him on the sidewalk. Then he passed Eden. For an instant, his stride faltered. Even without the elemental fireworks in the sky behind him, he crackled with intensity, a primal magnetism that was as alluring as it was disconcerting. She'd always considered herself immune to dark temptations, and yet when his gaze collided with hers, a tiny frisson of sensation danced along her spine.

"I almost forgot." He retrieved the smelling salts from his trouser pocket. "I daresay you'll never need them, but I hear they're requisite among Good Samaritans."

Eden blinked. She was uncertain what to make of his guarded tone . . . or the warm, calloused hand that took hers, gently but insistently closing her fingers around the bottle.

"Michael," Bonnie called. Her pout was thinly disguised. "You are coming, aren't you?"

Michael withdrew, and Claudia chuckled, watching Bonnie march her reluctant quarry down the street.

"Well, niece," she said, her cagey eyes bright with mischief, "looks like you and me have got a heap of fun ahead."

"I beg your pardon?"

"Oh, nuthin'." Claudia smiled like a certain Cheshire feline. "I was just thinking about the alley cats in this town. And yours is still up in that tree, ain't it?"

# Chapter 2

⌒~◯◯~⌒

**B**onnie Harragan was going to be the final nail in his coffin.

Gritting his teeth as thunder bludgeoned his brain, Michael hurried his horse away from the widow's driveway. Bonnie had insisted she was too weak to make the trip home alone. He'd suspected her only real ailment was a twisted imagination, and the minute she'd ordered Jamie away from her bedside, her roaming hands had proven Michael right. Unfortunately, he hadn't dared ignore her head complaints for fear she might have suffered a concussion. And Bonnie knew that, damn her. She knew Gabriel's death made him feel personally responsible for every fever, ache, and chill in this town. It wasn't the first time she'd cried wolf to try to lure him back into her arms. He suspected it wouldn't be the last, even though he'd told her in no uncertain terms he would never court her again, not after she'd jilted him for a wealthier beau. Instead, Bonnie chose to believe she was competing with another lover, and she needed to ply her charms harder.

Michael groaned, turning up his coat collar against the first pellets of rain.

43

Hell, he wished he *did* have a secret lover to make him forget the forbidden fantasies he still suffered over a certain red-haired healer. He wished his mysterious illness would let him muster enough lust to rid his memory of that innocent's touch. But he couldn't allow his thoughts to dwell on a lost moment. He had bigger problems to deal with now, namely: What was he going to do with Sera when he became an invalid?

Because Michael was sure his central nervous system was failing. He knew enough about electrochemical pathways to realize the recurring numbness in his limbs hinted at some grave disorder. At first, when the tingling began in his feet, he'd thought he'd been standing too much, chopping wood, treating patients, repairing Claudia's store roof. But then, during routine exertions like stair climbing, he'd noticed he'd grow uncommonly fatigued. And lately, he'd been experiencing vertigo.

The worst part, though, was having to lie to Sera. Michael didn't want his kid sister to start worrying she would lose him, like she'd lost everyone else: Mama, Gabriel, Papa—even Rafe.

Of course, Michael's half-brother wasn't really dead—at least, Rafe hadn't been dead six months ago, Michael thought grimly, recalling the letter he'd caught Sera sneaking to her bedroom. If any member of the Jones clan deserved to be dead, that member was Rafe, but Michael wasn't the kind of man who went looking for vengeance. He figured Rafe would eventually suffer his due punishment for all the heartache he'd caused the family, and that punishment would be far more thorough than anything Michael could dole out.

No, he refused to waste one precious second of his ebbing life on the wastrel who called him "brother." Michael's first concern was Sera. He wanted his kid sister to be safe and happily married before his illness took its toll. It frightened him to think he was losing ground, battling an enemy he had no way of overcoming, and yet for Sera's sake, he had to hold on.

Riding to the one-stall stable at the side of his house, Michael somehow managed not to slump to his knees while fumbling with the bridle. He gave Brutus a cursory rub and a pitchfork of hay and then, heedless of the mud and the drizzle, stumbled gratefully toward the bed that awaited him in the modest, two-story house he'd inherited from his father.

"Hello? Michael, is that you?"

His eighteen-year-old sister's voice, pitched above the clatter of rain on the tin roof, made him wince, and he turned reluctantly from the hall stairs. His sodden shirt and trousers were forming rivulets that snaked through the dust on the pinewood floor. He knew Sera wouldn't care, though. In fact, he suspected Sera wouldn't notice. She'd renounced mops and brooms shortly after Papa's death two years before, and he doubted whether she even knew what beeswax was used for.

"Were you expecting someone else?" he asked wearily, hearing her approach from the kitchen.

Her eager footsteps missed a beat, and when she appeared around the corner, he noticed her peaches-and-cream complexion had tinged a shade of rose.

"Of course not," she answered quickly, too quickly for his peace of mind. Like a shadow flitting behind the pain, he vaguely recalled a stranger, a Texican, and the reprobate's predatory smile. Michael wondered if Sera had planned a meeting with the man, but before he could challenge her, she threw a gauntlet of her own.

"Why are you home so early? What's wrong?"

He stiffened. "Nothing."

"Then how come you look madder than a rooster in an empty henhouse?"

He avoided her eyes. "I'm just tired, that's all."

Sera blew out her breath. Her exasperation suggested she suspected his lie. The idea worried him, so he retreated behind sternness. The Reverend Jedidiah Jones had often preached that discipline was the only way to curb a child's natural tendency toward rebellion, and Sera, unfortunately, had always been more rebellious than most. Thanks to the nearly twelve years that separated them, Michael had never been close to his sister, but he knew his duty by her. More than that, he loved her. Lying about his illness was putting a strain on their already tense relationship, but he had no choice. The truth of his condition would be too hard for her to bear.

He made an attempt to gentle his voice. "You know I prefer you not to pry into my private affairs."

"For heaven's sake, Michael, I wasn't pry—" She stopped herself. Pressing her lips together, she shook her head. "Fine. Whatever you say. Dinner's almost ready. I baked some cornpone and—"

"Thanks, but I'm not hungry."

"You're always hungry."

She sounded suspicious again, and he cursed himself for his mistake. It was too blasted hard to think when his head felt like an anvil.

"I ate some biscuits and gravy at Aunt Claudia's," he lied a second time.

"I didn't think Aunt Claudia and that long-lost niece of hers had come home yet."

"Look." The pounding in his head accelerated to near ramming speed at the mention of their neighbor's house guest. "I'll eat the cornpone later."

"Well, excuse me for caring. I thought you looked a

little peaked, but obviously, you're just in another one of your black moods."

"My clothes are wet, Sera. I want to dry off."

"Well, you don't have to bite my head off." Her chin jutted, and she planted her hands on her hips. "If this is the way you're going to act all night long, I'm going next door for some friendly conversation."

Michael's foot froze on the bottom stair. *Next door?* Eden might be next door by now.

A new worry seized him, one that had nothing to do with the secret of his illness. No, his longing for Eden Mallory was a secret of an entirely different nature.

"Sera," he blustered, "there's lightning outside."

"*You* didn't seem to mind it when you drove home."

"That's different. Besides, I don't want you catching your death of cold."

She tossed her black curls, which were slightly damp and more than a little wayward after her afternoon of baking. "I declare, Michael, you see catarrh in every drop of rain. I'm hardly the invalid Mama was, or that Gabriel was, for that matter. I've been cooped up in that kitchen all day long, plucking feathers, grinding corn-meal, and baking pies. It's high time I had a little fun. I'm not married to you, you know."

He winced. The child had a point. On the other hand, she had to learn how to run a household if he was to find her a decent husband.

"It was never my intention to make you a prisoner in our kitchen, Sera. As for being married—"

"Never mind," she interrupted. Her indifference to her most respectable suitor, Preacher Prescott, was another bone of contention between them. "I'm sorry I brought it up. Tell me what happened back in town. With the rain and all, Bonnie didn't stop by this afternoon. I feel like I'm the last person on earth to hear the news."

Michael sighed. If his head weren't doing its level best to split, he wouldn't have let Sera weasel out of the marriage topic so easily.

"What news are you referring to?"

"Honestly, Michael. What has everyone in this town been talking about for the last three weeks? *Eden Mallory.* Bonnie can't bear the fact that Claudia might add Eden to her will, especially at this late date."

A wave of heat rolled up his neck. Claudia's refusal to heed his medical advice was a constant needle in his side. Even though he knew that reversing her age was an impossibility, some part of him still couldn't come to terms with the inevitable. It meant facing an old demon named Failure.

"You know I don't approve of gossip, Sera."

"That's the trouble with you, Michael. You don't approve of anything." She tugged her apron over her head, letting a cloud of flour sift onto the puddle that was creeping across the floor. "If you weren't so blessedly good-looking, I don't know that any woman would want you to come a-courting."

"Is that the kind of 'friendly conversation' you anticipate at Aunt Claudia's?"

She gave a guilty start.

"Well, no. Not exactly." She pursed her lips. "If you really must know, I spend most of my time trying *not* to talk about you to the unmarried girls. One can only stand to hear so much sappy sighing over one's brother. Bonnie's the worst, although Aunt Claudia doesn't help matters any, the way she always brags about you 'taking care of her like a son.' Honestly, if she weren't more than twice your age, I think she'd try to marry you her-self."

Michael grimaced. He supposed he should be flat-tered that half the female population in this town hoped he'd set his cap for them, but he didn't think of himself as any great prize. The simple truth was, Blue Thunder was short on bachelors, and that meant the wedding-bell chasers had time to make mischief. Most bachelors in Blue Thunder considered the two-to-one ratio a dream come true. But for Michael, who knew his illness would prevent him from doing right by a wife, the surplus of love-starved women was nothing short of a nightmare.

"You know, Michael," Sera said, locking her slate-blue stare with his. It was a sure sign she was about to brave forbidden territory. "It wouldn't hurt you to start courting again—and it sure would make my life easier," she muttered under her breath. "Did you get to meet Eden? Is she the hootenanny Bonnie says she is?"

Michael nearly choked to have his kid sister stumble across his most shameful, secret fantasy about Eden.

" 'Course, I wouldn't want your heart stepped on by a hootenanny," Sera said quickly, misinterpreting his distress. "Bonnie says the only reason Eden left Colo-rado is 'cause the Injuns, Chinamen, and beggar-trash wouldn't have her."

Michael flinched. He didn't want to believe that the seventeen-year-old he still remembered so vividly had fallen into the desperate straits of prostitution.

"You have no right to spread such rumors, Sera."

"*I'm* not spreading the rumors," she corrected him primly. "Bonnie is. I'm just trying to find out more about Eden. Is she pretty?"

Michael tore his gaze free as the heat started building again in his face . . . and his loins. The devil take him.

How was he supposed to answer Sera? That Eden Mallory transcended "pretty"? That she was an angel, a vision of the divine? That he was an unholy bastard for taking an innocent's memory to bed with him every night, year after year, until the fantasies had eroded the reality completely? Crouching under that wagon today, thigh to thigh with the flesh-and-blood woman, he might not have recognized her at all, if it hadn't been for her cascade of auburn hair. And then to learn from Aunt Claudia that her niece, his fantasy, was named *Eden*, of all things . . .

"Michael Elijah, I declare." The unabashed amusement in Sera's voice brought him crashing back to the present. "You're blushing."

He snapped erect, towering over her in dire warning. She merely grinned.

"So, you liked her, eh?"

"Seraphina, I will not have you matchmaking for me."

"Of course not, Michael." She flashed impish dimples and turned on her heel, tossing the apron over the bannister.

"Sera! Where are you going?"

"To take a gander at this Eden Mallory you like so much."

Michael groaned to himself. The last thing he wanted was Sera growing friendly with a woman whose father had been a doctor. If any of Mallory's medical wisdom had rubbed off on Eden, she was the one person he could count on to see past his pretenses and warn Sera he was sick.

"Sera," he said sternly, "ogling strangers and carrying tales are not pastimes for proper young girls—"

"I know," she countered cheerfully. "That's why I do

them." Waving, she darted for the kitchen's outside door.

"Sera—"

"Bye, Michael," she called, her words floating above a receding rumble of thunder. "Have a nice sulk."

He muttered an oath. For a moment, he chased after her. But when the lower half of the back door slammed and he glimpsed her dashing rabbitlike through the puddles of their backyard, he halted, reconsidering. Short of raising Sera's suspicions, and acting like a horse's rear end in the process, what possible excuse could he give to prevent his sister from visiting their lifelong neighbor and her guest?

Giving in to the torment, Michael finally raised a hand to his head. *Hellfire.* Eden Mallory was bunking next door.

It was going to be a long summer.

Rubbing his temples, Michael turned once more for the hallway. The ceiling needed paint, and the primrose-dotted paper on the walls was starting to peel along the seam. He hadn't had time to see to the repairs, though, not between his patients and the various odd jobs he did for Aunt Claudia to repay her loan for his medical schooling.

His jaw hardened to think of the futility of that education.

Even after all these years, the thought of Gabriel's death hurt so much, he couldn't bear to look at his brother's daguerreotype. Sera had handled the loss better, but then, at ten years old, Sera hadn't lost her faith in God yet. During Gabriel's burial, she'd sworn she'd seen Mama taking his hand and leading him through the Pearly Gates. Papa, of course, had been livid; he'd told her lying to seek attention was a sin of vanity, and he'd forbidden her to speak of her visions again.

To this day, Michael still wasn't sure what Papa had been objecting to: the idea that Mama had entered heaven after she'd cuckolded him, or the notion that a mere child could communicate with angels while he, the town authority, had never even heard the whisper of wings. In any event, Papa had won: Sera stopped claiming she played with her dead brother, and Gabriel disappeared entirely from household conversations.

Despite his best intentions, Michael's mind drifted, conjuring forbidden thoughts of Eden. Now there was a paradise a man could believe in: autumn-colored hair, luminous green eyes, luscious breasts and hips. He'd known, of course, that Claudia was expecting kinfolk, but he'd never dreamed that visitor might be the object of his fantasies. For weeks after that night in Whiskey Bend, his dreams had raged like a fever out of control, filling his nights with visions of a tempestuous, red-haired siren who'd dried his tears with one hand and massaged his straining crotch with the other.

The very idea made him burn with lust and shame.

Of course, Eden had appeared closer to his own age in the dreams, which had finally dwindled over the years, but not to the point of stopping. In truth, some lonely corner of his soul welcomed their return. But then, he'd never expected to see the real, flesh-and-blood Eden again. He'd never thought he'd have to *face* her.

*But that's not what's troubling you, is it, Jones?* he jeered in self-disgust. *The real trouble is you took a gander at the live woman and came to realize what a poor substitute your imagination has been. She's beautiful.*

A poignant yearning stirred inside him. To the memory of the Tennessee woman-child who'd touched his soul, he could now add the vision of Eden Mallory running across the street, casting her life to the fates, wrestling a wild-eyed horse to save a child. Today he'd seen the strength, the courage, the magnificent spirit of the woman his fantasies had maligned.

He supposed he should be grateful Eden hadn't recognized him. No doubt his clean-shaven mug looked quite different from the cut and swollen face she'd washed in the livery. With eight years of aging to add to the change, he doubted whether Eden would ever recognize him. He hoped his luck held out. He wasn't proud of his behavior that night in Whiskey Bend.

If only Eden weren't so . . . special, he mused wistfully.

*Don't be a fool, Jones. Even if you were in the prime of your health, a woman like Eden Mallory wouldn't look twice at a failure like you.*

The thought lanced his chest, cutting so deeply he actually clutched his heart. Suddenly his knees buckled. He stumbled forward, his hip upsetting the hall table. A flower vase crashed and lamp fixtures tinkled; something wet and smelling of decay struck his cheek. An indescribable panic seized him as he lost all control of the muscles in his legs. He flung out his hands, groping blindly for the coat tree opposite the table. Instead, he fell like an avalanche, striking his temple, helpless to claw his way out of the darkness that flooded his mind.

Collie's head shot up and his hand froze, hovering above the kitchen door's handle. Thunder sounded like crumpling tin around him, but the crashing he'd heard hadn't been thunder.

His heart raced to his throat; he nearly strangled on the air that tried to squeeze by. Straining every sense, every instinct, he tried to isolate that noise again. Mountain sounds he knew, but city sounds confused him. They came from every which way, and they always meant trouble—like hounds on a scent. Or a shotgun blast. Was that crotchety old taxidermist still chasing him?

He crouched the way his cur dog used to, tasting the wind, sniffing the rain. He could run fast, if he had to—not faster than buckshot, but faster than people. And he could outsmart any lazy old city hound, too.

But nothing stranger than usual struck his senses. Just the smell of horse manure mixed with geraniums and cinnamon, and the clatter of rain mingled with the banging of a window shutter.

Collie loosed his breath, sagging back against the door. If he weren't so hungry, he wouldn't have come here. Sera was gone, he knew. He'd seen her run hand-in-hand down the street with a tow-headed man. That she wasn't home, in the kitchen, disappointed him; still, he knew she wouldn't mind if he took a loaf of bread. Or maybe one of her apple pies. Sera had said it wasn't stealing if he left something behind. And he always left flowers for Sera. They had an agreement. It was the others who didn't understand . . . like her brother.

Turning, he raised first his eyes, then his nose, above the half door. He sniffed longingly, his eyes trained on the golden crusts cooling at the center of a sawbuck table. Collie had stolen food a lot less appetizing than that before. But never from Sera, of course. The trouble was, with mud flooding all the ditches, he hadn't been able to find a flower pretty enough to leave her. And he couldn't leave her any of the apples he'd stashed in her rain barrel. He needed those.

He frowned, mouth watering, mind racing. Would

Sera be angry if he brought her flowers later?

A tiny pain speared his heart.

No. He couldn't risk that. Sera was his only friend. Maybe he could sweep the floor for her. He knew how much she hated "house drudgery," as she called it.

Glancing furtively behind him, Collie lifted the latch. The door wasn't locked. It never was. But even if somebody, like that brother of hers, had been mean-spirited enough to lock Sera away from him, Collie would have found a way in. He wasn't the kind who liked to brag, but lock picking was one of his best skills.

Every instinct on alert, Collie slinked inside the yeasty warmth. To him, the kitchen was Sera, all Sera. Eagerly, he sought the lingering signs of her presence: pink lip smears on a coffee cup, a strand of hair dangling from the water pump, dainty footprints in spilled flour. He breathed deeply, forgetting for a moment his gnawing gut and numbing toes. If he concentrated really hard, sorting through the barrage of odors, he could smell Lily of the Valley, Sera's favorite perfume, amidst the bacon grease and spices. He could also smell leather, hair tonic, licorice, and tobacco.

He frowned, sniffing again. Yep, man smells. Not the sort of odors he associated with Doc Jones, even though Collie knew the sawbones was around here somewhere. He'd seen the gelding in its stall.

He edged toward the table, careful to "walk Injun," as Pa used to call it. Sidestepping the flour, skirting a broken egg shell, Collie left no traces of his own on the bleached pineboards. Then he darted another wary glance around him. *So far, so good.* He was just reaching for a jar of strawberry preserves when a long, guttural groan made him jump out of his skin. He spun around, his bowie clutched expertly before him, until he realized no beast was lunging at him from behind.

*Dang.* He drew a shaky breath. *Did Sera own a hound now?*

Then his gaze lit on a piece of broken porcelain. And a puddle of water, mixed with crushed lilac petals. The debris led into the hall, where it was dim. Collie crouched again, his pulse racing. The groan-growl had come from that dimness.

With fourteen years of scrapping to bolster his nerve, Collie decided to investigate. It was Sera's house, after all. And if somebody was out there robbing it, he thought righteously, well . . . he'd do something. He didn't know what, exactly. But he would.

Creeping along the wall, Collie drew close enough to the entranceway to poke his head around the corner. What he saw made him gape. Toppled furniture littered the hall; coats and hats were strewn across a pair of boots. And attached to the other end of those boots, beneath a heap of posies and umbrellas, he spied Doc Jones sprawled on his back.

Collie sniffed suspiciously, looking for whiskey bottles.

*Well, he ain't drunk, at least.*

He edged closer, eyes darting forward and back. When he saw no blood, powder burns, or outlaws lurking in ambush, he squatted warily. Jones looked pale, but not as pale as death. And his breathing was regular. Collie cocked his head. He figured the doc wasn't dying so much as he was dreaming, especially when his legs flailed. *Dang.* Collie hastily jumped out of the way as a picture frame somersaulted off the end table. No wonder things were strewn all over.

Collie wandered back into the kitchen, cutting himself a slice of cornpone before he grabbed a broom. Munching as he swept, he tidied Sera's flour, as well as the blue vase scattered through the hall. 'Course, the skin on his hands and feet was all leather, but he worried that Sera, with her lady's fingers, might get hurt picking up porcelain. So, making sure every last sliver was swept, Collie straightened the furniture and hung the hats and umbrellas. When he'd finished, there wasn't much left of the mess except a watery smear and Jones, who was still snoozing like a baby. Collie shook his head. The doc sure had picked a strange place for a nap.

He leaned on the broom handle, suddenly wondering if Jones was sick. Sera had said Gabriel died of being sick, and Jones had gotten mighty riled when he'd overheard her say that Gabriel had become an angel who liked to play with lonely boys like Collie. That's why Collie knew the doc didn't like him. 'Course, Collie didn't like Jones, either, so that made them even—well, as even as they could be, he thought sullenly. After all, Jones knew all the Samaritans and could sic them on Collie in a heartbeat.

Still, if the doc really was sick, Collie mused, maybe he oughtta go find Sera. Even if *he* had no use for her nosy older kin, Sera did. And he didn't think she'd take too kindly to another dead brother.

Jones groaned again, his head lolling. Collie held his breath. He was just trying to decide whether to stay or run when Jones's glassy blue eyes flickered open and stared square at him.

"R-Rafe?"

*Uh-oh.*

"Am I in hell, or are you just visiting?"

*Satan's bloomers!* Dropping the broom, Collie fled, making sure to grab the cornpone and a pie on his way out the door. *The doc has gone plum loco!*

Michael grimaced at the clatter of wood so close to his ears. Squeezing his eyes closed, he tried to make sense of a senseless situation. *The boy. No, not Rafe. Rafe isn't fourteen anymore . . .*

Michael drew a shuddering breath as the memory of their sibling rivalry started to fade. Where was he? And why was he lying on the floor?

The scent of lilac wafted to his nose.

He raised tremulous fingers and rubbed his temple. He must be in the hall. Yes, he remembered now. He'd fallen. Struck his head, apparently. He'd been upset. He'd been shaken by his encounter with Eden, and when Sera had insisted on going to meet her—

"Sera!" He gasped, his eyes flying wide.

The kitchen door slammed. He was alone.

*Collie.* Michael struggled to sit. *The boy must have been Collie.*

Silence fell thick and fast, broken only by the tick-tock-ticking that droned endlessly from the wall. He glanced up to note the time, and the clock's hands faded in and out before his eyes. He battled a frisson of panic. *My God, what's happening to me?*

Shrugging off wet leaves and petals, he climbed unsteadily to his feet. His pulse was erratic, and his hands tingled as he leaned on the banister. For some reason, he was alive. Why that should be, he didn't know, except that whatever he'd suffered hadn't been an aneurysm.

He shuddered.

Spying the pile of porcelain chips, he heaved a breath and frowned. Collie had been sweeping? He suspected Sera's pie thief hadn't tidied the mess to help *him*. All those years ago, when Sera had tried to comfort Collie over the loss of his hunting hound, Collie had misunderstood Michael's reprimand. He'd been chastising Sera for claiming that Gabriel was in the room, talking to her. Michael hadn't meant to imply that Collie wasn't good enough to play with the "angel" that Gabriel Jones had become. In any event, Collie had gotten his feelings hurt, and matters had only worsened between Collie and Michael when he had stepped forward to help the boy after his father's murder.

Michael's hands shook, and his knuckles whitened on the banister. Just thinking about his seizure and how he himself might have become a corpse a few minutes ago renewed the pounding in his brain. That Collie, not Sera, had found him had been divine providence, but Michael knew his luck wouldn't hold out. Somehow, he had to stop Collie from telling Sera what he'd seen.

# Chapter 3

⸻⟡◦⟡⸻

**I**f Aunt Claudia's Trading Post and Notions was any indication, the residents of Blue Thunder were accustomed to oddities.

At least, that's what Eden told herself as she straightened the shelves in her kinswoman's store. The main counter—the foundation of which looked suspiciously like a chimney—was dominated by an enormous stuffed beaver bearing sawed-off antlers and a skunk's tail. "Cooter," as Aunt Claudia referred to this novelty, was fetchingly attired in doll-sized overalls and roller-skates. Colorful fishing lures dangled from his prongs, and a pair of spectacles teetered precariously on his snout. Eden couldn't help but chuckle every time Aunt Claudia swore to some wide-eyed youngster, "That's how them tree gnawers are grown in the backwoods."

To the left of Cooter and against the rear wall were racks of shotguns, hunting traps, and bowie knives—not so very odd, really—but the centerpiece of this manly display was a wooden bust bearing the latest calico fashion, a sheepskin hat, and snowshoes. To Eden's secret amusement, Claudia had forbidden her to repair this creation with more traditional female fare.

The right side of Aunt Claudia's store was relatively subdued, since its rainbowed array of fabrics, hair ribbons, and skin tonics catered to the fair sex of Blue Thunder. Still, Eden found herself shaking her head when she swept her feather duster over the placard that read, DON'T BE LOOKING FER ANY DANG BLOOMERS HERE. Apparently when it came to her female customers, Aunt Claudia was only willing to make limited concessions.

Eden glanced toward the main counter, where the store's proprietress stood rummaging around her jars of gumdrops, peppermint sticks, and saltwater taffy, Eden's personal favorite.

"Where the dickens is it?" Claudia growled, shoving Stazzie out of her way.

"Where's what?" Eden asked mildly.

"My snuff box, that's what!"

Turning, Claudia glowered at the ten-year-old who was solemnly sprinkling dead flies into his new toad's box. "Jamie Harragan, did you steal my snuff?"

The child's eyes grew bigger than silver dollars. "No, ma'am!"

"Yeah?" Claudia's cagey gaze narrowed, darting suspiciously from side to side. "Well, somebody sure did. Where'd that tow-headed Texican go?"

Eden cleared her throat. "I'm sure Mr. Cassidy was too busy admiring Jamie's toad to pinch your snuff tin, Auntie."

"Burro's milk. Cassidy was busy admiring my money safe. Er . . . not that there ain't nuthin' to admire about Georgie," she added for Jamie's benefit.

The boy looked up anxiously. "Georgie's not eating as good as he did last week." He used a forefinger to tumble the pile of insects closer to his pet. When Georgie made no move to pounce, Jamie bit his lip. "Do you reckon he's sick?"

Claudia harrumphed. "More likely, Georgie's tired of flies—barflies, that is," she added ominously, glancing toward her broken window shutter.

Eden glimpsed a blond head ducking out of sight.

"Dang Cassidy," Claudia groused, stalking to her gun rack and snatching up her scattergun. "And dang that pal of his, Quaid. I don't like the looks of 'em. Them two drifters are nuthin' but trouble, and I don't want them skulking around my store."

For emphasis, Claudia thumped the stock of her shotgun on the window ledge. The window's crank promptly thudded to the floor.

"Tarnation!" Claudia's face flooded with color. "The whole blamed store's falling apart. First the shutter, now this two-bit crank! And yesterday, for no blessed reason, the lid from a licorice jar got dashed all over the floor."

Eden started. She could have sworn she'd heard a boy's muffled laughter coming from outside the window.

Claudia, however, looked far from amused. Stomping over to Cooter's counter, she yanked open a drawer and flung the crank inside. "What deuced good is a handy man if he ain't handy? Michael promised he'd come over and mend my shutter—not to mention my rain-spout—before the week was out. Well, that was *last* Monday." She glared at Eden as if she were somehow to blame. "I ain't seen hide nor hair of that boy since you pulled in to town. Makes me think I'll have to stick that mouser of yours under a wagon wheel if I want to drag him out of hiding."

Stazzie's tail lashed indignantly against the pickle

barrel. Eden gave her a reassuring pat and offered a sprig of parsley to Georgie.

"I'm sure Michael didn't mean to forget you, Auntie," Eden said absently, watching the toad flatten itself on top of the herb, as if it were nesting. "He's probably just been busy."

"Yeah, he's been busy, all right. Busy mooning over *you*."

Eden knew she'd turned as red as Jamie's bandanna. "Really, Aunt Claudia. The man talked once to me, and that was at the stage depot," she said, carefully omitting her worry that he'd recognized her from some previous encounter. "I'd hardly consider our discussion of cuts and bruises grounds for rumors of a courtship."

"That's 'cause you ain't lived around here long enough to know better. Sera says he's sweet on you. And Bonnie's mighty sore about you being Michael's backdoor neighbor." Claudia's face split in an impish, sparsely toothed grin. "Yep, as fillies go, I'd say you're ahead by a nose."

Eden sighed, shaking her head. She didn't bother to point out for at least the tenth time that Michael wasn't behaving like a lovestruck beau. She wondered how much his mysterious first sighting of her was to blame, and how much could be credited to her recklessly altruistic behavior at the stage depot. He had made a point to chide her foolhardiness, after all. Maybe he didn't think her ladylike enough, since she'd charged a rearing horse, flopped in the gutter with her bloomers bared, and audaciously sought to revive Bonnie with a home remedy. To a university-educated doctor like Michael, her Spirits of Hartshorn concoction had probably smacked of quackery. Eden wouldn't have been surprised if he'd decided right then and there that she was a trouble maker whom he'd be wise to avoid.

She just wished he would be more civil about it. The day after her arrival, for instance, when she'd spied him hitching his horse, he'd greeted her with nothing more than a curt nod and a surly, "Mornin'." Later that afternoon, when she'd passed the open window of his clinic, he'd turned his back so hastily, she'd felt certain he'd meant to snub her.

Eden wished she could say Michael's opinion of her didn't matter. But as Sera's guardian, he could end Eden's budding friendship with his sister. Eden had warmed immediately to the younger girl, even though she'd suspected Sera's effusive praise of Michael had been a matchmaking ploy. Sera was the only unmarried young woman in town who didn't glare daggers at her, thanks to Bonnie, and Eden, who'd never lived in any town long enough to make a close friend, was eager to deepen their acquaintance.

The bell jangled over the front door, rousing her from her thoughts. A rosy-cheeked child with wheat-colored ringlets bounced into the store. "Hello, Miss Eden," the eight-year-old said brightly, her eyes already fixed on the candy jars. "Hello, Aunt Claudia. How are you today?"

Claudia grunted, apparently unimpressed by this elfin charm. "I've been better."

Eden hid her smile. "Hello, Amanda. Did you bring us your mama's shopping list?"

"Yes, ma'am." The child juggled a squirming blanket and dug the paper out of her pinafore's pocket.

Claudia tugged her pipe from her lips. "Amanda Jean, that bundle of yours ain't your little brother, is it?"

"Oh no, ma'am. I brought my puppy."

Amanda glanced at Jamie as she spoke. To Eden's

mystification, the children exchanged conspiratorial looks before Jamie blushed and dropped his gaze back to his toad.

Amanda knelt before Stazzie. "Puppy and me were wondering if you'd like to come to our tea party," she crooned as the dozing cat cracked open an eye.

"*Puppy?*" Aunt Claudia snorted. "Amanda Jean Buchanan, you can't go on calling that whelp Puppy."

"I can't?"

" 'Course not."

"How come?"

" 'Cause he's gonna grow up. Be a great big coondog someday. Coondogs need a respectable name."

Amanda looked perplexed. "What's 'respecabell'?" she whispered to Jamie.

"Grown up," he fired back.

"Oh." She peeled back the blanket, as if seeking inspiration from her hound.

Suddenly, a pink tongue darted out. The puppy tried to lick Stazzie, and the cat yowled, recoiling. Wearing a look of potent disgust, she leaped off the pickle barrel and padded to a safer napping place.

"I know!" Amanda was beaming with her newfound idea. "I'll call my doggie *Mr.* Puppy. That's grown up."

Claudia rolled her eyes.

The whelp sneezed.

"Uh-oh." The light in Amanda's face snuffed out. "I think Mr. Puppy has a cold."

"A cold?" Frowning like a hanging judge, Jamie dropped his jar of flies and hurried to Amanda's side. "That puppy wasn't sneezing last night. What did you do to him, Mandy?"

"Nothing!" She snatched the hound from Jamie's reach. "I gave him a bath, is all."

"What for?"

" 'Cause he was smelly on account of the way you—" She seemed to catch herself, clutching the dog closer to her chest and darting a furtive glance at the grown-ups. "Never mind. *Mr.* Puppy," she emphasized, "is my puppy now. And I won't have him being smelly."

"You have to keep baby animals very warm," Eden interceded gently, "especially when they're wet. Otherwise, they get sick like Mr. Puppy did."

"I didn't mean for him to get sick." Amanda sounded stricken. "Is he gonna die?"

Eden winced, caught off guard. Talk of death never failed to remind her of the futility of her training as a medicine woman. "Don't worry, Amanda. I'm sure your Mama can help Mr. Puppy feel better."

Amanda darted another glance—this one anxious— toward Jamie. He cleared his throat.

"Miss Eden, couldn't you help Mr. Puppy?"

Amanda nodded eagerly at Jamie's suggestion.

"Well, I'm not sure that would be—"

"Please?" Amanda chimed in.

Claudia struck a match and squinted at her pipe bowl. "Go on, niece," she mumbled, wreathing herself in smoke. "Michael ain't likely to know any more about puppies than you do."

Eden gaped at this vote of confidence. Only two days ago, Claudia had turned up her nose at Eden's best medical opinion, despite the fact that she'd found her aunt clutching her chest and panting on the stairs. "I'm seventy-five dang years old," Claudia had snapped between breaths. "So's my ticker. I ain't lookin' fer any miracle cures."

Eden had been too mortified at the time to believe that Claudia's reaction hadn't really been an objection to her niece's questionable reputation as a healer.

"I don't know a thing about puppies. I never had one of my own," Eden added lamely, unwilling to admit the truth: She feared she'd do more harm than good.

"Yeah?" Claudia blew out her match and leveled her with a piercing stare. "So what are ye saying? You know more about healing hoppy toads?"

Eden's ears warmed. In truth, the parsley had been more for Jamie's peace of mind than Georgie's well-being. If she'd been a competent medicine woman, she wouldn't have lost Papa. And she wouldn't have been forced to flee Silverton with her tail tucked between her legs.

*Auntie, why are you putting me in this position? You've proven you don't believe in my abilities any more than I do.*

Puppy licked her hand. Amanda sniffled.

Eden's resolve crumbled. To assuage her conscience, she tried to convince herself that curing a whelp's cold wasn't as daunting as trying to save her father from pneumonia. "Very well, Auntie. I'll mix a tonic for Mr. Puppy."

Amanda cheered.

"That's the spirit." Claudia nodded, her gaze canny with approval. "And while you're doin' it"—she rose, her pipe puffing like a chimney as she reached for her scattergun—"I'm gonna march down the street and see what's so jo-fired important that Michael's been holed up in his office like a bear."

"Um . . . do you really think the shotgun's necessary?" Eden ventured.

Claudia snorted. "Obviously, you ain't never hunted bear. C'mon, Jamie. We got critters to track."

Jamie's eyes bugged out as he jumped off his stool.

"Bear critters? The black, savagerous kind you taught Mr. Lincoln how to wrastle?"

Claudia hid a lopsided grin. "Sure as shootin', boy! Why, ol' Abe woulda been coon gone if I hadn't whupped that varmint fer 'im."

"Golly!"

Claudia smirked, tossing Eden a wink.

"Say, you like watermelon, Amanda?"

"Sure!"

Claudia waved her and Mr. Puppy to the door. "C'mon then. Me and Jamie'll show you the best patch to steal 'em from."

The door whacked closed before Eden could protest. A traitorous giggle threatened. Stealing watermelon, indeed. Claudia owned the only patch in town. And what was that nonsense about Abe Lincoln? Last week, Claudia swore she'd taught William Tecumseh Sherman how to tree polecats in the moonlight.

Eden's smile widened as Stazzie coiled like a spring, ready to pounce on an unsuspecting spool of thread.

Eden supposed Claudia's imagination had been a necessary cultivation, helping her through the lonely years of her young womanhood. Claudia had been dubbed the town whore once word leaked of her secret love affair with the widower Harragan. Claudia never did marry Henry Lucas, even though she'd "carried on" with him, as she liked to put it, for forty-five years. To Eden's mystification, Claudia had confided it was she who'd refused to let Harragan "make a decent woman out of her." Now that Eden knew her aunt better, she suspected Claudia had preferred the freedom her scandalous lifestyle had given her.

Then again, Harragan certainly hadn't hurt her independence any when he'd died twelve years ago, willing her his mercantile fortune.

Eden sighed, watching Stazzie scamper under the back room's curtain in pursuit of the spool.

She liked her independence too. But spinsterhood had definite disadvantages. Eden wanted to share her life with someone. Family was the one thing Papa had never been able to give her. Although she'd come to love the copper-skinned woman who'd shared his bed, just about everyone else who learned of Papa's affair with Talking Raven had spurned them like lepers. Eden often suspected that was the real reason Papa kept traveling from town to town, although she'd never once doubted his commitment to helping the sick and crippled in the clapboard villages they'd visited.

The old grief stirred as she recalled those years in the medicine show. For as long as she could remember, she'd heard nothing but praise for the foxglove remedy her father prescribed for his patients' heart palpitations. She refused to believe her last twenty-five years had been filled with lies. She wanted to vindicate Papa, to prove that Andrew Mallory *was* a good doctor.

But Claudia wouldn't touch the remedy, and Eden was terrified of offering it to anyone else. She didn't want a repeat of that dreadful Silverton experience. She wasn't the risktaker Claudia was—or that her mother had been, for that matter. Unlike Lacey Mallory, who'd delighted in stunts such as snowshoeing through avalanche country or chasing wild mustangs through Indian Territory, Eden wanted to live to a ripe old age.

A furtive creaking broke her reverie.

Eden started, spilling some syrup of onion she'd just finished measuring for Mr. Puppy's tonic. Had she heard a footstep in the back room?

She listened uneasily. A minute, perhaps two, dragged by. She heard only silence.

*How strange.*

She was just about to turn her attention back to capping and labeling the remedy when Stazzie loosed a yowl that made every hair on her head stand on end.

"Stazzie?"

Hissing and spitting erupted from Claudia's storage space. Next came a metallic crash that sounded suspiciously like canned goods. Eden hurried to the rear. Pushing back the curtain, she stepped across the threshold and froze.

There before the chaos of dented tins and toppled shelves crouched Collie. Barefoot and defiant, he glared at her through straggly blond hair. In his left hand, he held a ten-inch knife. In the right, he grasped the nape of Stazzie's neck. The cat was flailing for all she was worth. Collie was panting.

"M-my cat," Eden managed weakly, noticing how the boy's blade pointed expertly in her direction. "What are you going to do?"

"Eat it."

She swallowed, unnerved to hear such a gruff, uncompromising tone in a beardless youth.

"But she's my pet."

"Looks like it's time to get a dog."

Stazzie mewed piteously. Collie bared his teeth, looking ferocious.

"Um . . ." Eden did her best to breathe normally. The quarters were cramped, and the shelf he'd knocked over was barring his retreat to the alley. He had nowhere to go but forward. Through her.

She tried not to think about that.

"I don't mean to be difficult, but I'm rather fond of

that cat. Not as a meal," she added quickly. "As a companion."

He didn't look the least bit sympathetic. She thought fast.

"Are you hungry?"

This time, she saw the flicker of interest in those burning gray eyes. He tossed the hair off his forehead.

"Why?"

"Well . . ." She gestured carefully behind her. "I have some fried chicken and a cherry pie in a picnic basket behind the front counter. Aunt Claudia and I were going to eat them for dinner, but you're welcome to them. I suspect they'll taste a whole lot better than Stazzie."

Collie grunted. It was a noncommittal sound that didn't bolster her confidence. Even so, he wanted to eat. And God help him, he needed to. The boy was alarmingly thin, his cheekbones protruding beneath the canyons of his eyes, which themselves were rimmed with shadow. His Adam's apple jutted above skeletal shoulders, and his elbows looked too knobby for his arms. With each breath, his faded red gingham sank into a concave abdomen, and his dungarees would have fallen clean off his hips if his belt hadn't been double-cinched. Eden suspected he carried some intestinal parasite. At the very least, he was dehydrated and malnourished. Yet for all his apparent weakness, Collie gripped that bowie knife with the efficiency of a veteran butcher.

"If you don't like pie," she improvised, trying to recall what else in the store might appeal to a half-starved, wild man-child, "I've got tapioca pudding. And there're apples, canned peaches, licorice, and venison jerky. If you like, I can warm up some Arbuckles in the coffee-pot—"

"Cats is just fine."

"Oh."

Eden bit her lip. Although virtually helpless in the boy's fist, Stazzie nevertheless resumed her struggles, doing her valiant best to damage Collie's eardrums with her caterwauling.

"Are you sure?" Eden had to raise her voice. "I mean, I should think killing, skinning, and cooking a cat would be a bit troublesome. Compared to a nice plump chicken leg and an oozing slab of cherry pie."

Collie's tongue darted across his bottom lip. Then, as if recognizing his weakness, he gave her an even fiercer glare.

"You got any potato salad?"

"Well . . . no. But I have some deviled eggs. Will they do?"

"I dunno . . ."

"It wouldn't take but a moment to fetch them," she added.

Collie knitted tawny brows. "No tricks?"

"Of course not."

"You swear?"

Eden blinked, appalled that anyone, much less a child, should have to barter for meals. "I swear."

" 'Cause if you don't got no pie," he threatened, flicking the knife tip with his thumb, "it's gonna be kitty cat steaks fer the next coupla meals."

"Collie," she assured him quietly, "I'm happy to give you any food I have."

He started when she used his name. Jaw jutting, he looked her up and down.

"You ain't from any danged orphanage, are you?"

"No." She kept her voice soft. "Why would you think that?"

" 'Cause that's the only kind around these parts who

wants to help me. 'Cept fer Sera, of course."

"You mean Sera Jones?"

The distrust had crept back into his eyes. "Mebbe."

"I know Sera, too. She's my neighbor."

He harrumphed.

"It sounds like you and I have the same friend."

He said nothing.

She tried another tactic. "My name's Eden."

"So?"

A wave of warmth rolled up her face. So much for social pleasantries. Bless the child, was he always this hostile? She hated to think what had happened in his young life to harden him this way.

"I just thought you'd want to know. Because if you like the pie enough," she hinted broadly, "you might want to come calling at my house for more."

"Well, I can't know how much I like anything if you keep jawin' at me all day, now can I?"

"That's true." She hid her smile. "Wait here."

"Nuthin' doin'. I'm coming too. No tricks, ya hear?" He gave Stazzie a menacing shake.

"No tricks," she murmured.

Ferocious and stiff, he stalked after her through the curtain, Stazzie dangling impotently from his fist. He planted his back to the front door, still wielding his knife like a buccaneer, but as he stood before the licorice, it was a child's longing that stared out of those silvery eyes.

"You can have as much candy as you like," she called over her shoulder.

"Yeah?" He edged closer, seemed to remember his hands were full, and halted. "How come?"

She shrugged. "You want some, don't you?"

He hesitated.

"I said you could have any food you wanted."

His brows snapped together. "How come you're being nice to me?"

"Shouldn't I be?"

He fidgeted, his gaze riveted now on the pristine, golden crust she was lifting from the picnic basket.

"I was gonna eat your cat," he reminded her grudgingly.

"But you're not now, are you?" She skirted the counter to stand before him with her offering.

"I reckon not."

He dropped Stazzie, who bolted like lightning for the calico display.

Eden focused all the warmth of her smile on the boy. Like a wild animal, he shifted from foot to foot, torn between yearning and distrust. She could almost feel how much it cost him to yield the first step. Then the second. Finally, he stood quivering before her, his heart beating so hard, she could see the flutter of his gingham shirt.

"You can cut it yourself, if you like," she said quietly.

He licked his lips and raised the knife.

That's when the door bell jangled. A mountain of a man stepped forward, the setting sun carving his silhouette out of the doorway like an onyx wall. For a moment, she could see little more than that blaze of orange molding a magnificent torso.

Then sunbeams glinted off Collie's blade.

"Eden," Michael choked. "My God!"

Collie spun; Michael lunged, his work tools clattering around him. Two hundred pounds of muscle slammed into the half-starved boy, driving Collie back across the counter.

"Michael, no!" Eden cried as the blade clattered and

Collie snarled, kicking and punching with all the tenacity of a cornered cougar. Hastily, she pushed the pie onto a barrel. "Don't hurt him!"

It wasn't much of a contest. Michael simply clamped his fist over the boy's collar, and Collie wheezed, his face reddening as he clawed the bear paw squeezing the breath from his throat.

"Michael, please . . ." Eden tugged at his sleeve as the boy slumped, panting, his face full of humiliated fury. "He wasn't hurting me! He was only going to cut the pie!"

Michael pulled the boy to his feet, a handful of shirt still wrapped in his fist. "Is that true, Collie?"

Collie curled his lips like a dog. He tried to kick Michael between the legs, but Michael dodged, upsetting the pie. It thumped to the floor, splattering cherries and juice in every direction. Exasperated, Eden slapped Michael's bicep.

"Stop it! Both of you. Michael, let him go. You're two times his size."

"I ain't afeared of any prissy old preacher's brat," Collie rasped.

Their stares locked. Eden could have sworn she saw the smoke.

"Collie," Michael bit out, a thread of iron lacing his tone, "you need a bath. And a toothbrush. And what the devil is this?" He turned the boy and pointed to a circular bulge in his back pocket. It looked suspiciously like Aunt Claudia's snuff tin.

"Ain't none of your beeswax!"

"Collie," Eden interjected more gently, "you'd feel a lot better, I'm sure, if you ate a warm meal instead of, uh, snuff."

"Did you pay for that snuff?" Michael demanded.

Collie twisted snakelike. When his shirt didn't rip and Michael's grip didn't break, he scowled.

"Son, if you keep thieving, you're going to wind up like your pa. Is that what you want?"

"My pa was a *real* man, not some nancy-boy like you!" the boy spat.

Suddenly, Collie's elbow rammed up and back, cracking Michael's jaw. He staggered, and Collie broke free. Diving for his knife, he scrambled over Michael's tools and raced for the street.

Eden winced as the door banged closed after him. So much for earning the boy's trust.

"Um . . . Michael?"

He was working his jaw and shaking his head.

"Are you all right?"

"Yes. Of course."

He towered over her, the indomitable mountain once more. Eden might have doubted her first impression entirely, that Collie's blow had rattled him, if she hadn't seen the bruise purpling the soft underside of his chin.

She sighed. She supposed Aunt Claudia had convinced Michael to close his office for the day. Facing him in all his brooding intensity, she had time to notice he'd changed from his suit. Minus the dark coat, vest, and tie she'd seen him wear on every other occasion, he should have looked more relaxed. Instead, his unbuttoned shirt collar betrayed the rapid flutter of his pulse, and his thigh-hugging blue jeans accentuated the tension in his limbs.

She couldn't help but wonder what bothered Michael more: Collie's blow or her company.

"It was very chivalrous of you to come to my rescue, Michael," she said with genuine sincerity, "but Collie's harmless."

Color bloomed in his cheeks.

"Collie is *not* harmless. Not as long as he's running loose with an Arkansas toothpick sheathed to his hip."

"He's just a child."

"He's fourteen years old. And like it or not, that's man enough to be hanged."

"For heaven's sake, anyone with eyes can see the boy's starving. He's just trying to survive."

"I haven't met a man yet who needs snuff to survive," Michael said darkly. "Collie is his father's son. He won't go to school; he refuses to work; and he'd rather steal than take charity. At this rate, he's going to wind up like his pa did. Dead."

Eden's stomach turned. Surely Collie wasn't as bad as all that! During her medicine show travels, she'd treated gunfighters and thieves, men far less couth and a great deal more callous than the silver-eyed youth who'd stared with such longing at the licorice he couldn't afford. Collie might be wild, but he wasn't heartless. And being rebellious didn't make him evil. What it did make him, though, was hard to love.

"I've been a stranger in a lot of places, Michael. One of the things it taught me was to see things local people overlook. Like Collie. He's not just hungry; he's sick."

Eyes like indigo granite bored into hers. "He told you that?"

"No, but . . ." She hesitated, her sympathy for Collie vying with her reluctance to antagonize Michael. Presenting herself as a medical authority, especially if he'd witnessed her rallying crowds for Papa's tonic demonstrations, was a guaranteed way to earn Michael's scorn. "There were splotches of dried blood on Collie's . . . um, bottom."

Michael's chest swelled. She couldn't tell if he was indignant or contrite.

"If what you saw was blood," he said gruffly, "Collie could have gotten it any number of ways. He could have sat where he'd skinned his last meal, for instance. There's no telling."

"Someone could ask him."

"*Ask* him?" Michael sounded incredulous. "You heard the boy's mouth. You'll never get a straight answer out of Rafe—I mean, Collie." His ears reddened.

Turning abruptly, he stepped over his toolbox to begin gathering his hammers, screwdrivers, and nails.

Eden watched him speculatively. Wasn't Rafe Michael's half-brother? The one whose letter to Sera had arrived only that morning, addressed to Claudia's store? Good heavens, was the blood between Rafe and Michael so bad that Sera couldn't receive Rafe's letters in her own home?

"You know, Michael," she said carefully, "my papa once told me people use anger to keep other people from getting too close. Close enough to see the hurt they hide inside."

He set his jaw.

She gently prompted, "Maybe Collie's more scared than dangerous."

"Eden," he said tersely, "I wouldn't presume to debate your father's ideologies with you."

She winced. So much for mending fences with the man.

Shoving the last wrench into his toolbox, he stalked to the half-hinged shutter and set to work. Other than the clank of pliers, the rattle of wooden slats, and the scratching of Jamie's toad in its box, nothing could be heard in Claudia's store. Eden sighed, gathering a broom and dustpan to sweep up the cherry goo.

Stazzie, meanwhile, had apparently composed herself. Slinking out of her sanctuary, she darted a wary look around the store, her whiskers twitching. For some reason, Michael, not the fallen pie, captured her attention. He knelt on one knee, keeping his back turned. Eden might have been grateful for the consideration, except the ensuing silence clapped around them like thunder. Stazzie didn't seem to mind, though. She watched him intently, taking a tentative step forward. Then another. Suddenly she burst into a purr as rusty as the window's old crank. Bemused, Eden watched as her imperious, self-absorbed feline padded the rest of the way to the sawbones and butted her head against his inner thigh.

Michael jumped about six inches.

"Anastasia!" Eden's face flamed as red as Michael's neck. "Stop that!"

To her credit, the cat didn't ignore her completely. Instead, she sat down on her haunches against Michael's knee and continued to purr in affectionate little rumbles. Michael had to step gingerly around her.

"I'm, uh, sorry about my cat," *whose neck you'd be well justified in wringing right now,* Eden groaned to herself as Stazzie slinked back between his legs. *For heaven's sake, Stazzie. Show a little decorum!* "I don't know what has gotten into her," she added meekly. "Stazzie doesn't usually like people. In fact, she avoids them—unless they're sick."

Michael made what could only be described as a choking sound. Stazzie rubbed his ankle, purring all the louder.

"Um . . ." Eden set aside the broom, wondering what would be more scandalous, prying Stazzie from Michael's leg or watching the cat rub whatever sinewy, male body part she chose. "Would you like me to put Stazzie outside?"

"That would be appreciated, yes," he ground out, making a dexterous grab for the fur behind Stazzie's neck. The cat yowled in indignation, but Michael braved flailing claws and flashing fangs to thrust Stazzie toward the door. Eden held it wide, and the sullen feline stalked across the threshold, her tail slashing the air behind her.

*Thus ends another cease-fire.* In resignation, Eden dumped the dustpan, rubbed it clean of pie filling, then turned back to Mrs. Buchanan's grocery list. As much as Eden was dying to know where she remembered Michael from, she didn't dare ask him to enlighten her until she was confident they could both laugh over the incident as friends. Unfortunately, the chances of that happening were growing bleaker by the moment.

As if to verify her conclusion, Michael began hammering with a vengeance.

Wincing at the sound, Eden checked the onion bin. Finding it empty, she crawled up on Aunt Claudia's stool to complete Mrs. Buchanan's order. The perch was awkward with its wobbling three legs, but she needed its extra height to reach the onion sack that Aunt Claudia, or more likely Michael, had thrust on the top shelf.

"Blast," she muttered when her fingers fell short of their mark. Careful not to trip over her skirts, Eden eased herself back to the floor and moved the stool more directly under the sack. She glanced hopefully over her shoulder. Michael was busy cranking a wrench and didn't appear to have the slightest inkling of her dilemma.

"Um, Michael? Do you think you could—"

"Help you?" he finished for her, testing the window handle he had just repaired. "I was wondering if you were too stubborn to admit you weren't tall enough."

*Ooh*. Eden fumed. So he *had* been aware of her dilemma!

"Never mind," she retorted. "I may not be tall, but I'm resourceful." Grabbing a nearby wall hook, she leveraged herself higher, testing the strength of a shelf with her foot.

"Eden," Michael warned.

"Pray go back to grousing. I'm sorry I disturbed you."

"Don't be a fool."

She heard his boots thumping behind her, and she glared over her shoulder. "Michael Jones, you stay right where you are. I don't need or want your—"

She was interrupted by an insidious cracking. The hook twisted in her hand. Suddenly, the mounting ripped from the wall, and she gasped, flailing through a hail of plaster. She made a desperate grab for a shelf; the stool heaved, throwing her sideways. She might have crashed to the floor if her breasts hadn't struck Michael's shoulders first. His arms clamped over her waist, and she "oomphed." She found herself sliding down his torso.

For a suspended moment in time, she was locked in his embrace. Her heart hammered madly against his chest; her feet dangled helplessly beneath her. All she could see in that instant were his eyes, two molten pools of sapphire, so hot and hungry they consumed her senses, flushing her skin with fever.

She gulped, her breath rattling in her throat like dried leaves.

"Th-thank you."

His lashes fanned downward, inky spikes that did

little to impede the radiant heat of his gaze.

"Y-you can put me down now."

"You're bleeding."

His voice, husky warm with concern, rumbled deep in his chest and vibrated into hers. It was a heady sensation, one that distracted her almost completely from the throbbing in her left hand.

"I am?" She noticed then the ragged flash of her knuckles and the bruise purpling the base of her thumb.

He nodded. As he held her, she could feel the heat of his hands, reassuring but titillating too, as they spanned her waist. If she hadn't been so convinced the man disliked her, she might have wondered at his delay, as minute as it was, in lowering her to the ground. His breadth blocked out everything at this proximity, everything but the lightning-swift charge that seemed to leap from his belly into hers. She had little doubt he'd felt their fireworks, because when she tilted her head to gaze past his stubbled chin, she glimpsed the answering flame in his cheeks.

Breaking their contact, he abruptly turned and straightened the stool. "Wait here," he rasped.

His trip to the rain barrel gave her time to slow her racing pulse, but when he returned to her side with a valise and a sloshing bucket, her silly heart jumped like a rabbit.

"Are you hurt anywhere else?" he asked in a tone that was still too throaty to be entirely businesslike.

"I . . . don't think so." *Really*. What was the matter with her, letting the man's presence electrify her nerves? And what had she been thinking, letting him goad her into climbing shelves like a half-grown Indian? She wasn't a thirteen-year-old anymore, shimmying up elder trees to gather berries for Talking Raven. Besides, she was trying *not* to make a sensation in Blue Thunder. It unnerved her to think that Michael might already know about the past she was trying to flee. Part of her thought she should befriend him to woo his loyalty and his silence. Another part of her wanted to avoid him and his inevitable censure.

She watched him uncomfortably, trying not to notice how the sultry summer twilight had moistened his shirt, making it cling to the muscles of his back. He opened his valise and retrieved a cake of soap. After lathering and rinsing his hands, he turned to her.

"Let's see the damage."

She fidgeted. Michael had composed his voice again; he'd even managed to smooth his features into a semblance of professional courtesy. He was a fine actor, she decided, the way he appeared willing to put aside their differences in such a short span of time. Would he still be willing to help her, she wondered, if he knew vigilantes wanted to punish her for helping Papa peddle a homemade heart remedy?

"It's just a scrape," she hedged, peeking at the swollen knuckles she'd wrapped in her apron. "In fact, it looks a good deal worse than it feels."

"Let me be the judge of that."

"You needn't go to any trouble—"

"Eden." His voice was quiet, but it rang with an unmistakable authority. "Give me your hand."

She bit her lip. She suspected the only reason he hadn't dragged her hand out of hiding was because she'd tucked it between her thighs. "Very well."

He took her wrist. Much to her embarrassment, her pulse thumped wildly beneath the pads of his fingers.

His eyes raised to hers. They were warmer than ever, but wary too. "That was quite a spill you had."

She blushed, glad for the distraction when he cupped water over her scrapes with his hand.

"I suppose an 'I-told-you-so' is in order."

An endearing dimple creased his cheek. "You're your great-aunt's niece. That's all I care to say."

"Is that so bad?"

"Actually . . ." The dimple deepened, and he used his own shirttail to pat her knuckles dry. "It's quite refreshing."

In that moment, Eden couldn't recall a single reason to be annoyed with him.

"Does this hurt?"

She winced, nodding as he rotated her thumb. "I must have jammed it."

"Hmm." He shifted, and lamplight struck blue highlights from his hair. "Ice will reduce the swelling. And eucalyptus oil will soothe the bruise after that. If Aunt Claudia doesn't have any, come by my office tomorrow morning."

"I'm sure I needn't bother you over a bruise."

"You won't be bothering me, Eden. Your health is my responsibility."

As he reached into his valise for a jar of ointment, his seriousness struck her in an odd way. Part of her was touched to realize the depth of concern he must feel for his patients. But another part of her was troubled to think he held himself accountable for her healing. That's when she recalled something Sera had said. "Michael thought he could cheat God and keep Gabriel alive. But of course, he couldn't. The angels came, and . . . Well, I don't think Michael has ever been the same."

Odd, wasn't it, Eden mused, that she and Michael had each failed to save a loved one? She marveled that he had found the courage to carry on with his work—

a courage she feared she might never muster.

"Michael," she murmured, her respect for him growing by leaps and bounds, "I hope you don't really believe you're responsible for my health."

"I am Blue Thunder's doctor."

"Yes, but I was the careless one."

"How you were injured is irrelevant."

"Michael . . ." Her heart twisted for him. No one understood better than she how weighty self-blame could be. "Sera told me about Gabriel."

His hands fumbled with the lid of the jar. For the briefest of moments, his composure slipped, and she glimpsed the anguish he'd grown so adept at concealing.

"Sera talks entirely too much about private matters, especially mine."

"She's very fond of you," Eden said gently. "I think she worries and is looking for reassurance."

"Then she should speak to me."

Eden sighed. He did have a point. Still, if she were in Sera's shoes, she wasn't certain she would bare her soul to Michael, either. He might be a finely trained medical doctor, but he didn't possess the manner that encouraged a girl to divulge her secrets or her dreams.

"I'm very fond of your sister, you know," she said, thinking to give Michael a new perspective on Sera. "She's gone out of her way to be neighborly. Why, she came to the store with fresh-baked peach cobbler the day she introduced herself."

Michael's hand stilled, a dollop of salve quivering on his fingertips. "To the store, you say?"

"Yes. It was a lovely, thoughtful gesture on Sera's part."

Michael's face darkened, and Eden suspected he disagreed.

"Sera is delightful," she said hurriedly, not sure what had caused his ire this time. "And she's an excellent cook. We all ate the cobbler for dessert that evening. It was a shame you couldn't join us."

His lips twisted mirthlessly as he reached for a bandage.

"I'm glad to know Sera spent that evening with you, at least."

"I'm not sure I understand."

"It seems my sister hasn't been completely honest with me."

*Oh no.* Eden received an unwelcome insight. *Don't tell me Sera has been using me as an excuse to sneak out of the house at night with Billy Cassidy.* "Maybe you just misunderstood."

"No." He sounded upset. "I am very clear about where Sera said she was going the night of the storm. It's the one thing I am clear about," he muttered under his breath.

Eden watched him uncertainly. She could have sworn she'd sensed the rise of something panicky in Michael a moment before he'd tamped it down. She didn't know if his worry about Sera was to blame, or if something else was troubling him.

Releasing her hand, he abruptly stood. "You'll experience swelling in that thumb." His voice sounded unnaturally strained. "Soak it in ice for as long as you can. Tomorrow, begin applying hot water bottles to stimulate the blood."

Eden blinked at him. Was it her imagination, or did he look a shade paler than before?

He took several steps and swayed. Suddenly he was

grabbing for the counter. A jar of peppermint sticks crashed to the ground.

"Michael?"

She rose in concern. He stood with his head bowed and his eyes squeezed tightly closed. Every muscle in his body was taut and quivering.

"What's wrong?"

He waved her away, somehow managing to straighten, to open his eyes. They were glazed with pain.

"Did Collie's punch—"

"No," he gasped. "Not Collie. I apologize. That . . . that was clumsy of me. There's no need for you to be concerned. I'll pay for the jar and candy."

Eden suspected his sheer strength of will kept him from buckling at the knees. "Michael, please. Sit down. Aunt Claudia won't care about the—"

The front door banged open. The proprietress herself stood scowling on the threshold, her shotgun in one hand, a slice of watermelon in the other. Jamie and Amanda, their chins spattered with red juice, crowded in behind her.

"Lawd Awmighty," Claudia scolded. "It's loud enough to wake snakes in here. What's all the commotion about?"

Michael was breathing more heavily than usual as he packed his valise. "Eden took a misstep. Nothing serious. A couple scrapes and a bruised thumb. Would you fetch her some ice, please, Claudia?"

Claudia looked suspiciously at the glass shards scattered across the pinewood planks of her floor. "A misstep, eh?" She snorted. "It's more likely you two lovebirds were chasing each other around the room."

"Aunt Claudia, really." Eden was too worried about

Michael to do more than glance at her kinswoman. "Jamie, will you fetch a broom and dustpan, please?"

The boy scampered into the rear room even as Michael stooped, his hands shaking as he retrieved pieces of glass.

"Michael, you really should sit down," Eden urged softly.

"For what purpose?" He paused to match her stare for stare. For a moment, those blue eyes were so unflinching, she might have doubted his malaise if she hadn't seen the tremor in his hands.

He dropped the glass into the trash barrel. Then, as if fearing he really was too weak to continue his charade, he hastily latched his medical bag and turned for the door.

"Hey." Claudia planted her fists on her hips. "You just got here. Where do you think you're going?"

"My office. I forgot about an appointment."

"But my shelves! You promised you'd build me some in time for the jamboree."

"They'll have to wait." He gave a curt nod. "Ladies."

Claudia muttered an oath as the front door slammed.

Uneasily, Eden pushed back the shutter and looked out the window. Stazzie was dashing off the porch after Michael. The cat appeared to be mewing for his attention, but he ignored her as he hurried toward his office. Fumbling with his keys, he staggered inside, shutting Stazzie out so firmly that the window shade slapped against the door.

A minute passed, maybe two. Michael never turned the CLOSED sign around, but he did light a lamp. She could see his silhouette as he grabbed the arm of a chair, sinking heavily onto its seat. Stazzie scratched at the door. Then she paced the mat. Finally, she hunkered down as if keeping a vigil.

Eden swallowed. Even if she couldn't always trust her own instincts, she could trust Stazzie's. Something was ailing Michael Jones.

An insidious panic crept through her. What cruel twist of fate had brought her, a healer who had sworn never to heal, to a town whose doctor needed as much help as his patients?

*I'm not ready,* she shouted silently. *I'm not ready to fail the way I did in Silverton. Let someone else salvage Blue Thunder's broken hearts and bones.*

*But Michael's in such pain,* came the quiet response.

She hugged her arms to her chest, remembering Gabriel. *Yes,* she acknowledged uneasily. *Yes, he is.*

She gazed once more toward the silhouette holding its head in that lonesome doctor's office. What ailed Michael, she wondered. Did he know?

Did Sera?

# Chapter 4

Nearly ten days passed, and Eden saw no sign of Michael. Sera confessed she hadn't seen much of him either. He'd been arriving so late from the orphanage and waking so early to return, that some nights, she suspected he hadn't come home at all.

Eden didn't think it was wise for a physician to deny himself sleep, even if there was a measles epidemic, but she told herself Michael's health was a private matter. Besides, she preferred not to remind him, or anyone else for that matter, that she had once purported to be a healer.

Eden sighed. Honoring her truth, as Talking Raven used to call it, had been easier when the Cherokee was alive. Then Eden had had someone to champion her as she struggled to express—and believe—her innate wisdom. She couldn't always explain to her father why she'd instinctually known things about healing that he'd had to study for years. Most of the time, she couldn't explain her intuition to herself. But Talking Raven had told her the feminine spirit was a powerful force. "Woman must speak and be heard," the Cherokee would say whenever Eden balked, fearing the disapproval of her father. "Unless Woman speaks, the wounds of the people will not be healed. It is the spirit of the Earth Mother that speaks through Woman, teaching the two-leggeds and four-leggeds how to live in peace. Would you silence the message of the Great Mother?"

So Eden would try her best to express her opinion, but her confidence always wavered in the face of her father's skepticism. Maybe that's why Papa had so often dismissed her recommendations as simplistic. Talking Raven had encouraged her to follow the teachings of the Female Elders, that the body and the spirit must be addressed to effect a complete cure; Papa, however, had seen illness strictly as a physical malfunction. "A physician must look at empirical evidence," he'd counseled her and Talking Raven. "He must study which compounds are proven remedies for each complaint. I know you mean well, but prayers, rattles, and drums do not cure gout. Or dropsy."

Or pneumonia, unfortunately.

Eventually, Papa had learned to regard Talking Raven's shamanic rituals with amused tolerance, while Talking Raven had grudgingly conceded there was room for many approaches to the same cure. Thus they had lived together, teaching each other to think in broader ways. But until they'd reached that accord in the last year of Talking Raven's life, their arguments had confused Eden, making her feel torn between their ideologies. In the end, she'd dabbled in each method of healing and had failed miserably at both.

Haunting her now was Michael. He was eerily similar to the man her father used to be. But she wasn't Talking Raven. And her mistakes had proved she never would be. As advantageous as it would be to befriend Michael,

Eden wasn't sure she could endure his know-it-all attitude with the same aplomb that Talking Raven had learned to adopt toward Papa. Indeed, Eden wasn't convinced she should have to, not if Woman, as Talking Raven had claimed, must speak and be heard.

*But I still have so many questions about Papa's death. And Michael's the most likely person to answer them.*

Turning the store's key over and over in her hands, Eden paused on the threshold, deftly straddling the broken porch plank that had tripped many an unwary pedestrian and jolted countless packages from the arms of hurrying shoppers. The sun, spitting fire behind the jagged ridge of mountains, slashed lavender-pink ripples through unfurling wisps of clouds. She squinted westward, blinking toward the office with the boldly lettered, no-frills shingle: PHYSICIAN. Peach-colored streaks tinged the walls; for the first time in days, a golden glow radiated through the blind, that same blind which had silhouetted Michael as he'd sunk into a winged chair and so forlornly held his head.

Eden shook herself.

Michael Jones was a grown man and a university-trained doctor to boot. He wouldn't want her to fuss over him.

Besides, she still hurt too much over Papa's death to bear her soul to a physician who was more likely to condemn than comfort her.

Squaring her shoulders, she thrust the key in the store's lock, twisted it, and turned eastward for the shady lane of cobblestones that led to her aunt's red-brick cottage. Usually she'd be home feeding Stazzie by now, but she'd been delayed again by Amanda. Mr. Puppy, apparently, had stepped on a thorn. The day before, Amanda had rushed into the store, worried because the raccoon that Mr. Puppy had chased into a tree wouldn't come down. Two days before that, Amanda had brought Mr. Puppy to Claudia's back door, complaining her pet had a dry nose. Eden had grown suspicious, demanding to know how many dogs Amanda really owned, since Mr. Puppy had mysteriously developed white speckles on his muzzle. Amanda solemnly swore Mr. Puppy had always had the distinctive markings and that Eden just hadn't noticed.

Eden supposed the explanation was possible; however, she found it curious that Amanda had yet to bring the puppy back for a checkup, even though she herself appeared every day at the store, seeking a solution to some veterinary dilemma. Eden wondered if the child badgered Michael this way when he wasn't battling measles epidemics.

Passing Pine Mountain Bank on the other side of the street, Eden noticed Jesse Quaid. The drifter's spine rested against a porch post, the heel of one dusty boot tucked comfortably beneath his buttocks. His stance was relaxed, almost indolent as he struck a match, cupping the flame and tilting his head so his cigarette caught fire. Smoke spiraled across the slouching brim of his Stetson; a whispery breeze riffled the red-checkered bandanna at his throat. He might have been the subject of a Frederic Remington portrait, the Texas cowboy that figured in so many schoolboy dreams, but there was one unsettling exception. He wore his holster too low across his hips. Only gunfighters wore rigs the way Jesse Quaid did. After all the bullet wounds she'd helped Papa stitch out west, she'd become adept at recognizing the nervy, dangerous men who lived by the gun.

She stumbled at the thought, attracting his attention.

Although his head never moved, she knew the instant his gaze touched her, knew it with a trembly shiver. His eyes—a startling shade of green, as she recalled—probed her. Dismissed her. Looked beyond. Her breath released in a ragged whoosh.

A heartbeat later, she caught it again. Jesse was staring into the alley behind her. Staring at the couple conversing so animatedly in the shadows. Staring at Sera.

"Miss Mallory."

She whirled, nearly biting her tongue in two. The call had come from a doorway she had recently passed. She was only vaguely relieved when she saw Blue Thunder's sandy-haired preacher emerge from the headquarters of the Ladies Aid Society. But at least the dark sorcery of Jesse Quaid's spell was broken.

"Good evening, Reverend Prescott," she murmured as he doffed his black bowler and halted at her side.

Henry nodded, his nervous gaze sliding to Jesse, who paid him only passing interest. Eden suspected the drifter didn't see a preacher as a threat, particularly a preacher with the fuzzless face of a babe. If not for the indistinct creases around Henry's hazel eyes, one might have thought him no more than fifteen.

Eden had learned from Sera, though, that the lanky, dimpled preacher was close to twenty-five, a statistic which, apparently, failed to impress Sera. Like most folks in this town, Henry had grown up in Blue Thunder; he rarely rode beyond the city limits; and someday, he would be buried here. For an adventure-seeking belle, a stable, unambitious man like Henry was a dull prospect. In fact, Sera privately referred to her love-struck suitor as "Pestcott."

"I do beg your pardon, Miss Mallory," Henry said, his voice, at least, too sonorous for fifteen. "I was hoping to speak with you about Collie MacAffee."

Eden frowned. *Uh-oh*. Had Bonnie converted Henry into one of her minions? As president of the Ladies Aid Society, a meddling gaggle of matrons who had nothing better to do than pass judgment on their neighbors and bully them into stringent codes of behavior, Bonnie considered it her sworn duty to reform Blue Thunder Valley's "white trash."

Eden met Henry's gaze evenly. "Collie MacAffee, sir?"

"Yes. Sera—that is to say, Miss Jones"—Henry blushed like a properly smitten beau—"said Dr. Jones visited your aunt's store a week or so ago and found Collie. He mentioned there was some, er, misunderstanding over a cherry pie."

Eden casually maneuvered her stance so Henry's back was to Sera's tête-à-tête with Billy Cassidy. "Yes, I recall the incident."

"So it's true the boy was making trouble?"

Eden eyed the preacher dubiously. She suspected Sera hadn't said *that* about Collie. "Collie was hungry. And I don't think he's well."

"You've befriended him, then?"

"Is there a reason behind these questions, Mr. Prescott?"

Running his bowler's brim through his hands, he cast another uncomfortable glance at Jesse. "The boy's grown up ornery. Like his pa. He's been an outsider since the day he was born. I know he's had an unfortunate lot, what with his mama dying in childbirth, and then his pa getting lynched. Still, the boy's a problem. No one wants their sons and daughters influenced by his cussing and his willfulness. He defied the Ladies Aid Society's best Christian efforts to put him in an orphanage. And now that Berthold Gunther is accusing him of theft—"

"Theft?" Eden sucked in her breath. "You mean the canned peaches in the street, don't you?"

"That's the least of the charges. Collie has had several confrontations with Bert since then. The boy's been trespassing on Bert's spread, and Bert says his property's disappearing."

Eden frowned. Collie was stealing from Gunther? Somehow that didn't ring true. Berthold Gunther wasn't known for the luxuries he kept. He lived on the fringe of the piney woods, in a seedy, one-room shack, the offal-strewn yard of which was a health hazard to anyone foolish enough to pass through its gate. Certain upstanding males of Blue Thunder were rumored to slink out there at night, far from the disapproving eyes of their wives, and place bets. Their anonymous patronage was the only reason Gunther hadn't been jailed for baiting cocks, bears, dogs, and God only knew what other unfortunate creatures.

"I can't imagine," Eden said primly, "what property Mr. Gunther might own that would tempt a boy to theft."

*Unless, of course, Collie stole a gun . . .*

Henry fidgeted, apparently searching for a delicate way to broach the secret that every male in this town only *thought* they were keeping hidden from their womenfolk. "Bert says his . . . uh, taxidermy specimens have been disappearing."

*So that's what he calls them, eh?* "You mean the live ones?"

He started, giving her a searching look. "The ones Bert's been paid to stuff, yes."

Eden was beginning to understand why Sera didn't

respect Henry Prescott. "Mr. Gunther must have quite a backlog of business, to be keeping so many wounded and malnourished *specimens* in his pens. I wonder how he even notices when one of the poor beasts is missing."

"The animals are valuable to him."

*So valuable,* she thought snidely, *Gunther lets them gnaw their limbs off rather than shoot them when they're fevered?* "You'll have to forgive my skepticism, Mr. Prescott, but Collie strikes me as canny, not foolish. He knows he would be caught if he tried to sell Mr. Gunther's animals anywhere in this valley. And since Collie doesn't keep company with dogs or cocks," she added with a trace of irony, "I cannot believe he is Mr. Gunther's specimen thief."

"There is one other possibility," Henry insisted quietly. "Being hungry, as you say he is, Collie may be eating them."

Eden knew she'd blanched. She wasn't sure which disturbed her more: the idea that she'd inadvertently provided a motive for Collie's detractors to jail him, or that the boy was ingesting diseased flesh.

"I apologize if I've shocked you," Henry continued in that same quiet voice, "but if you are really Collie's friend, then you must see why it's important he eat home-cooked meals. I suspect yours is the only other kitchen he would dare visit in this town."

Eden swallowed, meeting Henry's green-gray eyes with a touch of chagrin. Perhaps she'd been too quick to judge the man. "Have you told Sera about Gunther's accusations?"

"Of course," he said. "But she's been . . . preoccupied of late."

So Henry knew about Billy Cassidy? Needled by guilt, Eden couldn't quite keep herself from glancing toward the alley. To her relief, Sera had disappeared. Cassidy, however, was strolling out of the shadows with a toothy, cocksure grin.

"Why, if it isn't Preacher Prescott," the Texican drawled, his thumbs hooked over his gunbelt. "And purty Miss Eden." His sun-coppered cheeks split even wider as his impertinent gaze fastened on her bodice. "Nice night for sparking, eh?"

Henry stammered something about the weather; Eden's face flamed. Billy Cassidy knew very well Henry was sweet on Sera!

Come to think of it, Eden thought, why was Billy leering at *her*, when he was supposed to be courting her friend?

Insolent brown eyes locked with hers, as if daring her to seek an answer. She rallied her indignation.

"Good night, Mr. Cassidy," she dismissed him coolly.

"See ya around, ma'am." Touching his hat brim, he winked. "Evenin', preacher."

Chaps flapping and spurs chinking, he sauntered across the street, whistling some off-key ditty. Jesse Quaid tossed his smoke into the gutter. Not a word was said between them, but they turned north together, taking a short-cut to the saloon district by way of the miller's alley.

"Well." Henry's complexion had mottled. "I didn't mean to detain you, Miss Mallory. The next time you see Collie, try to talk some sense into him. As little as he likes the orphanage, it's better than jail. Or boot hill."

Eden nodded, unable to quell her shiver of foreboding as she imagined Berthold Gunther taking justice into his own hands against a fourteen-year-old boy.

Inclining his head, Henry replaced his hat and strode

away, his long, gangly legs eating up the floorboards between him and the sunset.

"Pssst."

Eden jumped at that conspiratorial whisper. She turned slowly and spied Sera craning her neck around a stack of empty barrels that were piled before the cooper's shop one storefront away. She ventured a little further into the sunlight, her black hair catching indigo fire, and peered cautiously after Henry.

"He's not going to Michael's office, is he?" Sera whispered urgently.

Eden's lips quirked. "He didn't say."

"Well, I can't see him from here. Make sure he's not, okay? Please?"

Eden dutifully watched as Henry continued west along Main and finally veered onto Church Street, a gravel road that led to the rectory on the hill. "He's going home, Sera."

"Thank God. I mean . . ." She blushed prettily. "I thought he might have seen me. With Billy. But he couldn't have, could he? Do you think he saw us?"

"Well, his back was to the alley . . ."

Hope vied with dread on Sera's Valentine face.

*Oh, Sera, honey. Michael just wants to protect you from rounders.*

Sera edged around the barrels. A splinter snagged the yellow muslin of her sleeve, and when she tried to yank it free, a shredding sound followed.

"Bother." She poked a finger into the sleeve that had been neatly sliced at her elbow. "It's ruined. Now folks will say *Billy's* to blame. It's just the excuse they'll need to run him out of town."

"Um . . ." Eden glanced around them. Several shopkeepers were indeed emerging from their businesses, drawing their door blinds, heading to the livery or strolling east toward the residential district, as Eden had intended. Still, they hadn't been on the street two minutes ago. "I think I'm the only one who saw you with Billy."

"*That* won't matter. People know he's sweet on me. Someone will see my sleeve and leap to conclusions. They always do. That's how it is around here. Folks start rumors about outsiders." Her chin raised, quivering with indignation. "Folks want to hate Billy because he's different. Because he's *interesting*. I hate this town for that." The hurt in her tone undermined her vehemence. "Nobody will give Billy a chance—except you, Eden."

Eden dropped her gaze. After she'd weathered Billy's leering today, she wasn't sure she wanted to give the Texican a second chance. But for Sera's sake, Eden decided to withhold judgment. "I suppose we'll just have to get you home before anyone else sees your sleeve."

Impetuously, Sera threw her arms around Eden's neck. "Nobody here understands me the way you do."

A lump rose to Eden's throat before the younger girl withdrew.

Blinking rapidly, Sera linked her arm through Eden's. "I declare," she said, making a concerted effort to be more cheerful, "all these waterworks over a silly old sleeve. I'll just buy myself a whole new blouse." She giggled, leaning closer as they hurried away from the scene of her coquettish crimes. "When's Aunt Claudia getting home from Louisville with all the new fofarrow? I want first pick."

Eden couldn't help but laugh to picture pipe-smoking Claudia, adorned in her habitual overalls and coonskin, arbitrarily grabbing machine-sewn garments off the shelves of a big city emporium to satisfy "the dang bloomer wearers" back home. Maybe it was best that Claudia *hadn't* gone on a clothes-buying spree.

"I don't think Aunt Claudia will have much in the way of fofarrow," Eden said. "She went to buy a laundering machine."

"Oh." Sera made a face. "Well, what the store *really* needs is more hair combs, perfume, and a music box or two." She wrinkled her nose. "And a lot fewer canned peaches!"

Eden giggled. "I think Aunt Claudia eats most of them," she confided.

"Honestly, how can a woman who thinks canned peaches taste good judge a blue-ribbon pie? You *are* planning on entering one of the baking contests at the jamboree, aren't you? Why, I was bragging about that cherry pie of yours to Michael just this morning," Sera cooed. "I said, 'Michael, Eden's cherry pie is going to give Bonnie Harragan fits.' And he said, 'Why's that?' And I said, 'Because it's going to dethrone Bonnie as Pie Queen of the Independence Day Jamboree.' And Michael was suitably impressed, which is a feather in *your* cap, Miss Eden Mallory. Not a lot of things impress my brother, you know."

Eden's lips twitched. Matchmaking for Michael, she had discovered, was Sera's second favorite pastime, edged out in her affections only by mooning over Billy. "I'm not sure the birds will leave enough cherries on Aunt Claudia's tree for an Independence Day pie."

Sera nodded solemnly. "Ten days is a long time to be fighting off the sparrow hordes, huh?" The corners of her eyes crinkled. "Well, I daresay you'll just have to bring one of the pies you baked yesterday over to dinner tonight. I know Michael's dying to taste one. Why, he stood for hours by the back door, just sniffing at the crusts you had cooling on your windowsill. And you wouldn't want to deprive Blue Thunder's hard-working doctor of his cherry reward, now would you?"

"Sera, you're shameless."

"I am, rather." She giggled. They were standing by Aunt Claudia's gate now. The windows were still dark, and the usual flecks of pipe ash weren't littering the walk. Sera must have noticed.

"Auntie's not home yet," she announced, sniffing the air with mock gravity. "Nothing's burning on the stove."

Eden ducked her head, doing her best not to turn traitor again and laugh. "I'm really not expecting Aunt Claudia now that the sun is setting. She told me if she wasn't on the five o'clock stage, I wouldn't see her till tomorrow. She said she'd rather swap smokes with the boys in the taproom than have her bones jarred to pieces all night long on one of Angus's 'midnight express' runs."

"Then that means Angus stayed in Louisville too. 'Cause Angus knows better than to let Claudia out of his sight." Sera's dimples peeked. "Michael would have Angus's head on a pike if something happened to her on one of her 'dang shopping junkets.'"

As Sera mimicked Claudia's rusty grousing, Eden's mirth bubbled forth. So Michael was looking out for Claudia? By putting the fear of God in Angus?

The knowledge that Michael was doing his best to protect a seventy-five-year-old curmudgeon who refused to admit she was fragile, pleased Eden more than it surprised her.

"You're dawdling, Eden dear. Run along and fetch

your pie. There's no sense in your eating dinner in that big old house by yourself."

Eden had to admit, the prospect of laughing with Sera all night long was more appealing than watching Stazzie doze on the sofa.

"I don't know, Sera. Your brother and I really don't see eye to eye."

"Put some pie in his belly. He'll forgive you." Sera gave her a conspiratorial wink. "He is a *man*, after all."

Eden's smile was fleeting. She didn't share Sera's confidence that a mere slab of pie would earn her Michael's favor. Still, they had to start somewhere if they were going to bury the hatchet. Maybe then she could finally learn where the devil she'd first met him.

"Was he really trying to get a whiff of my pies," she ventured to ask, "or did you make the whole tale up?"

"Cross my heart and hope to die."

Hope fluttered in Eden's chest. "And he likes cherry?"

Sera rolled her eyes. "Let me put it this way. If my brother were faced with a shamelessly wanton woman who'd do anything he asked, and a succulent slab of cherries fresh from the oven, he'd pick the pie. Every time."

Eden smothered a giggle. She suspected Sera exaggerated. Still, it was nice to know Michael's appetites leaned more toward pie than sin. Must have been the preacher's boy in him.

"All right, Sera. But you have to promise you won't try any of your matchmaking tricks. If I see Michael in the yard tomorrow morning, I want to be able to look him in the eye."

Sera's grin was reminiscent of the Cheshire cat's. "I

wouldn't dream of interfering, Eden . . . once nature takes its course."

Thunder grumbled, and Michael woke with a start. *Eden.*

A clock's hypnotic ticking thrummed beyond the circle of gaslight. For a moment, he was lost. Confused. He must have dozed. Even so, he recognized nothing of the oakwood paneling or the black-rimmed licenses hanging by his door. Echoes from a carefree dream still haunted him, wooing him back to the sun-dappled field, where buttercups and larkspur danced amidst clover. The visions had been so alluring: the columbine sky, the crystalline brook, the rainbow of wildflowers . . . Eden. Her butternut toes peeked out beneath a robe of white; her hair, like liquid fire, tumbled across bared shoulders and arms. She wore a daisy chaplet and an effervescent smile, her laughter contagious as she twirled amidst a storm of orange and yellow butterflies. "Come, Michael," she called, opening her arms in invitation. "Come join me in the dance."

Forcing his eyes open, he drew a shuddering breath. Then another. The sweetness of that memory fanned the fire in his loins.

Eden. How he ached for her.

He wanted to consider the dream an improvement. He wanted to be encouraged by its variation on the theme that had plagued him for years. In the days before he'd known the woman Eden had become, he would dream of himself pining for love in the wildflowers, and she would appear, raising her skirts with a sultry smile and sinking her hips to mount him. But the Eden with the daisy chaplet was nothing like the Eden he usually envisioned unencumbered by bloomers.

Much to his chagrin, though, his pecker hadn't noticed the difference.

Michael grimaced, shifting gingerly. He could almost hear the ghost of his father shrieking, *"You are your mother's son!"*

Oddly enough, Michael couldn't remember the last time he'd wanted a woman—or rather, the last time he'd wanted one badly enough to consider some discreet relief. In fact, he'd been mortified to think his illness might have deadened his carnal urge. "Divine justice," his father would have called the irony. "Satan's revenge" had been Michael's moniker for it. He'd been so ashamed to think he might have become infertile, his hands had actually shaken when he'd reached for his medical books, forcing himself to research the symptom and its cure. He would have died right there on the spot if Sera had surprised him poring through those pages. But it looked like he wouldn't have to run *that* risk again. Thank God for Eden. He might have a brain tumor, but at least he wasn't impotent.

*Jones, you are one sorry, sick sonofabitch.*

He shook his head. Maybe his father was right. Maybe he had inherited his mother's fascination for forbidden fruit. As the clock chimed the hour, announcing him ninety minutes late for dinner, he wasn't thinking of the victuals his no-doubt infuriated sister had slaved to cook for him. No, he was thinking about Whiskey Bend.

And a certain livery that never failed to remind him of Eden.

And any memory of Eden so outshone the harsh, lurid reality he'd face on the sagging straw mattresses above the Jade Rose Saloon, that in the end, he would never make the journey, opting instead to writhe alone until his lust finally ebbed.

So, fornicate or abstain, he was damned either way. He supposed he'd have to reconcile himself to that fact as long as Eden Mallory plagued his dreams ... and most every waking moment, too.

Smiling ruefully, he unfolded his legs and pushed back from the cramped quarters beneath his cherry-wood desk. His captain's chair struck a cabinet, and a stack of patient records which he'd never found time to file toppled to the floor. He would have hired help if he hadn't been so worried an assistant might witness his vertigo and report it to Sera. But he needed the help desperately. His patient load was increasing, and because of it, the space in this two-room storefront was eroding. He'd had to make space for two more examining rooms by partitioning off the first and sacrificing the privacy of his study. In fact, many of his research books were at home now because his precious shelf space was crammed with ointments, sutures, bandages, and lollipops. He kept the latter on hand for children and Claudia.

Thoughts of his irascible neighbor made him smile a little, despite the sorrow that squeezed his chest. Because she'd refused to heed his warnings about candy, Claudia had lost most of her teeth. Because she refused to heed his warnings about her pulmonary arteries ...

Pensively, he fingered a sunny-yellow candy wrapper, his mind drifting to her physical examination two months ago. Waiting for his prognosis about her tingling limbs and shortness of breath, she'd sat on his examining table, her gnomelike face screwed up with glee as she kicked her feet and sucked a lemon lollipop. To see her so impish in the face of his news was almost his undoing. He wanted to fling his stethoscope across the room for verifying her sickness.

"It's your heart, Claudia," he announced, struggling to choke back his grief. "It's working harder than it should. You need to slow down. No more tree climbing. Or bear hunting. Or craps shooting with Angus."

She stopped her noisy sucking sounds to smack yellow lips and glare. "You tryin' to make me mad?"

"This is serious."

"So I'm a goner?"

"For Christ's sake, don't say that!"

Spinning away, he regretted his outburst. A physician needed to be calm. Indifferent. But how could he be? During those early years when Mama had doted on Rafe and Papa had been too bitter to recall he was raising other children, Claudia had been the one who'd patched Michael's scrapes and sheared his unruly hair. She'd given him his first whittling knife. She'd tucked forbidden dime novels into his Bible so Papa wouldn't be the wiser.

*No, goddammit! I won't let her die!*

"Here now." She joined him by the window and awkwardly patted his shoulder. "Ye're takin' this too hard, boy. A body can't live forever."

He shook his head. "You aren't going to die."

"Sure I am. But I ain't scared. Folks who fear dyin' are folks who ain't really lived."

*Then Gabriel must have been terrified.*

Staving off a fresh attack of guilt, he forced his attention back to the present by systematically packing his valise and shrugging into his frockcoat. He was just about to blow out the lamps when he spied the miniature rocking horse he'd painted and left to dry on the windowsill. He hesitated, his hand on the doorknob.

Ordinarily, when he wanted to apologize to Sera, he stopped along the side of the road and gathered wild-flowers. But he suspected the recent weeks of rain had pommeled even the hardiest daisies into the mud.

The toy rocking horse, on the other hand, would make a perfect peace offering. In honor of Sera's nine-teenth birthday, he'd been carving it for the Queen Ann–style dollhouse she was forever redecorating.

His throat constricted and he reached for the horse. How the hell was he supposed to tell Sera he was dy-ing?

By the time Michael arrived at his front yard, the clouds had unleashed a smattering of plump, splashy drops to slick down his hair and roll past his collar. He hurried Brutus through a currying and a sack of oats, then took the shortest route to the house through the kitchen. He found a pot of corn chowder on the stove and the lemony aroma of shortbread wafting from the oven. Chagrined to think Sera had wasted yet another afternoon in her apron thanks to him, he called her name as he crossed into the hall and prepared to lie about his impromptu snooze.

Fortunately, the deception wasn't necessary. Sera bounced out of the parlor, her flushed cheeks and shin-ing eyes making her look more like a smitten belle than an angry cook.

"At last!" she greeted gaily, rising on tiptoe to buss his cheek. "I thought you'd never come home."

Michael arched a brow as she grabbed the valise from his hands and tugged at a sleeve of his coat.

"A person could starve on a work schedule like yours, Michael."

"I'm sorry, I was—"

"Delayed," she finished for him. "Yes, I know. Gout

and chilblains are especially plaguey when it rains. Honestly, Michael, you might remind your patients you have a private life. Even if you don't mind a bowl of rewarmed stew, very few dinner guests do."

"Dinner guests?" he repeated warily. As exhausting as his practice was, he'd come to welcome the work as an excuse. The last thing he wanted was to field dinner invitations from the half dozen or more women who'd set their caps for him. But wedding-bell chasers, he'd learned, were relentless. They didn't comprehend tact. They certainly didn't understand a man's need for privacy. And Sera, who'd joined their ranks only last year, had a tendency to side with them. Had his sister let some besotted chit weasel her way to his table?

"Now don't get all grumbly," Sera said, her grin as impish as a leprechaun's. "You'll like this one. It's not Bonnie. Or Billy."

"Hmm." This gave him hope. Maybe Sera had finally allowed Henry Prescott to break bread with her. "You shouldn't be entertaining alone, Sera."

"My sentiments exactly. But if I waited for *you* to come home every night, I'd sprout cobwebs." She giggled. "Maybe even moss."

*She has a point.* He smiled reluctantly. It was good to see her in such high spirits. If the person waiting in the parlor had the power to spark that girlish blush in her cheeks, Michael had to admit he approved. Besides, any beau, at this point, would be an improvement over Cassidy.

"Sera . . ." He hesitated, remembering the rocking horse. "I really don't mean to neglect you."

She laughed, but surprise registered in those sky-blue eyes. "I should hope not. But just in case you do, be forewarned: I've been collecting recipes for turnips."

He chuckled. They'd shared the joke ever since last spring. Why God had placed such a curse on the vegetable kingdom, Michael would never know. But when Aunt Claudia's order of six onion bins had somehow turned into sixteen turnip crates, the only way she could rid herself of them was to give a dozen to each homeowner. For weeks, turnips were served on every dinner table in Blue Thunder. Now Michael couldn't walk into a patient's house and smell a steaming bowl of turnips without wanting to retch.

"I have something for you," he said awkwardly. "It was going to be your birthday gift, but...well, I wanted you to have it early."

"Early?" She clasped her hands, forgetting to be demure and ladylike. "What is it?"

He couldn't hide his smile. "See for yourself. It's in my coat."

Her beau apparently forgotten, she raced to the hall tree, and rummaged through the garment until she found the telltale lump. When she pulled out the miniature pony, she gasped, her eyes sparking like twin flames. "It's for my dollhouse!" Then her brows furrowed, and she grew very still, staring down at the tiny gray flanks, the black tail and mane.

"It...looks like Gabriel's pony."

"Yes," he said quietly.

She bit her lip, touching a forefinger to the red saddle and blue runners. "Gabriel's favorite colors," she said softly.

He nodded.

Her eyes glistened. Suddenly, she threw her arms around his neck. "I love it, Michael." She sniffled as he clasped her to his heart, and the old, familiar ache constricted his chest. "Thank you."

He tightened his hold, and she clutched him a moment longer before she broke free to give him a watery smile.

"Uh-oh." She dashed away tears and wrinkled her nose. "The shortbread!" A look of comical horror crossed her features. "It's burning!"

With a muttered oath, she dashed toward the kitchen, and Michael's humor struggled to the fore. Sera Jones was going to make some man a belly full of aches someday, unless her husband came to the dinner table with a cast-iron stomach.

Curious once more about Cassidy's replacement, Michael combed a cursory hand through his hair and turned toward the parlor. He had to admit, he was delighted to know Sera's infatuation for the drifter had finally run its course. Still, he did have one misgiving about the newcomer. He wanted to make perfectly clear that in the future, he would not tolerate unchaperoned sparking with his sister.

The gaslight flames danced in their sconces, casting wild, writhing shadows across the wall as he walked along the hall. The shades reminded him a bit too uncomfortably of a drawing from a college history text, one of naked pagans celebrating the rites of spring. Why he kept such garbage locked in his mind remained a mystery, since he needed every available brain cell to track the lies he'd been telling recently about his fatigue. If nothing else, he needed a clear head to discuss courtship etiquette with Sera's new beau.

Gathering his wits, he rounded the corner—only to freeze in midstride on the threshold. Sera's visitor stood with her hands clasped behind her back, her attention riveted on the book titles that ordinarily would have held no interest for Sera or her friends. Even though the woman's back was to him, Michael would have recognized that cascade of russet hair anywhere. How many times had he seen it blowing in the wind through his dreams? How many times had he imagined its taste, its scent, its feel as it tumbled across his face while Eden made love to him?

His response was instantaneous. He grew as hard as any randy youth. He wanted to believe his thoughts of writhing pagans had something to do with his lust; unfortunately, he knew better.

*Christ, Jones. She's an innocent. She won't notice the difference. Walk into the room, exchange a few pleasantries, and get out. She'd have to be deaf not to hear you panting out here like a bull.*

But Eden didn't hear him, thanks to the tumult of the heavens. Instead, she rose on tiptoe. Her tongue jutted in determination as she stretched her hand as high as it could reach. Somehow, she managed to grasp the first volume in his medical set. The one entitled *Compendium of Ailments: Abrasions (Aa) to Hemophilia (He)*. The one whose dog-eared corners clearly marked the sections on cranial pathology.

His heart slammed into his ribs. Too unnerved to concoct a lie about which patient's complaint he might have been researching, he flew across the room.

He had to stop her before she learned his most dire secret.

# Chapter 5

❧❧❧

"**W**hat the devil do you think you're doing?" Eden spun guiltily at that rumble of ire. She hadn't heard Michael come down the hall. In fact, she hadn't heard much of anything but the shrieking of her conscience and the hammering of her heart. Spying Michael's medical books high on the shelves in the family parlor had seemed like the answer to her prayers.

But guilt had made her sneak. How could she explain her interest in medical research to Sera without revealing her secret fear: that she had killed her father?

And so Eden had bided her time, half dreading and half hoping for an opportunity to pore through Michael's books without anyone—least of all Michael—standing over her, asking painful questions.

Unfortunately, the very last person she'd wanted catching her in the act was now stalking into the room like a smoking volcano.

"M-Michael." Thunder shook the walls, or did that quaking come from Michael's boots? "I'm sorry. I didn't mean to pry—"

"Of course you meant to pry. Prying is what females do best. And I have no patience for it."

**113**

He snatched the volume from her hand, and Eden winced. Looming over her, all muscle and menace, he practically steamed. She felt his heat like a furnace blast, flushing her skin and melting her nerves into a puddle.

"I'm sorry," she repeated. Good heavens, why was he so angry? True, she'd been handling his personal property, but it wasn't as if she'd been tearing out its pages. "I was just curious. About, um, respiration."

"This volume is clearly marked *A* through *H*. Respiration would be in another volume entirely."

"Yes, but bronchial inflammation—"

"Are you ill?"

Her pulse tripped as his gaze swept to her bodice. How could eyes so ice-blue one moment burn so scintillatingly hot the next?

She cleared her throat. "No. Nothing like that. I was just—"

His gaze snapped back to her face. "Then kindly refrain from snooping."

She managed to gulp a breath. "I wasn't." Honestly, the man might try to be civil. She was his neighbor, after all—not to mention his guest.

A sudden suspicion, one having to do with Sera and matchmaking, crept through Eden's mind. Her gut sank.

"I, uh, brought you a cherry pie."

His mood didn't improve in the least.

"For dessert."

Again, no reaction.

"Since Aunt Claudia's out of town," she prompted hopefully, "Sera invited me to dinner. She seemed to think it would help us mend fences."

He raised a pitch-black brow. "I wasn't aware we had fences to mend."

"Oh."

A moment of silence lapsed. Eden wondered if it was too late to slink under the rug.

But if Michael noticed her embarrassment, he didn't comment. He simply stretched above her, intent on shoving the volume onto an out-of-reach shelf. When his arm brushed her nipple, she jumped. He recoiled. The electrifying jolt made them both gasp. If she hadn't known better, she might have thought him edgy, not angry, his flash of temper little more than show.

"The kitchen's that way," he said, jerking his head toward the hall.

"I know where the kitchen is."

Their eyes locked. Again, that midnight brow rose. A thread of her patience unraveled.

But as much as her reluctant host deserved a tongue lashing, Eden had to concede that Sera was the real culprit. Sera's scheming had made her and Michael both pawns. Since Sera did nothing but try to marry him off, and Bonnie did nothing but try to trap him for the same purpose, was it any wonder Michael thought females were conniving? By Aunt Claudia's count, there were at least a dozen women in Blue Thunder—some as old as Claudia herself—who would have given their eye-teeth for one of Michael's kisses.

Eden's chin raised a notch. *Well, it's high time Michael learns that Eden Mallory isn't moonstruck—or desperate—like all the other spinsters in this town.*

She mustered the shreds of her decorum. "I completely understand your feelings, Michael. If I'd come home after a long day's work and discovered I was expected to entertain, I'd be put out too. If you prefer, I'll leave."

"That won't be necessary. You're my sister's guest."

*And clearly unwelcome by you.* The proof of her suspicions burrowed deep, a barb to nettle the defenses of her heart.

She told herself her hurt was ridiculous. She didn't care one whit for Michael. "I don't want to cause tension between you and Sera."

"Sera causes tension between me and Sera."

"Yes, well . . . I'm sure she believes she's acting in your best interests."

"By scheming to end my bachelorhood?"

Eden fidgeted. He did have a point.

"Dinner doesn't have to be difficult," she said, opting for a topic change. "Even though you don't like me—"

"Who told you that?"

She bit her lip. Whenever he used that tone of voice, it was hard not to feel like a child. "You did. Or rather, you do. Whenever you snap."

"You shouldn't take everything so personally."

Did he actually mean to say he *liked* her?

She had trouble hinging her jaw closed. "Well, that may be. But you have to admit, you've been short with me since the first day we met. It makes me wonder if . . . well, if I've done something to offend you."

"Are you asking me to apologize?"

"Well, no, I . . ." She caught herself. Why was she trying so hard to appease him? Clearly, even a neighborly relationship was out of the question. "May I speak frankly?"

"When do you not?"

*Ooh. Insufferable man.*

"Honestly, Michael, you would try the patience of a saint. Contrary to what you might think, I don't wake up each morning plotting some new way to aggravate you. And I certainly don't spend my nights dreaming up schemes to make you court me."

"Indeed?"

"Heaven forbid. Why on earth would I waste a perfectly pleasant evening with a man who's so *un*pleasant?"

"The question does give one pause."

Her irritation climbed another notch. "You see? That's just the sort of attitude I've been talking about. Rather than own up to your failings like a proper gentleman, you resort to sarcasm. Or arrogance. You're as high-handed as a tyrant. And you're more prickly than a porcupine."

"I see." He folded his arms across his chest. "Anything else you'd like to share before dinner?"

Her hands flew to her hips. "Well, if you must know, I find you completely lacking in humor!"

His laughter startled her. It was a warm, rich, rumble of mirth, so utterly masculine and thoroughly frustrating, she wanted to smack him.

"That wasn't supposed to be funny!"

"My dear Eden, are you certain you aren't the one lacking in humor?"

"Don't you dare try to turn the tables on me, Michael Jones. My sense of humor is expansive! It's the only thing that helped me survive the mob, and the ridicule, and the ransacking . . ."

To her horror, she realized she was on the verge of tears.

"Eden . . ."

He reached for her sleeve, but she spun away, battling the grief that washed over her. She hadn't meant to speak of Silverton. Certainly, she hadn't meant to give Michael Jones any more reason to disdain her.

"Are you crying?"

"No!" Her voice broke, humiliating her further. "I won't have you mock me, Michael. I won't!"

"I'm sorry."

Her chest heaved, and she halted before the window, squeezing her eyes closed. The rain had ceased again. The resulting silence clapped louder than thunder, leaving her at the mercy of her senses. She could hear his breathing, smell his cologne, feel his remorse. But she couldn't bring herself to confide in him. She couldn't bear his condemnation, his criticism, or worse, his platitudes.

"Tell me about this mob," he said more gently.

She gripped the bombazine with a shaking hand.

"Is that why you left Colorado?" He stepped behind her, his heat rippling over her in waves.

She shivered.

"Did they hurt you?" he prompted.

"It's not important."

"Do you expect me to believe that?"

"I don't want to tell you!"

"Ah." This time, his mockery was self-directed. "That I can believe."

She dashed away tears and wiped them on her skirts. "You can be very cruel."

"That's true."

She rounded on him. "Why? Why do you pretend to be cruel when you're not?"

She'd startled him. Chagrin flickered in the ocean-blue depths of his eyes.

"It's hardly pretense. I am what I am."

"No." She shook her head emphatically. "I've met cruel men before. They have no conscience. But you,

you'd blame yourself for every sickness you can't avert."

His shoulders grew taut.

"You'd lay down your life for a child," she added more gently.

"You can't possibly know that."

"I was there, Michael. I saw you. You would have torn that wagon apart, splinter by splinter, to dig Jamie out."

A familiar agony pierced Michael's chest. It was true—everything she'd said. But on the day of the accident, he hadn't seen Jamie under that wagon, he'd seen Gabriel. Ten years had eased none of the pain. In every cough, every sprain, every broken bone and wound, he saw the ghost of his kid brother. Gabriel's death had left a scorched abyss where his soul once had been.

And if he ever fell into that pit, Michael knew, he'd never crawl out again.

"I told you," he said curtly. "Healing people is my responsibility."

"Your responsibility or your passion?"

"You suffer romantic delusions about me."

"You'd like to think I do. You'd like to convince us both you don't feel any grief or pain."

He didn't like where this conversation was heading. "Are you sure you haven't set your cap for me?"

That derailed her from her track. Her chin rose, quivering beneath flashing, storm-flecked eyes.

"I told you I haven't."

"Good."

"Why?"

"Because you'd regret it."

"Why?" she demanded again.

His gaze roamed over her ribbon-bound hair, shimmering like molten copper in the lamplight. Renegade wisps curled softly in the hollow of her throat, just beside the flurry of her pulse, and his lashes fanned lower. He didn't want her to see the long-constrained hunger that would have made him feast upon that column of peaches and cream—or, God help him, the ripe, pouty handfuls that heaved just an arm's length away. Lightning surged to his loins as he envisioned the globes of her breasts spilling over his palms, their tender rosettes jutting into his mouth.

"Because I'm not the angel I was named after."

Red-gold brows fused, her forehead puckering. "What do you mean?"

He allowed himself a rueful smile. "I mean, my sweet Eden, that what you think you know about me is a honeycomb of lies. I'm cold. I'm callous. And I have no intention of changing."

She licked her lips. Nerves, he told himself, not guile. Still, to spy the pink tip of that tongue chipped at his straining self-control.

"You're just saying that," she said tremulously. "To make me think less of you. You couldn't bear it if anyone tried to hold you up to your own impossible standards."

Her insight, spoken with such hard-won defiance, was almost as unnerving as the realization that the seventeen-year-old who'd once bathed his wounds had grown into a woman wiser than her years, a woman who could see clear to the charred bottom of his soul.

But Michael had never cowered before a worthy opponent, and he wasn't about to start. He stepped closer. Then closer still. He halted only when his thighs were bare inches from her skirts, when his shoulders towered above hers and she was forced to crane her neck to meet his gaze. It was a deliberate tactic, one designed to press his physical advantage, and yet, at this proximity, he was forced to breathe her fragrance.

The intoxication of lilies, lavender, and cherry pie was almost his undoing.

"I'm not afraid of you, Michael."

"You should be, Eden," he said huskily. "Very, very afraid."

She swallowed, her eyes as dewy as meadows. They reminded him poignantly of the butterfly field from his dreams.

"Why?" she whispered again.

It was more than he could bear, her refusal to concede. That she would stand before him, rejecting what he knew to be absolute—that he was detestable because he had failed Gabriel—unleashed a raw, manic frenzy inside him. How dare she be so blind? So naïve? He needed her to run from him as he would have run from himself. He needed her to acknowledge his utter contemptibility. And he knew of only one way to make her see the light.

He locked his arm beneath her buttocks and dragged her forward for his kiss.

The breath slammed out of Eden as her breasts collided with linen-swathed musculature; her pulse pounded as relentless fingers gripped the base of her skull. She barely had time to gasp, to think, before Michael's tongue thrust past her lips, a velvet rapier intent on bringing her to her knees. Sandalwood soap and rain-scented hair flooded her senses. His thighs branded her hips; his palm burned its imprint through her silk stockings. She trembled, shock giving way to unease.

She tried to shove him back, to wedge a hand between them.

Then he moaned.

Tortured rather than threatening, the sound wracked her with confusion. It seemed to well up from some dark, tumultuous vault, a Pandora's box of denial and need. The healer in her recognized the pain; the woman in her heard the desire. Stunned by the proof of such raw emotion, she sagged, her chest sinking against his wildly beating heart.

"Eden," he breathed, freeing the fingers he'd tangled in her hair. He cupped her cheek, and his lips moved seductively now, nuzzling, sipping, caressing. Her mouth trembled open, tasting the heady tang of man. Somehow, the fist that had been so intent on pushing him away clutched a handful of his shirt. He rewarded her submission. Feather-light touches lured her hips forward until they, too, sank in intimate surrender. His arousal should have frightened her; she should have come to her senses, cried out for release. But the intoxication of his lips, the bonfire that spread from her belly to her limbs, numbed her virginal unease. He wrapped his spell around her, fanning the heat that sizzled between them until she dared to slide her fingers through his hair. Until she fit her length more snugly to his. And when she dared to push her tongue into his mouth, a guttural sound ripped from his throat.

*God help you, Eden. I want you.*

In that moment, Michael was lost. He couldn't help himself. He drove her spine into the wall, and she squirmed, her nipples hardening like pebbles against his chest. He reveled in the way she clutched his shoulders, in the way she gasped his name. He'd wanted to prove he was a bastard, and so he had, but he hadn't expected her to respond like a prairie fire in the wind. He hadn't expected the pretty little maid to explode into the siren from his dreams. That she was yet an innocent, he had no doubt, for her caress was a tentative one, sliding along his spine, hovering uncertainly above his buttocks. But the fact that this blushing woman-child would stroke him below the belt fanned his fever to a maddening pitch. To hell with the fantasy, he wanted Eden. *Eden.* And nothing less than this paradise-in-the-flesh would do.

He swung her toward the settee, his mouth feasting greedily on hers. He was intent on filling his lap with her, on gripping those coltish hips between his thighs and liberating those straining nipples from their buttons and whalebone. Had he been given five minutes more, just five minutes come hell or high water, he would have had her stripped to her stockings and writhing in wanton delight. Unfortunately, God chose that moment to answer his prayer.

"Michael," Sera called, "for heaven's sake, didn't you hear the doorbell ringing off the—"

Her voice trailed to a gasp. Michael spun, his face burning hotter than his loins. There on the threshold stood his bug-eyed sister with a rain-drenched, but equally slack-jawed Jamie Harragan.

Abruptly, Michael released Eden. She staggered, and he had to grab her again so she wouldn't topple over the arm of the couch. Sera's grin broadened. Michael ground his teeth. In that moment, he didn't know whom he'd like to kick harder, his sister or himself.

"Jamie, what's wrong?" he demanded, turning his back on his rumpled guest. He was annoyed to find his breathing so ragged.

The boy looked past him, blinked suspiciously at

Eden, then said, "I didn't know she was here."

"Yes, yes," Michael said crossly, "Eden's here. What's wrong?"

"I declare, Michael." Sera snickered. "There's no cause for you to take your embarrassment out on—"

"Is it private, Jamie?" he interrupted, tossing his sister a daggerlike glance. "Man business?"

The boy nodded hurriedly.

"Very well. I'll get my valise."

"Man business indeed," Sera taunted as he swept past her, clasping Jamie's shoulder.

He wanted to wring her neck. But he wanted to flee the scene of his crime even more.

He grabbed his coat and doctor's bag and let Jamie hurry him out the front door. Thunder rumbled, drowning out the anxious child's prattle of dogs and coons and bunnies. Jamie caught his hand, dragging him down the porch steps, and Michael followed automatically, his thoughts—and his eyes—straying to the parlor window and the blaze of lamplight that left nothing to the imagination of passersby. A sheepish, grinning Eden was being embraced by a laughing Sera. His sister's glee was punctuated by animated gestures that only added to Michael's humiliation.

*Wedding-bell chasers. Damn them both.* Despite all Eden's protestations to the contrary, she'd plotted to titillate him. She'd plotted it, and he'd fallen for it, even though he'd *known* what she was scheming. He'd walked into that room with his eyes wide open—and his pecker at full mast.

He cursed himself for his stupidity. For his lust. What game would the conniving little chit play, he wondered, if she found out he was ailing? How fast would Eden run from his embrace if she knew she'd be saddled with a dying husband whose only inheritance was a wayward sister and a mortgage?

Michael scowled, battling the crush of loneliness. Of despair.

It would be easy to play her game. Too damned easy.

But even Eden Mallory didn't deserve that.

Grimacing at the sunbeams bouncing so cheerfully off the mirror, Eden sat before the vanity in her aunt's guest room and gazed in resignation at the hollows ringing her eyes. She hadn't slept well the night before. Sera's squeals of triumph had echoed too loudly through her dreams:

*"I knew he liked you. I just knew it!"*

Michael liked her, all right. But Eden wasn't sure that was a good thing. How could she possibly tell Sera that the brother she so admired didn't hug . . . well . . . chastely? That the preacher's boy whom she thought preferred cherry pies to carnal pleasures kissed like white lightning, not melted butter?

*"I'm cold. I'm callous. And I have no intention of changing."*

Honestly. Could any man have sputtered a more baldfaced lie?

Eden raised wistful fingers, cupping her cheek. She wished she could recreate the branding sensation, the uncompromising possession of his hands on her skin. Even if she could have convinced herself Michael didn't feel one solitary spark of emotion, she'd be in the minority. Sera didn't think he was callous. Aunt Claudia didn't think he was cold. And Bonnie clearly thought he was the hottest prospect in town. So why did Michael purport such rubbish? To drive away marriage-minded women who annoyed him?

She raised her chin. As much as it hurt, she supposed Michael now placed her in the bell-chasing category. Never mind that he'd kissed *her* until she saw stars, not the other way around.

She bit her lip, partly to coax some color into her face, partly to distract herself from unmaidenly frustration. Michael wanted her to avoid him, and he'd been willing to play the cad to drive his point home. But why? Why would he go to such lengths to repel a woman who, frankly, had never even considered him a prospect until his kiss?

*His kiss.*

She sighed, propping her chin in her hand. All her life, she'd longed to be kissed that way, not shyly or piously, but hungrily, wildly, passionately. In her most romantic fantasies, she'd yearned for a man who would make her heart pound and her knees quake. A man who could kindle her senses and ignite her soul. A man who was giving enough, strong enough, *spirited* enough to love.

And Michael was such a man.

Only, Michael didn't want her. At least, not in the marriage sense.

This realization proved more depressing than Eden had thought possible. Why wasn't she someone Michael could love? Other men found her pretty. They seemed to enjoy talking with her, walking with her, holding her hand. She wasn't a prude, not after twelve years of traveling in a medicine show. She'd had to touch men to heal them.

Once, she'd actually thought she was in love. She'd impetuously confided her longings to Talking Raven. The Cherokee had never told her she was sinful or shameless to desire a man. She'd simply hitched the

horses and driven Eden to the ranchhouse of her
suitor—whose pregnant wife and two young children
had curiously greeted them at the door. Talking Raven
had proven that day that not all men were as committed
to their lovers as Papa had been to her. Eden had cried
for weeks to realize how Paul had humbugged her. Still,
in her stoic way, Talking Raven had averted what might
have been the greatest mistake of Eden's life. And Eden
had never again considered becoming some man's mis-
tress.

*Not that Michael is ever likely to propose such a thing. Not
to his backyard neighbor and sister's friend.*

In resignation, Eden pinned up her riot of curls and
pinched some color into her cheeks. In an hour or two,
Claudia or no Claudia, the people of Blue Thunder
would expect their general store to be open. And that
meant Eden would have to risk another morning encounter with Michael across the back fence. Her heart
beat wildly at the thought.

Would he really rise this early? He hadn't come home
for hours last night. She hadn't meant to spy on him,
but sometime around 3 A.M., after she realized sleep
was futile, she'd huddled in the darkness on her window seat, watching the rain roll down the glass. That
was when a lamp flared in a second-story window of
the Jones house. She'd held her breath, watching Michael pace like a caged tiger. He'd shrugged out of his
sopping coat, tugged off his cravat and the black silk
vest plastered to his powerful chest. He'd tossed everything in a heap on a chair. Then, just as he'd been reaching for the buttons of his shirt—that nigh transparent
swatch of dampness that clung so enviably to his belted
ribs—his head had jerked up. A slick, wet strand of hair
had spilled across one eye; still, she'd felt the full inten-

sity of his gaze, like blue cinders, burning through the night. He'd stared directly at her hiding place. What had clued him to his voyeur? She couldn't say. She'd been certain he couldn't see her. Nevertheless, while she'd sat there blushing, her private parts growing moist with the siren call in her blood, he'd stalked to the shutter, yanked on the cords, and . . . well, left her prey to an imagination that had only made the ache worse.

Really, what was the matter with her? Before she'd met Michael Jones, she'd viewed half-dressed men with the professional eye of a healer. Now a certain set of taut buttocks and brawny shoulders made her salivate—for all the good it would do her. Aside from sexual attraction and their mutual love of Sera, what did she and Michael share in common?

*Secrets,* came the unbidden response. *Scandal and failure.*

Even if Michael wanted to be her suitor, how could she let him without lying about her past? A university-educated physician was likely to become the ringleader of any new vigilante group that formed to keep her too terrified to sell Papa's tonic.

A high-pitched yowl shattered her musings.

Eden winced. "For heaven's sake, Stazzie, what is it now?"

A sequence of clattering, followed by a particularly virulent curse, answered.

Eden frowned. Had Aunt Claudia come home early?

Visions of smoking shotguns and dead cats dancing in her brain, Eden gathered up her skirts and raced down the staircase, only to slide to a halt when she reached the splash of sunlight on the kitchen's threshold. The back door had been thrown wide. Copper pots and pans littered the floor; so did dozens of forks and spoons. The linen on the dining table was smeared with dripping, red goo. Squatting in a puddle of that goo, and covered quite liberally with it, was the very last person she'd expected to see.

"Stay back, cat, y'hear me?" Collie snarled. "Stay back, or I'll cut yer dang tail off!" He brandished his bowie knife while scooping cherries, dust, and God only knew what else off the floor into the toppled pie tin at his feet.

Stazzie, meanwhile, crouched an arm's length away, her ears flattened, her tail lashing, and her eyes narrowed to topaz slits, which gleamed in striking contrast to the pink pie filling on her whiskers.

Eden cleared her throat. "Um, Collie?"

Pale gray eyes, as turbulent as last night's storm, glared at her through straggly white-blond hair. "What?"

"You, uh, aren't planning on *eating* that pie, are you?"

"It ain't no good to you no more."

Stazzie inched closer, her gaze riveted on her nemesis, as she sought to lick up more of the splattered ambrosia. Collie threw a spoon at her. It clanged off a table leg as Stazzie fled.

"Collie, really. Do you think we might call a truce long enough to eat breakfast? I was planning on baking some jelly muffins."

His head swiveled back to her, and those stormy eyes regarded her with wary interest. "Yeah?"

"Yes," she said firmly. "You might have let me know you would be paying a call. I would have put them in the oven by now."

"You ain't mad I came here?"

Actually, she was a bit unnerved that a wild man-child with a ten-inch knife had been stealing through her house while she'd been alone and naked. However, she was even more mortified that Collie was willing to eat her pie off the floor like . . . well, a common cur. But she didn't think it prudent to tell him.

"I told you you could come here whenever you were hungry."

"That old woman told me different."

"She did?" Eden frowned. *Is that why you've been raiding Gunther's animal pens? Because Aunt Claudia chased you away?*

Less nervous about the boy's knife now, Eden mustered a show of bravado and swept past him, sidestepping a kettle on her way to the pantry. "I'll just have to set her straight, then, won't I?"

She could feel his eyes assessing her as she hauled flour, sugar, and spices to the table, then pulled measuring cups from a drawer.

"Reckon Sera was right," he said.

"About what?"

"About you being like family. 'Specially after lip-smacking the doc last night."

Eden wheezed, nearly spilling a cup full of flour down her skirts. She hastily returned to the pantry for an apron. "S-Sera told you I kissed Michael?"

"Naw." His voice lilted. "That part I saw through the window."

Eden's knees wobbled on her way back to the table. "Collie, you should know better than to peer through someone's window," she said primly, tying her apron sash. "Peering is snooping. And snooping's impolite."

He raised the tablecloth to grin up at her. "That's what Sera says whenever *she* forgets to draw the curtains."

Eden groaned inwardly. She hoped she didn't look as embarrassed as she felt. Good Lord, who else had passed by in the storm to see her kissing Michael? She remembered Jamie's visit and cringed. If Jamie had watched, then Bonnie must surely know, which meant everybody in town knew.

*I wonder if Aunt Claudia's store really needs to be opened today . . .*

"Hey!" Collie was feuding again with Stazzie, who had sneaked up behind him and was sniffing the seat of his breeches. The boy's face turned bright red, and he scrambled backward so fast, his spine struck a table leg. Eden barely saved her eggs from rolling onto the floor.

"Git away from me, you mangy bag of fleas!"

Another spoon went flying; Stazzie sped for cover, and Collie bolted upright, smacking his head on the underside of the table.

"Are you all right?"

"Yeah," he sputtered between curses. He rubbed his crown and winced. "Dang good-fer-nuthin', pussyfootin' *varmint!*"

Safe behind the butter churn, Stazzie hid a smirk behind her paw as she washed her whiskers. Eden tried her best not to smile.

"Why don't you go and wash up? You've got more cherry pie on you than in you, I'll wager."

He glared at her next.

"By the time you've scrubbed your face and hands," she continued with careful nonchalance, "I'll have scrambled eggs, bacon, and grits ready for you. And a pan of jelly muffins will be on its way."

His face darkened. "What do I have to wash fer? This ain't Go-to-Meeting Day."

She decided to fight the battle over his grammar some other morning.

"Because you've got pie smeared all over you. Not to mention something—well"—she wrinkled her nose—"smelly."

He snorted. "You women are all alike. Actin' like a little river mud's gonna kill you."

She folded her arms. She suspected the stains on the boy's seat weren't from any river, God bless him. Still, the only way to know for sure was to get him out of his pants.

"Now see here, Collie McAffee, if you want to eat *my* cherry pie and *my* jelly muffins, you're going to come to my table with a clean face and hands. And a clean shirt and breeches too. You can wear a pair of Aunt Claudia's dungarees till we get yours laundered."

"I ain't that hungry."

"Suit yourself." She began to replace the lids on her spices.

His jaw jutted.

Next, she returned the milk and eggs to the icebox.

He scowled.

But it wasn't until she started to scrape the muffin dough into the slops bucket that he lunged across the room and grabbed the spoon from her hand.

"All right, all right, woman, I'll wash! Can't you take a joke?"

*"Woman,"* eh? She mentally added etiquette to the list of things she would teach him. "The pump is outside, behind the rain barrel. And Collie?" she added silkily.

He glared over his shoulder this time.

"You'll need this."

His reflexes proved lightning-fast as he caught the cake of soap in midair.

"All I can say is," he growled, wagging the soap like a finger, "those better be mighty good muffins."

She smiled sweetly. "Don't forget to wash the cherries from your hair."

"Dang women," he muttered, stalking out the door like a man marching for war. She giggled. Then she bit her lip. Considering how little he liked washing, he wouldn't be gone for long. That meant she didn't have much time to make up her mind.

Torn between her calling to help people heal and her fear that her best intentions might lead to someone's death, Eden fidgeted before the shelf over the window. Aunt Claudia had grudgingly removed the boxes of buckshot she'd stashed there to make space for Eden's herbs.

"But don't you be tryin' to sneak none of yer Injun heart wampum into my stews," Aunt Claudia had warned, sniffing suspiciously at the jar labeled PEPPERMINT. "Them herbs better be just fer cookin'."

Eden had bit her tongue, ashamed to admit that the idea had, indeed, crossed her mind. Each time her aunt wheezed or experienced a palpitation, Eden's fear of losing Claudia grew greater than her fear of prescribing herbal remedies. Fortunately for Claudia, or perhaps unfortunately, foxglove wasn't the sort of herb one could use for food seasoning. Eden wished she knew of a culinary herb that could treat Claudia's heart, because in truth, most of them did have medicinal uses. Mints were handy for fever, headaches, and insomnia. Rosemary was good for colic and indigestion. Thyme could ease sore throats and bronchial inflammation.

Wild buckwheat could cure diarrhea.

Reminded of Collie, Eden gritted her teeth and forced herself to reach for the dusty bottle three rows back. But when her fingers closed over the lid, a flash of panic jolted her. What the devil was she doing? She had come to Blue Thunder to be inconspicuous. The minute word spread that she might actually know something about healing, every desperate townsperson whom Michael couldn't cure would be pounding on her door, no doubt followed by an outraged Michael and Sheriff Truitt.

*But Collie will never seek help from a doctor, especially Michael,* the voice of reason whispered. *Besides, a cup of buckwheat tea won't hurt the boy.*

She tasted bile, but reached anyway for a second jar: sweet anise. A general physic, anise would make the tea taste like the candy Collie loved. It might even get him to drink enough to start healing in earnest. Perhaps she could put it by his plate and see if he was inclined to sample it.

She sniffed the contents of both jars. Although the herbs were well labeled, and in her own hand, the smell and taste checks were ritual. Talking Raven had taught her never to trust labeling. Mistakes were often made that way. In Papa's case, she'd determined—with mixed emotions—that the herbs had failed him, not her labeling.

*Okay, okay, I'll brew the blasted tea,* she decided. *I'll do it because the boy needs help. And because . . . well, in a way, I do too.*

By the time Collie had stalked inside, she had the tea brewing. By the time he'd run out of arguments, mostly about peeling off his soiled clothes and trading them for Claudia's, she had breakfast on the table. She suspected she won the battle only because the smell of bacon had weakened his will.

"Now there's plenty of everything," she told him, after railroading him into thirty seconds of prayer. Apparently a wild man-child didn't think to say grace when feasting on cats and coons. "You can have second helpings, if you like."

She passed him the plate of bacon, hoping to divert him from the steaming cup by his plate. But all his feral instincts were on alert.

"What's this?"

"Sweet anise tea."

"You didn't say nuthin' about no tea."

She shrugged, feigning disinterest as she sipped her own cup. "I thought you'd like some. It tastes like licorice."

He dumped the entire platter of bacon on his plate. "I like coffee," he retorted, unsheathing his bowie knife.

She almost choked when he reached to saw through the butter. "We don't have coffee," she said, gesturing toward the table knife by his spoon.

He harrumphed. Retrieving the silverware as bid, he dumped a whopping half of the butter on his grits. Next, he served himself a mountain of eggs. As might be expected, the scrambled yolks bounced off the bacon and into his lap. Unperturbed, he fished them out of his seat, popped them into his mouth, and licked his fingers clean.

Eden squirmed. Somehow, she kept herself from protesting. With Collie, it was clear she'd have to pick her battles.

As her guest shoveled down his breakfast, she tried not to stare at his hands, long-fingered and large-knuckled, like a man's. In fact, she tried not to stare at any part of him. Collie had washed up nicely. With his hair slicked back and tucked behind his ears, and God only knew how many weeks of filth scrubbed off his face, the boy was ... well, attractive. She suspected she'd be calling him handsome after a few home-cooked meals and a couple more years of growth had filled him out. Collie MacAffee was going to be a heart breaker one day, if he ever learned some manners.

He wiped his sleeve across his mouth. "So, how come you like the doc so much?"

She started. She'd been preparing to fight another battle over the neglected tea, not Michael. "Uh . . . l-like him?" She felt as stupid as she sounded. "Really, Collie, it's none of your business."

"I figured you'd say that."

"Well, it's true."

"So how come?"

She gave him a withering look.

"He's about as ornery as a mule colt."

She refused to rise to this bait. "I'm sure Michael has his reasons."

"Sure. Just look at him slantways."

She managed not to smile.

"Is it 'cause he kissed you?"

Her face flamed again. Honestly, how was she supposed to defend herself from a town full of gossips if she couldn't even put a fourteen-year-old in his place?

Determined to meet his eyes once more, she was mildly surprised to spy the keen mind at work behind them. More startling still, she recognized a youthful curiosity in those pewter depths. Collie wasn't embarrassing her out of malice. He wasn't trying to exhume any skeletons. He had some other purpose for prying.

Suddenly it occurred to her that he'd reached the age when kissing and . . . er . . . more robust intimacies would be of acute interest. And he had no father to teach him what he needed to know.

More shaken than she wanted to show, she went back

to drinking her tea, hoping he'd get the hint and do the same.

"Sera says you like him," he persisted, reaching for the marmalade.

"Sera shouldn't spread gossip."

His spoon froze in midair. "Don't you be saying nothin' bad about Sera," he warned, a warlike gleam in his eyes.

She blinked, amazed that he'd been so quick to take offense. Then understanding dawned. Why hadn't she guessed it sooner? The boy was crazy-mad in love. No wonder he wanted to know if kissing was what women liked.

"I didn't mean anything bad, Collie," she said soothingly.

"That may be. But I won't stand for nobody hurtin' her. 'Specially not *him*," he added under his breath.

Eden wondered if she'd misunderstood. Surely Collie didn't think Michael would hurt Sera?

He began plastering marmalade all over his muffin, heedless of the strawberry jam already oozing from its center.

"You don't like Michael much, do you?" she asked over the rim of her cup.

"Nope."

"Can you say why?"

He snorted. "What difference would it make? You wouldn't listen. Womenfolk get all mushy-headed after kissin'. Can't see the bees fer all that honey."

Amusement trickled through her—amusement, and a poignant sense of embarrassment as she remembered Paul. "Is that a fact?"

"Yep." He licked the orange goo that had plopped off

his knife onto his fist. "Don't say I didn't warn you," he added, wagging the knife at her.

"I wouldn't dare," she murmured.

He set the utensil down and reached for his cup. She caught her breath—a big mistake. Those canny eyes snapped back to hers.

"It's medicine, ain't it?"

Her whole body blushed. "What makes you think that?"

"Nobody drinks tea 'cause they like it."

Arguing that point, she realized, wouldn't win her the war.

"I won't lie to you, Collie. Some folks drink tea as a tonic."

He recoiled as if burned.

"But not always. I'm drinking it, and I'm not sick."

"That's 'cause you wanted *me* to drink it."

She sighed, half resigned, half exasperated. "Well, you don't have to drink it."

"Good."

"Only . . ."

He pressed his lips together.

"It'll stop the stomach pains you've been having. And the burning in your behind."

His jaw jutted. She held her ground quietly, compassionately.

"How come you know about them?"

She realized she was about to venture into embarrassing territory for him. "You've been eating bad food," she said carefully. "Maybe even drinking bad water. And you're thin. Too thin. A boy as tall as you shouldn't have to double cinch his belt."

He absorbed her answer in silence, suspicion flickering across his features. It vied with an almost pathetic need to trust. "You know about medicines, huh?"

"Yes."

*There. I said it.*

She drew a shaky breath. The admission felt good, unbelievably good, as if someone had lifted a hundred-pound yoke off her shoulders.

"And this tea's gonna make me feel good?"

"Good enough to eat here every night and grow some meat on your bones."

He sniffed the cup again and made a face. "What if I don't like it?"

"Then we'll find something you do like."

He still didn't look inclined to swallow.

"You could add some honey," she suggested.

He raised his chin, the very picture of a proud man standing before an execution squad. "Naw. You drank it, right?"

She nodded.

Her heart went out to him as she watched his struggle between the longing to be well and his abhorrence for bad-tasting medicine. Finally, he squeezed his eyes closed and gulped.

His eyes popped wide again. "Hey, that's not so bad fer tea." A sheepish grin spread across his face, and he drained the cup, setting it back on the saucer with a clatter.

"Am I better now?"

"Well . . ." She was hard-pressed not to laugh. "You may have to drink several cups, spread out over several days. But I'll try to have some cherry pie or blueberry cobbler waiting here to make it worth your while."

His disconcertingly insightful gaze met hers with a new kind of respect. "I reckon that'd be all right, s'long as that old woman ain't around to raise a ruckus."

He busied himself with stacking his dishes, a gesture of help that completely surprised—and charmed—Eden.

"I got another problem fer you to fix too, mebbe."

She wrapped the last muffin in a linen napkin and braced herself for the worst. "You do?"

He nodded solemnly, cast her a sidelong glance, then took great pains to scrape a splotch of marmalade off the table with his spoon. "The only reason I'm telling you is 'cause . . . well, you ain't like the other Samaritans."

She knitted her brows. "You mean good Samaritans?"

"Yeah. Them ones that try to cut my hair and change my talk and make me sit in a hot stuffy schoolhouse all day when I could be out hunting and fishing and jumping in the swimming hole."

She cleared her throat. From Collie's perspective, if from nobody else's, she suspected she'd just received a huge compliment. "Thank you."

"But you don't lie so good. And that could mean trouble."

"Uh . . ." She wasn't sure this observation was quite as flattering. "Why would that be troublesome?"

" 'Cause you ain't allowed to tell nobody."

"I see." She did her best to match his gravity. "I assure you, Collie, I believe in keeping healing matters private. They shouldn't be anybody's business but your own."

He dismissed her assurance with an impatient shake of his head. "Yeah, but do you *promise*?"

Her chest warmed with a feeling she recognized as maternal. Whatever ails the heart of a boy, Talking Raven had once told her, becomes a sickness in the man.

And Collie's heart had more reasons than most to be troubled.

"Of course I promise," she said softly.

His breath expelled in a rush. Apparently satisfied, he sat back, looked her square in the eye, and jabbed his forefinger at his cup. "What kind of teas do you got for coons?"

She blinked. "C-coons?"

"Yep. Hounds and rabbits, too. We got a whole passel of them, and they've got worms."

# Chapter 6

**M**ichael's first inkling that trouble was brewing came when he heard youthful voices squabbling ahead of him somewhere beyond the sunspangled mists of the forest. Spurring Brutus through the tangle of blackberry bushes that carpeted Blue Thunder Mountain, Michael strained his ears above the alarm cries of blue jays and scampering fox squirrels. The feud appeared to be escalating.

"A girl? You brought a *girl* to our hideout?" Jamie sputtered.

"Listen here," Collie snapped back. "Yer the one who started it all, giving that puppy to Amanda Jean Buchanan."

"That's not fair! Mandy *followed* me up here. What was I supposed to do?"

"Pay more danged attention, that's what."

Michael's lips quirked. He supposed he should have paid more attention, too. On and off over the last six weeks, Jamie had quizzed him about medicines, bandages, and splints. Amanda had asked about fevers, colds, and mites. They'd always had some reasonable excuse: Amanda, for instance, claimed her doll had a runny nose, while Jamie insisted he wanted to be a doctor when he grew up. Since both children were in the pink of health, Michael had dismissed their questions as idle curiosity. He supposed if he hadn't been so preoccupied with the measles quarantine at the county orphanage, he might have been more suspicious.

But it had never occurred to him that the children were sheltering orphaned animals. Nor had he guessed that Jamie had defied his mother's orders regarding the orphaned fawn he'd found starving in the woods. When Michael had examined the animal ten weeks ago, the fawn had been suffering from a malformed knee, which, apparently, had been a birth defect. He'd tried to explain to Jamie that shooting the fawn would be a kindness, since it would never be able to run from its predators. Jamie had cried, refusing to let Michael near the animal again, and Bonnie, at her wit's end, had asked Berthold Gunther to remove it from her stable. Strangely enough, the fawn's carcass had disappeared from the taxidermist's compound.

Last night, Michael had learned why. Jamie had confessed that Collie stole the fawn for Jamie to bury. Just as Collie had stolen the dozen or so other animals that Jamie had determined must be rescued from Gunther.

"Jamie, honey."

The liquid strains of a familiar alto snared Michael's attention more thoroughly than a bear trap.

"I thought we were friends," Eden coaxed in a tone that would have made castor oil bearable. "Don't you want me to help your animals? The way I helped Georgie?"

"Heck, no. That dried up old plant you gave Georgie turned him into a *girl!*"

"A . . . girl?" Eden sounded bemused.

"That's right! He laid eggs!"

Michael smothered laughter beneath his riding glove. He could see the three of them now, silhouetted against the backdrop of flaming morning, dew-laden conifers, a half dozen cages, and the dilapidated remains of a pioneer cabin. During the 1760s, so the story went, Daniel Boone came across Blue Thunder Valley while he was blazing the Wilderness Road, and he grew so fond of the region that he built himself a home amidst the mountain laurels and scented pines. Michael suspected that the chimneyless shack, with its half-hinged door and crumbling roof, had really been constructed by some long-forgotten mountain man who'd grown weary of his solitary life and had traded his beaver traps for a plow. Nobody but Collie thought about these ruins anymore, and the only reason he did was because his father had made a life for himself here nearly thirty years ago after running away from a Missouri orphanage.

"Uh . . ." Eden's face had grown a charming shade of rose in the dappled play of mist and morning. "I don't believe a pinch of parsley can make boy toads turn into girl toads."

"Well, something did." Jamie raised his chin, and his coonskin—or rather, Claudia's coonskin—fell across the bridge of his nose. "Ma says it's your fault. She said when you came to our town on the stage, God sent us a plague of warts, just like he did the locusts in Egypt!"

"Your ma's got sawdust for brains to say somethin' so stupid," Collie retorted, flipping his shaggy locks off his face. Michael noticed they actually looked grease-free for a change. Come to think of it, so did Collie.

"Don't you be saying nothing bad about my ma."

"You can't get warts from toads, Jamie," Eden interjected diplomatically. "Dr. Jones said so himself."

"Told you, brat."

"Quit calling me brat!"

"Then quit actin' like one."

Jamie scowled at Collie's taunt. If Michael hadn't already suspected the ten-year-old had defied doctor's orders last night, sneaking out of his bedroom to finish stringing wire mesh across the cabin's windows, he might have wondered at Jamie's uncharacteristic rudeness. The child had gotten no sleep. And he'd undoubtedly skipped breakfast. As selfish as Bonnie could be, she was a good enough mother to notice when her son was missing. Michael wondered how long it would take before she waxed hysterical enough to convince Sheriff Truitt and a posse of sawmill workers to comb the forest for Jamie's corpse.

"Well, this animal orphanage was my idea," Jamie said. "So whatever I say here goes."

"You wouldn't *have* no danged animals fer yer stupid orphanage, if it weren't for me," Collie flung back. " 'Sides, this here land belongs to my pa."

"It does not!"

"Does too!"

"Jamie." Michael ducked beneath a cascade of pine needles. "If you want to keep this place a secret, then I suggest you quit hollering at the top of your lungs."

Eden's features registered shock, even a faint uneasiness, when she spied him. Collie rounded, half squatting, reaching for his knife. Michael was gratified to see the boy's hand hesitate at the sight of the doctor's bag in his fist. Nevertheless, Collie grew as rigid as a railroad tie when he realized just who had invaded his pa's sanctuary.

"You told *him* about us?" he hissed at Jamie. "You said you'd only ask 'bout the medicine!"

"That was before last night's storm. Someone had to patch the roof in a hurry, 'cause your straw didn't work."

Collie's cheeks mottled.

"It is a bit of a surprise to have Dr. Jones join us," Eden said, placing a gentle hand on Collie's shoulder, "but I'm sure he only means to help."

"We don't need his kind of help."

Collie tried to glare Michael down. Not for the first time did the base of his skull prickle when the boy defied him. Collie reminded him too much of Rafe. Their eyes were the same color; their hair was nearly the same shade. But most troubling of all, Collie was the age Rafe had been when he and Michael had brawled on their mother's fresh grave. The memory of that fistfight, which Michael had provoked out of grief and jealousy, was one of the greatest shames of his life.

"Collie." He spoke softly, deliberately. "You know nothing about medicine."

"Miss Eden does. She cured me."

The blood rushed to Eden's cheeks. "Um, Collie," she croaked, looking like she might like to slink under a rock, "if you don't mind, I'd like to have Dr. Jones's help. When you asked me to mix a deworming tonic, I didn't realize you had so many animals."

She smiled shyly at him, and Michael felt his heart trip. The mere thought of lingering, of breathing her lily-and-lavender fragrance and watching the dimples flirt with her kissable lips, was enough to fire his blood.

He cleared his throat, doing his best to rally the discipline that had always been his salvation from temptation.

"Jamie, didn't I tell you not to come back here last night? Your ma's going to be worried."

"Ma thinks I slept over at Bobby Buchanan's."

"I don't like the idea of you lying to your mother. Or Mrs. Buchanan. Or anyone else, for that matter," Michael added sternly. "And you have no right to involve Bobby. It'll only get him in trouble too."

"Bobby ain't in any trouble," Collie retorted, "unless *you* plan on squealin', Doc."

Jamie looked aghast. "He swore a pinky oath!"

"Pinky oaths don't make no nevermind to him. Don't you know? He's on the *orphan committee.*"

Michael heated under his collar. Collie's dig had hit home.

Eighteen months ago, three men, wearing gunnysacks over their heads, had somehow breached the county jail's door, dragged Bartholomew MacAffee from his cell, and hanged him on the sycamore outside. An investigation ensued, but no one had much liked MacAffee, and no witnesses stepped forward. Some folks speculated that MacAffee's old gang of horse thieves had finally been freed from the Texas penitentiary and had hunted him down for turning state's evidence against them. Others had whispered that MacAffee had tried blackmailing one too many people in Blue Thunder.

In any event, someone had had to break the news to Collie. Michael volunteered, along with Henry Prescott and Lydia Witherspoon, headmistress of the Cumberland Orphanage. Sheriff Truitt had accompanied them. Riding out to the crumbling hovel MacAffee had shared with his son on Blue Thunder Mountain, they had found Collie faithfully bottling his father's latest vat of moonshine. A heartrending scene ensued, particularly when Truitt started shooting up MacAffee's illicit kegs of whiskey. Howling, Collie lunged at the lawman with his knife, and Michael was forced to tackle the boy to keep Truitt from beating him—or worse. Lydia, the most motherly woman Michael had ever met, sought to calm the boy with assurances that new brothers and sisters waited for him in her care, but the mere mention of the orphanage sent Collie into another fit. At a loss, Prescott suggested the boy be placed with foster parents closer to his home; this idea had led them all to swear pinky oaths at Collie's insistence. They'd promised he would only stay at the orphanage for a week or two, until arrangements could be made.

Everyone had sincerely intended to find Collie a home, even if Truitt had remained skeptical. But the boy's reputation, coupled with that of his father's, had made the task nigh impossible. Six weeks dragged by, and Collie ran away from the orphanage. Truitt tracked him down, brought him back to live with a grudging farmer and his miserly wife, but Collie ran away again. The pattern repeated itself several times. Nobody wanted Collie.

And Collie wanted nobody.

"You aren't gonna tell my ma, are you, Doc?" Jamie grabbed his hand and blinked beseechingly. "Not about the animals, I mean. Ma won't let me keep them. You know she won't! And no one else'll want them, 'cause they're orphans, like Collie." His brown eyes brimmed. "Please, Doc. Promise you won't tell!"

Michael fidgeted, glancing at Eden. The amusement had ebbed from her features, leaving them soft with compassion and an almost breathtaking beauty. Even in his dreams, she hadn't appeared half as desirable. The realization did something strange to his insides. In that moment, captured by the warmth in her gaze, needs he hadn't even known he possessed stirred in his chest— needs that transcended the physical.

*Damn.* The only reason he'd made his promise to Jamie in the first place was because he'd been so distracted by the memory of Eden's kiss. After so many torrid, lonely nights of writhing, of dreaming of her scent, her taste, her touch, kissing Eden had been a mistake. Indulging in his fantasy hadn't slaked his desire; if anything, it had stoked his loins to a fever pitch. He feared he would never rid himself of his dreams now. What was worse, some silly, infatuated part of him was eager to redeem himself so he wouldn't appear the villain in this episode.

"All right, Jamie," he said grudgingly. "I won't tell your mother. But only if I can trust you to keep your word. And that means doing your chores, and eating your meals, and going to Sunday meeting like you're supposed to."

Jamie nodded hurriedly. "I promise!"

Michael sighed. Collie was still glaring at him as if he were Satan's own messenger.

"I have a busy schedule, boys. I'm due at the orphanage by ten o'clock." He tucked his valise under his arm to roll up his sleeves. "And I suspect Miss Eden has a store to open shortly. Let's proceed with the examinations. Jamie, fetch the coons. Collie, bring me a bucket of water so I can wash up."

The younger boy scrambled to obey. Collie snorted.

"You ain't the boss of me." He folded his arms and turned his back. "Miss Eden, is there anything you need?"

She clasped her hands, the picture of diplomacy in her riding tweeds, ruffled white muslin, and cameo brooch. It was the lilt in her voice that belied her intent.

"Why yes, Collie. If it wouldn't be too much trouble, please fetch my satchel from Aunt Claudia's nag. I'll need to add garlic and honey to the syrup of onion. Oh, and I'll need to mix a preventative, too, so a bucket of water would be grand for washing up. I'll share it with Dr. Jones so you don't have to fetch two."

Collie "humphed" over his shoulder at Michael. Retrieving a rusted pail, he strolled with elaborate nonchalance toward the rain barrel. Eden tried to smother her giggle behind her hand, and Michael's lips twitched. Smug little trouble maker, wasn't she?

"If I didn't know better," he said, "I'd think you were gloating."

"That wouldn't be very professional, would it?"

"Professional?"

She avoided his eyes, her color on the rise again. "What I meant to say is, there's more than enough work here to keep two healers occupied."

Belatedly, he remembered what Collie had said: that Eden had cured him. He recalled, too, the wagon she'd directed him to all those years ago in Whiskey Bend, and the balding, spectacled man who'd stood on the stoop with his stethoscope. Did Eden think that growing up under the tutelage of a medicine show quack qualified her to diagnose and prescribe?

"So you've decided to follow in your father's footsteps?" he asked more cautiously.

"What do you mean?"

He bit his tongue. Wasn't the man's medicine show common knowledge? Michael wracked his brain to remember Sera's gossip. Damn, but he hated gossip. Still, he'd rather have Eden think he'd learned of Andrew Mallory's quackery through the grapevine. The last thing he wanted was for Eden to remember him as the "champion" who'd defended her from Black Bart in a Whiskey Bend alley. She'd only use the memory to further her fantasies about him. After he'd kissed her breathless the night before, she did, unfortunately, have good reason to think he would court her. He might be a bastard, but he wasn't cruel enough to mislead her.

"Your father operated a medicine show, as I recall."

She nodded, and he wished he'd kept his mouth shut as he watched the clouds roll across those candid eyes.

"He was a good doctor, Michael," she insisted. "People would condemn him because traveling physicians have become suspect. But Papa was wise in the conventional methods for treating the body. Just as his . . . uh . . . assistant, Talking Raven, was wise in the ways of treating the spirit. Together, they could heal almost anything, if given the chance."

Goosebumps scuttled over Michael's skull. He couldn't have said why he grew so uncomfortable; he knew only that he had to change the topic of conversation.

"Well. If you're determined to assist me, then I suggest you scrub up."

She arched a brow. He turned abruptly, striding through streams of sunlight filtered by tangerine clouds. She had a point about the workload here, and since he was on a tight schedule, he wasn't opposed to letting her help—under strict supervision, of course.

He headed for the center of the clearing. His goal was the hickory stump, but he slowed long enough to cast a critical eye over the emergency repairs he'd made the previous night. Since the boys had carried the animals and all their cages out to dry, he suspected his pine-needle thatch hadn't diverted the deluge any better than

Collie's straw. Still, even with last night's rain steaming from the roof, Michael could see by day what the lightning hadn't fully illuminated: substantial wood rot. It would take more than a barrel of tar to seal out predators and elements; it would take a whole new roof.

And four new walls wouldn't hurt, either.

He shook his head, setting his valise on the stump. The boys meant well, he knew. But they weren't thinking ahead to the time when their charges would outgrow their cages. Michael didn't know which was the lesser of two evils: keeping wild animals that yearned to be free, or loosing half-tame orphans to fend for themselves amidst the foxes, martens, weasels, cougars, and bears that prowled Blue Thunder Mountain.

Tugging off his gloves, he snapped open his valise and began the precise ritual of arranging his instruments: the thermometer beside the tongue depressor, the probang next to the eyedropper. He did all this to distract himself from the disturbing notion that he might not be able to work side by side with his living fantasy without pulling her into his arms. Above the clatter of his serum vials and chemical powders, he could hear Jamie crooning to the coons, Collie prying off the rain barrel's lid, a stream gurgling somewhere to his left, and bunnies scampering across the dried leaves in their cages. One would have thought all that racket would be enough to distract him from the sounds of the woman picking her way through the wildflowers to join him.

It didn't.

"You're not mad at me, are you?" Eden asked meekly. She halted at his elbow, and his palms grew moist.

Annoyed at these schoolboy jitters, he draped his stethoscope over his head. He wished he weren't so damned aware of Eden's perfume. "Do I look mad?"

"Most of the time."

He tossed her a withering look. She flashed an endearing smile. He wondered how much longer he'd be able to resist the allure of her charm. The woman was entirely too trusting to think she would be safe working within his reach. Little did she realize how many of his unspeakable fantasies had taken place in wild, woodsy locales just like this one . . . and how little subterfuge it would take to rid this clearing of their two witnesses.

He watched her flip open her satchel and kneel in a patch of buttercups. Her fist-thick braid swished against the swell of her buttocks, and his groin tightened as he envisioned that shy, tender flesh in his palms. He chastised himself, but it did little good. His eyes seemed to have a will of their own, conjuring erotic imagery from the sunburst of gold, red, and ivory that framed her against the eastern sky. He imagined her as some sylvan nymph, her skin pearlescent with dew, as she withdrew her mystical wares from the bleached doeskin in her lap. He half expected a Pan flute to materialize in her hands.

When she swept aside his instruments to make room for a mortar and pestle, he arched a brow at this take-charge attitude.

"Who would have thought Jamie Harragan and Collie MacAffee would wind up in cahoots?" she asked in conspiratorial tones, reaching once more inside the bag. "Have you ever seen a more unlikely pair?"

He shook his head and folded his arms, more interested in the curiosities she was unloading on the stump.

"Collie swore me to secrecy," she continued. "About the animals, I mean." A bone-handled knife replaced his thermometer. "Unfortunately, I took the oath before I realized what I was getting myself into." Next to the knife, she piled a collection of fringed rawhide pouches, each one bearing the painted replica of some flower or plant. "I don't like the idea of lying to Bonnie and Mrs. Buchanan, even by omission, but I don't dare break my word now that Collie finally trusts me." Her brow furrowed, which made her nose wrinkle and her freckles crowd together in the most appealing way. "Do you think that's a mistake?"

"I don't see any reason to raise an alarm—yet," he admitted, momentarily distracted from her Indian relics. "I made a cursory examination of the animals yesterday. None of them shows signs of fever. Gunther's animals have always been his bread and butter; he wouldn't have been negligent enough to let rabies spread through his pens. So the boys don't appear to be risking disease. And since Collie was careful to steal whelps, the coons and the pups aren't difficult to handle, like their feral sires."

"Well, that's a relief." Next to the pestle, she laid a notched measuring stick and a dipper made from a tan-colored gourd. Then she withdrew a corked bull horn and shook it, as if to mix its contents.

"Syrup of onion," she explained breezily. "Glass can break on the road." She nodded at the jagged crack working its way down his bottle of paregoric. "See what I mean?"

He muttered an oath, grabbing the precious opiate and casting about for another container. Without missing a beat, she handed him a tin box.

"I usually put my sage sticks in here, but this should do in a pinch."

*Sage sticks?* He bit his tongue on the question and nodded his thanks, his attention claimed by the liquid oozing from his bottle into the box. He didn't realize she'd taken the opportunity to rummage through his pharmaceuticals until a dainty hand smelling faintly of clover thrust a jar of white powder under his nose.

"What's potassium antimonyl tartrate?"

He slid her a sideways glance.

"Tartar emetic."

She made a face, much like the ones Sera used to make when he'd try to spoon-feed her black-eyed peas. "You don't actually think a puppy will *swallow* that, do you?"

He snatched the jar from her hand—a mistake. Lightning danced between their fingertips. The sizzle streaked all the way to his loins. He sucked in his breath. She staggered backward. *Damn.* How could such an innocent contact be charged with so much sexuality?

He rallied his wits enough to respond. "I take it you think you have something better?"

"Well, for purging parasites, yes." She sounded faintly breathless. "Honey and garlic for the coons, horse chestnuts for the rabbits."

"Horse chestnuts?" he repeated huskily, wishing he'd cleared his throat first.

"They cure worms."

He'd never heard of such a thing. Wormwood was the usual purge of parasites in this part of the country. But before he could question her claim, she added wistfully, "I'm fresh out of black elderberries. Couch grass too. They would have made marvelous preventatives."

He couldn't help but smile. "Are you practicing medicine or tossing a salad?"

She hiked her chin. "We'll just see whose elixirs get lapped up the fastest."

"And which ones have the desired effect."

She averted her gaze, dropping several cloves of garlic into her mortar. As she began to grind, several moments of silence passed between them. Meanwhile, Jamie was struggling to slide back the rusted door on one of the coon cages, and Collie, who'd discovered a hole in the bottom of his pail, was cursing like a muleskinner.

"Michael . . ." She hesitated, glancing over her shoulder as if to assure the boys were out of earshot. "What do you think Gunther will do if he finds out Collie took his animals? Press charges?"

Michael postponed his answer, unscrewing the lid of his magnesium hydroxide, a guaranteed dewormer. In all honesty, he didn't think Gunther would go to the sheriff. Cantankerous loners with questionable business reputations didn't arouse sympathy in judges and juries. The man was more likely to settle the matter himself. It was the "how" of that settling that worried Michael.

"Gunther," he said carefully, "will be hard to appease if he can prove the animals are his."

"But he can't, can he? I mean, coons, rabbits, and hounds are plentiful in this county. They could have come from anywhere, right?"

He glanced into her upturned face, so puckered with worry. He forced a smile. He didn't want her to share the burden of his concern.

"Proving ownership would be difficult," he conceded.

"That's what I thought." She nodded with a touch of asperity, and a flame-colored curl tumbled across her temple. It was a striking complement to the fire kindling in her eyes. "I know it's a terrible thing to say, but I'm glad Collie stole those whelps. Collie told me Gunther shot the mother coon because she tried to defend her babies. And Gunther's been throwing the rabbits—live—into a pit of ravenous dogs to whet his bettors' appetites for the coon-baiting event." Eden shuddered, edging closer, her voice lowering to a fierce whisper. "Berthold Gunther should be shot, or better yet, tossed into a pit with his hounds! What's the matter with Sheriff Truitt, letting that man get away with such cruelty?"

"There's no law in this state against baiting animals," Michael said grimly. "Only a law against stealing them."

"That's ridiculous. Basic human decency should prevail in these cases."

"I couldn't agree with you more. However, the fact remains, if Gunther can prove those animals are his, Collie could be arrested. Truitt already dislikes the boy. Jamie's got his mother's influence—and his father's money—to protect him. But Collie has nobody."

She was quiet for a moment.

"You care about him, don't you?"

He glanced at Collie. The boy was so busy keeping a wary eye on him, he didn't notice he was pouring water on the ground, instead of inside his new pail. A twinge of remorse tweaked Michael's chest. He'd been an orphan too—in deed, if not in fact. After his mother's death, and especially after Gabriel's, he couldn't remember gestures of affection from his father.

"Collie's young," he rallied gruffly. "Wayward. He needs a father. But most of all, he needs a mother. Someone to take the edge off his roughness and give him a good Christian upbringing."

"Have you . . . ever thought of telling him you care?"

Michael winced inwardly. He'd never been good at speaking his feelings; in fact, his profession frowned upon sentiment. But even if that weren't the case, what good would words accomplish? Collie's resemblance to Rafe didn't stop with his eyes and hair. The boy hated him.

Weeks ago, when Collie's prospects had looked particularly dim, Michael had thought about raising the boy. Collie had always gotten along with Sera, and Michael had hoped she might have enough influence to keep Collie on the straight and narrow. Unfortunately, that was about the same time Michael's illness set in. Without a definitive diagnosis, much less a cure, Michael decided he couldn't shoulder the responsibility of one more ward. He'd be lucky to find Sera a loving husband before news of his mysterious malady leaked. The last thing Collie needed was to have another parent die on him.

Michael understood that heartache only too well.

A splash sounded behind them. They turned in unison, watching Collie list sideways under the weight of the sloshing pail. His left leg was soaked from his knee to his boot, and he was muttering.

"Here's yer dang water," he growled at Michael, thumping the bucket on the ground. "I suppose you'll be wantin' me to get them rabbits fer you, too."

"If it's not too much trouble," he said dryly.

"It is. But I'll do it anyhow, seein' as how you'll leave quicker that way."

Eden dissolved into laughter as Collie strutted back to the shack. The sound sparkled, like sunbeams dancing across a wind-rippled river. Her humor made his heart yearn. She was more than beautiful, more than desirable. She was *alive*, possessing an easy, down-to-earth femininity he had always looked for, but never found, in Bonnie. Despite his rationales, all of which were excellent, he was having a devil of a time ignoring his attraction to Eden. Compared with her cheerfulness, he felt . . . well, jaded. But under his cracking veneer of weariness kindled a long-forgotten hope. Hope for renewal. Hope for happiness. Eden was like a tonic for his embittered view of the world, and the realization scared him—scared him to the rock-hard bottom of his soul. He hadn't allowed himself to harbor hope, much less dreams of love, for a long time.

He'd liked it better when his only interest in the woman had been carnal.

Like a man wading through quicksand, he forced himself to turn his shoulder, to call to Jamie, to encourage the boy to hurry, *hurry* with his coons.

"I'm trying, Doc!" Jamie panted, lunging after the five pound baby that had somehow unlatched its cage and was now charging playfully around the clearing.

"Head 'im off!" Collie shouted.

But Jamie's foot tangled in a surfaced root. He fell with an audible "oomph," and the masked prankster, making gleeful "whickering" noises, rubbed salt into the wound by dashing over Jamie's knees.

"Get up!" Collie called, abandoning the rabbit cages to lend a hand. "Dang it, he's gonna run straight fer that—"

The coon scampered up a hickory, and Collie slid to a halt, sputtering an oath about "townie boys."

Michael strode to the tree like a four-star general and ordered the boys to leave the coon alone. Eden didn't dare laugh when Collie ignored him and swung onto the lowest bough. She couldn't resist a smile, though, when Michael, in his gruff, paternal way, fielded Jamie's rapid-fire questions: What if Collie couldn't climb high enough? Did baby coons know how to climb down trees?

Collie proved more crafty than the inexperienced baby, however, and the coon, dangling as impotently from his fist as Stazzie once had, soon found itself locked up again with its masked cohorts. Jamie scolded it liberally.

Collie rolled his eyes. "That coon don't understand a word ye're sayin'."

"Sure it does. It knows its name is Vanderbilt."

"*Vanderbilt?*" Collie snorted. "What kind of name is that?"

"An important one! And I named his brothers Morgan, Rockefeller, and Harragan," Jamie said, beaming as he pointed at each coon in turn, the biggest one proving to be his namesake.

Collie made a derisive sound. "Didn't you know Harragan's a *girl?*"

"He is not!"

"Is too!"

Eden giggled. The horror on Jamie's face as he looked under Harragan's tail was, well, priceless. Besides, humor seemed the best way to diffuse the tension between the boys, not to mention her and Michael. She'd never dared to hope they'd meet so soon after their kiss; she'd assumed he'd avoid her with even more determination than usual. Now she wondered if today's chance meeting had really been by chance. Had he lain awake until dawn, as she had, thinking of their sparking? Had he followed her and Collie to this site, hoping to apologize—or better yet, to resume where they'd left off?

She watched him, so composed, so matter-of-fact as he diverted Jamie from the boy's grim new mission, gender identification, by producing carrots. Michael had stashed the vegetables like cigars inside the breast pocket of his suit coat, and for some reason, this creative camouflaging tickled Eden's heart. Her heart swelled even more to see this mountain of a man cradle a squirming, brown and white bunny against his chest, stroking its ears and murmuring encouragements, as Jamie held the carrot beneath the creature's quivering nose. Eventually Collie, his yearning overcoming his mistrust, uncaged another rabbit and accepted Michael's carrot offering.

Eden wished she'd had a way to capture the image forever: the three males standing elbow to elbow, their feuds forgotten, their faces split by lopsided grins, as they watched their bunnies munch breakfast from their hands. She sensed she was seeing a side of Michael the rest of the world rarely saw. His eyes had warmed each time he'd gazed at her, and his voice had grown husky as she'd moved near. She liked to think he was experiencing the same sweet infatuation she was, but with Michael, it was hard to tell. He was so intense. His secret self swirled with dark, mysterious undercurrents that lured her as irresistibly as the mountain laurels were drawing the bees. A woman could spend a lifetime learning to understand Michael Jones.

She wondered a little wistfully if he would ever let down his guard enough for her to try.

The rest of that morning passed in relative peace as the boys cleaned their charges' cages and Eden worked companionably with Michael, soothing the animals and searching for parasites. The rabbits were adorable, with their gigantic feet and velvet ears, and the puppies were fun, full of roughhousing mischief.

But the coons were Eden's favorites. Harragan proved to be shy and docile, while Vanderbilt, the smallest of the four, was the undisputed rogue. Ebony eyes glittering behind his mask, Vandy tried to steal Michael's watchfob. When Michael foiled that attempt, the unremorseful coon reached a grasping, handlike paw inside Michael's trouser pocket. This led to much sputtering and blushing on the good doctor's part. Laughing at their antics, Eden knelt by the tree stump to offer the baby a penny.

Michael watched in undisguised amusement as the coon scampered through the buttercups and dunked his prize in the water bucket.

"That one is going to be a bad influence."

"Honestly, Michael. What a terrible thing to say," she teased.

Finished now with their examinations, there was nothing left for them to do but pack their bags—or play with the babies. She watched her favorite coon rear up and hook his forepaws over the pail's rim. Whiskers twitching, Vandy was presumably sniffing for the coin he'd sunk; however, the appearance of a watery rival distracted him. With a territorial bellow—which from Vandy sounded more like a squeak—the baby swatted at his reflection, spraying water all over himself and Eden. She ducked, laughing.

But Vandy was outraged to see his rival shimmer back into focus. Loosing a baby battle cry, he scrambled into the pail before Michael could grab his ruff. The bucket toppled, water gushed, and Vandy howled, somersaulting nose over tail until he landed at Michael's boots with a soggy thud.

He whickered sheepishly at the wet human looming over him.

"Oh, no you don't," Michael growled as the baby bolted for the nearest tree. Michael swooped, and Vandy squirmed, protesting vociferously as he was thrust into the ignominy of his cage. His black eyes blazed with indignation as he wrapped his forepaws around the bars. He looked every inch like an outlaw in a jail cell.

Eden grinned as Michael squatted, offering her his handkerchief. "It's going to be curtains for you, Doc," she quipped, "the next time Vandy the Varmint gets loose from his cage."

"Much obliged for the warning." The dazzle of perfect teeth and masculine dimples made Eden's heart take a giddy skip. "But that rascal won't be seeing daylight for . . . at least a coon's age."

She was delighted. He treated her so rarely to his sense of humor that she'd begun to think she brought out the worst in the man. "Admit it. Vandy's your favorite."

"Vandy, eh?"

"Sure. Vandy, Rocky, Morgie, and . . . Harry."

His brow arched. "You mean Harri*ette*."

She winked. "Only when Jamie's not around."

He chuckled. She was captivated. The dark, brooding façade he favored had magically melted, and she knelt beside a charming, urbane man. A man who, less than twelve hours ago, had kissed her until her head had spun and sparks had showered her nerves like shooting stars. *Oh Michael,* she pleaded, *please don't retreat inside your armor again.*

She wondered if he'd heard her thought. As they laughed together, he rocked forward, his head nearly touching hers. He stilled. Her heart tripped. A breathless moment lay suspended between them. She watched his eyes, indigo now with a touch of silver, as they traveled over her hair, which was damp and no doubt wind-tossed; her nose, which was probably freckling in the sun; and her cheeks, which were growing warmer by the second. His expression softened, growing so tender, that when he raised his hand, she hardly dared to breathe.

"A souvenir from Vandy, I suspect," he murmured, his thumb brushing a dab of mud off her chin.

"Thank you," she whispered.

His inky fringe of lashes lowered. Her pulse skyrocketed. It pounded so hard, she could hear nothing of the birds, the wind, the boys. There was only Michael and the singing in her blood as his head moved closer and his breath grazed her lips.

"Eden." His voice throbbed around her, as deep and rich as the fertile earth. "I—"

A bucket clanged beside them.

"Are you two gonna start smacking lips again?" Jamie demanded.

Michael reared back, his face crimson. Eden blinked, slightly dazed. She hadn't heard the boys' approach. Jamie, his coonskin cap draping his left ear, looked as repulsed by the kissing idea as he had when Michael had tried to explain what worms could do to a dog's heart. Collie, his muscles quivering like a wildcat ready to defend its young, halted beside her. Eden wasn't sure whether it was Collie's narrowed stare or sheer embarrassment that made Michael climb so hastily to his feet. All she knew was a crushing disappointment, because whatever he had meant to say, whatever he had meant to *do*, were lost to her now.

"Did you finish watering the animals, Jamie?" Michael demanded, sweeping up his instruments with an economy that made Eden wince.

The boy nodded, growing contrite before that blazing blue glare.

"Good." Michael checked his pocket watch and muttered something that wasn't meant for children's ears. "Jamie, you'd better ride to the city limits with me before your mother hires a posse to bring you home." He jerked his head in the direction of the trees. "Fetch Brutus."

Eden's brow furrowed. *Brutus?*

A half-formed memory niggled at her mind. As Jamie scurried off, she started to rise, her thoughts chasing dim, elusive specters. Unfortunately, her inattention made her catch her heel in her petticoat.

Even more unfortunately, Collie was the one who grabbed her arm before she pitched headfirst over the stump.

Michael, as distant as Mars, closed his bag with a sharp *snick*. "Collie, I trust you can see Miss Eden home?"

"I brought her here, didn't I?" the boy growled.

"My point exactly."

Michael gave her a curt nod. She felt like Alice must have felt when she'd shrunk to six inches in size.

"Michael, wait—"

She bit her lip. The gaze that met her own proved as dispassionate as . . . well, a physician's. She struggled with the frustration that welled inside her.

"You were going to say something," she reminded him.

Those placid, blue pools never wavered.

"Right before Jamie interrupted," she prompted huskily.

An alpine spring couldn't have been any cooler. "I don't recall."

She choked. She wished he'd slapped her. A slap wouldn't have stung half as much as his words.

"Please, Michael. Don't go back to being—"

"It's better this way."

*Why, damn you?*

Tears threatened faster than she could blink them back. He was walking away. He was leaving her, his message unmistakable. What more could she say? What *dared* she say, with Collie standing like a guard dog at her side?

She stomped her foot. She hated the tear that slipped past her lashes, but she couldn't stop it any more than she could stop the maelstrom of yearning, the girlish hopes and fantasies that churned through her chest, unleashed after these eight long years. Finally, she'd put two and two together. Finally, she'd remembered the importance of Brutus. The man who'd saved her life that night in Whiskey Bend—the unarmed hero who'd bluffed his way past Black Bart—had ridden a bay gelding named Brutus.

Collie scowled like a gargoyle after Michael. The boy must have noticed her damp cheek, because his expression grew even more dire. He shook his head.

"I told you he ain't worth it," he muttered.

But Collie was wrong. Just as Sera had been. Just as *she* had been, Eden realized, recalling her romantic dreams of a mighty champion, a dashing gallant who'd return some moon-splashed midnight to love her and cherish her and carry her off on his bay-colored charger.

Michael wasn't ever going to be that gallant.

He wasn't even going to love her.

The knowledge pounded her with the force of a battering ram. Shaken, she was certain she'd heard something crack.

No doubt that sound had been her breaking heart.

# Chapter 7

❧☙

As the Independence Day jamboree approached, Eden did her best to reconcile her fantasy Michael with the Michael who was her neighbor. She told herself she was older now, wiser. She shouldn't have to keep herself company in the wee hours before dawn with dreams of a heroic longrider and his toe-curling kisses. Michael was a man. A hard-working, intensely passionate man. And while she admired the way he championed orphans and young women in peril, she was angered by his arrogance and outraged by his callousness. She'd cried for two whole nights after he'd flung that "It's better this way" barb at her defenseless heart.

She tried to tell herself he was right, that it *was* better for him to avoid her, building Aunt Claudia's shelves behind the closed doors of his toolshed, or riding to the animal orphanage during peak merchant's hours when Eden was needed at the store. After all, Michael's salad wisecrack that day at the animal orphanage proved he didn't approve of her healing craft any more than Papa had approved of Talking Raven's. Eden wanted desperately to believe that her success at curing Collie's dysentery over the last week had been no accident; to face Michael's disapproval, even if unspoken, would have been crushing. She didn't need to be challenged to prove she was a medicine woman. In fact, she'd begun to hope secretly that some respected physician, preferably Michael, would take her under his wing and help her nurture her fragile confidence.

Sometimes, she wondered if she approached Michael meekly, confessing that she'd been the gawky seventeen-year-old who'd bathed his wounds and comforted him that night in Whiskey Bend, that he might see some potential in her. At other times, she'd recall her shame over the medicine show scandal, and she'd be cured of her foolish notion.

She just wished there was a cure for her youthful fantasies about him. Now that she knew Michael had been the magnificent, blue-eyed hero who'd saved her life in Whiskey Bend, the dream specters returned: visions of a mighty, virile champion, seen through a woman's desire. He would come to her on a thunderous night, his hair whipping rakishly on the wind, his shadow-cloaked frame as awesome as a mountain in the electrical sizzle of storm. She would glimpse his smile: arrogant, seductive, daring her to surrender to him, her secret fantasy. Her knees would quake before his primal masculinity; his arms, like oaken boughs, would root her to the earth. He would taste of rain and radiate fire; her senses would combust as they reveled in her danger. She'd hear the crashing of her heart; she'd mark his low, feral growl as his lips devoured hers. Then he'd lay her down beneath a flaming arc of heaven, and the night would shatter with her innocence, an explosion of ecstacy, light, and sound.

The dreams were almost unbearable, considering that

the real kiss she'd shared with Michael apparently meant as little to him as . . . well, the offer of her friendship.

Fortunately, she had plenty of things to occupy her hands, if not always her mind, as the residents of Blue Thunder descended on the general store to prepare for the jamboree. The booth builders bought every box of nails, even the cobwebbed ones, while the Decorating Committee swarmed over the sewing shelves like locusts, devouring every scrap of red, white, and blue fabric—including Cooter's bandanna.

Then there'd been the flour frenzy. Blue-ribbon hopefuls had mobbed the poor miller's son as he tried to deliver the weekly shipment to the store. Apparently less concerned than Eden about coronary stress, Claudia had climbed on his wagon, leveled her shotgun at the crowd, and threatened to cancel all store credit before the two-legged alley cats meekly retreated to the line of humanity waiting to purchase butter, sugar, and eggs from Eden inside.

"Happens every danged year," Claudia muttered, wreathed in her habitual cloud of blue smoke as she stumped back across the threshold. Cradling her shotgun over her arm, she leveled a ferocious glance at the next customer then smirked furtively at Eden. "I charge 'em double, just to spite 'em."

Eden had never dreamed a little county jamboree could be rife with so much intrigue.

"Eden? *Eden!*"

She cringed. That ear-ringing shout could have belonged to none other than Bonnie. No one else's lungs could outbellow shrieking children as they romped on rope swings, the clamor of booth vendors barking their wares, the report of a pistol starting the three-legged race, or the catcalls of rival firefighting companies as they competed in the jamboree's baseball tournament.

Pasting on a wary smile, Eden forced her eyes from the boys' tug-of-war, in which Jamie, Collie, Bobby Buchanan, and a ferociously growling Mr. Puppy were being dragged, inch by inch, toward the mud that had been slopped over the freshly mowed hayfield. She figured she was about to be blamed for Jamie's imminent mud bath.

But Bonnie wasn't immediately visible in the crowd. Eden shaded her eyes against the noonday sun, squinting at the rainbowed hues of muslin gowns and satin bows, the painted faces beneath fluttering parasols, the neatly coiffed and aproned legions that were manning the food booths that circled the hayfield's wooded perimeter. As for the men, most of them were either competing in one of the races or cheering the contestants from the sidelines. Eden suspected there'd been slim pickings at the Kissing Booth. Why else would Bonnie abandon her coveted post to hound her?

"*Eden!* Good heavens, didn't you hear us calling you?"

A caramel apple cart rolled by, and Bonnie, her lips kiss-swollen and her eyes spitting fire, materialized in its place. A smirking Sera stood beside her.

"You have *got* to do something about your aunt!" Bonnie said, racing forward. "Claudia was supposed to be the chaperone. Now she's ruining everything! She thinks she can raise money better than us, and she won't listen to reason."

"Or to Bonnie," Sera deadpanned.

Eden didn't dare succumb to the twitch in her lips. "What's she doing this time?"

"See for yourself!"

Eden followed the line of Bonnie's quivering finger. As the crowd shifted again, the seventy-five-year-old rascal could be seen stomping her feet, shaking her gun-stock, and hollering at the top of her lungs. She'd climbed onto the Kissing Booth's counter, her dunga-rees billowing in the wind, her iron-gray hair frizzing in the humidity. Apparently she was taunting any man too foolish not to give the booth a wide berth. It was a wonder she hadn't had a seizure.

"She's going to break her fool neck," Bonnie grum-bled, concern actually creeping into her tone. Then her accusatory eyes drilled through Eden. "Did you let her drink corn mash again?"

"I think Auntie ate Sally McGloughlin's mincemeat," Sera interceded glibly. "Sally always overdoes the rum."

Bonnie muttered something about *that* blue-ribbon pie winner that would have made the members of the Ladies Aid Society blush.

Suddenly, a cheer rose from the circle of children be-hind them. Bonnie turned, saw her giggling son sprawled face down in the mud with Mr. Puppy licking his ear, and grew as white as the pearls on her kid gloves.

"*Jamie Harragan!* What have you done to your clothes?"

Jamie knuckled the mud out of his eyes. Bobby grabbed Mr. Puppy and made a beeline for the woods. Collie grabbed Jamie and disappeared as the other boys closed ranks, gathering around the winners to dicker over marbles, river stones, and penny candy.

Now Bonnie looked aghast. "Did you see what that MacAffee boy did? He got Jamie involved in ... in a wager!"

"Oh, Bonnie." Eden was sorely pressed not to roll her eyes. "They're only trading marbles."

"It's gambling! And you know it." Cunning vied with the resentment on Bonnie's features. "It's no secret you've been feeding that MacAffee boy. How dare you encourage my son to commit sin with that no-account white trash?"

"Your son," Eden responded coolly, "is one of the brightest, dearest, most compassionate young men I have ever had the pleasure of meeting. If he should choose to befriend a homeless boy, then I think God must be smiling on them both."

Bonnie's eyes narrowed. Sera coughed delicately.

"Um, Michael works with orphans all the time, Eden. Maybe you can get his advice on how to dissuade Collie from vices."

"*I* shall speak to Michael," Bonnie said quickly. "My son's the one whose future's at stake. Collie's is clearly hopeless."

Snapping open her parasol, she swept into the young bettors' midst, demanding to know where Jamie had fled.

Sera winked at Eden.

"Just mention Michael whenever she whips out her stinger," the younger girl said cheerfully. "It works all the time. Besides, Bonnie can't stand the thought of you and Michael getting close enough to kiss again."

"Honestly, Sera. Must you keep bringing that up? I can fight my own battles. You shouldn't have put Michael in the middle."

"Michael was already in the middle, Eden honey."

Eden tossed her friend a quelling look. Sera giggled.

"Speaking of Michael," the younger girl said slyly, "he's likely to be a big bidder in the picnic auction today, seeing as how the proceeds go to the orphanage. You didn't happen to pack that lovely but *plain* picnic hamper with the daisy linens inside, did you? The one that weighs half a ton thanks to all the cherry pie?"

Eden's cheeks warmed. "Sera," she warned, "don't you dare. None of the bidders are supposed to know who donated those lunches."

"What good are rules if you can't break them?"

"Your brother would throw a fit if he heard you say that."

"Only my oldest brother. Rafe would applaud."

Sera's grin was shameless. Eden shook her head.

"I think it's time I went and talked with Aunt Claudia," she announced diplomatically.

But Sera didn't take the hint. She trotted at Eden's heels as tenaciously as a bulldog puppy.

"You know," she mused aloud, "you might have to spend the whole afternoon with the man who buys your hamper. That could be a perfect dream—or a nightmare. I mean, imagine if Berthold Gunther suddenly got a hankering for daisies and cherry pie."

Eden doubled her pace.

"Of course, there's always the possibility nobody will bid on your hamper. If they don't know it's yours, I mean." Sera heaved a gusty sigh. "Last year, Johnny Dufflemeir did the charitable thing and bid on a hamper without knowing who'd packed it. A day later, when he was able to crawl back out of the privy, he told all the other sawmill workers he'd been poisoned by bootleather boiled in kerosine. Eventually, word got around that Sammy Jo Proctor had made that lunch. She had to move to New York City just to catch herself a beau!"

Eden slid her friend a dubious glance. "Honestly. Don't you think that's a bit extreme?"

"Well, yes. Can you imagine having to kiss one of those vulgar, strutting Yankees?"

Eden hid her smile.

"A Kentucky gentleman—like my dear brother Michael," Sera gushed unabashedly, "would know how to kiss a lady. But then, I don't have to tell *you* that, do I, Eden?"

Eden's belly quivered just to imagine kissing Michael again. She couldn't help but notice him then, chatting companionably with Lydia Witherspoon. He stood with the orphange's plump, good-natured headmistress in the shade of the daffodil-colored orphans' tent. Some of the older children, who'd survived the measles epidemic unscathed, were selling the rag dolls and peashooters they'd made to raise money for their home. Michael had already magnanimously contributed to the cause: a Y-shaped stick with a leather sling poked out of his trouser pocket.

In spite of the toy—or maybe because of it—Eden couldn't take her eyes off Michael. The peashooter was so contrary to the Michael he wanted her to know that it made her wonder. Beneath his gruff facade and prickly armor, did a charming rascal long to break free and wreak mischief on the world? Or perhaps the rascal had escaped years ago and had been lampooning Blue Thunder ever since.

The idea was an intriguing one. She already knew that Michael wasn't the stern, steely-eyed tyrant he pretended to be. A man made of steel couldn't boast the sensual magnetism, the smoldering virility that radiated from every inch of Michael Jones. Blue Thunder's doctor could tie a woman's tongue, buckle her knees, and fire her pulse all with a single glance. Indeed, Eden wondered that Lydia Witherspoon could withstand the dazzling flash of one of his unpredictable smiles without melting into a puddle at his feet.

Michael Jones was an inveterate heartbreaker. But did he know it? That was the question. For today's conquests, he hadn't dressed in a relaxed or colorful way. He'd chosen pinstriped trousers, a pearl gray coat, and the charcoal-colored silk of a cut-away vest. At his throat was the requisite black ribbon bow tie, a striking contrast to his pristine white shirt, but his head was bare, its thick, cropped mane riffling like a wheatfield in the breeze. The ensemble wasn't as formal as his habitual black business suit; even so, it lent him an air of authority—one that faded blue denims and a checkered workshirt might have had trouble evoking, except, perhaps, from a man like Jesse Quaid.

As Eden covertly sighed over Michael, Bonnie rounded the orphans' tent, dragging a sulking Jamie in her wake. She must have spied Michael's broad back and the unmistakable shock of his blue-black hair, because her scowl suddenly dissolved into a poignant, almost whimsical longing. She called something to him; he glanced over his shoulder; and his face lit with a welcome that, frankly, made Eden's heart crumble. Whether his greeting was for Jamie or Bonnie wasn't clear. Still, Eden couldn't help but remember the rumors: how Michael had once courted Bonnie with marriage on his mind; how she'd spurned his affections to elope with Justin Harragan; how she was determined to correct her mistake and win Michael back again.

Perhaps, Eden thought as her spirits deflated, Bonnie already had. When Jamie pointed shyly at the peashooter, Michael tugged it from his pocket and offered it to him. The boy gasped with delight, and Bonnie, magically forgetting her distaste for slingshots, popguns, and other toys of destruction, couldn't make a big enough fuss over Michael's gift. To watch Bonnie's fawning was more than Eden could bear.

Sera, of course, had missed none of the byplay between the former sweethearts. With an unspoken empathy that took Eden by surprise, the younger girl gave Eden's waist a firm squeeze. She was grateful for the sentiment, even though she suspected she'd turned as red as the polka dots on Sera's blouse.

"You can be as nice to me as you like, Sera Jones," she rallied lamely, "but I am *not* going to tell you which picnic basket is mine. And that's final."

"Oh bother. Are you sure?"

"Quite sure."

"Fine." Sera made a great show of pouting as they continued toward a fluttering pink and blue canopy and the Cupid-laden banner that read KISS A GIRL AND RAISE THE ROOF. "I guess I'll have to use deductive reasoning, like Michael uses on his patients." Gazing at the clouds, she furrowed her brow, the very picture of concentration. "Let's see. I donated a hamper, and so did Bonnie. That leaves fifteen more from the unmarried girls, and most of them aren't hard to guess." She glanced at Eden, smiled cherubically, then continued ticking off names on her fingers. "Every year, Mary Blackburn embroiders watermelons on her napkins, 'cause she's sweet on Smitty McCann. And Betsy Frothingale always paints her hamper with red-and-white checks, 'cause Tony Mattuchi's too nearsighted to see a little slip of checkered cloth if he has to bid from the back row. Maggie York wraps her handles with green bows—"

"Sera"—Eden battled a sinking feeling—"don't you have anything better to do besides torment me?"

Sera beamed. "I can't think of a thing."

Eden sighed. So much for the good-natured suspense surrounding the picnic auction. Cherry pie or no cherry pie, if Michael could deduce her basket as easily as Sera had, he would never try to win it.

But then, what did she care, Eden asked herself staunchly. It was a lovely afternoon. Why waste it mooning over a heartache named Michael Jones? Any number of attractive, unmarried men might bid on her lunch and spend the day with her. The whole county had turned out for the jamboree, after all.

By this time, she and Sera had drawn close enough to the kissing booth to hear Claudia heckle passing bachelors from her stance on the counter.

"You there," the spinster bellowed in a voice three times her size. "Tony Mattuchi! I see you skulkin' behind that draft horse. C'mon over here and kiss me, dadblast it! The orphanage needs a new roof. Hey! *Hey!* Johnny Dufflemeir. I saw them moths fly outta yer wallet. Git yer scrawny arse over here. Kissin' me'll cost you a buck. Fer three bucks, you can go home without my buckshot in yer britches!"

Eden smothered a giggle as Claudia leveled her barrel with deadly accuracy. She could see the coins glinting in her aunt's kisses jar. Claudia and her shotgun had amassed more silver dollars than all of the younger, prettier volunteers combined. No wonder Bonnie wanted Claudia chased from the booth.

Eden nodded politely at scowling, red-faced Johnny as he stalked forward, dug a fist in his trouser pocket, and plunked three coins into Claudia's jar.

Claudia shook her shotgun after him as he fled. "My picnic basket's the one with the coon tail 'round the handle! Be sure to bid on it, if you want my bear traps on credit!"

Chortling, she squatted, her gunstock balanced across her knees and a sparsely toothed grin creasing her cheeks. "Hello, niece. Hello, neighbor. Dang. I don't know what the deuce Bonnie was gripin' about. Raisin' money fer them orphans is easier'n shootin' fish in a barrel."

Sera laughed, a bubbling, carefree sound that turned more than one masculine head. In her red and white blouse, with its ribbon-edged ruffle and leg-o'-mutton sleeves, she was stunning, a vivacious young belle ripe for romance.

"Um, Sera." Eden phrased her question carefully, surprised to see no kisses jar bearing her friend's name. Had strait-laced Michael forbidden his sister to lend her kisses to the cause? "You didn't cry uncle, did you? I mean, Aunt Claudia may have the fullest jar in the booth, but I'm sure she'd tolerate a little friendly competition—for the sake of the orphans."

Sera grew wistful. "I can't. Billy's coming from the sawmill soon."

"*Billy?*" Claudia snorted. "That no-account horse thief?"

"My sweetheart is not a horse thief," Sera retorted primly. "I'll thank you to quit spreading such rumors."

"Most rumors are based in truth, young 'un. And 'horse thief's' the nicest thing I've heard said about that Texican. Why don't you git yerself a kisses jar and catch yerself a worthwhile beau?"

Sera raised her chin. "Billy wouldn't like me kissing other men. Not even for the orphanage."

"Billy ain't put no ring on yer finger that I kin see, girlie. And his kind ain't likely to, even after a tumble in the hay. So don't be doin' anything stupid."

Sera blushed. Eden cleared her throat. Honestly, Aunt

Claudia might be a bit more tactful, since Sera fancied herself in love with the man.

"Well, I'm sure there must be other ways to raise money," Eden interceded. "I was going to volunteer at the lemonade booth until the auction."

Sera's and Claudia's jaws both dropped.

"The *lemonade* booth?" Claudia grimaced, shaking her head. "No wonder you ain't married, niece. Why in the name of Sam Hill would you want to squeeze some dang old lemons when you could be kissing the socks offa some bachelor?"

Sera nodded. "*And* making Michael jealous."

"I don't want to make Michael jealous."

Claudia folded her arms. "Why not? Didn't you like the way he kissed ya the last time?"

Eden sputtered, tempted to crawl under the counter and die. Who had turned traitor and tattled? Sera or Jamie?

"It's hard to believe you got the Collier blood running through yer veins," Claudia continued in dire tones. "I ain't never met a woman who needs more schoolin' than you do in the ways to catch a man."

"I think I do perfectly well on my own, thank you."

Sera covered her mouth and giggled.

*Is there a law against throttling friends?* "This conversation is unworthy of you both," Eden retorted.

"Being hoity-toity ain't gonna win you any fellers," Claudia snapped.

"Oh, Eden. *Someone's* got to marry my brother. Why shouldn't it be you?"

*Why shouldn't it, indeed?* She tried not to stare too forlornly at Jamie, whose hand had all but disappeared in Michael's bear-sized fist. Bonnie was beaming as she chatted beside them, and Eden couldn't help but imagine the family they might make: Michael with his feet propped up, relaxing with the evening paper in his father's old, red and green–striped armchair; Jamie kneeling on the carpet, staging a mock battle with tin soldiers; Bonnie humming an off-key lullaby as she rocked her new baby by the hearth . . .

Eden blinked the vision away and drew a shuddering breath. Jamie idolized Michael. And Michael clearly doted on the boy. Even Sera couldn't deny that Michael's affection for Jamie gave Bonnie an edge over all her female competitors.

"Maybe I will fill a kisses jar," Eden said in resignation. With Michael's lips haunting her dreams, she hadn't thought she could bring herself to kiss another man—at least, not until Cupid's arrow struck her for some other beau. But maybe Claudia was right. The kissing booth was a perfect opportunity to invite a flirtation. After all, she wasn't getting any younger.

"That's the spirit," Claudia crowed, jumping off the counter and rummaging through a box beneath the columbine-blue crepe of the drapery. After a series of clanks and rattles, she straightened triumphantly, plunking an empty canning jar in front of Eden. "You got at least an hour to convince some man to bid on yer basket, so pucker up and get to work."

Eden sighed, reaching for the paintbrush to label her jar. *One hour to hope that Michael comes by. One torment for every minute he doesn't.*

Claudia heaved herself back onto the counter. "Git me my shotgun," she fussed at Sera, who grimaced, reaching for the barrel the way she might have reached for horse dung. Claudia snatched it from her hand. "Now git outta the way. I'll show you fillies how to rope a stallion."

Eden and Sera exchanged wary looks.

"Hey!" Claudia thumped the gunstock on the counter for attention. "You there in the tight breeches. Yeah, *you* know who I mean, Four Eyes. You didn't put them pants on to be ignored, I'll wager. Get your pretty mug over here for a kiss."

The sodbuster straightened his spectacles, took one look at Claudia, and fled.

She scowled. "Dang. That boy must be deaf as well as blind. Bad breeding stock."

Sera's nails dug into Eden's arm. She was trying so hard not to laugh, she looked like she might cry.

"Hey!" Claudia bellowed next at the blacksmith's boy. "I got a round of buckshot with your name on it, son. Git yer big, brawny self over here fer a kiss!"

"I'll kiss you, old woman."

At the sound of that rumbling Texas drawl, Eden caught her breath. She suspected she didn't hide her shock particularly well as Jesse Quaid strolled out of the crowd. Lithe and rangy, he moved with a predatory grace that exuded a titillating danger. Claudia stiffened at his approach. Sera turned an intriguing shade of pink.

"Afternoon, ladies." He tipped his hat, a black Stetson bearing the trace of some pleasantly pungent tobacco.

"Git on with ya," Claudia growled, swinging her barrel into point-blank range. "You ain't kissin' nobody. Least of all, me."

Jesse didn't even flinch. He simply gazed up that long double barrel yawning six inches from his chest, and grinned. His smile was a slash of white in a face nearly blackened by the sun. "Now don't go getting coy on me, ma'am."

She glared back, her iron-gray eyes locking with emerald steel. "I know what ye're about. Don't think I don't. 'Sides, You ain't got the money."

In answer, he fished inside his breast pocket and slapped three silver dollars on the counter. "One for each of you."

Sera tossed her head and sniffed.

Claudia grunted. "Yeah? So where'd you steal 'em from?"

"Auntie." Eden gingerly pushed the gun barrel away from Jesse's chest. "That's enough. If Mr. Quaid would like to spend his money at the kissing booth, he has every right."

"We're closed," Claudia growled.

"That's right," Sera chimed in loftily. "I was just saying how blazing hot it's getting—wasn't I, Eden?—and that we could all use a splash of lemonade. I'm sure you understand, Mr. Quaid. Will you excuse us? I do believe I see Billy waiting for us by the sycamore."

"Must be one of those heat mirages, ma'am," Jesse said. He leaned against the counter, unconcerned that Claudia's shotgun dangled a hair's breadth from his jugular vein. "I've known Billy since he was in short pants. He never did cotton to family picnics and such."

"You're wrong about Billy," Sera flared. "He is too coming to the jamboree. He promised."

"I reckon you'd know best, then."

Eden fidgeted. She wasn't sure what to think of Sera's antagonism. She was even less certain what to think about Billy.

"Come along, Auntie," Sera said crisply.

When Claudia squatted, as if to jump down, Jesse offered her a hand. She slapped it away, grabbing Sera's shoulder instead.

"You *are* coming, aren't you, Eden?" Sera demanded, her arm now linked through Claudia's.

Eden glanced at Jesse. He returned her gaze evenly, no ire, no prevarication. She suspected there was something more to the man than Claudia and Sera were seeing. *Strange.* Why would Jesse offer to kiss Sera if it meant subjecting himself to her public contempt? Surely he must have known by now she didn't hold him in the same high esteem she reserved for his childhood friend.

Eden took a deep breath. And a leap of faith.

"Perhaps you could bring some lemonade back for me," she answered quietly.

Sera's mouth formed an *O.* Claudia's eyebrows slashed down like twin thunderbolts.

"Have you lost yer cotton-pickin' mind?"

"Oh look, Auntie," Sera exclaimed, the high pitch of her tone a thin veil for her warning. "I see Sheriff Truitt just over there." She nodded in the direction of the caramel apples cart, where the pot-bellied lawman was doling out confections to three eager, jumping toddlers. "I suddenly have quite the taste for apples."

Claudia slapped her shotgun on the counter. "Truitt or no Truitt," she growled, "if this slanty-eyed bastard lays a hand on you, niece, don't think twice."

Eden blinked, taken aback. Sera dragged Claudia in the direction of the sheriff.

Jesse said nothing. He simply watched them go.

"Um . . ." She caught herself twisting her skirts. The habit was a deplorable one, developed at the age of six, when her father had first coaxed her onto his medicine show stage to sing. Hastening to smooth out the wrinkles, she cleared her throat and tried to seem at ease with this man whose cartridge belt rode so low across his hips.

"I'm sorry about my aunt. She can be a bit crotchety at times. Please don't take her rudeness to heart, Mr. Quaid."

"Jesse's good enough for me."

While his features remained as serene as any veteran poker player's, a hint of bitterness roughened his voice.

"I'm sorry," she said more gently this time.

Sun-crinkled eyes, more sharp and green than pine needles, at last darted her way. She wondered if Comanche blood ran through his veins, the way his bones sat so high in his cheeks. With his crooked nose and square jaw, she wasn't sure she'd classify him as handsome. He looked to be about twenty-six, not an incompatible age for her—or even for Sera. But Sera didn't like her sweetheart's best friend. Eden wondered if Jesse's sixshooter was to blame. She had to admit, the Texican didn't exactly fit the average husband seeker's definition of *civilized*. He was too unpredictable, too unnerving. He smoldered with an undeniable sensuality, like an ember waiting to combust. His mere presence made women stammer. Eden had watched her neighbors gather their skirts and hurry across the street to avoid passing him on the sidewalk. Even so, they'd tossed hungry, covetous looks his way.

Why was it that Jesse Quaid, in a town short on bachelors, didn't have a single bell-chasing sweetheart trotting at his heels?

Thin, predatory lips curved, as if he'd intuited her train of thought.

"Mind if I smoke?"

He was fishing in his breast pocket again, the gingham of which precisely matched his eyes. She hesitated. In polite society, a gentleman would never light tobacco in a lady's presence. But Jesse didn't strike her as the byproduct of polite society. He already had the cigarette and matchsafe in his hand.

"Well," she said slowly, "I suppose it would be all right. If you stayed downwind."

"Reckon you mind, then."

She couldn't tell if he was amused or annoyed. The cigarette disappeared back in his pocket. He did, however, pull a match from the safe to chew on the headless end.

"Lots of folks here today," he observed companionably. He'd turned his back to the counter and leaned his elbows upon it. The pose let him do what he liked to do best: study his surroundings. She realized she'd never seen him do much else. He was always watching, always vigilant. Each time he'd come into the store, his gaze had roamed continually from the windows, to the customers, to the door. While Billy liked to boast and flirt, Jesse shunned attention. He preferred corners, shadows, and silence, like a man who . . . well, like a man who had reason to wear a gun.

"The whole county must have turned out for this shindig," he added casually. "Sodbusters and horsetraders. A couple of cowhands, too. Say, have you seen Black Bart yet?"

"B-Black Bart?" She choked on the outlaw's name.

"Sera said he's an old friend of yours."

"I can't imagine why she would say such a thing." *Least of all to you!*

He was observing her subtly. He hadn't shifted; he hadn't even turned his head. Even so, she recognized his heightened awareness. It loosed a shiver down her spine.

"I ran into Black Bart once," she felt compelled to defend herself.

"Yeah? Must've been exciting, meeting a war legend."

"Black Bart isn't exactly known for his heroics around these parts."

"You don't say?" The matchstick rolled nonchalantly to the other side of his mouth. "So how'd you meet him?"

She blew out her breath, loath to continue the conversation. Unfortunately, her righteous side felt obligated to cure Jesse's idyllic image of the man. "Bart tried to steal my horse about eight years ago in Whiskey Bend. To be honest, I didn't know who he was. I figured it out a day or so later because of the gossip. Apparently a stagecoach had been robbed just outside the town limits. Everyone said Bart's gang did it. But I never saw any other road agents that night. Just Bart. He was limping—bleeding, too—and dragging a burlap sack."

Jesse had grown still, as still as a pond in midwinter. Even so, she sensed the rise of something dark in him, something primal and potentially savage. She might have been frightened if he'd changed his stance or his manner. But he was careful, extraordinarily careful, to betray no outward sign of feeling. Without the evidence to validate her intuition, she preferred to give him the benefit of the doubt.

"Did he hurt you?" he demanded quietly.

"Oh no. Michael—that is to say, Dr. Jones—came along and scared him away."

"Jones, eh?"

Eden blushed. "I'm sure he doesn't remember."

The ghost of a smile lightened the shadows that chiseled Jesse's face. "You must've been just a kid."

"Well . . . not *exactly.*"

Those keen eyes flickered her way. "I meant no offense."

"I know. It's not your fault. I mean . . ." She heated another degree. "Never mind."

He shoved his hat back with his thumb and bent his knee, tucking his heel under his backside. A moment passed as he surveyed the three-legged race, the leap-frog tournament, the quilt-judging team . . . and Sera talking a mile a minute to Sheriff Truitt. She kept glancing anxiously toward the Kissing Booth.

"I've heard it said Doc Jones is sweet on you."

Eden started. "You have?" She was momentarily elated. Then her most logical deduction sank in and crushed her fledgling hope. "Sera must have told you. She does talk a lot. I'm afraid she has a tendency to see things that aren't always . . . well, there."

"Oh, it's there all right." He directed her attention back to the orphan's tent. Michael was ignoring Bonnie completely, despite the widow's skillful coquetry. In fact, he was staring in Eden's direction, his brow so thunderous, one might have thought he'd spied her committing some heinous sin.

*Irritating man.* She turned her shoulder. She knew he disapproved of her, but did he have to telegraph his feelings to the entire county?

"I'm sure you're mistaken," she told Jesse firmly.

"Do you want me to be?"

"Well, no, it's just that . . ." She fingered her empty jar and tried to ignore a pang of longing. "Michael has been very clear about his intentions. He's my neighbor, nothing more."

Amusement punctured Jesse's preferred armor: indifference.

"I usually make a point not to tell a lady she's wrong. But in this case, I figure you won't mind. Besides. You've always been nice to me."

"I have?"

"You don't think so?"

An unaccountable shyness washed over her. She couldn't remember treating Jesse differently from any of the other men who came into the store. Then again, most women crossed the street, refusing to share a sidewalk with him. Did Jesse receive so little kindness in Blue Thunder that mere courtesy seemed remarkable?

"I know what it's like to be an outsider," she said quietly.

A faint grimace marred his features. It was a glimpse into his private pain, and it surprised her.

"Reckon you would," he said after a moment, "what with the way folks treated you in Silverton."

She sucked in her breath. "You . . . know about that?"

His lips twisted faintly.

"You never mentioned it before," she added uneasily.

"Don't like to talk about it much," he admitted. "I'm trying to put Colorado behind me, too." Knowing eyes, discerning eyes, touched hers. "Fact is, I was locked up in the county jail, waiting to stand trial, about the same time your pa got sick. The reason I know about him is the marshal tossed a couple of rowdies into the cell next to mine. After they slept off their rotgut, they got to scheming. Said they could make a heap of drinking money once they got free if they told that grieving Mallory girl her pa owed them money for testifying to the crowd.

"I always reckoned," he added softly, "you'd want to know about that."

Eden's eyes brimmed. That he was willing to expose his own sins to exonerate her father touched her deeply. "Thank you," she whispered.

He nodded, gazing once more into the crowd, his

coarse, coal-black hair rising on a puff of wind.

As he gave her the space to compose herself, she thought of Papa's heart tonic, and excitement kindled in her chest. Jesse's tale could mean her father's successes had been valid. Perhaps the elixir would even help Claudia, despite her advanced years. The trouble was, how could she convince her aunt to try it?

Eden ventured another glance, this one hopeful, at Michael. He hadn't taken his eyes off her, or maybe Jesse was the one he was really glaring at. It was hard to tell.

"Want to try an experiment?" Jesse drawled.

She started, realizing he was watching Michael, too.

"An experiment?" she repeated uncertainly.

Dimples carved Jesse's cheeks. He turned his head her way. "Lean over the counter, closer to me."

A vague suspicion snaked through her mind. "Why?"

"Just do it."

"Jesse, I'm not sure . . ."

Devilry glimmered in the stare that captured hers. "You want Jones or don't you?"

Suspicion turned to understanding, and her heart tripped. She tried to look at Michael.

"No," he murmured. "Look at me. That's it." He gave her a smile that would have melted Lucifer's heart. "Now then. Smile. Like you mean it."

His instructions, so matter-of-fact, were at odds with his expression: provocative, tantalizing. She couldn't help but wonder which was playacting and which was real. Was he genuinely attracted to her?

"Good. Now shimmy out here a bit."

Her pulse quickened. "Are you going to kiss me?"

"If that's what it takes. You game?"

She drew a long, tremulous breath. She didn't like the

idea of trying to make Michael jealous, but he wasn't likely to care, so she couldn't bring herself to regard it as much of a crime—especially after Jesse had gone out of his way to give her peace of mind.

She nodded her consent. "I don't understand," she whispered, feeling more than a little traitorous. "Why are you doing this?"

"I've got my reasons." He turned his body to face hers, and her breath caught in her throat. He was broader than she'd first thought. Broader, taller, and more formidable.

"Now," he murmured, his lashes fanning lower, "I'm going to come closer." He tossed aside his matchstick, and her pulse leaped. His lithe sinews hinted of a restrained strength that made her stomach flutter. "Steady." The corner of his mouth curved. "I'm going to touch your cheek." She caught a whiff of leather and woodsmoke as a dark hand, calloused but gentle, tilted her face up to his. She swallowed as his thumb brushed her chin. "You're a beautiful woman, Eden," he said wistfully. "Jones is a damned fool to—"

*"Quaid!"*

Jesse smirked. He barely had time to raise his head before two hundred pounds of muscle and menace grabbed his shoulder, spun him around, and shoved him backward. Jesse recovered his balance with the grace of a puma, while Michael, heedless of the younger man's sixshooter, planted himself like a grizzly bear between Jesse and Eden.

"Stay away from her," Michael growled.

Jesse feigned indignation, raising his hands in a placating gesture. "Now see here, Doc. I don't know what you're getting so riled about. I paid my dollar. Paid three dollars, to be exact. The lady owes me three kisses."

"Your money's no good here."

"Oh, I get it," Jesse said amicably. "Don't worry. Those silver dollars are the real McCoy. Got them straight from the sawmill for a day's worth of work."

Michael swept up the coins and flung them at Jesse's boots. "No orphan in this county is in dire enough straits to take charity from the likes of you."

"Michael!" Eden gasped. "That is entirely uncalled for."

"Well now." Jesse arched an onyx brow. "I think my feelings are hurt. But I hear Miss Eden's cherry pie's the best medicine a man can buy. 'Specially for Cupid cramps." He gave her a naughty grin. "Which one of those picnic lunches did you say was yours again, hon?"

"*Miss Mallory* '—Michael emphasized the formality—"and her picnic lunch are spoken for. By me. Now be about your business, Quaid."

"Is that a fact?" Jesse stooped, picking his coins out of the grass. "Reckon you've got some competition then, Doc. Good thing I saved up two months' worth of wages, eh?" Pocketing the silver, he tipped his hat, giving her a furtive wink. "See ya at the auction block, Doc."

Hooking his thumbs over his gunbelt, Jesse sauntered away, nearly colliding with Sera, who'd come racing up behind her brother, Sheriff Truitt huffing in her wake. Jesse exchanged a few terse words with the lawman, while Sera, turning red with guilt—or perhaps it was triumph—hurried out of Jesse's path.

Eden, meanwhile, was so furious, she was shaking. She rounded on Michael, who was glaring like a hanging judge after the younger man. "How dare you?" she sputtered. "How *dare* you come over here and order my customers around?"

He turned slowly. The full force of sapphire steel clashed with her ire; she felt the vibration all the way to her toes. Still, she refused to be cowed by his ever-ready scowl.

"You had no right to banish Jesse from the booth," she said. "He paid his money, just like everyone else."

"Eden, honey," Sera interceded anxiously, "you don't know what you're saying."

"I most certainly do! Your brother is a common bully. What's more, he has the manners of a boor!"

A disturbing gleam kindled in Michael's eyes. She suspected if she'd been less angry, she would have considered it a warning. Instead, she proceeded to seal her own doom.

"I shall kiss any man I please, Michael Jones. And I shall picnic with whomever I please too! Don't you dare tell another beau I'm spoken for, least of all by you!"

"Are you finished?" he demanded in a low, fierce undertone.

She hiked her chin, hating that the traitorous thing quivered. "For now."

"Good."

He turned on his heel and strode away.

She gaped. Then she choked. How dare the arrogant cuss turn his back on her and walk off without so much as a grunt in apology? She stomped her foot, wishing she could satisfy her outrage in a more visceral way— like punching him in the gut.

"Eden . . ." Sera twisted her hands. "You shouldn't have said all those things. Michael did the right thing."

"I can't believe you're condoning his behavior!"

Sera fidgeted, glancing toward Jesse. He was arguing

now with the sheriff and two deputies for the right to keep his gun. In the end, he was forced to surrender the weapon. Sera hugged herself, hastily averting her gaze as those pine needle-green eyes stabbed through the crowd to accuse her.

"You just can't trust Jesse," she said, although she didn't sound entirely convinced. "I know he seems nice sometimes. But you can't let that fool you. He can be cruel. Vicious, too. He's not safe to be around. Especially if you're a woman."

"Sera, really. Is that more gossip from Bonnie and the Ladies Aid Society?"

"No, I . . ." Sera shook herself. "It was—*you* know"— she lowered her voice—"one of the visions I told you about," she finished in a rush. "Michael says I shouldn't speak of such things."

"Michael's not here."

"I know, but . . ." She bit her lip. "Well, I could have been mistaken. I mean, the things I see don't always make sense. Still, Billy said Jesse served time in the penitentiary. And when he got out, the woman who put him there mysteriously *died.*"

Eden's heart tripped. *Jesse . . . a murderer?* She frowned. He'd as much as admitted he was an outlaw. She'd even thought him a tad shy of frightening. But that was before she'd glimpsed his private pain for being ostracized. Seeing that ember of humanity in Jesse, she wasn't sure she believed Billy's accusation that his companion was a cold-blooded killer. In fact, she wasn't sure she believed anything Billy Cassidy said.

"If Jesse's so dangerous, then what's Billy doing, riding around the country with him?"

Sera blinked, growing pink with indignation. "You heard Jesse. Billy's his friend. They grew up together."

Eden decided to keep her opinion on that particularly lame explanation to herself.

Suddenly, a towering shadow darkened the stall. Eden glanced up in time to see Michael eclipse the sun. Striding out of the crowd with a bulging picnic hamper in his fist, he halted before her, hoisted the box, and banged it down on the counter with a challenging thud. Dishes clattered inside, so did the silverware. He didn't seem to notice, though. Nor did he seem to care that he might have broken Aunt Claudia's china. He was too busy locking stares with her.

"Forgive the intrusion, ladies," he said, deceptively pleasant, "but there's been a slight change in Eden's plans. This afternoon, she'll be picnicking with me."

# Chapter 8

E den was so stunned by Michael's audacity, that for a moment, all she could do was blink. Even Sera looked aghast. She gazed up at her brother as if he had just committed some unforgivable crime.

"Michael," she said, her usual bravado wavering, "what have you done? Put Eden's basket back. If you disqualify her, she'll be ruined in this county!"

He didn't look the least bit disturbed. "I'm sure Eden's reputation will survive."

"But you can't just steal her basket—"

"I don't consider a one-hundred-dollar investment to be a steal."

*One hundred dollars?* Eden gulped a shallow breath. She hadn't thought it possible for a corset to grow so tight.

"Can you do that?" Sera breathed.

"I just did."

"But the auction hasn't even started—"

"The auctioneer," Michael interrupted dryly, "had the good sense to take my one-time offer, since he, as the president of the Raise the Roof Committee, recognized that Eden's basket was unlikely to earn as much income from any other bidder, Mr. Quaid included."

Eden's heart hammered so hard against her ribs, she feared one would break.

"So . . ." Sera's eyes had grown as wide as the Ohio River. "You didn't disqualify her?"

"Like I said. Eden's reputation is likely to survive this episode. It might even be enhanced. Coming, Eden?" He stretched out his hand. "I believe you owe me the pleasure of your company."

Sera giggled. Eden pressed her lips together. If Michael Jones were any other man, not the fantasy she'd been longing for night after restless night, she would have told him to go choke on her picnic lunch. He was reenacting the role of her hero, but that didn't mean she had to approve of his methods.

Hiking her skirts, she swept past his insufferable hand, taking some small satisfaction in the fact that he'd now have to haul her twenty-pound hamper of fried chicken and cherry pie to some distant spot of shade.

To watch him fall into step beside her, though, the wicker swinging effortlessly from his arm, proved disconcerting.

She set her jaw, trying not to appreciate the way his tailored suitcoat accentuated the broad planes of his shoulders, or the way the late morning sun struck flinty shades of blue from his hair.

"Well, you've had your way and impressed your authority once more on Sera," she said tartly as they passed the rear entrance to the orphans' tent. "Now that she's out of sight, you can return my basket to the auction block so some serious-minded beau can offer for it."

"I'm afraid I can't do that."

His drawl, like Kentucky's finest bourbon, was

golden smooth, intoxicating. She did her best to ignore the nuance, even though it melted her nerves.

"Why not?" she demanded.

"Certain factions in this county would find a cure for Cupid cramps . . . inconvenient."

She stumbled at his jest. A dimple creased his cheek, which only heightened her aggravation. She halted, planting her fists on her hips. Courtesy forced him to stop and face her, even though they were now the object of speculation for several gawking bystanders and at least a dozen couples who'd slowed their strolls to listen. She decided not to care. In fact, some ornery part of her refused to play the docile female to Michael's high-handed male.

"You are a pirate of hearts, Michael Jones. If my cherry pie did indeed have curative powers, every female in this town would be lined up for a slice."

"And that is precisely why your cherry pie shall never see the light of day."

She glared at him, refusing to laugh at this disarming humor. "Your diabolical plot is doomed to fail. Because while I was perfecting my recipe, I tasted plenty of cherry pie, a fact which, I assure you, has made me thoroughly immune to the charm of irksome male neighbors who prefer to mind *my* business instead of their own."

He arched a coal-black brow. "Selling kisses to outlaws, in broad daylight, does not connote a sound business sense."

"That is your opinion, sir. Contrary to your belief, I think the orphanage would be enormously grateful for any donation it receives, including one from Jesse Quaid. The man can't be all bad, if he is willing to commit a charitable act."

"Charity was the farthest thing from Quaid's mind."

"So you're a mind reader now?"

"Eden." He gentled his voice. "Your willingness to see goodness in the blackest of hearts is one of your most endearing qualities. But it can also be a peculiar blindness. Quaid is dangerous—to you, to Sera, to anyone who crosses his path. Men wear guns for a reason. Don't put yourself in the crossfire."

She swallowed. The concern in his voice vibrated into her being, touching her in a dangerously romantic way. She had to remind herself he'd included Sera among the people he was trying to protect.

"Are you trying to make me crazy?"

She'd taken him by surprise. She could see his guard waver in those breathtakingly blue eyes.

"I'm not sure I follow you."

"All protestations to the contrary, you're behaving like a beau. A *jealous* beau."

Amusement curved his lips. "I'm behaving like a good neighbor."

She blew out her breath. "Fine. Call it what you like. But you are not responsible for me, Michael. Besides, Jesse wasn't doing anything I didn't give him permission to do."

"Jesse, is it?"

She rolled her eyes. "You're missing the point. Deliberately, I think."

He shifted her basket to his other arm. "As much as I enjoy sparring with you on a public fairground," he said evenly, glancing at the eavesdropping children who huddled, bug-eyed and mouths agape, at the rear of the orphans' tent, "might I suggest we find a cooler location?"

Eden could ignore the trickle of perspiration sliding

under her whalebone to dampen her chemise. But she couldn't disregard the orphans, especially when one chubby ten-year-old with brown, sausage-style ringlets waved to Michael. "Hi, Doc!" she called shyly. "Is that your new sweetheart?"

The whole tent tittered. Michael weathered the giggles with aplomb. Mrs. Witherspoon appeared, tossed Eden an apologetic glance, and ushered the girls back into the shade for cookies. Eden suspected Michael the Pirate had stolen a couple of adolescent hearts, too.

"Honestly, Michael." They began strolling toward the nearest stand of trees. "You might have told the children the truth."

The glance he slid her way was veiled. "That you prefer outlaws to doctors?"

She glared back. "Must you be so difficult? I don't have to picnic with you, you know. After removing my basket from the auction and fueling a virtual prairie fire of gossip at my expense, I think I'd be well within my rights to leave you standing in the dust."

"Hmm. I suggest we drive, then."

Her lips twitched at this sally, despite her staunchest resolve. "You're impossible. Did you really pay one hundred dollars to save me from Jesse Quaid?"

"I'm afraid so."

She caught her breath, uncertain whether to be elated or deflated. He'd neatly foiled her accusations that he was jealous, and he still refused to acknowledge he was behaving like a beau. Maybe he'd planned to spend the money at one of the half-dozen auctions, anyway.

"Well . . . thank you. I think."

"You have nothing to thank me for."

"You're not the lesser of two evils?"

"Not necessarily."

He caught her elbow, guiding her toward the carriages parked along the perimeter of the field. "While it's true your reputation will survive Jesse Quaid," he said, "the question remains, will it survive me? That, my dear Eden, would be your dilemma—if you still had a choice."

He gazed fully at her then, and the heat of those blue cinders melted the protest that had bubbled to her lips. She wanted to believe Michael was making light of himself, but after that night in the parlor, she wasn't so sure. She couldn't help but remember his warning, *I'm nothing like the angel I was named after.* Then he'd proved his devilry with his kiss.

A thrill prickled her arms at the memory.

"Where do you propose to take me?" she demanded as he handed her into his phaeton.

The smile he flashed her was sinfully male.

"Somewhere we won't be disturbed."

As he climbed into the driver's seat, sweeping Eden's cream-colored skirt off his cushion, inhaling the delicate floral fragrance that drifted out to entrance him, Michael steeled himself against his pleasure. He'd paid one hundred dollars to keep her out of mischief, by God, and so he would: by removing her from the bad influences at this jamboree. Michael Jones he could trust—more or less. The rest of the male population was questionable.

Besides, Eden had proven herself susceptible to wolves. It was high time someone showed her the error of her ways. With Sera in Claudia's capable, anti-Cassidy care, Michael had the freedom for once to indulge in a personal whim, namely, to educate Eden about the baser instincts of men. A young woman couldn't go about kissing physicians *or* convicted felons without placing herself in peril. To think Eden was a

tease at heart absolutely galled him. He realized he had
no business being angry, that the very reason he'd ignored her shy greetings and sweet smiles for the last
six weeks was to encourage her attraction to another
beau. But Jesse Quaid, for God's sake? What lunacy had
possessed the woman?

As much as it nettled Michael's pride, he had to admit, he wasn't good at self-sacrifice. Watching Eden
delight in another man's attention had made him
greener than a poisoned apple. He'd thought he could
step aside and let another beau woo her, marry her,
*make love to her*, because in the end, she'd be better off
without an invalid husband. But that was before he'd
realized she took a fancy to reprobates. And that was
before he'd seen, with his own eyes, some other man
touching her. God help him, he would have ripped
Quaid's head off if given half a chance.

Michael scowled as he gazed over his shoulder, backing the phaeton out of the shade. He knew he had to
rein in his jealousy. If Eden suspected he had an ulterior
motive while he was trying to talk sense into her, she'd
simply laugh.

In the meantime, Eden was his private joy for an entire afternoon. It was a heady realization, since the part
of him that had been longing for her company, for the
cheerfulness that could coax him beyond his secret misery and help him glimpse the rosy complexion of life,
was dangerously close to gaining control. He was glad
Eden was Eden, because she couldn't stay mad at him
for long. In truth, it amused him to watch her bounce
on the cushion beside him, striving so hard to be prim
and aloof. She didn't know how.

At first, she maintained a stoic silence, retreating into
some polite caricature of her more amicable self if a fair-

goer hailed them. But the minute they were on the road, winding through the fallow fields of wildflowers, she would gasp with the wide-eyed appreciation of a child and point to the flash of oriole wings or to the nigh-transparent masterwork of a spider that had stretched its web between two milkweed pods. Michael chuckled to himself. Eden found wonder in the simplest things, things that, he vaguely recalled, had fascinated him once too, when he'd roamed these hills in knickers. Funny. He couldn't remember the last time he'd reined in his horse just to count the seconds a hawk wheeled overhead, her russet wings gliding for what seemed like forever, before she finally flapped to sail the winds.

"Michael, listen," Eden breathed, cocking her head. Her bonnet had long since spilled down her back, allowing her nose to freckle endearingly in the sun. "Do you hear it?"

"What?"

"The brook! There's one nearby. Oh, let's picnic by the water!"

She was right—sort of. He'd halted the phaeton about a stone's throw from Smitty McCann's irrigation ditch, and the recent rains had helped it bubble over its banks. The physician in him smiled at her conclusion. Certainly there was nothing wrong with Eden's hearing.

"I know a better place," he said, slapping the reins. "That is, if you don't mind a spot of shade with your wildflowers. Or sharing your crumbs with a presumptuous magpie."

She treated him to a shy smile. "I like magpies. They remind me of Colorado—and the days when it was fun to go there."

He waited curiously for an explanation, but she gave none other than a wistful sigh as she gazed at the clouds wreathing Blue Thunder Mountain. He wondered if she was thinking of the mob she'd mentioned in the parlor that night he'd been so intent on playing the bastard. He realized he had no one but himself to blame if she refused to let him heal her wounds. For some reason, the knowledge hurt.

He worried his physician's pride wasn't the only source of that pain.

No doubt due to the Independence Day festivities, Blue Thunder Valley's most popular swimming hole was deserted. Michael reined in, uncertain whether to be anxious or relieved. Part of him relished the idea of strolling the grassy streambank with Eden alone, of sharing her delight over tadpoles and dragonflies, of holding her hand or combing his fingers through her wind-mussed hair. A smaller, increasingly less vocal part of him demanded to know if he'd lost his mind. The environs of Blue Thunder Creek weren't as erotic as his dreamscapes, but the reeds and boulders made the lagoon secluded enough for skinny dipping. How many times had he jumped butt-naked into the water as a morally uptight youth desperate to prove to the other children that he could—and would—defy his father?

Michael tried to draw some spiritual fortitude from the rope swing that dangled from a long-suffering cottonwood, from the childhood memories of water fights and crayfish hunts and raft floats under a full moon. Unfortunately, he also remembered the stolen clothes pranks. Claudia had kept his humiliation from his parents, but in private, she still ribbed him about the time she had gone in search of him—worried because he hadn't arrived to chop her firewood—and had found him hiding miserably in the bushes, scratching the poison-ivy welts that covered his nakedness. To this day, Michael wondered if Rafe had filched his breeches. Although he was two years Michael's junior, Rafe had always been the popular Jones, the ringleader among the other children. Michael had been less welcome in their circle because he'd taken more seriously his father's sermons on youthful malfeasance and the road to damnation.

"Michael? Is something wrong?"

Eden's gentle query nudged him back to the present. He drew a shuddering breath. In truth, Rafe wasn't the only reason Michael had stopped coming to this swimming hole. After all these years, he'd thought he'd be able to stand on these banks with equanimity.

Loath to appear weak, he pasted on a smile and did his best to blink away the vision of a coughing but exuberant Gabriel romping through the shallows with his speckled hunting hound.

"Of course not." He crossed to her side of the phaeton and reached to help her down. "It's beautiful here, isn't it?"

Her brow furrowed, as if she recognized his diversion. "Yes." She placed her palm in his. It felt like sunshine against his skin. "I guess there're a lot of memories for you here?"

"A Pandora's box full of them. Hardly the sort of fare to inflict upon your ears."

"I don't mind."

He heard her sincerity. More than that, he heard her caring. The combination helped to salve his wounds, strengthening his resolve not to ruin their precious afternoon together.

"I'd much rather you told me what the devil weighs so much in this picnic hamper."

She blushed, charming him.

"I think it's the bottle of wine. Aunt Claudia smuggled it in when I wasn't looking. Apparently lemonade doesn't attract high bidders."

"I didn't realize Claudia was so philanthropic," he said dryly.

"Actually . . ." Her dimples peeked. "I don't think Claudia likes having another unmarried female in the house. Too much competition."

He chuckled, and they strolled, taking a leisurely, meandering direction toward the bubbling sounds behind the cattails. Michael carried the hamper; Eden clutched the quilt Sera had thought to put in the phaeton that morning. At the time, Michael had been amused for once to learn the lengths to which his sister would go to trap him into a romantic liaison.

"We're going to steal away from all the chaperones," Sera had declared boldly. "Me, Eden, Bonnie, and all our beaux. We're going to have a perfectly lovely group picnic, then we're going to sneak off with our sweethearts, hold hands and probably *spark.* Because you're such a wet blanket, Michael Jones, you're not invited to come along. Unless, of course, you get the gumption to be a beau instead of a brother and outbid all Eden's other gentleman callers for her hamper."

He smiled a little, remembering how she'd worked the protective-brother and the jealous-beau angle all into one sentence. Not to be manipulated, he'd sicced Claudia on her, making his neighbor promise to keep her eye on Sera and chaperone the bell chasers, especially if Billy Cassidy joined their ranks.

And yet, knowing that money raising for orphans was a secondary consideration for Sera, Bonnie, and every other picnic maker in town, here he was, of his own free will, strolling side by side with Eden Mallory.

Alarm bells should have been making him deaf by now.

Instead, the usual warning noise had fallen strangely silent. It was just one more indication that he'd lost his mind.

Eden's gasp of delight broke his reverie. His lips quirked as he watched her crane her neck, gazing up through the shifting leaves of an eastern redbud tree. Amazingly for the time of year, one tenacious twig still bore a spray of purple flowers.

That Eden had spied the miniature bouquet nearly ten feet above them cued him all over again that her observations were keener than most people's. He wondered how much about his illness he inadvertently betrayed every time he risked a moment in her company.

"I think we should spread our lunch here," she announced.

"And why is that?"

"It feels good. Don't you think?"

He arched a brow. He wasn't opposed by any means to the location. He'd just never heard anybody choose a picnic site because it "feels good."

"What feels good about it?" he asked, humoring her as she spread the quilt.

Her hands paused where she knelt, smoothing the wrinkles from the fabric. "Well . . ." She glanced up at him, her smile growing shy. "It's green and growing. Talking Raven, the Cherokee medicine woman who taught me about herbs, used to say that healing happens when we sit on the earth. And it makes the earth happy to be so remembered."

Michael had never heard that before, either. He chuckled to himself. Eight years might have passed since the seventeen-year-old innocent had braved his best growls to bathe his wounds, but the sweetness of that maid still lurked in the eyes of the woman sitting at his feet. *Now I know why bees can't resist nectar*, he mused, succumbing to the silken tug on his heart that made him join her on the quilt.

He finished unfurling the folds and ripples on their blanket while she busied herself with the hamper. A virtual feast lurked inside: potato salad, watermelon, fried chicken, canned peaches, deviled eggs, smoked ham, cheese, pralines, apples, and cornbread. But the *pièce de la résistance*, as far as he was concerned, was the cherry pie. The tin practically buckled from the weight of its fruit.

Persuaded by Eden's carefree nature, he yielded to temptation and reached for that pie.

"What are you doing?"

He grinned, cutting himself a slice. "Beating the ants to my investment."

"Isn't it customary to eat the main course first?"

"Not according to Sera. 'Life is uncertain,' she tells me. 'Eat dessert first.' "

She laughed at him. "Honestly. Blaming your kid sister for your table etiquette. I think you've rubbed off on Collie. Last week, I found him scraping up cherry pie splatters from my kitchen floor—before breakfast, yet."

Michael sucked the cherry filling from his fork. "The boy does have good taste, I'll grant him that."

"So it's true. Cherry pie's your favorite."

"Let me put it this way. I wouldn't have spent one hundred dollars on peach cobbler."

He was rewarded by another peal of mirth. He couldn't remember the last time he'd felt so at ease with a woman, so eager to please her. Even if Eden was a bell chaser, she didn't raise his hackles the way the others did.

"So how did a woman who grew up in a traveling medicine show learn to bake a blue-ribbon cherry pie?"

She adopted a conspiratorial tone. "I practiced a lot. Especially on miners and ranch hands. If they showed up on Papa's doorstep with a bellyache, we left town in a hurry."

He chuckled, enjoying her humor. "So you weren't deliberately trying to drum up business for him?"

"Oh no. Quite the contrary. Most of the time, we had more patients than we could handle. That's why I want to patent Papa's heart tonic," she added eagerly. "We got hundreds of testimonials about it. I really do believe he was on to something."

"What was in it?"

"Oh, some herbs and wildflowers. Mostly foxglove." Her color rose, and she slid him a veiled look. "You don't believe my father was a charlatan because he mixed home remedies, do you?"

Michael toyed with his fork. The conservative physician in him was unwilling to give Andrew Mallory an unconditional endorsement. But only wild horses could have dragged an answer from him that he knew would hurt Eden's feelings.

"Well, a lot of plants have validity as curatives. Many pharmaceuticals have been derived from the chemical compounds researchers have isolated in plants. But without knowing the active ingredients in your father's heart tonic, I would hesitate to advocate it as a drug."

She seemed encouraged by his answer. "If I gave you the recipe, would you . . . would you be willing to analyze it? In the hopes of prescribing it to your patients, I mean. I think Aunt Claudia would be willing to try the remedy, if you were the one to prescribe it. And I know there are other folks in this town who are suffering from weak hearts. But you see, they don't *have* to suffer. The foxglove works.

"Of course, I realize you'll want to prove it to yourself," she amended hastily, a childlike vulnerability vying with her determination. "I know you wouldn't want to give your patients false hope."

That newfound part of him, the part that wanted to please her, couldn't conceive of anything more heinous than saying no.

"I'd be happy to look at your father's recipe," he said quietly. "Nothing would make me happier than cheating the Angel of Death out of a few more souls." *Before the bastard comes here for mine.*

Her smile was misty. "Thank you, Michael. I so want my father's work to live on. Even if . . . even if I'm not the one to do it." She tried to hide the shadow of grief that crossed her features. Ducking her head, she spooned potato salad onto her plate. "I know you probably believe that unscrupulous men run medicine shows. But Papa wasn't bilking people. He wasn't running from the law, either. He took his medical practice on the road to protect Talking Raven, because none of the white communities would accept her. Talking Raven used to say that traveling with Papa was part of Great Spirit's plan because they could help more people that way. And they did help a lot of people, contrary to the lies spread about Papa in Silverton."

Her jaw jutted.

Lost in thought, Michael uncorked the wine. He remembered her outburst in the parlor and the tears she'd tried to hide as she'd mentioned a mob. She'd refused to answer his questions then, and he wondered how to broach the topic now without causing her additional pain.

"Do you think you'll go back to Silverton? To set the record straight?"

Her shoulders tensed. She took an inordinately long moment to smooth a napkin across her lap, to balance her plate with its Spartan helpings of salad, chicken, and watermelon. He poured her a glass of wine. When she was forced to accept the goblet from his hand, her troubled gaze finally rose to his.

"I don't feel safe there."

This disturbed him more than he could say. He leaned his spine against the tree. "Why don't you tell me about it."

She bowed her head, and the reflection of her flame-colored hair rippled across the pale, sweet libation she swirled in her glass. "They threatened to lynch me."

Michael's glass froze half way to his lips. "Who?"

"Some men who . . . claimed Papa owed them money after he died. But I know they were lying. Papa didn't have to pay people to . . . to sit in the audience and pretend to be cured. Besides, I'd never seen any of those men at our shows, and I assure you, I would have remembered them if they'd testified. I was keeping careful records, you see, so Papa could improve his tonic.

"I can't prove it," she added tremulously, "but I'm sure those men were the ones who ransacked the wagon the day of Papa's burial. It was horrible. They smashed the bottles and burned my herbs; they stole Valentine and shoved the wagon over the cliff . . ." She swallowed, her hand shaking on her glass. "I went to the town marshal, but he wasn't any help. He said mining towns were full of drunken rowdies, most of whom were transients. How was he supposed to track them down? The county sheriff wasn't any more help. He made a few cursory inquiries just to placate me. The next morning, I woke to find a rag doll with red yarn for hair hanging from a rope outside my hotel window."

Something cold settled in the pit of Michael's stomach. He recognized it as rage. "And you were all alone? With no one to protect you?"

She nodded, biting her lip. "I fled town with Stazzie that night. I hate that I had to run," she added miserably. "I'm sure the people of Silverton took it as proof of some crime. But I swear, Michael, I never knowingly mixed or sold an elixir that I didn't truly believe would help someone heal."

"I know," he said in soothing tones. Inwardly, he had the overwhelming desire to buy a train ticket to Silverton and beat the bloody hell out of some miners.

He struggled to keep his tone gentle. "Were these rowdies responsible for your father's death?"

"No. Pneumonia killed Papa." She was quiet for a long moment. "Sometimes, I wonder if I didn't help."

He frowned. "What do you mean?"

"I tried everything, Michael, *everything*, but nothing brought him around. I keep wondering: If I'd chosen hellebore instead of bloodroot, or if I'd been more adamant that he rest, would he be alive today? He was so stubborn, you see, working long into the night, refusing to admit he suffered more than a chest cold. By the time the sickness forced him to his bed, liquid had seeped into his lungs. He only lived two more days."

Michael's throat constricted as her grief triggered the memory of his own failures. How many times had he blamed himself for Gabriel's decline—and over the same lung complaint that had killed his mother?

"Sometimes you can do everything conceivable to save a life," he said grimly, "but Death defeats you anyway. Death and God."

Her brow furrowed, as if she wasn't quite certain she agreed. "I know faith is part of the healing process. Faith and God. Still . . ." She bit her lip. "When I lost my faith in myself, I swore I'd never heal again."

His scalp prickled. It was eerie the way her experience paralleled his.

"I swore the same thing after Gabriel died," he admitted, his voice roughened by emotions he was still desperate to repress.

"What changed your mind?"

*Sad little faces. Love-starved eyes.* "Cholera broke out at the orphanage."

"Oh," she whispered.

He forced his gaze back to his plate. The understanding in those glistening, emerald eyes had nearly been his undoing. "Practicing medicine isn't quite like climbing back on a horse; still, the fear will pass."

"I hope so. Thinking about mixing Papa's heart tonic still gives me the jitters."

"And yet you prescribed for Collie."

She sighed, using her fork to push a potato across her plate. "Brewing that tea was the hardest decision I've made since Silverton. I know it might seem wrong to you, since you're university trained and licensed. But I couldn't bear to stand by and watch his pain, Michael. Not when I knew a remedy that might help."

"Spoken like a dyed-in-the-wool, it's-in-my-blood medic."

Her mood lightened a little. "Talking Raven used to say healing's more about compassion than pills and tonics."

"I'd say you're a natural, then."

The sudden burst of sunshine from that smile melted another plate of armor around his heart.

"Thank you, Michael. Your saying so means a lot to me."

Feeling that uncustomary warmth fill his chest, he wondered why he hadn't been insightful enough to praise her abilities days earlier.

They managed to speak of more pleasant things then, of fireworks displays and three-footed races, of childhood games and Indian celebrations, of mountains and cities and eccentric old relatives. She could mimic Claudia's throaty grumblings to perfection, much to the amusement of them both. Her laughter charmed him. He wished he could bottle it. He was half convinced it was a revolutionary cure, one that could eradicate every ailment known to man. Certainly its carefree nature soothed his spirit, allowing him to forget his regrets.

When they'd eaten all the food they could possibly swallow, she suggested they walk along the stream. The breeze beneath the sheltering canopy of cottonwoods was a godsend. He'd stripped off his suitcoat an hour ago, and frankly, shade or no shade, he wondered how she'd survived the heat this long in ten pounds of underwear. He probably should have worried more about her alcohol intake than heat stroke, though. Flushed with Aunt Claudia's wine and a smattering of sun freckles, she kicked off her shoes, declaring herself scandalous in the extreme. A moment later, to his secret amusement, her determination to wade barefoot wavered, and she asked his permission in a shy, hesitant voice. He nodded gravely. As a physician, he told her, he'd seen his fair share of women's ankles; nevertheless, he offered to turn his back so she could roll down her stockings with modesty. This act of gallantry gave free rein to his imagination, and he spent sixty seconds of sheer, wicked delight, straining his ears for every crinkle of muslin, every whisper of silk. His fingers itched at his sides, and he wished heartily that he was doing the unrolling.

"Do you climb trees?" she called, cueing him with her splash that she'd finally completed the task.

He ventured a glance over his shoulder, half-relieved, half-disappointed, to find her ankles buried in the swirling current and her ivory skirts, with their strawberry embroidery, spread demurely over the grassy bank.

"I used to." He settled beside her and stretched his legs out.

"*Used* to?" She feigned indignation. "Good heavens, Michael, if I were a person in pants, I'd climb trees all the time."

He suspected mischief in the making. Relaxed and playful, she reminded him of a kitten, minus the whiskers dripping with cream.

"A person in pants, huh?"

She nodded solemnly. "Talking Raven had me climbing elder trees for berries and cliff tops for eagle feathers. Then I grew up. And Papa made me stay earthbound."

"A man of surpassing wisdom, your father."

She sniffed. "Beastly boring, that's what growing up is. When's the last time you did something outrageous? Something *scandalous*, just for the fun of it?"

He fought back a grin. Well now, *this* was a side of Eden he hadn't anticipated. However, his kid sister's friend—not to mention his kid sister herself—shouldn't be privy to the sorts of skeletons rattling around in his closet: ale-chugging contests in the church chancellory, prize fights he'd won after the women and children had left the county fairgrounds, naked widows he'd romped with through cornfields, the hundreds of times he'd wound up snoring with a bottle of rotgut in the Jade Rose Saloon. In fact, he wasn't sure he wanted anyone to know what he did as "Mick" when he slinked off for another round of Commandment breaking in Whiskey Bend.

"Well, let's see." He rubbed his chin. It was already growing rough with evening stubble. "I hid a dime novel in my Bible, once."

"And?"

"And Papa was livid."

"That's it?"

He cast her a sideways look. "You've never seen Jedidiah Jones livid."

She wrinkled her nose. "I suppose that's true."

Thanks to the breeze, a tendril of hair kept slithering across her cheek, and while it didn't seem to bother her, it was a sore temptation to him. He had to lean his weight back on his hands just to keep from reaching for her.

"I fell in love with a married man, once," she volunteered.

A bolt of jealousy crackled all the way to his toes.

"Of course, I didn't know he was married at the time," she admitted.

He was relieved to hear that.

"Loving Paul was probably the most wicked thing I've ever done. But I stopped loving him when I realized how he'd lied to me. I don't think there should be any room for lies in love. I mean, if you have to lie, you can't really love the person, can you?"

He squirmed inside. *But what if the lie serves that person better than the truth?*

"Have . . . you ever been in love?" she ventured.

He dared to meet those ocean-sized eyes and quietly, helplessly, drowned. Even if he could have forced some answer from his collapsed throat, he wasn't sure it would have been coherent.

He managed a weak nod.

"With Bonnie?" she whispered, sounding faintly hurt.

He nodded again, hating himself for the truth. Hating that he'd ever found anything at all appealing in Bonnie's catty, underhanded ways. He'd been so green, even at twenty, thanks to all the garbage he'd digested from Papa's pulpit. Some part of him had wanted to believe Bonnie would see the error of her ways. Just like some part of him had wanted to believe the meek would inherit the earth, that goodness would prevail, that God actually did care about humanity. But then Gabriel had died. And Michael had wised up in Whiskey Bend.

Eden plucked at her skirt. "Bonnie is very pretty."

"That has nothing to do with it."

He winced. He hadn't meant to sound so harsh.

"What I mean," he said, "is that things were different then. I was preoccupied with school, studying feverishly, reading everything I could get my hands on to save Gabriel . . ." His voice trailed as the old grief pushed its way to his throat. All the medical knowledge in the world had been at his disposal, and yet he'd still stood helplessly by, witness to his brother's agonized coughs, watching Gabriel's flesh stretch tighter and tighter over his ribs. "I'm sure," he said hoarsely, "Bonnie grew bored waiting for me to notice her. I wasn't much of a beau."

"I'm sorry, Michael," she murmured.

She pulled her feet from the water, and he turned his face away, grateful for the distraction. Was it the wine or the heat that was making him maudlin?

She rose, giving his shoulder a gentle squeeze before walking away. He swallowed, wondering why she was leaving him, wondering why the hell he was letting her go. She picked her way across a patch of wildflowers, her damp hem trailing behind her, gathering yellow pollen. Each time she stopped to bend over a petal or finger a leaf, her hair slipped further out of its knot, cascading in burnished waves over her left shoulder. He could almost imagine that shoulder was bare as he shielded his eyes against the sun, because her bodice was only one shade deeper than the alabaster-cream of her skin. She made an alluring picture against the backdrop of cloudless sky and rainbowed grasses.

A crushing sense of loneliness seized him. He couldn't bear for her to slip away, to vanish as she had so many times in his dreams. He rose, thinking to follow. He thought he should at least retrieve the shoes and stockings she'd left behind.

Her gasp of excitement stopped him. "Michael, look!"

He did, and his chest constricted. A swallowtail butterfly had fluttered onto her hand. It beat its wings for a moment before launching again for the sky. Laughing, she gave chase, disrupting what he'd thought had been a palette of orange and yellow flowers. Suddenly, she was surrounded by saffron wings. She threw her arms wide, spinning in the golden storm, rousing more butterflies from their slumber.

It was the scene from his dreams. The realization exploded through him with the force of a cannonball. He cursed as his legs failed.

"No, dammit," he panted, groping desperately for the nearest tree trunk. He fell hard to his knees anyway.

"Michael!"

He barely heard her. The weakness had attacked out of nowhere, knocking his legs out from under him as easily as an ax cleaves through kindling. He couldn't feel his feet. The knowledge made his head pound. "Stay back," he choked.

But she didn't. She was kneeling beside him. "What is it?"

He stuttered something nonsensical, pushing feebly at her hands. It did little good. She tugged his cravat loose, ripped unceremoniously through the buttons on his shirt.

"Breathe," she commanded.

He sank earthward, clutching his head; she straddled his hips as if to still his muscular seizure. A sound, some sort of chant he realized dimly, was coming from Eden. Her humming vibrated through him like a gut-deep sigh, loosening the knotted muscles at the base of his skull, dispelling the fear that had locked his limbs. To his amazement, he began to feel his feet again. When he opened his eyes, he was able to discern color and shape.

She slowly swam into focus: the cascade of autumn that was her hair, the luminous emerald that was her eyes, the pale, trembling rose that was her mouth. She clenched her bottom lip between white teeth, and the resonant chanting stopped. He might have been disappointed if she hadn't leaned closer, practically stretching herself on top of him.

"Does it still hurt?"

He swallowed. She'd shifted her hands. One tenderly stroked the damp curls from his forehead; the other nested atop the wiry hairs on his chest, as if to check his heartbeat. He could feel her breath against his chin. "No," he rasped.

"I can get your doctor's bag—"

"It's in the orphan's tent."

"Oh." Her troubled gaze held his for an uncertain moment. "Was it something you ate?"

He might have laughed at her fear, that he'd been poisoned by her picnic lunch, if he hadn't been so shaken by his seizure.

"No," he murmured, brushing the hair from her cheek. "It wasn't the food." He tried to smile. "I'm better now."

"You're so pale," she whispered. "Like that day in the store."

He drew a shuddering breath. He knew he should sit up. He knew he should find some argument to dispute the evidence she was starting to piece together. But the effort to lift her, to move her, to separate the welcome heat of her thighs from his hips, was gargantuan. Instead, he averted his gaze, watching as his fingers twined one of her satiny curls. "I'll survive."

"That's nothing to joke about," she said tremulously. "I thought—"

Her voice broke. He spied the track, if not the tear itself, and a humbling sense of awe washed over him.

"You're sick, aren't you?" she whispered hoarsely. "Really sick."

The lump in his throat nearly suffocated him. As hard as he tried, he couldn't lie to her.

"It's not your concern," he forced out.

"It is."

She rocked forward, and his heart skipped a beat. The beams of sunlight that danced behind her head seemed to rush toward him as she lowered her lips. And when her mouth settled over his, he was gifted with the taste of paradise.

He cradled her head, his pulse thundering in his skull. Strangely, the pressure brought him no pain. His awareness telescoped to the moment, to her sweet offering, to the scent of larkspur and lilac that spilled from her like some midsummer bounty. She was the very essence of the season, brimming with life, resplendent in full flower—magical. All his hopes and dreams woven into one ripe and luscious lover. He cautioned himself to remember her innocence, to enjoy her kiss and nothing more. He was even careful to keep his quaking hands above her shoulders.

It was the flavor of her tears that undid him.

"Eden. Honey." He choked. "Don't cry for me."

A sob shuddered through her anyway. His own emotions dangerously close to the surface, he clasped her length, rolling her to her side. She clung to him as if the ground were spinning and he were her only anchor. He tried to soothe her with his hands, to murmur consolations. She pulled him closer. A muffled warning knelled in his brain, but he was too busy needing, wanting, *feeling* for the first time in forever, to heed the alarm. He thought only that holding her was better than his dreams. And he didn't want to let her go.

His hands took on a will of their own. He wasn't sure how her gown slipped off her shoulders. Or how his shirt wound up crushed on the grass beneath her. He delighted in the feel of her skin, peach velvet. She tasted as sweet as she smelled. She groaned when his mouth steamed through her chemise; he took the sound as permission to continue, to slip the straps and bare her breasts to his tongue. She arched, gasping. Her naked calf somehow brushed his arm; he recalled the vision of elfin feet kicking up butterflies, and he couldn't deny himself the pleasure of exploring that coltish limb: pearl-shaped toes, exquisite ankles, bashful knees . . . bloomers.

The unmentionables should have come as a white flag. They didn't. When her fingers roamed lower, kneading the musculature of his spine, his hands trembled, pushing higher. To his visceral satisfaction, she wore nothing else beneath the cotton. She squirmed as he touched the silken down that shielded her innocence. His mouth swooped, sealing off her moan.

She was all woman now, fiery moist, riding the instinct of her own pleasure. As he petted her, it thrilled him to realize she would take as much as she gave, that she would be a lover who reveled in the unleashed power of her own femininity. He was a man who needed such a lover, a woman unfettered by the chains of a guilt-ridden upbringing or the religious beliefs that would make her view the most sacred act of love as something dark and twisted.

She thrust her tongue into his mouth, and a low, needy growl welled up from the most primal part of his being. He blamed the sound for deafening him to the world beyond Eden. In that moment, there was only her heart drumming time with his, her panting echoing his labored breaths, her body singing the same siren's song that shrieked through his veins.

Something wooden creaked. Vaguely, he heard a horse's snort. He forgot them instantly, swept away by the rhythm of Eden's hips against his hand, knowing she was close, so close to her first avalanche of desire. It was the light, airy sound of female laughter that finally punctured the fog in his brain. Eden sucked in her breath. Somebody emitted a strangled gasp. Long-legged shadows obliterated the sun from the sky.

"Merciful God," came Henry Prescott's unmistakable baritone.

Another male coughed. Eden turned to petrified wood. Half dazed by unslaked desire, Michael let instinct prevail. He grabbed his shirt, shielding her naked breasts from the voyeurs who'd stumbled across their fevered petting. Somehow, he marshaled his nerve, rallying thirty-one years of repressed antagonism toward the Almighty. Rolling over, he tossed the hair from his eyes, prepared to defend Eden from the neighbors who loomed over them like God's own jury.

That's when he spied his kid sister, her blue eyes wider than the whole damned sky above the hand she'd pressed to her mouth.

"M-Michael," she stammered.

Shame splashed like ice water against his loins.

Bonnie, standing with Luke, the mayor's youngest son, looked ready to lunge at Eden's throat. Luke fidgeted, staring sheepishly at Bonnie's picnic hamper in his fist. Claudia elbowed her way forward with Johnny Dufflemeir, who toted her hamper like a man dragging leg irons. Prescott, meanwhile, had waxed a cherry shade of righteous. He dropped Sera's basket with a clatter.

"May God have mercy on your soul, Eden Mallory," the young cleric sputtered, doing his best to turn Sera's head away.

Claudia harrumphed, thumping her gunstock on the ground as she halted to stare down at her niece's dishabille and her niece's debaucher.

"Hallelujah's more in order, preacher." Claudia

smirked, and Michael's humiliation burned as her cagey gaze fastened appreciatively on his bare torso. "Looks like these two young 'uns are gonna have one heck of a weddin' night."

# Chapter 9

**M**ichael's bedroom clock knelled the eleventh hour as Eden paced the wedge of moonlight that splashed the hand-loomed rug. How she'd managed to survive her hasty wedding ceremony and the ten hours since she'd been labeled the town whore was a mystery, although she suspected Aunt Claudia's wine had helped.

On second thought, maybe the wine had been to blame.

Her stomach churned.

Beyond the open window, crickets chirped raucously, making the utter stillness of the house feel like a tomb. The sticky summer air begged for a breeze, but Eden shivered anyway, hugging her arms to her chest. Her new lace and cotton nightdress had sat on Claudia's store shelves for weeks because no woman in town had dared to purchase an unmentionable that everyone else had fingered or seen. Bonnie had snidely suggested it was the perfect gift for Eden's wedding night. Claudia had told Bonnie to dunk her head in the pickle barrel, but she'd given the gown to Eden anyway with an awkward pat and the disgruntled promise that they'd round up a proper trunk of "girlie things" the next time they visited Louisville.

Sera had been only slightly more enthusiastic. After her initial shock, she managed to generate a spark of excitement for the scandal-steeped marriage.

"I guess this makes us sisters now. I always wanted a sister, you know, so . . . here. It was Mama's ring. A bride should have a ring on her wedding day, and I know Michael didn't, um, have time to buy you one."

Eden's hand shook as she stared down at the battered gold band that branded her a Jones. *Eden Jones.* Michael's wife.

She wondered if her husband hated her.

The lamp flickered in the sconce on the wall, chasing voluminous shadows across the Spartan, hand-hewn bed. No posts adorned the pine headboard, although a pair of scratches, like a dog's claws, marred the footboard. The quilt bore faded blue chintz squares, patched with an occasional piece of denim or gingham. It was so tightly tucked around the straw-filled mattress, she could have bounced a marble off it. Above the headboard, across the sun-faded wheat sheaves that papered the wall, a discoloration clearly marked the space where a cross had once hung.

No other signs of deity were visible in this room that, she was certain, had once belonged to Jedidiah and Catriona Jones. She wondered if Michael had changed anything else to make the space his own. The window seat was bare of cushions. The shaving stand was topped by plain white porcelain. The chest of drawers was little more than a giant box with black knobs. The Michael he liked to show the world, the brooding cynic who rarely smiled, haunted this space. But not the Michael from the animal orphanage. Not the Michael from the swimming hole . . . nor even Michael from the church chancellory.

Her heart quickened as she remembered him standing in the rainbowed hues that splattered the stone floor in a cross-shaped pattern. The stained glass had seemed so small and narrow to make such an impact upon the room—upon Michael himself. Facing that window, he'd awaited her arrival like a man bound for execution, his shoulders squared, his hands clasped at his spine. He'd changed from his rumpled gray suit into his habitual black broadcloth, and her heart bled to see the pallor beneath his newly formed tan.

"Please sit down," he'd finally said as she fidgeted on the threshold, uncertain whether to join him or flee on the first westbound stage. She'd been entertaining the notion of flight all the way from the swimming hole back to town. After all, Talking Raven had never married Papa. And Claudia had never married Henry Lucas. Eden reasoned she didn't have to marry Michael just because everyone expected it. Or because some preacher thought she was going to hell.

In fact, she'd been prepared to tell Michael the very same thing. Claudia had already said she'd stand behind whatever decision Eden made, even if it meant "losing the best dang store help I ever had." In truth, Eden had seen no choice but to leave Blue Thunder: She'd realized she couldn't bear to live in Michael's hometown if she had to watch him hang his head each time he was forced to share a sidewalk with her.

But when he'd turned from the stained glass cross to face her, his eyes had blazed blue fire, and her nerve had vanished in a puff of smoke. She'd practically tiptoed across the chamber to take the seat he'd offered.

Even if she didn't think she was going to hell, Michael most assuredly did.

"Eden."

She swallowed as he came to stand before her, as solemn as a hanging judge. He must have intuited the uneasiness his mood was breeding in her, because he did try to smile. He even knelt on one knee, clasping her right hand tightly between both of his. She could see the effort he was making to remain calm while his world imploded.

"I am profoundly sorry," he said quietly, "for the shame my behavior has caused you. You deserve better, Eden."

Her throat constricted so forcefully, she had trouble breathing.

"I can offer you little in the way of consolation," he continued in that same, tightly controlled voice. "Of course, I will take you as my wife, if you desire it. But you must be made to understand, without illusions, what you will face, and . . . what hardships may arise."

She squirmed inwardly, longing for the inspiration to leaven his mood, for some quip about brides and grooms and their traditional feelings of impending doom. But the torment in his eyes paralyzed her tongue.

"You guessed correctly at the swimming hole. I am sick," he said flatly. "I may be dying. There is no cure."

Her heart completely stopped before heaving once more into an agonizing rhythm.

"For this reason, up until now, I have chosen to stop courting. Nobody knows about my condition except a few doctors. One in Chicago. One in Boston. One in Louisville."

Understanding flooded her mind. It all made sense now, his gruffness, his aloofness, his switch from witty, urbane companion to wintry stranger at the animal orphanage and his enigmatic reasoning for leaving her behind: *"It's better this way."*

She managed, somehow, to wield her tongue. "What is the diagnosis?"

"None of them can say for sure. The symptoms—general malaise, lethargy, numbness in the limbs—are progressing. It's hard to say how much longer I'll be able to . . . function normally."

He spoke so matter-of-factly. So bravely. Only when he averted his gaze was she able to glean the depth of his despair.

"But there are other doctors—"

"Don't you think I would have followed every lead?"

She bit her lip as bitterness crept into his carefully modulated tone. She suspected that for him to admit he couldn't heal himself, especially to another physician, had galled him. It might even have humiliated him. She wondered how much of him took grim satisfaction in searching out colleagues who would diagnose his illness the way he had . . . and then tell him he was right.

"Advances are made in medical research every day, Michael. Perhaps—"

"Eden." His smile was bleak. "You must not enter into this arrangement hoping for miracles. You must be practical. Your entire future lies before you. It need not be dire. You are a young, beautiful woman capable of attracting any number of robust beaux. I hazard to guess that your dreams of marriage did not include nursing an invalid husband who should have been in his prime. I will not force you into any bargain that is repugnant to you. But . . . if you agree to become my wife, I will ask that you honor the vows you make before God. So if you pledge yourself to me in sickness and health," he added softly, his voice thickening around the words, "make your promise with your eyes wide open."

She blinked back tears. He shimmered before her, the powerful shoulders, the chiseled jaw, the hauntingly beautiful eyes. As he knelt there, so proud but so vulnerable, so noble in his despair, a flash of heat unlike anything she had ever known burst through her soul. In that moment, she was certain she fell in love with Michael Jones. How could she not care for this selfless, fiercely courageous man? And how could she turn her back on him?

She lay her hand against his cheek in a tender gesture. "I will marry you, Michael," she said quietly, "because you are so very dear to me. Because you make me proud to know you. Because sharing your life now is more important to me than worrying about the future."

He blinked. She guessed she'd shocked him, and she smiled, hoping to touch him with all the warmth that fairly poured from her soul. In that moment, she'd never felt more confident about a decision in her life. She would be Michael's wife, not because she pitied him, but because she loved him. Because she wanted to spend every precious moment with him. Because she wanted to laugh with him, and see the hope kindle again in his eyes. She only prayed that someday, somehow, he would fall in love with her, too.

"We will have to tell Sera," she said, striving for a lighter tone.

He blanched. "No." For the first time since he'd knelt before her, his reservoir of strength drained enough for her to glimpse his gnawing dread. "You mustn't tell Sera. Please. Eden, promise me."

"But—"

"She mustn't know I'm sick."

His hand shook as it tightened on hers. She swallowed. He'd misunderstood her. She'd meant to say they should tell Sera the good news about their arrangement. But his illness . . . that was another matter entirely.

"You can't keep it a secret much longer," she said gently.

"I have to. For as long as I can."

She could feel the desperation in his grasp. "She's my friend."

"She's my sister," he countered hoarsely.

Uneasiness coiled through her. She hated secrets and lies. How could she pretend to Sera? Then again, how could she refuse her husband his request for privacy?

"All right, I promise," she said reluctantly. She rationalized that if Michael were her patient, she would have kept his health matters confidential as a matter of course. Still, she felt duplicitous. And she worried that if she did become his healer—an inevitability—she wouldn't be up to the challenge.

"Thank you," he murmured, drawing her to her feet. Color, in the form of relief, rolled back the grayness in his cheeks, and he raised her hand to his lips before tucking it in the crook of his arm. "Let's get married, then," he said huskily.

That had been nearly five hours ago. The ceremony itself had been a hasty affair; Claudia and Sera had served as witnesses, and Henry had presided without looking her once in the eye. Eden hadn't cared. She hadn't cared, either, that a thin crowd had dragged themselves away from the square dance at the fairgrounds. Apparently scandal was more scintillating than promenading with your best sweetheart. The handful of couples who had gathered outside the church came mostly to gawk, although some had remembered their manners long enough to stammer an insincere congratulations. Bonnie, sitting in her carriage at the top of the hill, had watched venomously as Michael handed Eden into his phaeton and had driven her to her new home. At the time, as Eden recalled, he'd grown unsettlingly pale. She wondered if shame or his illness had been to blame.

She wondered, too, if resentment for her or yearning for an old sweetheart kept him from coming to bed now, at this late hour, on their wedding night.

The clock chimed the quarter hour, sounding strident in its reminder of the passing time. She wondered if Michael had fallen asleep in his study. Or worse, if he'd had another seizure. She halted before the door. Should she venture down the stairs to check on him? She knew he was alone. Sera had volunteered to stay with Aunt Claudia for several days, "to let the lovebirds nest," as she'd so cheekily put it.

Eden shifted from foot to foot, trying to imagine what illness she would have diagnosed based on Michael's unrelated set of symptoms. Shortly after they had foiled Sera's hastily plotted shivaree by chasing Aunt Claudia and a handful of noisy mischief makers off the porch, Eden had gathered her courage and asked Michael's permission to examine him by lamplight. He'd grown stiff with insult, telling her to put away her tom-tom and prayer drum, that he was her husband, not some greenhorn seeker, and that their marriage was not a circus side show. Excusing himself curtly, he'd retreated behind his office door, leaving her to feel inadequate once more as a medicine woman.

Perhaps her secret longing for his approval was just

a pipe dream. Perhaps it was better to forget Talking Raven's teachings, Eden mused, and ignore her inner guidance, which was so rarely based in logic or fact.

No matter how many times she'd seen Talking Raven emerge from a trancelike vision with new insights that eventually helped her patient, Eden couldn't quite shake her father's belief that faith healing held no medical validity. And Michael clearly shared her father's view. So if she were ever to earn Michael's respect, she would have to make a choice.

She would have to sacrifice her female intuition.

She sighed, deciding to seek out her husband for a reconciliation. But as she reached for the handle of the door, she heard a creak on the stairs. She hastily retreated, her heart ricocheting off her ribs. His footfalls were almost soundless, despite his size, despite the hush in the house. If not for the occasional protest of the timbers under his feet, she might not have been able to track his approach: past the family portraits—all preachers—who frowned down upon the narrow stairwell, past the shrinelike alcove where a vase of wild roses guarded his mother's dog-eared prayerbook, past the closed door of the bedroom in which Gabriel had breathed his last.

Michael halted, and Eden held her breath. In her mind's eye, she could see him standing on the other side, silent and somber, haunted by all his ghosts. Torn between fascination and dread, she riveted her gaze to the doorknob and waited for it to turn. When he quietly knocked instead, she almost jumped out of her skin.

She licked her lips. "Come in."

He didn't. Instead, he towered on the threshold, polite, erect, and unrumpled. Even his cravat remained tied. So much for her worry that he'd collapsed, or that he'd forgotten about her because he'd been dozing, his dreams filled with happy memories of making love to Bonnie.

"I thought you'd retired, but then I heard you stirring," he said, the resonant echo of his voice chasing tingles down her spine. "Do you need a sleeping draught?"

She blushed, shaking her head. *Of course* she was awake on her wedding night! She hadn't been this nervous since Papa had first coaxed her to sing, "Oh, Susanna!" to a boot-stomping crowd of miners. Now that her doctor husband had finally come to their room, she couldn't help but wonder: Did Michael offer a potion so she'd relax for the intimacies he planned, or did he want her to sleep so he could avoid the ordeal of lovemaking altogether?

She did her best not to look crushed. "I was waiting for you."

Some elusive emotion flickered over his features, touched his lips, was quickly gone. As careful as he was to stand beyond the lampglow, she couldn't read his mood. He stood split between shadow and light. *Half man, half angel.* She wondered which Michael, the mortal or the seraph, would determine his behavior tonight.

"I didn't want to disturb you," he said, as if to explain his delayed arrival. "You've had a trying day."

"No more than your own," she murmured, wishing he'd step inside, wishing he'd kiss her the way he had that afternoon, passionately, unabashedly, without apology or excuse. In the butterfly field, she could believe he'd felt affection for her. Here, in the room where Jedidiah Jones used to sleep, she wondered if that affection had turned to contempt.

Bruised to her core at the notion, she tried another

tactic. "I'm sorry, Michael. I didn't mean to offend you about . . . about the examination. I wanted to help."

"I know." His response was the closest thing to an apology she figured she would ever hear. "It will take time for us to get used to each other's ways."

"I'm willing to take that time," she offered shyly.

The shadowed side of his mouth curved. "I've left you little choice, it seems."

Was that what was bothering him?

Encouraged to think he didn't despise her for being sexually forthright, she gathered her nerve to speak candidly. "Michael, I'm not ashamed about how we touched today. I don't care what other people think. You and I know the truth of what happened. That's all that matters."

"Bravely spoken. But the months ahead won't be easy. Bonnie will make life difficult for you."

"She'll try," she corrected him. "Papa used to say lies are like weeds: They wither in the light of a strong truth. Let Bonnie say what she likes. People will see she's speaking out of spite. Eventually, they'll discount her."

He bowed his head. For an uncomfortably long moment, he stared at the floor. When he sighed, she wondered what he was thinking. Did he regret that Bonnie had been among the picnickers who'd found them together? Had he hoped for more time to explain the truth before she'd leaped to the worst possible conclusion?

"I won't always be around to protect you, Eden."

His reminder, so poignant with regret, made her vision sparkle and blur. It had never occurred to her he was worrying about her rather than Bonnie. It had never occurred to her he was contemplating the future she would face without him at her side.

"I want to make the most of our marriage, Michael,"

she nearly pleaded. "I want to be a good wife to you—if you'll let me."

He stepped into the room. The lamplight swirled around him in a harsh, gilded blaze, exposing the stark emotion on his face. A heartbeat later, the breadth of his shoulders blotted the lamp from her view, and she blinked, adjusting to the dimmer dance of moonbeams that feathered over his chiseled jaw and torso. When he halted, leaving less than an arm's length between them, his eyes were in shadow, yet they glowed with an elemental yearning too captivating to ignore.

"Eden." His voice held a throaty cadence, throbbing with an intensity that made her knees weak. "Do you know what it means to be a wife to a man?"

She could only nod, her breath raveling somewhere in her throat.

His lashes fanned a mesmerizing degree lower to veil the glittering hunger in his eyes. "When you agreed to marry me, I did not presume you would let me share your bed."

"B-but why?"

"Because I've wronged you. In more ways than one."

"It takes two to touch, Michael."

The smile flickered again, a slash of irony before it faded into self-reprisal. "I have wanted to touch you that way, and other ways, for a long time. Ever since the first night I met you. I'm sure you don't remember. It was years ago, near the livery at Whiskey Bend. You couldn't have been more than seventeen when you knelt beside me in the straw."

"I remember," she said softly.

He started. But his surprise couldn't completely dispel the grim, brooding irony. "I had hoped you wouldn't. I wasn't exactly gracious."

"You saved my life. You didn't have to be."

He shook his head. "I'm not the man you think I am, Eden. I've whored, I've brawled, I've gotten stinking drunk—"

She started to protest, but he cut her off.

"I know. You won't listen to me. You won't listen now any more than you would then"—amusement vied with his frustration—"any more than you would in the parlor. I tried to send you away for your own good. I've been trying to send you away ever since that night in the livery. But you're stubborn—my own stubborn angel. You insist on giving me assistance whether I want it or not. Now look at what your goodness has brought you." He swallowed, and for the first time, he allowed her to glimpse the anguish and the longing he'd bottled up inside.

"You haunt my dreams, Eden," he confessed fervently. "You've filled my nights since Whiskey Bend. I tried to stop the fantasies, but I couldn't help myself. At times, loving you seemed so real . . ." His voice trailed, and his fists clenched at his sides. "I never thought I'd see you again. I convinced myself the dreams weren't sins because the woman I'd conjured could never be human. And then you came to Blue Thunder, all summer and sunshine. You *are* my fantasy made flesh. It nearly killed me to have you within reach, to realize I might never be well enough to make you my own, to picture some other man touching you, kissing you, loving you into the night—"

"Michael . . ."

His chest heaved. His struggle against his inner demons was almost tangible. "I can't help but wonder," he whispered hoarsely, "if I didn't somehow create this marriage to keep you for myself."

She fought back tears. His pain was like a knife in her chest, and she didn't know how to help him. She didn't know how to heal the self-contempt that festered beneath his rationale and led him to shoulder the onerous burden of a dead brother, a rebellious orphan, and a young woman who'd secretly fantasized about loving him, too. Here was his real illness, she reasoned: the merciless judgments he heaped on himself.

"Michael." She chose her next words carefully, sensing that he would balk if he misconstrued her love for him as hero worship. "To blame yourself," she murmured, "is to deny that I have a mind of my own. I didn't choose to be your wife out of pity. And I didn't choose to marry you out of shame or fear. I made the decision to let you touch me, and I would choose to let you touch me again. I would *marry* you again, Michael. You're the husband I want, for however long God blesses us both with life. Nothing else matters. I want to be with you. *You*, Michael. Will you let me?"

His breath hissed in with a groan, and he opened his arms. She hurried inside, her throat aching as he folded her closer, as his lips buried in her hair. Waves of emotion broke over her; she would have crumpled to her knees if his arms hadn't wrapped her so fiercely. She felt his chest shudder beneath her, felt the tempest in her own breast.

And then, as if from far away, she heard his rough, choked rumble of sound: "You're more than I dreamed of, Eden."

She raised her head, and his mouth courted hers. The velvet penetration of his tongue chased a bolt of desire down her limbs. He possessed her with a restrained hunger even while his calloused palm trembled against her cheek, a tender affirmation of his own onslaught of feeling. She let his kisses enthrall her; she let the thrumming of his heart speak to her in ways that manly pride would have silenced. She did not fool herself into believing he'd forgotten Bonnie, nor did she believe that her single declaration of love could wipe out the failures with which he tortured himself. But she dared to hope that she could reach the part of him that still listened to Jedidiah Jones's condemnation. If God were kind and Michael were willing, maybe she could find the courage to be the healer he needed, to help him forgive himself before time and circumstance conspired to take him away.

He slid his hands down her neck, his thumbs spanning the base of her throat. When the pads of his fingers glided beneath the unlaced ribbons of her collar, her stomach clutched with a tingly thrill. He raised his head. His eyes blazed with an odd combination of tenderness and desire as he gazed upon the modest rise of her bodice and the contrast of pristine white cotton against the sunbronzed fingers that disappeared beneath the placards of her gown. "May I undress you?" he murmured.

She nodded, too choked to speak, and he slipped the buttons one by one, baring her shoulder. For a long moment, he did nothing but gaze upon the smattering of freckles there. Nerve-spawned goosebumps sprinkled her arms as she wondered if the flesh-and-blood reality had disappointed him after all his years of fantasies. Then a tender smile curved his mouth, and he pressed reverent lips to the hollow where her throat and shoulder joined. "Let down your hair for me," he whispered.

Her hands shook as she tugged the white ribbon free. The braid unraveled, spilling across her breasts. When he raised his hand to smooth the strands, her gown spilled from her hips. She stood before him in nothing but bloomers now, and her heart did a dizzying little dance as he reached for his cravat.

"No, please, I . . . want to undress you too."

The sparks that flared in his eyes made her private places yearn.

He let her peel off his coat and unbutton his shirt. The wiry curls across his well-muscled chest were plush and soft; in fascination, she pulled his shirt tails from his breeches, eager to follow the chocolate trail that marched lower, disappearing beneath his belt. He kicked off his shoes, catching her hands with a crooked smile before she could reach for his buckle. Then he led her to the bed, sweeping the linens back with a single toss.

"Shall I blow out the lamp?"

His voice was satin and smoke, a pure throb of sensual persuasion. She had trouble breathing at the sound. She almost begged him not to take the two strides that would put him out of reach. He was different somehow. The self-abasing sinner who'd stood on her threshold was not the accomplished lover whose tenderness wove a shimmering web of seduction around her. He'd crossed the line of light and shadow. She didn't want him to go back.

"I'm not afraid to look upon you, Michael."

A ripple of anticipation trembled through her body as the hunger in his eyes climbed another notch.

"You are a marvel to me, Eden."

As he laid her down, she had a split second to wonder at his meaning. But then his body covered hers, and she was distracted by the exquisite sensation of male musculature pressing her down. She squirmed with delight to feel her nipples bury in the sable thatch on his chest, to feel his palm rasp over her belly and fuse its heat to the thin cotton shielding him from her buttocks. She rubbed against him, eager to repeat the frenzied petting of the afternoon, when he'd eased his fingers so deeply into her milky heat that ecstacy had taken hold of her, making her tremble like a leaf in a fierce storm.

"Slowly, sweet. I want to savor every part of you."

His hands steered clear of her waistband, and she didn't know whether to be titillated or disappointed—until his tongue swirled inside her ear. She sucked in her breath, exhaling it in a shaky rush as he bit the lobe with great delicacy. She'd barely recovered from his teasing nips before his mouth was on the move again, mapping the trail his hands had blazed. Tingly thrills swept through her, leaving her skin flushed and deliciously sensitive. She sank beneath him, raking her fingers through his midnight mane, surrendering to the goosebumps his pleasure play raised. When his lips at last nuzzled the puckered bud of her breast, a throttled groan tore from her lips. The hot, tender rhythm of his mouth sent pleasure stabbing to the center of her being, and her eyes fluttered closed in shameless rapture.

With each suck, with each prickly tug of his teeth, she felt a pull deep inside the most female part of her. He was seeding a divine sort of restlessness, one that roused her primitive instincts and numbed her reasoning mind. Her hands itched for the feel of him, and she succumbed to the lure of his flesh, touching him as he touched her: long, luxuriating caresses that made his breaths come in swift, ripping sounds and his heart drum an ever wilder rhythm against her ribs. His skin was satin stretched across steel; she reveled in the tiny tremors her explorations loosed across his abdomen and the pads of muscle surrounding his nipples. When she cupped his maleness, thick and hot and mysteriously engorged, his breath went harsh and shallow. The reaction was all the invitation she needed to hug him closer, to try to bypass his belt. Her efforts proved unsuccessful, and he loosed a throttled growl, raising his hips and yanking on his buckle.

She was certain her eyes bulged when his trousers fell away.

"Your turn." His smile fairly smoked, wickedly male, promising sin.

She licked her lips. Even if she could have squeaked some protest, she wouldn't have. He drew leisurely on the laces of her bloomers, slipping one loop, then the other. It was a scintillating torment, combined with that smile and those eyes. When the first draft of midsummer rippled across her innocence, she gulped and blushed. He must have known even before she did that she'd try to shield herself, for his fingers were already twining through hers, gently but insistently peeling her hands away.

"Let me look at you."

He took his time, and she grew hotter, wondering what it must be like to lie on his examining table, to experience his touch as a female who'd already been initiated in the rites of womanhood. Did his patients squirm as she did now, teased by elusive whiffs of sandalwood, tormented by sensual fever? Jealousy streaked through her at the fantasy, startling her almost as much as the sight of his head dipping lower—and his first sultry breath across her maiden's flesh.

"Michael!" She shied as far as the prison of his knees

would allow, aghast and yet mystified by her suspicions. She tried to tug her wrists free, only to find them both pinned in his bearlike paw, and her most impious imaginings giving way to something far more wicked . . . and wonderful.

He sipped her as if she were ambrosia, stroked her as if she were a pampered pet. With each languorous lick, each artful thrust, pinpricks of fire streaked to her soles. Her thighs trembled wider; her hips pitched with a knowing she had yet to understand. She convulsed in blissful torment each time his slick fingers danced over the knot he'd coaxed from her innocence. Crazed by fever, she begged him to let her touch him, but he crooned something in the negative, rhythmically stoking the fire, methodically driving her mad.

"Michael, please." She half sobbed, half laughed. Like some black sorcerer, he dangled the lessons of magic before her, only to keep the spell's intrinsic secret to himself.

"Let go." His voice was a rough, throttled sound that vibrated intimately through her. "Trust me."

She tried, but she didn't know how, didn't know what she was holding, didn't want to disappoint him. A sweet violence coiled between her legs. Relentlessly it spiraled upward, twisting, stretching, arching her like a bow upon the bed.

Suddenly, her worries imploded, and her mind blazed white. Shards of sensation splintered through her, and she fell helplessly back, tumbling into a well where sounds merged as two heartbeats and impulse ruled all rationales.

He took her down again and again, mercilessly patient when she balked, gently insistent on her surrender.

He coaxed pleasures from her body she'd never dreamed it could feel, until his touch became her only goal, release her only need.

Once, when he slowed his conquest enough to catch his breath, she gathered her wits to wonder at his restraint. She could feel the sheen of perspiration as she clutched his shoulder and the tremor of his thighs, cramped and straining under his weight. But when she tried to reach below his waist, to stroke him as he'd so insidiously done to her, he growled, hooking her hips with his knee and fastening his mouth to her navel. She shrieked at the ticklish onslaught, and he smiled against her skin.

"You're not ready yet," he said hoarsely.

"I . . . I'm not?"

"I don't want to hurt you."

She didn't understand, couldn't imagine how he would. Her fingers trembled as they wove through the damp, inky strands of his hair, and he nuzzled higher, dragging an involuntary groan from her core as he drew her breast deep into the velvet, shifting textures of his mouth. Forerunners of ecstacy eddied deep in her milky heat.

"God, how I want you, Eden."

His thickness fell between her thighs; instinctively, she recoiled. But he'd become the sorcerer again, captivating her with kisses. His fingers snaked deftly past the flushed petals of her innocence. Undulating, bewitching, they conjured nectar from the flower within, and a throbbing force gathered at her core. She pitched urgently against his hand, only to realize, dimly, it wasn't his hand any more. He tempted her first, little nudges against the hot, steamy sheath of her, and she began to writhe, desperate to create the friction that she'd learned would ease the deeper throbbing.

"Eden," he rasped, gripping her hips, anchoring them beneath his.

She rolled her head on the pillow.

"Eden," he commanded again, his breath warm against her cheek. "Look at me."

She blinked, and he swam into focus. For one mesmerizing moment, all that he was, the unequaled power of his soul, poured its radiance from his eyes. She couldn't look away. She didn't want to. He bent his elbows, lowering himself with scintillating slowness. When his lips hovered a hair's breadth from hers, she nearly drowned in a whitecap of feelings.

He was moving inside her. They were one.

"Paradise." The husky catch in his voice left no doubt of his own awe at their joining. "You were aptly named."

Her heart burst open in a soul-shaking rush. She might have wept at the magnitude of her love for him if his mouth hadn't slanted across hers, if his primal, mystical rhythm hadn't wooed her attention back to the bolts of rapture that smoked down her nerves. She abandoned herself to his body, so potent with life, to the kisses and whispers and the sweet searing sorcery of unleashed emotions that flashed around them in the night like heat lightning.

The sacred, spellbinding mystery hovered and whirled. Elusive, yet so achingly close, it promised heaven if she could only reach above the horizon. She begged him to take her higher, to love her the way he would in his dreams, and he became an elemental force, beyond taming, beyond control.

Suddenly, she soared. His name ripped from her lips

as he catapulted her into the all-consuming miracle of creation. In wonderment, she beheld the wild, alchemical transference of flesh to spirit. Their very souls merged.

Michael trembled, swept up in the roaring, rushing force. Within that boundless moment, he lost his Self. He became one with the woman who'd pledged her life to his, and he knew the true essence of the divine. Never had he felt such reverence, such unspeakable gratitude. The rapture of their first union would be forever etched on his heart and mind. In Eden, he'd found the purest source of all love.

And in several months' time, he was doomed to lose her.

He rolled to her side, and she sighed, a long winding ribbon of bliss. When she opened her eyes, they gleamed softly, luminously, like sunlight dancing on water. He couldn't help but think how beautiful she was, how undeserving he was to have communed with anything so sacred. She raised her hand, stroking his hair, touching gentle fingers to his lips. When he kissed them, she smiled, an expression so tender, it made his heart kick.

"I love you," she whispered huskily.

He swallowed. How could that be? How could that *possibly* be?

He tried to force a response past the lump jamming his throat. But as the seconds ticked by, her smile never wavered. Her eyes never dimmed. She snuggled closer, resting her head on his shoulder, placing a soft, freckled hand over the unsteady pounding in his chest. Dimly he realized, with a humbling sense of awe, that she hadn't been seeking a response from him. She hadn't been seeking anything more than his willingness to hear a heartfelt truth.

As she drifted into a peaceful sleep, he buried his face in her hair. And for the first time since Gabriel's death, he let tears roll down his cheeks.

# Chapter 10

The next morning, Eden woke to a stream of sunshine and the aroma of freshly brewed coffee. Her husband, impeccably dressed in his ebony broadcloth, greeted her with a breakfast tray. It was laden with muffins and fruit, a vase of wild poppies, and two round-trip tickets on the Louisville and Nashville Railroad.

"We shall have our wedding tour in Louisville," he announced, his gaze warm with approval as it caressed her tumbled hair. "I've arranged for old Doc Perkins to come out of retirement and handle all medical emergencies for the week. He grunted only once at the prospect, which I took as a sign of pleasure."

Michael's grin was uncharacteristically boyish. She was so smitten by the expression that she nearly forgot herself and let the quilt slide off her nakedness.

"But Michael," she whispered, her vision growing misty as her heart turned over with love for him, "you spent a fortune on me yesterday. The picnic basket—"

"Was purchased to benefit the orphanage," he finished for her firmly. "You are my wife, and you shall want for nothing as long as . . ." His smile wavered al-

247

most imperceptibly. "For as long as we are man and wife."

She might have missed his fleeting melancholy if her ears hadn't pricked to the sound. She swallowed, forcing brightness into her tone to match his good spirits.

"If you keep spoiling me like this, I shall come to expect it," she said, stretching her hand for a muffin.

He swept the tray out of her reach, a thoroughly wicked gleam lighting his eyes. "One must work up an appetite before one eats breakfast in bed."

"Is that a fact?"

"Doctor's orders."

He lowered the tray to the floor and tugged at the quilt, peeling it playfully from her breasts. "Considering our shortage of time"—his teeth flashed, more feral than civilized—"we may be eating breakfast on the road."

He wooed away her morning shyness, taking special delight in leading her down new paths to pleasure. In her innocence, she had never considered that lovers might tease each other with poppy petals. She had certainly never dreamed that she would ever be licking whipping cream off . . . well, a male's virility. He must have waked unusually early to set the love traps that waited for her in scandalously public corners of the house. At nine o'clock, their panting echoed like tribal tom-toms in the stairwell. At eleven o'clock, he had her writhing so ecstatically on the kitchen counter, that the unwashed muffin pans bounced to the floor. They might have made the one o'clock stage, if he hadn't grown so insidiously helpful with her garters and stays. Not until three o'clock was she finally hurrying, flushed and giddy with romance, on the heels of her husband's ground-eating stride.

As they raced up the stage depot's porch, he gripped her hand firmly, his carpetbag flung over his shoulder, her portmanteau swinging from his fist. She marveled that any man who was robust enough to romp until late afternoon, who carried two sets of luggage as effortlessly as if he were toting sacks of feathers, could be gravely ill. What was wrong with his doctors, that they could hypothesize such rubbish? Surely Michael was too healthy to be knocking at death's door.

And yet she knew, from painful experience, how quickly an illness could strike a man down.

She wanted to rail at the sheer unfairness of it all, of losing her heart to a man who might not live to see the new year. Wasn't it enough that she'd lost Mama, Papa, and Talking Raven?

But she didn't give in to the grief. She refused. Michael was still alive, and as long as there was breath in him, there was hope.

Louisville proved a refreshing change from Blue Thunder's bygone architecture and Puritan minds. Eden breathed a sigh of relief when they disembarked from the train that had whistled through the rolling bluegrass country during the last leg of their journey. Modern gas lamps held the dusk at bay along cobbled, dogwood-lined streets, while gaily lit windows lured weary travelers to sample continental cuisine. Against the imposing brick edifice of the museum, a billboard announced the arrival of some mummified pharaoh from Thebes, while the windows of the playhouse gleamed a fiery topaz, bearing testimony to the popularity of the Kentucky Rattlers Minstrel Show. Eden was particularly impressed to know that the hotel Michael had chosen boasted all the modern conveniences: piped hot water, indoor privies, electric lighting, and a telephone that rang in the office of the town's most venerated physician.

She couldn't help but wonder, with a pang of unease, if the telephone service had cinched Michael's decision to lodge there.

He'd planned numerous outings during their stay: an auction of thoroughbred yearlings at Churchill Downs, a paddlewheeler cruise past the Ohio River's falls, a hot-air balloon exhibition at the University of Louisville, and a box-seat vantage for a sold-out performance of *Shenandoah*. When she asked that they take time to visit his physician's office, he grew dark and silent.

"Michael," she said more gently. "I'm your wife now. Whatever you face, we'll face together."

His jaw twitched as he stared past her to the burgundy bombazine that draped the breathtaking river view from their hotel window.

"I have told you all there is to know."

"Michael, please. Maybe your doctor overlooked something. Maybe all you both need is a fresh perspective . . ."

When those cinder-hot eyes at last locked with hers, she realized she was treading dangerous ground.

"Your intentions are honorable, I'm sure. However, you do not possess sufficient medical knowledge to understand such a complex malady."

She wanted to box his ears. "Try humoring me. Isn't your life worth saving?"

"That is a question I cannot answer."

She gaped. He'd stunned her so thoroughly, she couldn't rally her wits in time to keep him from changing the topic.

Although the doctor issue was far from settled, Eden

decided to drop the subject. She didn't want to spoil their outing to the museum.

But as they strolled out the hotel's main door, he surprised her, announcing he was taking her instead to Madam Letitia's Ladies Shop.

"M-Michael," she stammered. Never in her life had she worn a gown that wasn't home-sewn. "I don't need any new—"

"Wednesday night, you'll be sitting in the theater box that President Lincoln reserved when he came to town. I think the occasion warrants a special frock."

He arched a brow, as if challenging her to defy him, but she'd already lost. When he spoke in that smoky, chest-deep rumble, her mind sighed in surrender and her knees turned embarrassingly weak. She supposed she'd have to learn to resist that provocative drawl—someday.

In the meantime, she marveled at her husband's largesse. Although Sera had never wanted for anything as long as Michael had been her guardian, Eden had seen, with her own eyes, the patches in the soles of Michael's black boots and the crack in the glass of his silver-plated pocket watch.

Her husband, it seemed, gave generously to everyone but himself.

Unused to baring her corset and bloomers to strangers, Eden blushed for nearly the full two hours that Madam Letitia's assistants fluttered around her with green satin taffeta, measuring sticks, and pins.

In all honesty, though, the heat lapping over her skin had been kindled by her husband. While she stood awkwardly on her stool, her composure challenged by the half-circle of mirrors that surely magnified her every freckle, he lounged in the velveteen chair directly across from her, his off-center smile an earthy enticement. She couldn't help but think that Michael had made an astounding change since his arrival in Louisville. Perhaps she simply hadn't known him well enough, but the man who sat watching Madam Letitia's legions strip, swaddle, and pin her, was certainly not the man who'd ducked his head and hurried past her on the sidewalks of Blue Thunder. If the young assistants hadn't been so flirtatious, Eden might have reveled in the pleasure Michael took in his voyeurism.

Unfortunately, their interest in her husband was painfully clear: she received a pinprick each time Letitia's girls cast hungry, covetous glances his way. One even called him "Mick." Later that afternoon, while she was walking arm and arm with him through the commercial district, he sidestepped her question about the nickname, explaining instead that the girls had been raised in Lydia Witherspoon's orphanage, and that he'd convinced Madam Letitia to apprentice them.

He wasn't quite as artful about avoiding her "Mick" question the second time, though.

They had no sooner crossed the street for a French restaurant, when a beautiful brunette in a crisply starched apron rushed out of the nearby boarding house.

"Mick? Oh, Micky, it *is* you!" she squealed as he turned in reflex. She hurried down the sidewalk, her dark eyes warmer than melted chocolate, her porcelain cheeks blooming a captivating pink. Eden tried not to stiffen as the woman, her demure brown bodice straining over a pair of breasts that would have made a eunuch salivate, checked herself just one footfall shy of Michael's arms. Although Eden stood at Michael's elbow, the brunette didn't seem to notice. She was too busy clasping her hands and smiling with unabashed adoration at the man she'd called "Micky."

"You've been away so long," she chided in an alluring alto. "And you sent no word of your return. Shame on you! Did it ever occur to you I might have filled your bed?"

Michael reddened, and jealousy spiked Eden's chest. She wanted to believe the brunette had been referring to a long-term lodging agreement; even so, Eden couldn't help but mark the double meaning in the woman's words. Had it been intentional?

"I've taken a room at a hotel, Sofia. With my wife."

Shock widened Sofia's eyes. "Your wife?" she repeated thinly. At last forced to acknowledge Eden, she managed a weak smile. "Oh. I see. That's . . . understandable, I suppose."

Sofia didn't loiter much longer. With a polite smile and a half-hearted invitation for dinner, she excused herself and headed back to the boarding house.

Eden made a concerted effort to keep the accusation out of her voice. "Let me guess. Sofia's another orphan."

He slid her a wry glance. "No. A widow."

She took the elbow he offered her. "And . . . you were one of her boarders?"

His dry smile didn't reassure her. "Briefly."

They walked several more paces in silence. The restaurant was a quarter-block away, and she sensed he was using its proximity as an excuse to end their conversation. "You're not going to tell me, are you?"

"Tell you what?"

"What she meant to you. And why she calls you 'Micky'."

The gaze that met hers resembled a blue-black twilight. "Am I to be interrogated about every female acquaintance I've struck up over the last thirty-one years?"

She raised her chin. "You say that as if you have something to hide."

"I do. All men do. Premarital skeletons are best left in their closets, away from doting young brides. But if it eases your mind . . ." He lowered his voice to a dark, throbbing murmur. "While I was still at the university, Sofia became a young immigrant widow, desperate to feed two toddlers and appease her husband's creditors. When one of them gave her . . . an infection, she was too ashamed to visit a doctor. I only happened to deduce her condition, because one of the"—his voice dripped acid—"*gentlemen* had been bragging about their liaison in the saloon. Shortly afterward, he returned from the privy complaining of . . . difficulties there. So I looked up her address and took my valise. She was in a bad way."

Eden swallowed, and those dusky eyes pinned hers.

"When she was strong enough to work, I convinced the boarding-house owner to hire her as a cook so she could pay her debts and keep a roof over those babies' heads." Michael halted, reaching around Eden for the brass handle on the restaurant's door. "Satisfied?" he demanded softly.

She nodded, feeling the heat of his stare to her bones.

Reflecting back on that conversation, Eden found another reason to love her husband. He was willing to champion anyone who needed him—widows, orphans, raccoons—and yet he shunned all praise for himself. His kindnesses were surely the best-kept secret in Kentucky. Why, half of Louisville seemed to owe him some debt of gratitude. The moment the train conductor had recognized Michael, the man had marched them straight up the row of Pullman cars, insisting that they take the plushest compartment at no extra cost because Michael had once set the man's broken leg so well that he'd suffered "nary a limp."

Then there'd been the paddlewheeler's captain. He'd invited them onto the bridge of the ship, chattering enthusiastically about his son, a university student now, but a ten-year-old when Michael had saved him, diving into the murky waters of the Ohio to breathe life into his lungs.

At the hotel, the wealthy owner had arranged for fresh fruit and flowers to be brought to their room every afternoon with a gratuitous bottle of champagne. Apparently Michael had counseled him not to take his own life following a crushing loss at the racetrack.

Clearly, Michael was well loved in this town. He grew less guarded and more lighthearted under that affection, as if the dark cloud of Blue Thunder had finally rolled beyond the horizon. She wondered how much this new, easygoing Michael owed to six days of relaxation and romance, and how much he owed to Louisville itself. If the city represented to him all that was curious and carefree, then surely Blue Thunder was his prison sentence. Being well-traveled herself, she marveled that Michael had suffered for so many years in a house—in a community—where the ghosts of his mother, brother, and father eroded his peace of mind. Part of her understood the need, even yearned for the opportunity, to settle in a place she could call home. On the other hand, didn't Michael ever dream of life beyond the graveyard that Blue Thunder had become?

She worked up the nerve to ask him that very question on the last night of their wedding tour.

He shifted behind her, the broad plane of his naked

chest cradling her spine. She loved the erotic contrast of his rock-hard musculature beneath the downy softness of his hair and the way his arms and thighs possessively hugged her. They sat entwined on the window seat in their hotel room, the casements thrown wide, the stars shining down. All of Louisville slept; not a single light could be seen winking beyond their lovers' sanctuary, although somewhere, across the glittering black expanse of the Ohio River, she heard the distant clang of a boat's bell.

"Oh, Michael." She snuggled closer, sated and dreamy, but melancholy too. She didn't want their wedding tour to end, didn't want to return to the gossip, the stares, the small-minded judgments so rampant in Blue Thunder. In fact, a dark, elusive premonition niggled her mind every time she entertained the notion, and no amount of yearning for Aunt Claudia, Sera, or even Stazzie was able to dispel it. "I hate that our honeymoon's almost over."

She dropped her head back against his shoulder, letting him stroke her hair. The rhythm of his great, calloused hand soothed her in a way that was profoundly primal—as primal as the pleasure that pooled inside her each time he stole her breath with his slow, tender lovemaking.

"Do we have to go back?" she murmured wistfully.

She could almost feel his smile somewhere above her in the warm, velvet womb of the Kentucky night.

"I'm afraid so."

"But . . . I like it here."

"It is beautiful, isn't it?"

She sighed, watching the stars glow. If she squinted and called on her imagination, she could discern the rugged limestone bluffs of Indiana against the horizon.

"Have you ever thought about living in Louisville? I mean, for more than the few months you spent here each year while you were studying at the university."

He didn't miss a beat. "I have obligations in Blue Thunder."

She wrinkled her nose at his soft but uncompromising response. "Sera would love it here."

"Claudia would not."

She sighed again, defeated. He was right about Aunt Claudia. She'd been too stubborn to leave Blue Thunder during the hard times, when she'd been considered the town's pariah. Claudia wasn't about to quit the valley now that Henry Lucas's fortune had turned the tables and folks were kowtowing to her. Besides, she wasn't as healthy as she pretended to be.

"I suppose the orphans would miss you if you left," Eden conceded reluctantly. *Not to mention Bonnie and Jamie . . .*

"There is that, too."

She fell silent. She would go wherever Michael chose to go, of course. But after only six days of marriage, fear had entrenched itself on what should have been a wondrous journey. What if she was of no more use to her husband than the physicians who'd pronounced his doom?

That afternoon, Michael had grudgingly yielded to her pleas to introduce her to his physician. Peter Vandergraaf had surprised her: the blond, reticent Viking was the same age as Michael. Apparently they'd studied together at the university. She'd had to bite her tongue on her protest that Peter didn't have enough life experience to diagnose Michael's ailment, for the implication would have been that Michael didn't either.

And if Michael, who was six years her senior with

four years of medical schooling to his credit, didn't have the wherewithal to determine his own illness, what would that say about her competence?

So Eden had listened politely, doing her best not to squirm as Peter recounted the tests he had performed on his colleague and friend. She hated that her stubbornness had forced Michael to sit through the discussion again. In spite of his cool, composed silence, she knew that Peter's findings, all of which were inconclusive, caused Michael a bitter frustration. Peter had done his best, just as Michael had. But neither of them could discover the cause for his vertigo or his bouts of weakness.

Sitting now in the circle of strength that was her husband's arms, Eden wondered if Michael's Chicago and Boston doctors were also classmates from the University of Louisville. In her opinion, Michael's mysterious condition called for someone . . . well, wiser. She wasn't at all confident that she possessed the requisite wisdom, though. She wished fervently that Papa and Talking Raven were alive to counsel her.

"You never did tell me why everyone in Louisville calls you Mick," she murmured.

"Papa hated it. So I preferred it."

This surprised her. She tilted her head back but could discern little more than the square of his jaw. "You didn't get along with your father?"

"Most of his life."

She was glad for the darkness. She was sure she must have looked like a carp the way her mouth had dropped open. "But after everything Sera told me, I thought you were close to him."

"Sera likes to think so."

"And she's been wrong all these years?"

"It's kinder to let her remember the family the way she wants to."

Eden knitted her brows, pondering this bombshell. If Sera had painted too rosy a picture about Michael's relationship with Jedidiah, then maybe her stories about Michael and their half-brother were wrongfully colored, too.

"Tell me about Rafe."

His chest rose quickly beneath her shoulders, as if he'd drawn a sharp breath. For what seemed like eternity, he didn't answer. He didn't even acknowledge her request. She might have become lost in the echo of his heartbeats if their tempo hadn't noticeably increased.

She was just about to try another tactic, when he finally spoke.

"He was Mama's favorite."

Of all the things he could have said, those four quiet words were painfully telling.

"But everyone says you were your father's favorite," she reminded him gently.

"I resented my father. For the way he treated Mama. She deserved better."

"You must have loved her deeply."

Again, silence.

She bit her lip, not daring to indicate the depth of her insight into the confused, wounded child he must have been or the stern, dispassionate man he sometimes became. As a two-year-old, had he blamed himself for the bitter feuds that must have erupted between his mother and his father after Jedidiah learned Catriona had become pregnant by another man? As their firstborn child, had Michael learned to shoulder responsibility for the entire world? And later to blame his half-brother for his mother's unhappiness?

"Is . . . that why you hate Rafe?"

She counted his heartbeats, watched a shooting star streak across Scorpio. Somehow, the pulsing red sun at the heart of the constellation seemed significant. It spit and sparkled close to Mars.

"I don't hate Rafe. Not really."

"Not . . . really?"

Michael sighed, a long, weary sound.

"Rafe never had a chance under Papa's roof. And I wasn't much help to him. I was jealous about Mama."

She slipped her hand into his. Thick fingers closed around hers, holding on tight, as if drawing strength for a more shameful confession.

"On the day of her burial, Rafe and I quarreled at her gravesite." His voice roughened with the guttural, uncompromising tone she'd come to associate with his self-condemnation. "He never came home that night. I was sick about it, thinking he'd been lost in the snowstorm. I rode out the next morning, hoping he'd reached the orphanage. It was the first time I'd ever been in an orphanage, and I was horrified. All those children, all those sad, hungry eyes . . ."

A tremor moved through him.

"Anyway," he continued gruffly, "no one there had seen Rafe. And no one in town had heard from him. I thought he was dead. I blamed myself for . . . Christ, at least six months. Then one day he wrote to Aunt Claudia, bragging about the stage career that was making him famous." Irony edged Michael's voice. "Papa was livid. He'd always preached that thespians were drunkards and thieves. He vowed once and for all to wash his hands of Rafe's corrupt soul. But I knew, even if Sera couldn't see it, that Papa hated the thought of Mama's bastard being happy. The only way he could strike back was to forbid Sera to answer Rafe's letters."

Eden's stomach knotted. The more she learned about Jedidiah Jones, the more she marveled that Sera and Michael hadn't grown into bitter adults.

"Have you ever told Rafe?" she murmured. "That you don't hate him?"

"No."

She winced. His voice had been a quiet thunderclap. "Why?" she persisted stubbornly.

"He hates me."

Every fiber of her being rebelled at this reasoning. If there was one thing she'd learned, after watching Talking Raven suffer for years as an outcast from her people, it was that fear and hatred only bred more of the same.

"But you haven't set eyes on Rafe for what, ten years? How can you be sure his feelings haven't changed?"

"I'm sure."

She was hard-pressed not to shake her head at the finality in his tone. Why did Michael let pride stand in the way of a reconciliation that might lead to some peace of mind? Pride was such a poor consolation for happiness.

"Well, I'd like to meet Rafe someday," she said firmly. "He's family. And I've always wanted family."

"You have Sera and Aunt Claudia," he reminded her more gently.

"Yes, I know, but . . . I always wanted a brother, too."

Michael grew contemplative. She imagined his dark expression; she envisioned the shadow of Jedidiah looming over him just as it must have during his childhood, when the preacher-turned-cuckold had deliberately spawned resentment between Michael and Rafe.

But Michael surprised her again.

"I always wanted a brother too," he said quietly.

Her heart went out to him.

"It's not too late, Michael." She turned as best she could in his arms. "You can erase Jedidiah's legacy. You can end the shame and bitterness and give an uncle to your children."

He grew impossibly still. The hammering of his heart became her only indication that he hadn't turned to stone. She couldn't say why, but uneasiness snaked through her innards. Maybe it was due to his stare, transformed to glittering black onyx by the shadows.

"Y-you do want children, don't you, Michael?"

He drew a shallow breath. The smile he gave her was so raw, so afflicted, her throat grew tight with tears.

"Of course," he whispered huskily.

"Michael, I—"

"Shh." He kissed her. His hands stroked and soothed her. In that masterful way he had, he made her forget all her questions, all her worries. He carried her to the bed, wrapping himself around her, loving her into the moment where there was only him and an aching kind of pleasure. He worshipped her with his body, bringing her to such a state of erotic frenzy that she sobbed his name, streaking across the heavens like the shooting star that had blazed over Scorpio.

It wasn't until later, much later, that the questions crept back to haunt her.

And she realized then, as he lay sleeping, that he hadn't spilled his seed in her.

# Chapter 11

～◯◯◯～

They arrived quietly in Blue Thunder: no fanfare, no public stonings. Eden might have been relieved, except her husband's mood had darkened visibly with each signpost their stage ponies passed. She'd tried to distract him from his thoughts with questions about the Pine Mountains, but Michael had confined each of his responses to two or three terse sentences. Meanwhile, his hooded gaze had remained fixed on the coach's other passengers: a tow-headed baby dozing in his mother's arms.

Eventually, Eden had fallen silent herself.

After the hustle and bustle of a city hotel, the Jones home was positively tomblike beneath the slate-blue clouds that choked the twilight from the sky. Trying to ignore her usual sense of foreboding about storms, Eden stepped through the front gate as Michael swung it open. But when he let it close behind them with a bone-jarring bang, she cringed, unable to resist a glance toward the welcoming glow in Claudia's kitchen window. She wondered longingly if Sera was baking cookies, if Claudia was smoking her pipe and cleaning her shotgun, if Stazzie had survived her seven long days cooped up with an irascible old woman and a double-barreled Whitney. But Eden didn't dare leave Michael's side to find out. Not yet.

She smiled uncertainly as he halted in the hallway, grimacing at the foot of the stairs.

"Um . . . would you like me to fix you some dinner?"

To his credit, he tried to smile. But weariness weighted his shoulders. Hollows ringed his eyes. He adjusted his grip on their luggage so he could rest a hand on the bannister. "I could use some refreshment," he admitted.

She watched uneasily as he trudged up the stairs, the carpetbag and portmanteau he'd hoisted so effortlessly one week earlier now dragging on his arms like anvils.

A traitorous mist stung her eyes.

She shook her head to clear her vision. *Peppermint*, she told herself staunchly. An invigorating tonic would do them both a world of good. And then perhaps, if she could persuade him, she'd draw a rejuvenating bath. *Blackberry leaves, dandelion, nettle, lemon verbena, comfrey, raspberry leaves . . .* She was so busy ticking off the herbs she would need to stuff in a muslin bath pouch that she didn't notice the lanky blond shadow quietly observing her from the kitchen doorway. She practically collided with it.

"Collie!" she gasped, scrambling backward. "Good heavens. You gave me such a fright!"

Those gray eyes held hers solemnly. In the splintered light that arched behind him in the kitchen window, she beheld the ghost of the man he would someday become: rangy, untamed, and more canny than a coyote. He'd put on a pound or two in the week since she'd seen him. She was glad to see him looking so well and wondered if Sera had invited him to dinner.

He quickly dispelled that notion. "Did he force you?"

She nearly choked on her next breath. Only then, as her eyes grew accustomed to the flash that shimmered over the rose-patterned wallpaper, did she realize he gripped a shotgun in his fist.

"C-Collie," she said hoarsely. "What are you doing with a scattergun?"

"Takin' care of you. 'Cause you ain't got no man to do it."

She pressed shaking fingers to her lips. She wanted to throw her arms around him. More than that, she wanted to make this man-child understand he couldn't solve his differences with Michael—or anyone else— with a gun.

"Thank you," she whispered, her voice tremulous with the realization that he'd come prepared to kill on her behalf. "Collie, thank you for caring about me. But nobody forced me to do anything. I love Michael."

His gaze roamed over her quickly, impersonally, and yet she sensed he missed nothing. She thanked God she'd worn a high lace collar to hide the love nip Michael had given her.

"You sure?"

"Of course I'm sure."

"It wasn't the kissin'?" he insisted in dire tones. "Or the spirits?"

She dropped her hands to her sides and drew a steadying breath. "No, Collie. It was none of those things."

He harrumphed. Then he tilted his head, his eyes narrowing to flinty shards. "Does he love you?"

It took every ounce of self-control Eden possessed not to flinch and look away. Despite the half dozen times she'd assured Michael of her love, he'd never once echoed her sentiments. She hoped his feelings would change. Still . . . the honeymoon was over. Life would get harder from this day on. Already she was struggling with the knowledge that her husband's deepest feeling for her was a sense of responsibility.

"If you aren't satisfied with my answers," she told Collie primly, "then I suggest that tomorrow, when he's feeling up to it, you have this same discussion with Michael. But leave your gun at home."

Rebellion chased skepticism across his features. Then something else, something more boyish, kindled in his stare.

"It ain't mine."

"It's not?"

"Nope."

She found her pulse was at last starting to slow. "Whose is it, then?"

"The old woman's."

She started, peering more closely at the gun. She'd assumed it had belonged to Collie's father. "But how—"

"I won it. Fair and square," he added smugly. "We had a peashootin' contest. She ain't as good as she thinks she is. But I told her I'd give her a chance to win it back."

"You did?"

"Sure." The grin he flashed her was all boy. "Right after she fixes me a sweet potater pie."

Eden laughed. Claudia hated to cook almost as much as she hated to lose. Collie must have deduced this fact and settled accordingly on Claudia's comeuppance.

He followed her into the pantry, opting, as she did, to snack from a box of saltwater taffy rather than Sera's tin of fresh biscuits. He barely waited long enough to chew the first piece before he'd unwrapped two more and shoved them into his mouth. She laughed when his cheeks swelled up like a chipmunk's; still, he managed to chat about Sera, the raccoons, and a host of other topics as he shucked corn and she shelled peas. By the time she had the corn roasting and a savory vegetable chowder boiling on the stove, Collie had devoured all the taffy *and* the biscuits and was eyeing the bread and cheese she'd sliced for Michael's dinner. She shook her head at the boy.

"Honestly. And you were trying to live on roots and berries in that ramshackle hut you call home."

"Naw. I just told you that so you'd feel sorry fer me and bake me more pies."

"*What?*"

He giggled, grabbing a handful of apple slices and dodging the towel she smacked after his rump.

Suddenly the bottom half of the kitchen door crashed open.

"Where's that dang boy?" Claudia snapped, her sterling-colored hair crackling with storm static. She stomped inside, wreathed in a cloud of blue pipe smoke. How she could see anything through that eye-stinging fog was a mystery to Eden; still, Claudia grunted absently at her, as if the sight of her errant niece, newly returned from her wedding tour, wasn't much of a surprise.

"MacAffee," Claudia growled, squinting and puffing at the same time, "I got a bone to pick with you."

"Yeah?" Collie dropped back into his chair, propped his ankles on the table, and munched indolently on an apple wedge. The shotgun, Eden noticed in secret amusement, lay draped across his thighs.

Claudia scowled. "Hey! Ye're getting sticky juice on my scattergun!"

Collie popped a finger into his mouth and sucked

noisily until it was clean. "Whose scattergun?"

Claudia muttered something unfit for ladies' and young gentlemen's ears. "Listen here, brat. Sera said she's plumb out of sweet taters. And they ain't in season fer another three months."

Collie shrugged. "Ain't my problem. No pie, no rematch."

Claudia grew livid and began to push back her sleeves. Eden decided she'd better intervene.

"Um, Auntie?" She cleared her throat. "Perhaps you and Collie could settle your differences another way. Say, over . . . croquet. I believe Michael set up a few wickets for Sera in the backyard."

Claudia's cagey old eyes grew speculative. The ghost of a smirk twisted her lips, and she harrumphed. "That's a sissy's game. I got me a better idea. Unless, o' course, the boy there's too *yaller*."

"I ain't yaller," he retorted, dropping his feet to the floor in a fighting stance.

"Good. Then mumblety-peg it is. Hand me a pig sticker, niece."

Eden balked at the idea of her seventy-five-year-old, health-compromised aunt tossing butcher knives in the backyard. But Claudia ignored her protests and shouldered past her. Grabbing a bone-handled blade from Sera's arsenal of utensils, she stabbed it toward the door.

"Git on with ya, boy. Double or nuthin'."

Collie snorted, hiking the barrel over his shoulder. "What am I gonna do with two shotguns?"

"I meant two *pies*, you uppity pup!"

Collie's face creased with a sly smile. "Well now. That's different. Should be a cinch," he taunted as he sauntered for the door, "whuppin' a girl at mumblety-peg."

"Who you callin' a girl?" Claudia bellowed after him as he stepped beneath the lowering clouds.

"*Old woman*, then," his voice floated back to them over a rumble of thunder.

"That's better!"

Claudia wiggled her eyebrows at Eden. "Afore you know it," she confided with a grin, "I'm gonna have that boy raised to be a bonafide man."

"Ye're burning daylight, old woman!"

"Hold yer dang horses," she hollered after him, donning her best crabby expression and stalking into the fading light.

Mystified, Eden watched her aunt go. What on earth had happened over the last seven days to make Claudia tolerate Collie?

Not ten minutes later, as the wind started to knock the shutters against the house, Sera appeared, flushed and flour-dusted, to stick her head inside the door. "Eden!" she exclaimed, the stark white of her pinafore a striking contrast to her shining black hair. "Auntie's such a pill. She didn't tell me you were home. I had to see the light in the window!" She rushed inside and threw her arms around Eden's neck.

"Um . . ." When Sera withdrew, her gaze was riveted to the window. "Why's Collie pulling a butcher knife out of the dirt with his teeth?"

"Apparently Claudia made him eat crow at mumblety-peg."

"Oh." She frowned. "But do you think she should be playing with *knives* in her condition? I mean, your Papa's tonic has done wonders for her and all, but—"

"*What?*" Eden blinked at her. "Claudia's taking the heart tonic?"

"You mean you didn't know?"

Eden frowned, and Sera burst out laughing.

"Oh Eden, honey. Auntie's been humbugging you. Apparently Collie came looking for you a day or two before your wedding tour. He found Claudia clutching her chest and panting in the kitchen. He asked what was wrong, and she told him it was her heart. After her spell passed, they got to commiserating about medicines and how awful they taste—except for some kind of tea you must have brewed Collie. He said if he had the gumption to drink one of your tonics, she should too. In fact, he called her yellow. So to spite him, she grabbed one of the bottles from your medicine chest and took a spoonful. They've been fast friends ever since."

*Friends?* Eden wasn't exactly sure she'd describe Claudia's relationship with Collie as friendly.

"Why didn't Auntie tell me any of this?" she demanded, hurt creeping into her tone.

"You know how she likes Michael to make a fuss over her. Maybe she figured he'd stop doing it if she got better. Honestly, Eden, the only reason I know about the tonic is because I caught her red-handed with a spoonful last night."

Eden pressed her lips together. She and her aunt needed to have a little talk about self-medicating.

But if, as Sera claimed, Claudia's condition had improved as a result of Papa's foxglove elixir ... Eden's heart raced as her excitement grew. She couldn't wait to tell Michael. He'd promised to test the tonic as soon as they got settled into their family routine. Maybe Claudia's improvement would be all the proof he needed.

And maybe the tonic's proven curative powers would earn them enough money to search out an *experienced* physician to treat Michael!

Sera tossed her a sly look as she poured herself a steaming cup of Arbuckles coffee. "Well?"

Eden checked her elation. Better to keep her excitement hidden than to pique Sera's curiosity, especially about Michael. "Well what?"

"You've stalled long enough, Eden *Jones*. Tell me everything! And don't you dare leave out a single detail."

Eden blushed. The idea of sharing with Sera the absolute wonder, the soul-soaring bliss, she'd felt whenever Michael loved her seemed . . . well, traitorous. She wanted those moments to stay special, and hence, private.

"We had a lovely time," she hedged. "We saw the mummy, and the minstrels. We took a paddlewheel cruise and saw a balloon exhibition—"

Sera rolled her eyes. "Do you think I care about some crumbling old *mummy*? Or an overinflated *balloon*?" She sank on the bench, her elbows propped on the table, and blew spiraling puffs of steam off her coffee. "Was Michael wonderful?"

"I love him, Sera," she countered quietly.

"Well, I know *that*. Everyone loves Michael. Except Michael, of course. He's funny that way. Sometimes I think he enjoys being moody and cussed. Just like Aunt Claudia."

Eden averted her gaze, busying herself with the cornpone batter. She used to think the same thing, until Michael had confessed he was dying. Until she'd seen, with her own eyes, the pain and frustration he suffered and his valiant struggle to keep the truth from the people he loved.

"I think he bought you a souvenir," she said casually, hoping to change the subject. "Something from Madam Letitia's."

The ploy worked. Sera drew a whistling breath. "You mean the French seamstress? The one who designed Frances Folsom's gown for President Cleveland's inaugural?"

Eden arched an eyebrow. Michael had said nothing of Madam Letitia sewing ballgowns for the president's ward. "I suppose they're one and the same."

Sera squealed, jumping out of her chair. "*Eden!* For heaven's sake, why didn't you tell me? Where's Michael?"

Before she could answer, Sera was already speeding toward the parlor, calling her brother's name. Eden shook her head, chuckling. Sera could be so predictable, especially when it came to gewgaws and presents.

A moment later, Eden's merriment wedged in her throat. Sera's calls had shrilled, turning from eagerness to panic.

"Michael! What is it? What's wrong?"

Her heart slamming into her ribs, Eden raced down the corridor toward the blaze of gold that lit the parlor. The first thing she noticed, when she rushed through the doors, was that Michael was sagging nearly to his knees. Medical volumes tumbled down around his ears as he grabbed for the bookshelf. His face was ashen. His chest heaved like a bellows. He would have collapsed if Eden hadn't reached him in time to slide her shoulder beneath his arm. The impact of his two hundred pounds nearly threw her into the shelves, but Sera grabbed his other arm, countering his weight with a strength that

Eden hadn't thought possible in such a petite frame. Sera's face looked as gray as his, though.

"Michael, good heavens—"

"I'm fine," he rasped.

"You are *not*—"

"Sera," Eden interrupted more sharply than she'd intended. "Help me take him to the settee."

Somehow, and Eden could tell the effort was gargantuan, Michael got his legs to stumble under him. He protested their assistance, trying to straighten every step of the way, which only made them meander off course several times before they finally bridged the five feet to the couch. If Eden hadn't been so worried, she would have boxed his ears for his willfulness. As it was, she had her hands full settling him on the couch.

He shook his head, as if trying to clear it, while she climbed up behind him on the cushions.

"Get smelling salts," she ordered Sera.

She hoped the diversion would earn her several minutes to help Michael compose himself. As it was, he was growling something unintelligible, trying to fight his way off the couch. She wrapped him in her arms, rocking and chanting, using her voice the way Talking Raven often had to soothe wild animals. The trick must have worked, because Michael's grip eased on her wrists, and he heaved a shuddering breath. The color began to return to his cheeks.

Sera flew back across the threshold just as he was starting to growl something new about not needing help. The tracks of her tears shimmered in the lamplight.

"Michael, *what is wrong with you?*" she cried, falling on her knees in a heap of peach muslin.

His smile was more of a grimace, especially when the

stink of the salts assailed him. "Tired," he lied hoarsely, pushing her hands away and accidentally dislodging his pocket watch.

"Don't give me that. You haven't—" she gasped, recoiling from his watch as if its gentle bump had scalded her fingers. "M-Michael."

In growing concern, Eden watched her friend's eyes glaze over, changing from a briny indigo to a cloudy sapphire. Even Michael must have noticed the difference, for he struggled out of her arms, his hand shaking as it stretched for his sister.

"Sera—"

She made a tiny broken sound, like a child whimpering through a nightmare. He grabbed hold of her shoulders, pulling her against his chest in a bundle of pastels and lace. She shuddered. Her black hair, the exact color of his own, gleamed in stark contrast to the pallor of his cheek.

"Sera . . ." Torment crossed his haggard features. "Honey, don't."

"You're sick," she choked, her fists clenching great handfuls of his starched shirtfront.

"No," he murmured, stroking her hair.

"You are! I can see when you were alone in the hall. You fell. Y-you knocked over the flowers and all the umbrellas. And then you just . . . just *lay* there! And you fell in your office. And you almost fell by the swimming hole. Eden was there . . ."

She gasped, jerking out of his embrace, the tears streaming down her face. She rounded on Eden. *"You knew he was sick!"*

Eden swallowed, more than a little unnerved by her

friend's visions—and the accuracy of at least one of them. "Sera, I—"

"You didn't tell me! You're supposed to be my *friend*. Why didn't you tell me?"

Eden bit her lip, her luminous jade stare pleading for the truth. She looked like she might cry herself, and Michael struggled with his guilt. More than that, he struggled with his dread. The numbness was at last receding from his feet and legs; his tongue no longer felt like a piece of cotton gauze. Still, his gut churned, hot enough to process steel. This time, it wasn't due to the eery coincidence of Sera's insights, concocted by an overwrought young woman with more imagination than was healthy. No, this time the nausea was due to the fear that his illness, whatever it was, had taken a decided turn for the worse. And there wasn't a damned thing he could do about it.

"Sera." His voice cracked, harsher than he'd intended. He couldn't bear to see her cry, couldn't bear to know she was feeling every stab of the pain from which he had fought so long to spare her. "Eden is my wife. I made her promise to say nothing. To anyone."

"But I'm your sister!"

Eden shifted uncomfortably behind him. "Sera—"

She threw off Eden's hand, as if it were some kind of insect. The glare she shot his wife pierced Michael to the bone.

"I have a right to know if you're sick, Michael. You're not just my brother, you're my guardian!"

He averted his eyes. He could see her tears anyway. They dripped onto the fists she'd clenched in her lap.

"I'm sick, Sera," he confirmed bleakly.

Her swallow was audible. "Is it bad?"

"Yes."

"Bad enough to . . . to die?" she finished in a tremulous voice.

Self-loathing roiled through him. He'd been unable to ward off illness, cure himself, or protect his sister. Now Eden was caught up in the lies his failures had spawned.

"Yes," he said flatly, clinging to the dispassion his profession demanded. "I may die."

"But you can't!" The hand she pressed to her mouth was shaking even harder than the rest of her. "You have to see a doctor!"

"I have already consulted three—"

"Then consult a fourth. And a fifth! I don't care how many, only . . ." Her voice broke. "Don't die, Michael. Promise me you won't die."

The mantel clock chimed, six grim strikes of its mechanical innards. Between each one, an eternity fell away. Michael stared at the blank whiteness of the wall. He could hear Eden's uneven breaths behind him, feel her valiant struggle to hide her own upset. Sera's tears burned like acid where they fell on his knee.

He thought of his mother, who'd died so young. He thought of Gabriel, who'd died even younger. He would have gladly surrendered his life to save either one of them. And now, for her sake, Sera was demanding that he fight this debilitating curse that no doctor could name. Should he make yet another promise he couldn't keep?

"I'm sorry, Sera." Thirty-one years of cynicism, bred by good intentions gone awry, crept into his tone. "Would you have me lie to you again?"

A primitive keening ripped from her throat, rolled through the room, mingled with the thunder. Eden reached for her. This time, Sera let Eden hold her.

"I'm sorry, Sera," he whispered again.

Rain began to pelt the tin roof. He rose shakily. Drained by the endless effort to quash his own grief, he turned away. That's when he spied two shadows hovering in the doorway that led to the hall.

"Michael Jones." Claudia sounded more grim than he had ever heard her. "I ain't ever known you to run before."

Collie's eyes gleamed, ghostly in the pale yellow wash of the lamplight. He said nothing. He just stood with a shotgun by his side, barring any retreat.

"Let me pass," Michael growled.

"Ye're too young fer that."

"I meant . . ." He felt the old rage starting to build. He might be a failure, dammit, but he wasn't any coward. "Step aside."

"I'm writing to Rafe," Sera sniffled. "I'm telling him to come home."

"No!" The word exploded from Michael's mouth. Watching his half-brother gloat while he grew progressively weaker was more than he could bear.

Claudia harrumphed, folding her arms across her chest. "Rafe's got duties toward Sera. She'll need a male guardian."

"*I'm* her guardian."

"Not fer long, the way ye're talkin'."

"That's enough." Eden's voice cut like glass through the rain, the thunder, the weeping. "Michael needs support, not an interrogation. I will not allow you to bully him. If you choose to grieve, do so when he breathes his last. God willing, he'll outlive us all."

Michael's throat constricted. If ever there was an avenging angel, his wife was it. He silently thanked her with his eyes.

The love her gaze poured back to him buckled his knees.

With a garbled oath, he shouldered past Collie and Claudia. He didn't know where he was going when he flung open the door and stalked out into the storm. He knew only that he felt a primal kinship with the wind that ripped his clothing and the rain that knifed his face and throat.

No one spoke much about that day. Not in Michael's presence, anyway. Eden refused to let Sera wallow in woe, speaking of her brother as if he were already buried. Eden insisted that they focus on living, rather than dreading an uncertain future, and she sternly counseled Collie and Claudia, who'd been eavesdropping to begin with, to keep silent about Michael's secret. After all, a runaway wagon could strike any one of them down, Eden argued, just as Berthold Gunther's had nearly killed Jamie.

But rumors spread anyway.

At first, most people didn't pay much attention. Michael's hasty marriage gave the gossips more fat to chew than a couple of missing pounds off his broad-shouldered frame. When Bonnie blamed Michael's pronounced cheekbones on Eden's kitchen skills, Claudia just as vociferously pointed out that Michael was spending more time in bed of late—romping with his wife. Eden wasn't sure that Claudia's rumor mill was the lesser of two evils, but she kept her peace, hoping that the illusion of her happy marriage would bore Blue Thunder Valley, and folks would start grumbling again about the mosquitoes, drunken lumberjacks, and the stench of Gunther's animal compound.

By October, however, folks couldn't rely on Michael,

as usual, to be holed up in his office, waiting to treat their ills. Eden, who'd been dividing her time between Claudia's store and Michael's medical practice, briskly explained away her husband's shortened hours and brooding preoccupation, claiming that Michael was making more time for his family. But his clients lost patience with his odd behavior. They started turning to her for their treatments.

The most unsettling defection of all was Bonnie.

Eden rose early to prepare the clinic for Michael's return. The previous night, he'd been called to the bedside of an elderly sodbuster, and he'd slept at the ailing man's farm.

At least, that's what Eden wanted to believe.

Michael's long hours continued to be a bone of contention between them. It worried Eden to watch him ignore his fatigue, to see how he slumped over what little food he spooned onto his dinner plate, to see the hollows that ringed his eyes when he woke. Living under her husband's roof had proven eerily similar to living under her father's: Both men were driven to save lives, and both were too selfless to worry about their own. The similarity only intensified Eden's fear that her herbs were failing Michael.

And that she was, too.

As if to drive this point home on that particular Tuesday morning, Bonnie dashed through the clinic's back door. She didn't knock. She didn't even call out a greeting. She simply rushed around the corner, her crimson taffeta and trailing cape rustling like autumn leaves against the bleached pine of the floor.

"Oh." Bonnie slid to a halt before she could bowl over Eden, who was dutifully scrubbing medical instruments in a soapy basin of water. "I didn't know *you* were here."

Eden's hackles rose. Shaking the suds from her hands, she forced herself to count to ten before she spoke.

"Michael isn't here. He had to pay a call on Farmer Garretson."

"I wasn't looking for Michael."

Eden arched a brow.

"I was looking for Jamie."

*She's lying.*

Eden frowned. As usual, the insight was hard to substantiate. She had nothing to base it upon, except the unusual timing of Bonnie's call. Still, the knowledge that something was amiss rang inside her head with the vibrancy of an alarm bell.

Reaching for a towel, she struggled to maintain an air of professional courtesy. "Jamie isn't here, as you can see."

Bonnie moistened her lips. "Are you sure?" She edged toward Michael's desk, her knuckles nearly bloodless as she steadied herself against the scarred wood. Her complexion looked as pale as her hands. "Perhaps you should go in the other room and . . . and look for him."

Eden's suspicions climbed another notch as Bonnie's gaze darted furtively to the medicine jars filling the glass cabinet over the instruments. "I'm quite certain we're the only ones here. Is Jamie missing from the schoolhouse?"

Bonnie started, some of her color returning. "Um . . . missing?" Her gaze snapped back to Eden. "Of course not. He's probably under Auntie's porch, playing with that wretched toad. He . . . had a bellyache this morning. And he disobeyed my order not to leave the house."

"I see."

Bonnie audibly swallowed. "Anyway, since I'm here, you might as well give me a bottle of citrate of magnesia. For Jamie."

"You know very well Michael doesn't hand over medicines without a thorough examination. As soon as he returns, I'll tell him you'd like to set an appointment for Jamie—"

"I think I know my son well enough to determine what ails him. Besides, there's no telling when Michael will get back," she added hastily, "and my son is suffering now."

Again Eden counted to ten. She decided not to point out that a child who felt healthy enough to crawl under a porch with a toad probably wasn't suffering. At least not from dyspepsia.

"Very well. There are other remedies for bellyaches. The apothecary should be opening his shop soon. And you won't need Michael's prescription for peppermint, valerian, yarrow, or blue flax."

Bonnie wrinkled her nose. "I couldn't possibly stomach . . . I mean, *Jamie* couldn't possibly stomach the smell of boiling flax seeds this morning."

Another one of Eden's insights struck. This one was more ominous, more shattering. It made her stomach roil.

"This isn't really about Jamie, is it?" She choked out the remainder: "You're in the family way."

Bonnie retreated so hastily, her shoulders struck the wall. "N-no!" Her hand dropped to her abdomen, belying her protest. "How dare you? I'm not even married!"

Eden lowered her gaze. To a man-hungry widow like Bonnie, what difference would marriage—hers or anyone else's—make?

Dread gnawing at her innards, Eden tried not to draw the most heartbreaking conclusion about Bonnie and her real reason for visiting the clinic before business hours. "Have . . . you told the father?"

Bonnie spun away. For a moment, she looked like she might bolt out the back door for safety. Instead, her steps faltered.

"No."

"You won't be able to keep the baby a secret for long."

She faced Eden again, her eyes glistening a haunting green. "Aunt Claudia said your tonic stopped her chest pains."

"Um . . . yes," Eden admitted warily, her mind shrieking for answers that she wasn't sure she wanted to know. Was Michael really the father of Bonnie's baby? Or had Bonnie come here merely to get medicine for her nausea?

"I didn't believe Claudia at first," Bonnie rushed on. "But Sera said it was true. And Jamie says you're some kind of Indian medicine woman. Didn't you mix potions for people in Colorado?"

Eden squirmed. The very mention of Colorado was enough to deflate what little confidence she'd managed to build under Michael's tutelage. Although she still tried to refer all patients to him, the sheer volume of Michael's practice made her assistance necessary. After observing her for several weeks as she treated minor maladies, he'd insisted she had the skills to treat rashes, bee stings, head colds, and sprains. Part of her had been excited to think Michael was giving her an opportunity to grow her skills and prove herself to Blue Thunder's skeptics.

But the rest of her had begun to wonder if he were just too sick, too exhausted, and he didn't care who helped him shoulder his patient load. For surely if Michael believed in his heart she was competent, he would have heeded the medical advice she gave *him*. Instead, he opted for coffee instead of the rejuvenating teas she brewed for him each morning; he paid lip service to their agreement that he would come home each afternoon for a nap; and he refused to soak his weary muscles each evening in an herbal bath because he didn't want to smell like a "dandelion." Her confidence wavered every time he dismissed her ideas, and no matter how kindly he declined her offers of help, her pride stung.

"Bonnie . . ." Adulteress or no, the beseeching look in the older woman's eyes was nearly Eden's undoing. "I'm not the expert that Michael is. You should really consult with—"

"No! Not Michael. He'd never understand!"

Hugging her waist, Bonnie began to pace in an agitated rhythm, the heels of her kid boots scoring the soft pine boards. "This shouldn't have happened," she muttered under her breath. "I was so careful. I could *kill* that old mountain woman for convincing me her preventatives worked."

She turned abruptly, a tear staining her cheek. "It's not fair! I don't want this baby."

"I know you don't think so now," Eden countered shakily, not liking where this conversation was leading. "I know you're worried about the things people will say—"

"I *can't* have this baby, don't you see?" Bonnie's eyes

brimmed. "Birthing Jamie nearly killed me. I can't do it again. I can't let him grow up alone!"

*Oh, Bonnie.* Eden's chest ached. Never in her wildest dreams had she thought they'd find common ground in an age-old female fear. "I helped Talking Raven midwife several women out west. They were scared too, because the first child came so hard. But the second came easier. And so did the third."

Bonnie's brows knitted. "So you could make me live?"

"No, but you can. By fighting for life. By refusing to leave Jamie at any cost. Isn't that how you got through those first three months after he was born?"

Bonnie blinked at her. Eden blushed. She didn't know where that fount of wisdom had come from. Even so, some part of her knew, as surely as if Talking Raven had stood congratulating her, that her insight had been truth.

"I guess so." Bonnie bit her lip. "But I don't put much stock in prayer. I mean, I prayed till I was blue in the face that Michael and I would . . ." Her voice trailed, and she had the decency to redden. "Anyway, it's not like I have a choice. I can't go to him now. Doc Perkins is half blind. And that old mountain woman's clearly a charlatan. Maybe your Indian ways can . . . can eliminate my problem."

Eden cringed. Even when she'd failed, her intent had always been to save lives with her herbs. "I'll do everything I can to help you, Bonnie, except . . . something we'll both regret."

Bonnie straightened her spine, but her show of mettle was undermined by the quiver in her chin. "I thought you hated me. Why are you being nice?"

"Well . . ." The question was a good one, considering

the circumstances. "I suppose it's because I see the good in you. The part that loves Jamie and worries about Aunt Claudia. I try to ignore the rest."

"I suppose you think I should ignore your bad parts, too," Bonnie said petulantly.

The front bell jangled before Eden could respond. Bonnie jumped hard enough to make her straw boater bounce.

"Promise," she hissed, clamping a hand over her hat and backing for the rear door.

A footstep rattled the floorboards beyond the curtain that separated the rooms.

"Promise you won't say a word, Eden."

"But—"

"*Promise!*"

She nodded, too choked to speak. Bonnie fled in a flurry of crimson, the back door banging closed behind her.

"Mama?" Jamie poked his tousled curls around the curtain. "Oh. Hello, Miss Eden. I thought I heard Mama's voice."

Balling her fists in her skirts, Eden gulped a steadying breath and steeled herself against glancing toward the rear entrance. "She's not here, Jamie. Why aren't you in school?"

"Mr. Luke said I didn't have to go. He paid me a whole nickel to find Mama!"

*Mr. Luke?* Eden's heart stuttered even as her brain pounced on that grain of hope.

"Uh-oh." Jamie was gazing out the side window toward Claudia. She stood wreathed in her habitual smoke cloud as she unlocked the door of her general store. "I gotta scoot. If I don't get over there 'fore Auntie eats her breakfast, there won't be any peppermints left!

Bye, Miss Eden. If you see Ma, tell her Mr. Luke's looking for her."

Eden watched the boy dash back the way he had come.

*Luke! The mayor's son!*

Her momentary relief was checked by an insidious doubt.

*Just how many lovers does Bonnie have, anyway?*

The widow had been seen clinging a bit too cozily to a number of prominent bachelors since Independence Day. Eden had heard folks whisper that Bonnie didn't care one whit for any of them, that she was just trying to hurt Michael the way he'd hurt her when he'd gotten caught with his hand up Eden's skirts.

*Maybe Bonnie doesn't know who sired her baby.*

Eden's eyes stung. She didn't know for sure that Michael had spent the night at Farmer Garretson's house. And last night hadn't been the first night her husband hadn't come to their bed. In fact, he disappeared during business hours, too, leaving Eden to stammer excuses to his patients. Because he refused to speak of the circumstances surrounding his absences, she'd tried to convince herself that a patient's confidentiality was at stake. She even allowed herself to believe that he'd been called to some medical emergency at the orphanage. Circumspect questioning of Lydia Witherspoon, however, always proved there'd been no emergency and worse, no visit from Michael.

But the hardest lie of all to face came in the wee hours before dawn.

Michael had stopped making love to her only a week after their honeymoon. He'd used Sera as his excuse, pointing out that his unschooled sister was liable to hear them in a bedroom only two doors away. When Eden tried to seduce him during less conventional times—the Saturday afternoon, for instance, when Collie first sneaked Sera to the animal orphanage to meet Vandy—Michael claimed he'd agreed to repair the leaks in Claudia's roof. Other times, he pleaded an appointment he'd forgotten to mention. Or a headache. Or fatigue.

As if to apologize, he usually brought her flowers the next day. He never actually said he was sorry; she supposed he was too proud for that. But in truth, she didn't need him to say the words. She just needed him to hold her.

She remembered the last time he'd allowed himself to touch her in their bed. On that predawn morning in mid-August, the harvest moon had long since bobbed behind the horizon. The candles had guttered; even the crickets had hushed. Daylight couldn't have been more than an hour away. Something roused her from a dream—the usual restless dream—about him.

She realized his breath was stirring the curls on the nape of her neck.

Tingles streaked to her toes. She lay on her side, not daring to move. Not since Louisville had he eased himself beside her in this way, a *hungry* way, as if his long weeks of abstinence had finally taken their toll. His hand skimmed her cheek, so feather soft, she thought she must have imagined it. But then the hair he'd been brushing back from her ear snagged on the button of her gown. She swallowed.

He froze.

Half afraid to breathe, she lay waiting, hoping. She listened to his heart—or was it hers?—thundering around her in the night. The heat between his thighs nearly scalded her buttocks, but she only craved more.

How many nights had she lain smoldering like this, longing for him to set her aflame?

Finally his voice, low and husky, crooned above her ear. "I'm sorry."

Tears crowded fast and thick into her throat. He said nothing else, *did* nothing else.

It was more than she could bear.

"Michael."

He tensed.

"P-please touch me again."

She felt a tremor move through him.

"I didn't mean to wake you." The tone was very different this time, so distant. So . . . polite.

"I don't mind. Truly." She rolled on her back—and checked her next impulse. Something in his manner warned her against reaching for him, against pressing her lips to his or weaving her fingers through his hair.

"I love you so much," she whispered fervently.

His chest heaved above her. As dim as it was, she could see his features contort. Was he in pain?

"You are"—the rasp of his words grew almost guttural—"more than I deserve."

She tried not to frown. This wasn't the first time he'd alluded to such a thing. That he might honestly harbor the belief was starting to unnerve her.

She tried to focus on her love, not her upset. "Sometimes you make me so happy, I wonder how I could deserve you," she countered gently.

He bowed his head. She didn't need to see his face to realize his turmoil. Struggle was etched into every rigid sinew, every ragged breath. She ached to know what was tearing him apart.

"Would you . . . tell me if I'd done something

wrong?" she whispered uneasily. "Something that hurt you?"

"Oh God." His gasp was half laugh, half sob. "You're the one blessing in my life."

"Then what—?"

His lips swooped. Her head reeled with the tender savagery of his kiss. Dizzy with delight, she barely noticed the taste of salt on his tongue. She barely noticed how he shuddered when she arched her hips against his.

He loved her in every possible way that early summer morning—except one. The one that would join them completely. The one that she yearned for so much, she ached physically whenever he stood within reach.

Her husband had denied her his legacy. And in the weeks that followed, as he'd returned home later and later from his business, he chose to sleep in Gabriel's old bed.

Eden's suspicions made her heart bleed. It could no longer listen to the scant excuses Michael offered. It couldn't be salved by his flowers and trinkets. News of Bonnie's baby had been the final assault.

And this time, Eden's wound was mortal.

# Chapter 12

〜○〜

The morning following Bonnie's visit to the clinic, Eden was still grappling with her conscience, wondering if she had the right to breach a patient's confidentiality to confront Michael and question his fidelity. She thought she might explode with the feelings at war inside her. That's why she was glad, for once, to be refereeing the usual coon-and-cat feud that erupted after Collie's breakfast visit and his subsequent request to "mind Vandy for a spell."

But another, more unsettling diversion soon arrived at the back door to test her patience.

Feathers of frost speared the kitchen window, distorting all but the lean build and tawny hair of the person who approached the house. She didn't know who was more surprised when she answered his playful, Morse-code rapping. She'd been expecting the return of Collie. The stranger had obviously been expecting . . . someone else.

For a long moment, keen pewter eyes searched hers. They were so clear, she actually glimpsed her reflection: flushed cheeks, stray damp curls, flour-dusted gingham. If not for the broom she clutched, sticky with syrup and fragments of porcelain, one might have thought she'd been baking instead of chasing Vandy around the war zone that had once been her pantry. Stazzie was still hissing behind one of the few canning jars that hadn't rolled off the top shelf. Vandy heckled her from below, shoving broken lemon cookies into his mouth. Eden expected to hear another crash any minute. She didn't have time to entertain.

And yet the man's smile, a dazzling flash of rogue dimples, chipped at her resolve.

"My apologies, madam." His drawl was a captivating blend of southern elegance and western twang. "I thought this was the Jones residence."

"It . . . uh . . . is." She chided herself for stammering like a moonstruck maid. "Dr. Michael Jones lives here."

"Ah. Well, I was looking for Miss Sera Jones."

Eden's curiosity climbed another notch. This *gentleman* was looking for Sera? For surely the stranger's impeccably tailored gray wool, silk cravat, gold wrist cuffs, and bouquet of zinnias were the marks of good breeding. Michael would be overjoyed to know his sister had finally cast her eyes toward a beau of merit—perhaps one with an honest-to-goodness bank account—although she did worry that Michael might object to the stranger's age. He appeared close to thirty.

Even so, Eden guessed the man's mouth-watering good looks had won over Sera's resistance to mature beaux. She'd been moping for weeks, ever since Billy and Jesse had quit their jobs at the sawmill to ride out of town. Sera had informed anyone who'd listen that Billy was riding back to Texas to ready his ranch for a bride—namely, her. Michael had informed her in his gruff, hard-headed way that cattle ranchers spent the

summer driving steers to market, not sawing down
Kentucky pine trees.

"Well, I admire Billy for learning a new skill," Sera
said staunchly. "There's not much timber in Texas, so
he couldn't very well practice there. Besides, Billy wants
to build a big new corral for his mustangs."

"Any livestock that reprobate possesses," Michael retorted in dire tones, "was probably rustled."

"That's a terrible thing to say! Especially about the
man I'm going to marry."

"You'll marry Billy Cassidy over my dead body, Seraphina."

Wincing as she recalled the ensuing tears, oaths, and
door slammings, Eden hoped that argument was finally
behind them.

Something splashed behind her. Startled, she glanced
over her shoulder, following the sound of Vandy's gleeful whickering. He was washing the pork rib Stazzie
had left unguarded by her water bowl. Meanwhile,
fierce cat growls rattled the pantry door that the coon
had so cleverly pushed shut.

Eden mustered a smile for the stranger. Sera would
kill her if she let Vandy and Stazzie drive the man away.

"Um . . . Sera ran next door to borrow some eggs,"
Eden said, raising her voice above the animal feud behind her. "I'm sure she'll be back any minute. You're
welcome to wait inside. It's safer than it sounds, I promise." Heartened by the amusement in his eyes, she
opened the door wider. "I'm Eden, Sera's sister-in-law."

Shock registered on the man's sunbronzed features.

"Mrs. Jones." He gave her an off-center smile. "That's
very gracious of you. I wasn't aware Michael had married. No doubt my invitation was lost in the mail," he
added with dry aplomb. "I realize they're not much of

a wedding gift, but I hope you'll accept these flowers as a token of esteem from . . . your brother-in-law. Raphael."

Her breath hissed between her teeth. She could have kicked herself for her reaction. She hadn't meant to be rude. Even so, he didn't bat an eye. No doubt he'd expected worse.

"Oh, Rafe." She hastily accepted his bouquet. "I'm so sorry. I should have guessed."

"You've heard of me then," he said wryly.

"Yes. Yes, of course. Please come in."

He inclined his head, stepping past her. She had the fleeting impression of feral grace and sandalwood cologne. He didn't look the least bit intimidated as he entered the lion's den—or perhaps she should say the grizzly's den—and yet, like the wily fox, she sensed his every instinct was on the alert. She hastened to juggle her broom and bouquet so she could take his hat and gloves.

But the minute her arms were loaded, Vandy, to her consternation, chose to pester her guest. Fearless of humans, he galloped over to Rafe's shoes, which were polished bright enough to catch a raccoon's eye, and yanked at the shiny buckle fastening his gray spats. Eden was mortified, but Rafe's lips quirked.

"I see you've had more than one visitor this morning," he drawled as Vandy wrestled with his prize.

"I'm so sorry." She lunged for the coon, who'd been forewarned by her shadow, and was making a beeline for cover. Somehow, she grabbed his ruff before he charged through the razor-sharp fragments of cookie jar she'd been sweeping. "He keeps escaping from his cage," she added, blowing out her breath. Vandy had grown into a hefty, twelve-pound adolescent. "Collie left to put a new latch on the door, but I'm afraid it's hopeless. Vanderbilt is just too smart to stay behind bars. And the truth is, he shouldn't have to. If he weren't so trusting of people, we would have released him back to the wild by now."

"Hmm." Rafe cocked his head, addressing her masked ward. "I daresay it's no fun climbing trees when you could be locking cats in the pantry, eh?"

"Stazzie! Good heavens, I almost forgot."

"Allow me, would you?"

To her bemusement, Rafe offered to take the raccoon from her arms. Beady black eyes regarded him solemnly, and Vandy stretched out a paw, as if recognizing a kindred spirit.

"Are you sure?" Eden suspected her bundle of mischief would leave Rafe's expensive silks and wools the worse for wear. "I mean, Vandy won't bite or anything, but he will try to rob you of every button, coin, and gewgaw you own."

"I rescued a baby otter once and had to teach her how to swim. She's surviving quite well in the forests near Aspen these days, but . . ." He cast her a sideways glance as he let Vandy wrap a miniature hand around his thumb. "Sometimes I miss her. Tavy was fond of buttons too. Buttons and crayfish and . . . imported French soap bubbles."

Wistfulness crept into his tone. She tried to imagine this well-heeled sophisticate kneeling by a copper bathtub to teach an otter how to swim. It wasn't the sort of picture Sera had painted of her wayward, oat-sowing brother. And it wasn't at all like the bitter, angry young man that Michael had painted.

Eden smiled in understanding. Rafe smiled back. Vandy got busy ransacking his pockets.

With a curious coon to thwart the formalities, it wasn't long before Rafe lounged on her settee in an arrestingly male pose. Charming and debonair, he proved the model guest, acting as if it were an everyday occurrence to have the contents of his pockets strewn across the carpet, the spoils of a ring-tailed marauder. Sipping coffee, munching sticky buns, he regaled her with comedic tales: his stage debut as Shakespeare's Juliet, his five-month misery as a saddle-sore cowpoke, his adventures in a haunted silver mine, and his otter's frolic in the bath of his outraged bride-to-be. His stories had Eden laughing so hard, she feared she'd split a seam. It surprised her that she could strike up an instant camaraderie with the black sheep of the Jones family. Part of her felt guilty, considering the bad blood between Rafe and her husband. Another part of her empathized with Rafe. She supposed the reason was Talking Raven. The Cherokee had shown her how painful it was to be an outsider.

Perhaps a half hour slipped by before Rafe set his empty cup and saucer on the serving tray. Vandy had curled up at his boots, chewing the last of the sticky buns; Stazzie dozed in Eden's lap.

"I fear I've been rather selfish," Rafe drawled, "rambling on about myself. My only defense is that you've been an attentive audience. More attentive than I deserve."

"I've enjoyed your stories, Rafe."

"I take it laughter has been in short supply here these days?"

His question, so matter-of-fact and yet so insightful, caught her off guard. She'd guessed that Sera had written to him, of course; still, she hadn't had a moment to think how she should address the cause: Michael's illness.

"How is he?" Rafe asked quietly.

She averted her eyes. She hadn't meant to be cowardly. In truth, the feelings that wedged in her throat were so familiar now, she'd learned to talk around them.

But whether for good or bad, this time, she was spared from one of her discreet rebuttals. The back door slammed. Stazzie jerked awake. Sera's laughter floated down the hall. She was talking to someone about eggs and pumpkin pie. Eden felt every hair on her head prickle. She prayed that "someone" was Collie.

It wasn't.

Sera's gasp came next from the hallway. Rafe had already risen, silhouetted against the stream of autumn sunshine like some bronzed Apollo. Eden's introduction fizzled on her tongue as Sera squealed. A streak of pink tarlatan and lace ruffles, she flew into the parlor and launched herself into his arms.

Rafe laughed, swinging her around as effortlessly as he might a child. Eden watched nervously, her gaze flickering to her husband. Michael stood motionless on the threshold, his face chiseled granite.

"Oh Rafe, oh Rafe, *you came!*"

"Of course I came. I told you,'whenever you need me,' remember?"

Michael's chest heaved. Other than that, one might have thought he'd turned to stone.

Sera stepped back, clapping her hands together. "Oh, what fun. I bet you surprised Eden, huh?"

"You might have told me about my new sister-in-law," he countered.

She dimpled endearingly. "You didn't like my surprise?"

Rafe's gaze flickered to Michael, then back to Sera. A refined roguery crept into his smile. "Your surprise has been delightful."

Eden cleared her throat. Stazzie was rubbing affectionately against Michael's ankles, but he didn't appear to notice. His eyes fairly smoked, riveted as they were to Rafe.

Unable to postpone the inevitable any longer, Rafe turned at last and faced his older brother. The air crackled between them.

"Michael," Rafe greeted dryly.

"Raphael."

Eden held her breath. She knew what this reunion could mean for Michael if he'd only drop his pride.

The silence lengthened. For the first time since meeting Rafe, Eden actually sensed the presence of some bottled tumult inside him. She suspected he'd exercised no small amount of courage to show his face at Michael's door.

"Well." Rafe folded his arms across his chest and critically eyed the brother standing apart from them in the shadows. "You don't look sick."

"Disappointed, are you?"

"Oh, for heaven's sake." Sera rolled her eyes. "Rafe didn't come to gloat. He came here to talk some sense into you."

Michael's smile was mirthless. "About Cassidy?"

She tossed her curls over her shoulder. "That would certainly be a start."

"Um . . ." Eden found herself twisting her hands in her skirts. She hated when she did that. "I'm expecting Collie to return any minute with Vandy's cage. He might even bring Jamie. Might we call a truce for the children's sake?"

"A splendid idea." Rafe's smiled dripped mockery. "We'll postpone the dagger throwing till after luncheon."

Sera giggled. "That should give us plenty of time to march *you* down to the general store. I declare, Aunt Claudia will bite her pipe stem in half to see you all grown up and looking so fine."

Sera took Rafe's arm. He acquiesced, turning to say his farewell.

"Eden." The gaze that rose to hers was apologetic. "I look forward to knowing you better."

She nodded and swallowed, uncertain whether to be relieved or frustrated when Sera rushed Rafe out the front door, leaving her to deal with Michael.

He held her gaze for an excruciatingly long moment. "Did you know he was coming?"

His question was unsettling. She couldn't tell if he was angry or weary, resentful or hurt. But then, her husband was a master at hiding his feelings. She supposed all doctors had to be dispassionate to some degree. But Michael was also a man. He didn't have to pretend he never feared. Or yearned. Or despaired.

At least, he didn't have to pretend with her.

"No," she answered warily. "Sera never tells me anything these days."

Stazzie's purr sounded unnaturally loud in the unwinding silence.

"I'm sorry your friendship has suffered." He drew himself taller, like a man waiting for the lash. "Let's hope this is the last of Sera's surprises. I trust Rafe made arrangements for his lodging at the hotel?"

"He . . . agreed it would be best."

Nodding, Michael turned for the stairs.

"Michael?"

His heart tripped to hear the quiet determination in her query. Either she was about to ask him to make some kind of promise regarding Rafe, and he'd have to deny her; or she was about to demand some explanation he'd been avoiding, and he'd have to lie. Neither prospect sat well with him. The alternative—watching her grieve when he discussed his mortality—was more devastating than his disease.

That's why he'd been secretly arranging for the inevitable. He'd signed his last will and testament, ordered his grave marker, and paid the remainder of his debts. While he wouldn't leave her and Sera wealthy, at least they'd be comfortable until they fell in love more wisely the next time and married.

He prayed Eden wouldn't waste time in mourning.

Even so, the thought of her in another man's arms was likely to kill him before this damned, lingering plague did. He didn't know which was the lesser hell: barring himself like some prisoner from their bed, or watching her shutter her heart as she slowly fell out of love with him. Christ, that love had come to mean everything to him, even though he couldn't quite believe he deserved it. He wanted to feel worthy of a woman like Eden.

And for that reason, he couldn't risk another night by her side. He couldn't bask in the sweet enticement of her warmth, ignore the longing in her eyes, listen to her half-sobbed pleas for him to touch her, without crumbling in his resolve. Just the scent of her hair drove him mad. Eden was, and had always been, the one temptation that could vanquish him.

But by God, not again. This time, he would not fail.

He loved Eden too much to burden her in death as he had in life.

He would not—*could* not—risk spilling his seed in her.

Steeling himself against the raw, raging torment of leashed passions, he turned to face his priceless gift, his one blessing, and pretend he was too strong to need her.

"Yes, Eden?"

She twisted her apron. The habit was an endearing one, all the more so if she caught herself doing it, because her cheeks turned rosebud pink. But the habit also betrayed her inner agitation, and it made him want to drop everything, to wrap his arms around her, murmur consolations, and kiss away her fears.

If only he dared.

"This is your chance, you know," she said quietly. "To heal your grievances with your brother."

He drew a long, steadying breath. "It's not that easy."

"Why?"

"Rafe would rather gloat."

"I didn't get that impression."

"You don't know him well."

"Michael."

Again, he froze in midturn, cursing his inability to ignore the entreaty underlying that single word.

"Four months ago, you told me you'd always wished you had a brother. He's here now. Don't let pride stand in the way of your reconciliation."

Michael's throat constricted. "Rafe didn't come for reconciliation. He came for Sera."

"Is that so wrong?"

"Yes! He has no right to take her away."

Michael ran a rough hand through his hair. He hadn't meant to sound peevish. But how could he make Eden understand? While Rafe disappeared for years at a time, becoming heroic in his absence, Michael had shouldered the responsibility of raising his younger siblings. If familiarity bred contempt, then imagine how discipline was viewed through the eyes of a child. Sera had often threatened to run away after Papa's death and live with Rafe. Her outbursts had hurt Michael deeply. He'd done everything he'd known to be a good guardian. It galled him to think that Rafe could show up anytime on a whim, expend minimum effort, and convince Sera to leave with him.

Just as it galled Michael to see how easily Rafe had wooed his wife's esteem.

"Michael, a man can change in ten years. You're not even giving Rafe a chance. Besides, if I understood you correctly, you were as responsible as your father for driving Rafe away."

He scowled. That particular truth didn't make welcoming Rafe home any easier. "So you're taking his side?"

"What I'm taking is a God-given opportunity to help you heal old wounds."

"By singing my brother's praises?"

She pursed her lips. "You're being contrary. On purpose."

"*I'm* being contrary? By my estimation, my prodigal brother has been home less than an hour, and already he's turned you against me."

"That's ridiculous. If anyone has turned me against you, it's *you*."

He stiffened. Color bloomed in her cheeks. He suspected she hadn't meant to let the truth slip out in quite that way.

"So." He struggled to keep the hurt from his voice.

"You grow weary of the vows you made to an invalid?"

"Oh, for heaven's sake. You're not an invalid. Why do you persist with such nonsense?"

"It is hardly nonsense, madam. I have four medical opinions, including my own, that confirm the inevitable."

"So you'd rather be right than be healthy, is that it?"

"What the devil are you talking about?"

Never in his life had he seen a sadder smile. It clawed at his heart, shredding the iron defenses as easily as if they were a net veil.

"We've lived under the same roof for four months. And in all that time, I can't remember you seeking out pleasure. I can't even remember the last time you laughed. You've grown angry, bitter, and full of self-hate. Clearly, you don't want to heal, Michael."

"*What?*"

She sighed, dropping her gaze to the floor. "Not every illness resides in the body. But even if, as you believe, yours is strictly physical, how many times have you denied yourself treatment? How many times have you refused my tonics and my baths, or ignored Sera's pleas to let an older, more experienced physician examine you for—?"

"Let me get this straight," he interrupted harshly, feelings of futility spiraling dangerously close to rage. "You're saying I have *allowed* myself to get weaker, to suffer vertigo, to lose the sensation in my legs and arms?"

Her chin raised a notch. "Yes. I am."

He blinked, disbelieving. "That's not only untrue, that's . . . cruel."

"No crueler than you are to yourself."

"My God, Eden, I have done everything humanly possible to heal this plague!"

"You lie to yourself. You've done nothing but prepare to die."

The accusation, as gently as it was spoken, slammed into his gut with the force of a sledgehammer. He reeled, thinking she must have learned somehow that he'd paid a visit to the stone carver.

"I have taken steps, yes, to make sure you and Sera are provided for—"

"That's not what I mean. You stopped living a long time ago. I don't know what it was, exactly, that killed your spirit. But you allow yourself no kindnesses. You suspect gestures of caring. You drive yourself past exhaustion. You refuse . . . love. These are the things that siphon away life, Michael. The physical illness you're experiencing is just another symptom of the problem."

An odd tingling crawled across his skull. Every inch of his flesh prickled with goosebumps. He ignored them. "So now you're saying I deliberately got sick? That I brought upon myself an illness that couldn't be cured?"

"In a manner of speaking. It's all a matter of perception. You tend to see the worst in a situation. But what if this illness were the answer to a prayer? What if it were your greatest teacher, coming at a time when you most needed to rediscover the value of living? We all have to die, Michael. Dying is easy. Living's what's hard. It takes courage."

The raw truth of her words ripped at his chest. In that moment, his wound went so deep, he couldn't begin to separate his rage from his fear, his sense of betrayal from his self-contempt. All he knew was that his wife, the woman he loved enough to sacrifice his every need, had called him a coward.

He spun on his heel.

"Michael, wait." Eden hurried after him. "Where are you going?"

"I am not in the habit of being called a craven, madam."

"For heaven's sake, is that all you heard me—"

The front door slammed, cutting her off. She winced. The windows rattled around her.

*Damn him.*

She battled tears of frustration, watching his stiff, ground-eating stride carry him past the frost-coated hedgerows, through the white picket gate, and out of her sight.

Perhaps out of her life.

Was he going to Bonnie?

She smothered a sob. She couldn't live like this any more. She couldn't *hurt* like this any more.

Michael turned her away, denying her any part of his inner world. It killed her a little each day to watch him grow more distant, more disinterested in their marriage. From the beginning, their union had been doomed. Perhaps she should have listened to that inner voice that had urged her, on Independence Day, to flee Blue Thunder and never look back.

But she'd wanted so desperately to help him. She'd hoped that somehow, some way, she could make him feel love again and that her love would make him happy. Even that dream had finally died with her suspicion that he'd been unfaithful. She no longer believed Michael wanted happiness, at least not with her. In her company, he preferred to wallow in grief and nurse old wounds. A spirit couldn't thrive in the darkness with which he armored himself. As much as she loved Michael, perhaps the time had come to . . . love herself.

Dashing away tears, she gathered her skirts and climbed up the stairs for a traveling bag.

If she hurried, she could have her belongings packed by luncheon.

*He* was back.

Observing the tow-headed longrider below, Collie shivered on his belly as he clung to the frosted pine limb and cursed Billy Cassidy. Collie's flannel shirt front was damp, thanks to the way his own heat steamed through the ice crystals, and his gloveless hands were raw with the bite of wind. Still, he held on to the swaying bough, doing his best to keep his breaths from puffing like Injun smoke signals and giving his hiding place away. He knew, with the instinct of the hunted, that Cassidy and his cigarette-smoking pal were looking for him.

The coons whickered nervously as the men swung down from their horses; the rabbits scampered to the corners of their cages. Collie narrowed his eyes and flattened himself further. His heart pounded so hard, he imagined the icicles shook with each beat.

"Well now." Cassidy's unbuttoned duster flapped like buzzard wings as he strode past the coon cages and the rickety trough Doc Jones had built to bring water from the stream to the clearing. "Ain't this quaint. Boxes of bunnies."

"Looks like the boy's been raising them," Quaid said, strolling in a casual half circle—the same circle Collie's boots had traced only minutes ago, before he'd heard the horse snorts and the cracking branches and had loosed the hounds, hoping their romping would wipe out his tracks. Now they were somewhere off in the woods, snuffling for sport.

Cassidy's attention was fixed on Millie, the plumpest doe. "Looks like dinner to me."

Quaid propped his shoulder against Collie's pine and flicked ash into the carpet of needles. He said nothing as Cassidy flipped the latch on the cage and pulled out the squirming rabbit.

"You checked the shack?" Cassidy crooned, stroking Millie's ears. She started to relax. She started to trust him.

Quaid grunted in the affirmative.

"Little bastard." Cassidy cuddled Millie to his chest. "The brat's got weasel blood, just like his pa."

Quaid blew out a long, leisurely stream of smoke.

"Hell, Jess. I didn't bust your ass out of jail so you could piss away time. What are you waitin' for? Find the brat's tracks."

"Already did."

"Yeah?"

Quaid jerked his head in the direction of the stream. "Took off through the water."

"You mean you *lost* him?"

"He's probably freezing his tail off downstream."

"Christ, that's all we need. The kid catches pneumonia before we can beat the answers outta him." Cassidy scowled. "I'm sick of this town. Why did Bart's trail have to lead us back here? There ain't a damned thing in Blue Thunder worth stealing. We could be having a lot more fun—not to mention a lot more *money*—in Mexico, if you'd just remember what happened that night."

"So you've said."

Cassidy shook his head. "You're some piece of work,

Jess. Ain't you itchin' to kill the bastard yet?"

"I want to clear my name, not do more time."

Cassidy rolled his eyes. "Yeah, well, you can do that right after the brat tells us where his pa stashed our loot."

"I'm not convinced Bart MacAffee's our man. Black Bart was getting old. He wanted to stop running. Any man canny enough to settle in a sleepy little town till he thought the last of us were hanged wouldn't have kept a name that was posted on every tree in two states. The gossips would have sicced a marshal on him faster than a prairie fire with a tailwind."

"You know something? You think too much."

"Saves bullets."

Cassidy sneered. "Shit. If you got any softer, folks would spread you on toast."

Quaid said nothing. He just took a long draw on his smoke, tucking his boot heel under his buttocks.

"Where do you reckon the brat's hiding out?"

Quaid shrugged.

"Sera would know." Cassidy's smile oozed with new cunning. "Sera knows everything that goes on in this pissant town."

"Gunther's a better bet."

"Yeah?" Cassidy frowned, and his hand hovered in midstroke above Millie's head. "How come?"

"Where do you think the boy goes for his pets?"

Understanding dawned on Cassidy's coyote face. "Reckon ol' Bert did have a heap of rustling trouble awhile back. And for once, nobody thought to finger you and me." He smirked. "Tell you what. I'll talk to Sera. You talk to Gunther."

"I figured you'd want to call on Gunther," Quaid

countered, "seeing as how he made a laughingstock out of you last July."

Cassidy's eyes narrowed. "I got bigger fish to fry than some two-bit card cheat. 'Sides, I can't do every damned thing myself. The sooner you help me find that boy, the sooner we'll find our lost bullion—and the sooner you can go kiss some judge's ass to clear yourself of murder."

Quaid flicked more ash into the frost-coated needles. "You know," he drawled, "with a ribbon and a bow, that rabbit would make a nice gift for a sweetheart."

"You mean Sera?" Cassidy snorted. "That skirt can't kiss worth shit. But she can cook."

Suddenly his hand dropped. Millie screamed, flailing, until her neck snapped with an audible crack.

Cassidy purred. "I love it when the bitches scream."

Collie's eyes burned with tears of outrage. If he hadn't clamped his teeth over his sleeve, he would have retched all over Quaid's black Stetson, ten feet below.

"Christ, Jess. You gonna stand there all day?" Cassidy was tying Millie's carcass to his saddle horn. "Get yourself a rabbit, or get your ass to Gunther's."

Quaid dropped his smoke, rubbing it out with his boot toe. As he did, his gaze rose slowly, unerringly, pinning Collie like a striking panther pins its prey. Chills scuttled up and down Collie's spine. When the outlaw turned, padding past the cages with his soundless gait, Collie's heart hammered so hard, he felt dizzy. But Quaid didn't stop. He didn't open a cage. He headed straight for his horse.

Every muscle in Collie's length was shaking as the outlaws spurred their geldings and rode away. His tremors had nothing to do with the cold, though. Hatred seeped into his bones, burning hot enough to repel an alpine blast.

Something changed in him that day. Something hardened. He vowed to make Billy Cassidy pay.

He vowed to keep him away from Sera.

# Chapter 13

$\sim\!\!\odot\odot\!\!\sim$

S treaks of rose-tinged tangerine fanned across the western sky, heralding the end of day. Michael barely noticed. He stood where he'd been standing for the last hour, his fists shoved into his coat pockets, his breaths curling around his head like miniature geysers. The temperature was sinking with the sun, but Michael couldn't feel the change.

Or maybe he didn't care.

He simply continued to stare at the tombstone, bleached white by the years, deepening to a luminescent gold in the twilight.

HERE LIES GABRIEL JONES. BELOVED SON AND BROTHER. HEAVEN KNOWS A BRIGHTER SMILE.

Sera had insisted on the epitaph. She'd gone toe to toe with Papa for it, the only time in Michael's memory that she had fought Jedidiah Jones and won.

"Gabriel didn't understand scripture," she'd argued. "He hated stuffy old churches and prayer. Stop trying to make him an *angel*, Papa. Just let him be Gabriel."

Later, Sera had confided to Michael that Gabriel, in all his otherworldly glory, had floated down to sit on her bedpost the night of his death and had told her that heaven was a happy place where everybody smiled. "He likes it there," she said, beaming. "He said to tell you not to cry."

Sera had been ten years old at the time. Of course, Michael hadn't believed her.

His throat aching, Michael wondered how his life had gone so wrong. How had he lost his brother's friendship, his sister's respect . . . his wife's love?

*I'm no damned coward.*

Still, there were times when he envied the people who died in their sleep, never suffering the pain or loneliness of a lingering illness.

*Maybe it's true*, he thought ruefully. *Maybe in some ways I do wish for death.*

The gravel path crunched behind him. He tensed. Usually he was immune to flights of fancy. Nevertheless, he felt every hair on his scalp rise. Boot hill wasn't the most comforting place for surprises.

"Figured I'd find you here."

He recognized Collie's mutinous tenor before he spied the boy over his shoulder. Grim and pale, Collie stood silhouetted like an avenging fury against the backdrop of sun, dogwood, and neatly sculpted graves. He was coatless and gloveless, despite the garments Eden had purchased for him, and he gripped the barrel of Claudia's shotgun in a white-knuckled fist.

"Collie," he greeted cautiously. *Careful what you wish for, Jones.*

The boy narrowed his stare. Michael couldn't ever remember seeing that particular gleam in the boy's eyes.

"How come you always come here?" Collie demanded.

Michael turned slowly to face him. Was it his imagination, or were Collie's cheeks moist with tears? "I come to visit Gabriel, mostly. Sometimes my mother. Don't you ever visit your pa?"

"Shoot no. Pa ain't lying in some cold, lonely patch of ground. He's racing with the wind and howling at the moon. I take my pa with me wherever I go."

Michael averted his eyes. Racing with the wind sounded like paradise compared to rotting in a pine box for eternity. The trouble was, he couldn't believe in paradise, much less in God. And he'd never found any tactile proof to convince him that he possessed anything remotely resembling a spirit—despite Eden's belief that he'd killed it.

"You know I ain't ever liked you much," Collie blurted.

Michael braved the boy's hostile stare. "Yes."

" 'Course, *Jamie* thinks you hung the moon."

"Jamie misses his father."

Collie's jaw jutted. "He's got that Luke feller wantin' to marry his ma. He don't need no fathers anymore."

Michael's smile was fleeting. "And you do?"

"I didn't say that. Don't go puttin' words in my mouth."

"I'm sorry."

"Humph."

Collie cocked his head. That suspicious, half-wild stare pierced Michael like an arrow. "I'm man enough to own up when I'm wrong, I reckon."

"What makes you think you've been wrong?"

"I got eyes. Cassidy's back."

Michael sucked in his breath.

"Sera ain't gonna like us interfering, but it's fer her own good. You were right all along about that bastard."

Something in the boy's manner chilled Michael more

than the wind that kicked up the fallen dogwood leaves. "Where is he?"

"Headed to your house, I reckon."

Michael muttered an oath.

"You got a gun?"

Michael froze in midturn on his way to Brutus. "Why would I need a gun?" he demanded, forcing neutrality into his tone.

The boy shrugged. The gesture did little to detract from the canniness that hardened his features. "Rat huntin'."

"Collie . . ." The boy was already loping into the blue-black shadows of the coming night. Michael raised his voice above the wind. "Where are you going?"

But if Collie answered, the words were lost in the eerie scraping of the dogwood's barren branches.

The warmth of the sun was a distant memory as Michael dismounted, slapping Brutus toward the stable. Although Claudia's cottage glowed behind its overgrown hedgerows, every window in his house was dark. Both chimneys were smokeless.

Dread seeped into his bones.

Shoving open the door, Michael fumbled with half-frozen hands to strike a matchsafe and illuminate the foyer. No rosemary or cinnamon wafted from the kitchen hall. Stazzie didn't saunter out of the shadows to greet him with a stretch and a yawn.

"Sera?"

His call reverberated through the two stories, making them sound as hollow as a dry well. He had to force the next name from his lips.

"Eden?"

Facing the woman he loved, the woman who thought

him a coward, would be harder than burying Gabriel.

But the echo of her name sighed into a silence that was broken only by the chiming of the parlor clock. Seven bells.

The general store had long since closed. She should be home by now.

Frowning, he removed the lamp from the wall. He liked to think Collie's talk of guns was the only reason for his growing unease. After all, Rafe was most likely keeping company with Sera—and hopefully, distracting her from any rumor of Cassidy's return. Thus, for the moment, Michael was less worried about his sister than he was about the unusual silence in his house.

He headed for the bedroom, the lamp's circular, saffron glow bobbing at his feet. It was the peculiar absence of Stazzie, he decided, that had triggered his alarm.

"Eden?" he called again.

The door was cracked open; he pushed it wider—and froze. Stazzie's pillow was gone. So was the portmanteau Eden kept under the armoire. A quick inspection of his footlocker and chest of drawers proved that she'd removed her shoes and bonnets, skirts and blouses—in short, everything she owned.

Except those things he'd bought her.

Realization knifed him. He searched for a letter and found a sheaf of paper propped against his shaving bowl.

*I love you too much to watch you waste away your life,* she'd written in a shaky hand. *Since you don't want me, or even need me, I think it's best that I leave.*

He ran his thumb over the ripple where her tear had fallen. Was this some sort of test?

Crumpling the letter in his fist, he crossed to the window. His neighbor's guest room was lit. Perhaps Eden had merely fled to Claudia. Who else might be occupying that spare bedroom? Not Collie, certainly. The boy had yet to overcome his aversion to "fancy living." Although he'd agreed to do chores in exchange for shooting lessons and board, he'd flat-out refused Claudia's offer of a feather mattress, instead making his bed with her nag.

Michael scowled. That the spinster and the orphan had struck up a friendship still dumbfounded him. He didn't approve of Claudia's efforts to school the boy in gun play. In fact, he'd argued vehemently against the arrangement.

"Mind your dadblasted business, Michael," Claudia had flared, her chin jutting and her chest thrusting forward like a Bantam rooster's. "That boy'll turn fifteen come November. It's high time he traded his peashooter for a Peacemaker."

"Peacemaker my eye," he'd retorted, secretly impressed that the seventy-five-year-old curmudgeon could do battle with him without suffering mottled skin or shortened breath. Andrew Mallory's heart tonic was a phenomenon. "Collie's got his father's blood running through his veins. Why do you think Sheriff Truitt confiscated every firearm MacAffee owned?"

"Collie's a good boy, and you ain't got no right to deny him his passage to manhood."

"*Deny* him? I'm trying to see he lives long enough to *be* a man."

But because Michael had no legal right to assert his guardianship, he'd lost that argument. Collie had been eager for Claudia's shooting lessons. Unfortunately, the more proficient the boy became as a marksman, the less interest he showed in the veterinary trade that Michael had hoped he'd pursue.

Muttering an oath, Michael dropped the curtain. He recalled Collie's eyes, as hard and gray as the barrel of the scattergun he'd carried. Did the boy mean to force a showdown with Cassidy?

His head throbbing with a low-level pain he'd come to recognize as a warning, Michael headed for his neighbor's house. Leaves swatted his face and hands; muffled laughter whipped past him on the rising wind. He braced himself on Claudia's doorstep. The gaiety emanating from her kitchen beyond made him feel more intruder than neighbor, more outcast than brother.

Still, he wasn't a man who shirked his responsibilities. He rapped twice and pushed in.

The blast of warmth that assailed him was far more welcoming than the silence.

Sera's lips formed a startled O. Rafe arched a tawny eyebrow. Claudia squinted and scowled, while Eden averted her gaze, twisting her hands in her lap.

"Dadblast it, Michael, close the door," Claudia growled.

The wind yanked it out of his hands, slamming it so hard, the windows rattled.

Sera gasped in irritation, jumping up with potholders to peek inside the oven. "For heaven's sake, Michael, are you trying to flatten Rafe's welcome-home cake?"

"Or tear the house down," Claudia growled, tugging her pipestem from her teeth. "Between you and Collie blowin' in here like black blizzards, I ain't gonna have nuthin' but *toothpicks* left for walls—"

"Where is Collie?" he interrupted, his own irritation getting the better of him as he watched his wife train her gaze on anybody but him.

"Gone rat huntin'," Claudia said. " 'Course, I told him a shotgun would shear a little bitty varmint clean in half."

Michael bit back an oath, his worst fears confirmed—fears that he didn't dare divulge in the presence of Sera and Eden.

"You'll have to blame someone else, brother," Rafe drawled. "I haven't been here long enough to be a bad influence on the boy."

Michael scowled. *Always the smart-aleck.* If he'd had nothing better to do, he would have taken Rafe aside and demanded what his intentions were, particularly toward Eden. Michael considered it no small coincidence that he'd found his charming, devil-may-care brother sitting cozily beside his wife twice in one day.

Fortunately for Rafe, Michael didn't have time to indulge in their sibling rivalry.

"Eden." He turned to face her, steeling himself against his surge of hurt, against any loss of composure that would make him a target for his brother's rapier wit. He didn't have time to dally. And yet, he couldn't walk out the door without at least trying to bridge the distance between him and Eden. What if she fled on the morning stage while he was still hunting for Collie?

"Would you grant me the favor of a private word?"

The reluctance in her manner twisted the knife in his chest. He found himself grinding his teeth as she rose silently and sailed before him down the narrow hallway to the parlor. The sweet, unconscious swaying of her hips sharpened the lover's hunger in him. But then, he'd been smitten by Eden Mallory ever since he'd first laid eyes on her. How he could have fallen in love with an exasperating, seventeen-year-old healer, he'd never know, but what else could explain his heart's secret, eight-year affair with her? She was special in ways that defied understanding; still, it was the little things that were indelibly etched on his mind: her autumn fringe of lashes, the smattering of freckles across her breasts, her fascination with spider webs, the way she twisted her skirts when she was upset.

But when she crossed to the mantel, facing him at last, her hands hung loosely at her sides.

The observation rocked his world.

"Yes, Michael?" she asked quietly.

His palms grew moist. He reached for the cherry-wood doors to buy himself time, and they rolled closed with a raspy *snick*. The only other thing that could be heard above the unnatural tattoo of his pulse was the hissing of the pine log in the hearth.

He let another moment lapse as he struggled to erase the desperation from his features. When he forced himself to face her, he had to compromise, masking his despair with sternness instead of the serenity he'd been striving for.

"I want you to come home."

"I can't do that."

"You're my wife."

"I'd thought you'd forgotten."

His frown was wary. "Meaning?"

"My God, Michael," she whispered. "That you could stand before me and pretend not to know what I mean, is, perhaps, your cruelest blow yet."

"I never meant to hurt you—"

"But you have. Deeply."

He swallowed. While it was true he couldn't be the husband she wanted, the husband she *deserved*, he'd tried to be the mentor she so desperately needed. There were times when he'd challenged her medical opinions, playing devil's advocate, for instance, on the days that Jamie had complained of a sore throat and Amanda had swelled up with hives. But Michael had done so to teach Eden that a doctor couldn't earn her patients' trust until she learned to stand by her diagnoses. He'd wanted to encourage her independence, so he'd made her responsible for treating minor maladies. He'd even supported her quest to patent her father's heart tonic by writing to colleagues in Cincinnati, Chicago, and New York, where the country's most prominent patent medicine companies operated. He'd been hoping to surprise her with good news.

But now it looked like his attempts to make his bride a self-reliant widow had backfired. Eden had gathered the courage to walk out his door.

"You can't forgive me, is that it?"

Her chin quivered. "Is that why you've come? To ask my forgiveness?"

He blew out his breath. Hell no. He'd never done a damned thing but try to provide for her. And he'd been called a coward for it.

On the other hand, she obviously wanted his apology.

He conceded, trying not to sound as grudging as he felt. "I'm sorry you're unhappy. But I told you how it would be before we married. In the chancellory, I gave you your chance to back out. Instead, you swore an oath before God. 'In sickness and health, till death do us part.' That's what you promised."

"I know what I promised, Michael." As soft as her voice was, he could hear its underlying bitterness. "You promised things, too. Namely, to be my husband. But I can't remember the last time you shared my bed."

He was surprised. "Is that what this is all about?"

"I know it's not sickness that keeps you from . . . from lying with me."

*Jesus.* Relief flooded him so fast, he was hard-pressed not to laugh. She was *jealous!*

"Eden, honey, I have never been unfaithful to you."

Her hands splayed on her hips. "You mean to tell me that all those times you disappeared, never once giving me a good reason, you weren't really rendezvousing with Bonnie?"

"Good God. Of course I wasn't."

Her eyes narrowed. "Or with anyone else?"

"Eden," he said huskily, his throat aching as the words struggled through, "I swear. There has never been any other woman but you. I love you."

Tears brimmed, spilling crystal rivulets down her cheeks. "Y-you do?"

"Yes." His heart swelled with the admission. How could she not know it? How many times had he whispered it as she'd slept? How many times had he breathed it into her ear as she'd dreamed? In truth, he died a little each minute he denied himself her touch. After she woke and went about her business, he would slip into her bedroom and inhale the scent of her pillowcase. He kept an oriole feather in a dry inkwell at his office, and a milkweed pod in his valise, just so he could recall the wonder he'd felt to be with her on their fateful Independence Day. How could she not know how he warred with himself, trying to keep the burden of his legacy from her womb?

"Then why—"

"Can't you guess?"

A sob bubbled past her lips. "I don't care if I get sick too."

"My God. If I had ever thought that was possible, I

would never have allowed you to marry me."

"Then why won't you let me touch you?"

She edged forward, her eyes pleading. A cyclone of needs and desires, regrets and fears, funneled through him. It took every ounce of will he possessed to stagger away from her fingers.

"I can't. Don't you see? I'm trying to spare you!"

"S-spare me?"

"By the time you and Sera split my property, there won't be enough left to make a good dowry. And a baby will only make courtship more difficult."

"*What?*"

"A bachelor your age won't consider a widow with a child as desirable a match as a maid."

She halted dead in her tracks, her ears growing red enough to steam. "Michael Jones, that is the most egotistical excuse I have ever heard in my life! How dare you make decisions about babies without consulting me?"

He blinked, stunned by this about-face. "I am your husband."

"Yes, my *husband!* Not my warden. Stop punishing me for marrying you!"

"It was never my intent—"

"Did it ever occur to you that bearing your child might be the greatest happiness of my life?"

He jolted, knocked off balance by such an inconceivable truth. "You're not being practical."

"*Practical?* All this time, I thought you had taken another lover! I thought I didn't *please* you. Do you know what that was like for me?"

Shame burned its way to his soul. "I did what I thought was best for you."

"That's because you're just arrogant enough to believe, *really believe*, you know how to live my life better than I do." The tear she flung off her cheek splashed him. It felt like acid on his chin. "You treat us all like children. You take care of everybody but yourself. Whether you realize it or not, you've been using me, Sera, and Collie as your excuse. As long as you're trying to run our lives, you don't have to take a good, hard look at your own."

She pushed past him, wrenching open the doors, then paused, as if thinking better of storming out.

"Ever since I was seventeen and you saved me from Black Bart," she said raggedly, "I've loved you. You've always been my hero. But the difference between you and me, Michael, is that I don't expect you to be infallible. I just expect you to be a man."

"I'm sorry—"

"No! No more apologies," she choked, grabbing hold of his coat lapels and shaking him with both fists. "Just live life—your *own* life, damn you—before it's too late!"

She turned with a sob, knocking aside the hands he reached to embrace her with, and fled up Claudia's stairs.

His next breath shuddered through him. Slumping against the doorjamb, he watched in agony as all that he treasured, all that he held worthwhile, disappeared from his view—and perhaps from his life.

"I declare. That might have gone better, don't you think?"

Michael grimaced, spying his kid sister as she crept from the shadows, shoving her face up against the stairwell's balusters, much as she used to do as a three-year-old. Only this time, she hadn't been eavesdropping on their parents' argument. She'd been eavesdropping on his.

"You heard?" he asked bleakly, too dejected to feel guilty.

"It was hard not to."

He sighed, rubbing his temples. They were throbbing with a vengeance now. "Will you speak to her for me?"

"Absolutely. I didn't go to all this trouble to find you the perfect wife so you could chase her away."

She climbed two steps, apparently thought better of it, and hurried back down to throw her arms around his neck. "Honestly, Michael," she whispered against his cheek. "We all love you. It's just a little harder when you're being such a *bear*."

He smiled faintly, watching her bound up the stairs. All dimples and mischief, she turned on the landing and blew him a kiss.

*Billy Cassidy isn't fit to shine that girl's shoes.*

The thought sobered him instantly. He'd forgotten Collie and his other mission. Michael just prayed he'd have another chance to talk sense into Eden, because he didn't dare wait around for her to calm down while Collie was running loose with a shotgun.

With Sera and Eden safely out of earshot, Michael waded back through Claudia's habitual smoke cloud on his way to the kitchen. He found his brother and neighbor huddled like conspirators over their coffee mugs, Rafe's golden head nearly bumping Claudia's silver one. Michael wasn't sure whether his shadow or his footstep alerted them to his presence. But he didn't like the accusation in the pair of eyes that rose to challenge him.

Once again, he found himself struggling with his temper. All Rafe had to do was arch that insolent brow—like he was doing now—and Michael wanted to explode. Never mind that his black sheep half-brother hadn't said a word. Or that ten years should have been long enough to heal old wounds. Standing there, Michael was twenty-one again, facing down the nineteen-year-old upstart who'd dared to show his face after a five-year absence and had announced he was taking Gabriel to Texas so the child could have his wish to be a cowboy before he died. All the pain, all the fury, all the futility Michael had been feeling for those two long years as he'd watched Gabriel's decline, had culminated in a release of such volcanic proportions that Rafe was lucky he was alive today.

Michael supposed Rafe still had good reason to hate him. God knew, if he were Rafe, forgiveness wouldn't have come easily to *him*.

"Do you have a gun?" he blurted.

Wariness flitted through Rafe's mirrorlike gaze. He was too accomplished an actor, however, to drop his sardonic mask. "What would I need a gun for, brother?"

"To protect your sister from an outlaw."

Claudia's face darkened. "Cassidy's back?"

Michael nodded.

"Why didn't you say so in the first place?"

"Because there's more, Claudia." He fought down his own agitation, doing his best to gentle his tone. "Collie's gone looking for him."

*"What?"* The old woman turned nearly as gray as her hair. "Cassidy is Collie's rat?"

Michael glanced at Rafe. Judging by his brother's narrowed stare, Michael suspected Rafe had grasped the urgency of the situation.

"I'm going to find the boy. Talk some sense into him. In the meantime, I need you both to stay here, in case Cassidy comes looking for Sera—or worse, she gets wind he's in town. Rafe, if I'm not back tomorrow,

you'll have to keep her occupied. Especially come sun-
down. She'll try to sneak out her window."

"Why wouldn't you be back tomorrow?" Rafe demanded.

Michael hesitated. Claudia's gnarled hands were actually quaking. Never had he seen her looking so helpless, so . . . old. It bothered him more than words could
describe. She'd come to dote on the boy. If Collie did
something to get himself killed—with Claudia's gun,
yet—Michael knew it would destroy her.

He forced a smile. "I'm due at the orphanage tomorrow morning. Sometimes, I'm detained there all day."

"You're a poor liar," Claudia croaked. "Do you have
a gun?"

Michael cringed inwardly. He was in the habit of
patching up men, not plugging them with bullets. Still,
she had a valid point. "I keep a .45 in my office."

"And when's the last time you oiled it, much less
fired it?"

He opened his mouth, but she cut him off.

"Never mind." Shoving her chair back, she stumped
to the sink, tossed a sleepy Stazzie off the windowsill,
then knocked over a couple of spice bottles to reach for
the ammunition box behind them. Next, she grabbed
her own six-shooter and holster, which were hanging
too high for even Vandy's curious paws, from a peg
amidst the dried herbs on the rafters. "Here." She thrust
them both into Michael's hands. "The safety's on. Try
to keep it that way."

Michael hardened his jaw to stave off his uneasiness.
A preacher's boy–turned-doctor didn't have much occasion to fire a gun.

Rafe must have drawn a similar conclusion. He rose
as Michael headed for the door.

"Might I suggest," he said casually, barring Michael's way, "that your first stop be the sheriff's office?"

Michael shook his head, reaching around Rafe for the knob. "Truitt will throw Collie in jail without asking questions."

"Better jail than a gallows."

Michael's heart skipped a beat. As much as he hated the idea, he knew Rafe was right.

The trouble was, Collie would never forgive him.

He yanked open the door. The wind slammed into him like a cold fist. Shivering, he tugged up his coat collar and grimaced at the roiling, charcoal sky. It had already been one hell of a night.

Now it promised to get worse.

# Chapter 14

❦

Lightning flashed false daylight, and thunder battered the window sash, rousing Eden from an exhausted doze. She shivered, for the coals in the bedwarmer had long since burned out. She guessed dawn was an hour away.

Sitting gingerly in the ghostly half-light, she tried not to disturb Sera, who sprawled at her side. How her friend could have slept a wink through last night's cacophony mystified Eden, since, at one point, she'd thought Claudia's roof would blow off. She hated storms. They always seemed to portend some dire circumstance.

But lightning had been spitting long before Michael slammed into Claudia's kitchen last night, so Eden tried to put her superstitions behind her. Hopefully, the confrontation with her husband was the worst that would come of this storm. The thunderheads sounded like they were finally chugging over the mountain. With any luck, sunshine would soon warm the valley, and a crystal-clear autumn day would follow.

The trouble was, she was dreading this day almost as much as she'd dreaded last night's storm.

327

With Stazzie weaving sleepily through her ankles, Eden crept into the dressing room to tug on a skirt and blouse. The only reason she didn't dare pad to the kitchen in her night wrapper was her brother-in-law. Claudia had insisted Rafe sleep in her house, rather than a hotel, and for all Eden knew, Rafe was already on the prowl, hunting for Arbuckles and jelly muffins. It wasn't that she didn't trust Rafe; quite the contrary. Last night, she'd been so desperate for a sympathetic ear, that when she'd found him building a fire in Claudia's parlor, she'd spilled her heart to him. Although she'd divulged confidences about Michael she'd had no right to divulge, her excuse was that she loved him. And that she worried he was too stubborn to take the first step to reconcile with his brother.

God knew, he hadn't been terribly conciliatory to her last night.

She sighed. As angry as his reasoning had made her, she'd believed his claim that he'd been abstinent rather than unfaithful. She'd been more than a little ashamed, too, to realize what an appalling image she'd had of her husband, that he'd seed his bastard in a widow who was already rearing a fatherless child. Knowing Michael's overblown sense of responsibility, Eden wondered how she could have thought that he cared so little for the price Bonnie would pay if he died. As exasperating as her husband could be, Eden loved him even more to realize he had shouldered the consequences and leashed his desire to spare her the burden of raising his baby.

Still, Michael had to learn that his shoulders were only so broad—and that she possessed a perfectly sturdy pair herself. She just wasn't sure that trotting back to his kitchen and his bed was the best way to teach him those lessons.

Hurrying along the chilly corridor, she tried not to trip over Stazzie as she descended the stairs to the indisputably warmest room in the house: Claudia's kitchen. To her surprise, her aunt was already seated at the sawbuck table. Her sparrowlike frame was hunched beneath the weight of a patchwork quilt, and her bony fist trembled as she sipped a mug whose contents looked more like Texas crude than coffee. Eden grew concerned. It wasn't like Claudia to let her hair hang in limp strands. More to the point, she couldn't ever remember seeing Claudia looking so grim, gray, or haggard.

"What's wrong?" she greeted, her eyes straying anxiously to the bottle of tonic at Claudia's elbow.

Claudia started. Catching her aunt unawares was another telltale sign, and it worried Eden.

Claudia, however, was too canny to stay disadvantaged for long. She pasted on her habitual scowl. "This danged roof, that's what. I paid that MacAffee brat three whole shooting lessons to fix the leaks. Hell, that kid's worse at carpentry than gunplay. You seen him?"

"Uh . . . no." Eden doubted the roof was the problem. "But it's still early, don't you think?"

"I went to drag him by the ear outta my hayloft, but he'd already run off," Claudia said. "You suppose he's hiding at his pa's shack? Last night weren't any kind of night to be holed up on a mountain," she muttered to herself.

Eden crossed to the stove. Furtively watching her kinswoman, she tossed in another log. Despite the tonic at her elbow—or maybe because of it—Claudia didn't seem to be suffering any coronary distress. "Are you worried about Collie?"

"Nah. Just want to take the work he owes me outta his hide. Here now," she added irritably, glaring under the table. Stazzie was butting her head against Claudia's ankles. "Danged varmint thinks I'm gonna give her milk. Scat. *Scat*, you mangy cat!"

Eden giggled as Stazzie, rumbling affectionately, flopped like a rag poppet across Claudia's heavily darned socks.

"See, Auntie, Stazzie's helping you stay warm."

"Yer furball's giving me fleas, that's what," Claudia said, scratching sullenly at her calf. "And that coon of Collie's is worse. Say, where'd that critter run off to? I've been meaning to make me a hat."

"Oh, stop it, " Eden said, spying Vandy snoozing in the copper soup kettle hanging over the wash tub. She shook her head. It really was odd that Collie hadn't come back for his pet. He knew that Stazzie and Vandy were likely to tear the house down if left unwatched for a solitary second. They feuded worse than Rafe and Michael.

*And speaking of Michael . . .*

"You seen that husband of yours?"

Eden winced. Usually it was Sera who did the mind reading.

"No."

"Humph. Thought he'd be back by now. Maybe he holed up at Widow Witherspoon's last night. He would have needed somewhere warm to sleep in that typhoon. When are you two gonna kiss and make up?"

Eden blushed, distracted from asking why Michael had ridden to the orphanage. "Really, Auntie." She poured herself a cup of coffee.

"Don't 'Really, Auntie' me. I want nieces and nephews to bounce on my knee. I ain't gettin' any younger, you know. It's high time you and Michael stopped squabbling and started acting like man and wife."

Eden winced, recalling the letter she'd left her husband. Still, what choice had she had? She'd told Claudia how he'd slammed out the door, refusing, as usual, to listen to advice about his health, Rafe, or anything else. His stubbornness was making her miserable. "It's not like I haven't *tried* to be a good wife to him."

"Bein' a good wife ain't the same thing as being a good pretender."

She frowned, sitting across from Claudia. "What do you mean?"

"I mean this problem you think you're having with Michael ain't about him. It's about you."

"*Me?*"

Claudia nodded, her deepset eyes disconcertingly keen above her grizzled cheeks. "It takes two to argue, child. The minute you started pretending you didn't know about herbs, or healing, or anything else that might cost you yer man's approval, you started living a false life."

"I hardly think—"

Claudia snorted. "Now who ain't listenin' to advice? You want the truth, girlie? Michael ain't the one makin' you miserable. You are. God gave you certain gifts, and He expects you to use 'em."

"But I *did* try to use my gifts! I tried to be a good healer."

"Sure. You did it yer pa's way. You did it that Injun woman's way. But you never did it yer own way. You got a knack for helping folks that can't be bottled or prescribed. Someday Michael's gonna wake up and see that. Just like I did."

Eden shook her head, her throat constricting. "He won't even try my tonics."

"So you're gonna let that fool husband of yours make you doubt yerself? Even though your remedies cured Collie, Jamie, Amanda, half a dozen coons, and God only knows how many other critters?"

A tear slid down Eden's cheek. Claudia reached over and awkwardly patted her arm.

"There now," she said, her voice growing rough with discomfort. "I don't mean to say nuthin' against Michael. I ain't forgettin' he's fightin' a battle he don't think he can win. But don't you see, child? He's scared. Scared you won't be able to go on. Deep in his soul, he wants to know you've got the gumption to make a life without him. That's why you've got to stand up to him. You've got to prove that while you love him, and you want him, you don't need him by your side."

Eden swallowed a sob, averting her eyes. She'd never stopped to consider that Michael might worry about her future, thinking she lacked backbone. All this time, while he'd been challenging her diagnoses and refusing to heed her medical advice, she'd believed he was contemptuous of her methods, and more importantly, of her. The great irony in this misunderstanding was that while she'd tried never to cross him, thinking she was being a loyal wife, she'd only roused his frustration. Was it any wonder they'd grown so far apart?

A long silence passed while she furtively wiped away tears. Maybe there was still a chance for their marriage, if she dared to be the healer she'd always wanted to be.

"Is there anything else bothering you?" she asked meekly. "Besides my marriage troubles, I mean."

Stazzie jumped up on the table to lick a dribble from

the pitcher of cream. Claudia reached absently to pet her.

"Cassidy's back."

Eden's heart slammed painfully into her ribs. "Does Sera know?"

"You think she would've spent all night in this house if she did?"

Eden uneasily stirred her coffee. Sera didn't confide secrets the way she used to. Still, Eden liked to think her friend would have told her if she were contemplating . . . well, more than a hug and a kiss from Billy Cassidy. "Michael will be livid when he finds out."

"Who d'ya think told me?"

Eden bit her lip, glancing toward the kitchen window and the Jones house, its chimney tops gilded by streaks of dawn.

"Did Michael . . . um, say what he might do?"

"I voted on tar and feathers weeks ago, but nobody listened to me."

Something about Claudia's evasiveness made Eden doubly uneasy. "Auntie? What did Michael do?"

"Nothing yet, God willing."

"I'm not sure I follow—"

"Collie took my scattergun. Gone to hunt rats, he said. Who's the only two-legged rat you know worth huntin' on a night like the last one?"

Eden choked. *Cassidy.*

A board creaked in the hallway.

"Eden?"

Eden and Claudia both jumped. Their stares locked.

"I declare." Sera stumbled into the room, rumpled and yawning. "It's like an icebox in that bedroom. You might have told me you were waking instead of leaving me to freeze to death."

"Serves you right," Claudia rallied, making a furtive sign for Eden to keep quiet. "In my day, young girls were up before dawn, gathering eggs."

Sera rolled her eyes, meandering to the pantry. "We don't have chickens, Aunt Claudia."

"You got a horse to feed, don't ya?"

"Brutus is Michael's horse. And even if he wasn't, I'd hire a hand. Maybe *two* hands. That's what Billy does on that big ol' hacienda of his."

"Told you that, did he?"

Sera cracked open a jar of marmalade. At the sound— or perhaps the smell—Vandy's snout poked out of the kettle and his forepaws hooked over the rim.

"Well, you can hardly run a ranch house the size of Louisville's train depot without a servant or two," Sera said loftily.

Vandy dove from the kettle and scampered down the plumbing to tug the hem of Sera's nightgown. She ignored his plea.

"Besides." Arms now laden with butter, jam, and cornpone, she flopped onto the bench beside Eden. "Down in Texas, the wives of wealthy ranchers *never* gather their own eggs, much less cook them."

Vandy, however, was not to be ignored. He vaulted onto the bench and clambered over Eden's lap, making her slosh coffee all over the table.

"*Vandy!*"

Eden's scolding went unheeded. Tiny black fingers snatched the cornbread that Sera was doctoring. She squealed, dumping a tablespoon of marmalade down her robe as Vandy scampered across her thighs and fled with his prize.

"Ugh!" Her cheeks mottling, Sera fished an orange glob from her decolletage and shook it from her fingers.

"That coon needs to be spanked. After that, he needs to be dunked in a pennyroyal bath. The last time Vandy sat on my lap, I got fleas. And yesterday, after I caught him chewing a hole through my straw boater, I found a tick crawling along the headband!"

"Probably got it from the cat."

"Auntie, Stazzie does *not* have..." Eden's voice trailed.

*Ticks?*

Her flash of insight was followed by an unbidden prickling that crept over her skin and made her heart trip.

Although she herself had never treated such a case, Colorado trappers often complained of headaches, high fever, chills, pains, and growing weakness. Rocky Mountain spotted fever, as it was called, was caused by ticks. It usually disappeared after about two weeks, but recovery could take several months. Even so, the illness was serious. If left untreated, heart or brain damage could result.

She frowned, her mind racing.

Ticks could cause other problems, too. Papa had once described a rare case. A crippled outcast of the Ute tribe, who earned her keep sewing rabbit and squirrel pelts for East Coast curiosity seekers near the reservation, had suffered bouts of headache, muscle ache, cough, sore throat, eye pain, and numbness. There appeared to be no rhyme or reason for the illness; it would manifest every couple of weeks, causing what Papa had termed "relapsing fever." Although Papa had thrown up his hands—the squaw had refused to let a "white medicine man" examine her—Talking Raven eventually earned the Ute's trust. Acting on a hunch, the Cherokee prescribed a powerful blood cleanser, echinacea, St. John's wort, and goldenseal among the ingredients. The Ute's recovery had been practically instantaneous.

Eden grew so excited, she began to shake.

What if Michael weren't suffering from some disorder of his central nervous system, as he believed? What if he were suffering from . . . tick fever?

"Good heavens, Eden. The whole table's rattling. Did something crawl down your shirt?"

She blushed at Sera's complaint. "Ticks! I mean, no. But it could be! I have to find Michael."

Claudia arched a brow as Eden jumped up, running for the gray woolen coat she'd left hanging on the hall tree. "That ain't so smart, considering."

"Considering what?" Sera demanded.

But Eden didn't hear the rest. She was too busy shoving her arms into her sleeves and running out the door. Somehow, she had to find Michael and convince him to take the blood-cleansing tonic she already had on the window shelf in her kitchen.

But as she threw open the back gate, a desperate pounding shattered the crisp, autumn dawn. "Doc!"

Eden slid to a halt, her heart racing. The voice, pitched high with fright, sounded like Jamie's.

"Open up, Doc!"

She hurried around the corner of the house to find the boy all but hurtling himself against the front door.

"Jamie, what is it? Why aren't you in school?" she asked as he spun around, wild-eyed and tear-streaked.

"He found out! You gotta help me!"

Eden gripped his shoulders, steadying him as best she could. "It's okay, honey. Who found out? About what?"

"Gunther did! About my animals!"

Eden's stomach roiled as Jamie grabbed her hand and began dragging her toward the porch steps. "You gotta help," he panted. "You gotta help me hide them 'fore ol' Gunther gets there!"

"But how—"

"Cassidy! He told. And now Gunther's gunning for Collie!"

Michael jerked awake, his lungs heaving, his pulse pounding.

*Jesus.*

He sat quickly, shaking enough to make his narrow cot squeak. In the pale streams of morning that filtered through the chinks in the Cumberland Orphanage's barn, he stared at his hands. He turned them over twice, just to be certain.

*Still flesh. Still bone. Thank God.*

He squeezed his eyes closed, gulping breath after shuddering breath. The dream had seemed so real. Too real.

*"Where am I?"* he'd demanded of the beautiful young man who'd walked out of the iridescent pink and gold mists veiling the eastern sky.

The young man smiled. Dark-haired and fair-complected, with eyes bright enough to rival the sun, he seemed familiar somehow. And yet his sculpted features were so breathtaking, so hauntingly ethereal, that Michael trembled, hard-pressed not to drop to his knees. Surely only the Son of God could be so beautiful.

The youth laughed, as if knowing his thoughts. "I'm Gabriel," he'd greeted in a rich, liquid tenor. "Your brother," he added wryly, "not the angel."

Michael blinked, dumbfounded. Was this some sort of sick joke? Gabriel was dead. Ten years ago, God had sent a lung plague to rob him of his youth. Murdered at twelve, that's what Gabriel had been. But this youth looked to be—

"Twenty-two. Yes, that would be about right, wouldn't it?" The youth grinned as Michael gaped. "Normally, we don't pay much attention to time here in heaven, but I figured you'd listen to me a whole lot better if I appeared . . . well, older than twelve."

*Incredible.* Michael latched on to anger to snuff out his rising fear. "Are you reading my mind?"

"I've had more pleasant assignments, I assure you. But since I volunteered to be your guardian angel, there's no helping it, I suppose. Hey," Gabriel continued glibly, "now that we're on the subject: Would you mind concentrating a little less on the doom and gloom?"

"This is ridiculous."

"No more ridiculous than you walking around blaming God for all the misery you've heaped on yourself. I assure you, nobody up here determines your future. That's your job. You make all the choices. We just try to steer you clear of the ones you'd have trouble living with."

"So now you're telling me you *communicate* with me?"

"Sure. All the time. You just don't listen. Lucky for you, Sera does. And Eden does too, to an extent."

"What do you mean . . . to an extent?" he asked suspiciously.

"Well . . ." Gabriel shoved his hands into the front pockets of his blue jeans. For the first time, Michael noticed his self-professed guardian angel was wearing his kid brother's favorite red neckerchief and blue gingham shirt—only several sizes larger than the originals, of course.

"Usually I've got my hands full just trying to hammer truth into your skull," Gabriel said, "but every now and then, while you're sleeping, I can sneak off to chat with Talking Raven. She's the one Eden listens to best, so if I need you to hear something—like, you're a stubborn old billy goat and need to have your head examined—Talking Raven whispers it into her ear, and she tells you."

"Eden has never called me a billy goat."

"She will."

Michael scowled, more hurt than miffed. How dare his guardian angel tell his wife to call him names?

"I suppose you and Talking Raven told her to find a new husband, too?"

Gabriel sighed, shaking his head. "If you only knew how much she loves you, you'd kick yourself right off this cloud."

Michael started, noticing for the first time that Gabriel was buried up to his calves in fluffy white nothingness. "Where the devil am I?"

"I told you. Heaven. See how you don't listen?"

"But . . ." His voice cracked. "If that's true, then I'm dead!"

"Nah. Well . . ." Gabriel seemed to change his mind. "If you keep wanting to be dead, we can help you get *really* sick. But the fact is, Eden's in a fix. She needs you to ride out to that animal orphanage before she does. So if you don't put your spirit back inside your body—"

"My *spirit?*"

"Sure. You still don't think you own one? Look at your hands."

Uneasily, Michael spread his palms and nearly bit his tongue in two. His fingers, wrists, and forearms—even his chest and legs—were crackling currents of white.

*Pure energy. Like the cloud.*

Shuddering again on his cot, Michael clenched his

fists. He dug his fingernails into his palms until he felt the good old earthbound pain of flesh.

*It was a dream. Just a dream.*

*Stubborn old billy goat.* The unbidden thought flooded his mind.

He bolted upright, and chills scuttled down his spine. Youthful laughter rang in his ears before it faded into the twitter of sparrows and the jangle of halter rings. Brutus shook his head again, gazing curiously at him from the adjacent stall.

Michael smiled weakly. "Remind me never again to visit Gabriel's grave and then try to sleep on a stomach full of Lydia's chicken dumplings," he told his horse.

Brutus snorted.

Michael raked a hand through his hair. The act jogged his memory.

*Collie. What the devil am I doing, wasting time thinking about dreams?*

He reached for his saddle.

If he hadn't been riding Brutus, Michael would have searched all night long for the boy. However, he wasn't callous enough to force his horse to weather the storm. Blue Thunder Mountain hadn't been named for its hospitality in weather. Even nestled in the foothills, a good five miles away, the orphanage had been pommeled by howling winds and rain. The lightning displays had sent most of the children diving under their beds. Michael had hoped that Collie would come down off the mountain to find sturdier shelter. Even though the boy hated the orphanage, it was still the closest outpost between Bartholomew MacAffee's hovel and town.

But Collie hadn't shown his face on Lydia's doorstep. And that had worried Michael.

The odds were good the boy wasn't in jail at this

hour. Although Michael had paid a call on Truitt, as Rafe had urged, the storm had probably chased the sheriff and his deputies indoors before they could collar the boy.

Now the question was, had the bad weather stopped Collie?

Michael led Brutus into the blooming golds of dawn. If Collie had waited out the storm, there was nothing keeping him from his "rat hunt" this morning. Michael had to find the boy before Collie found Cassidy.

Or a bullet found Collie.

As if to echo his thought, a shotgun blast rolled off the hills to the northwest. Brutus stomped. Michael strained his senses. He had no earthly reason to think of the animal orphanage in that moment. But he did.

Had Collie fired the gun? Had he gone at first light to see how his wards survived the storm and found one that needed to be put out of its misery?

His heart speeding—for no logical reason—Michael vaulted into the saddle and spurred Brutus for the road.

It wasn't until he'd cleared the first ridge two miles later that he spied an ominous black tendril of smoke curling over the white oaks and pines.

# Chapter 15

**T**he gunshot drove Eden's heart into her throat.

 Even Jamie, cradled in her arms astride Claudia's nag, jumped as if he'd been hit. The whole forest hushed, and for a moment, there was nothing but the mare's labored breathing, Jamie's chattering teeth, and the ominous rumble of that dying echo.

"It came from the clearing," Jamie whispered, twisting anxiously beneath their wool blanket.

Eden did her best to soothe him, to soothe Nag, as Claudia called her mare. The beast was skittering as if the blast had gone off right under her silly nose. "Collie was probably just practicing."

They both held their breath, listening. But the only sound beneath the stunned canopy of pine was the whispering of the needles in the wind.

"I dunno. If it were just Collie practicing," Jamie said, tilting his head so his coonskin tickled her nose, "there should've been another shot."

Eden feared he was right. But she didn't dare say so. The boy—Nag, too—had been jumpy enough during the six-mile ride.

"Then I'm sure there's some other logical explanation," she said firmly, spurring Nag forward.

"Yeah. Gunther."

"Jamie Harragan," she scolded, "don't be a goose."

The boy grew quiet after that, but his heart pounded harder against her forearm with each step Nag took during that last half mile.

"Do you smell smoke?" he blurted finally.

The wind had shifted. Nag was snorting, tossing her head.

"Maybe Collie's cooking breakfast."

"I don't think so," Jamie said in dire tones. "A fire would make him easy to track, and he's supposed to be hiding out from Gunther."

Eden's nerves tensed another notch at this news.

"Well, there's only one way to find out," she said in her best matter-of-fact voice. Ignoring the queasiness in her gut, she urged Nag faster up the trail.

It was the stench of blood that hit her senses first.

Jamie jumped down, running for the clearing. She hurried after him, dread making her knees wobble. She heard him gasp, saw him slide to a halt.

Muddy boots, attached to scarecrow-like legs, protruded from the door of the shack.

She collided with Jamie's spine, pressing her glove to her mouth.

The body—a male—had fallen face down, struck from behind by a gunblast. Meanwhile, dancing macabrely around him, flames licked the inside of the shack.

"No!" Jamie cried, charging for his trapped animals.

"Jamie, wait!" Ripping off her riding gauntlets, Eden ran to the man's side and fell to her knees.

*My God. My God. It's Gunther.* Nausea hit her so fast, her head spun. *Somebody shot Gunther!*

"Collie, what have you done?" she half sobbed, trying

to drag the taxidermist to safety. *"Jamie!"* she shouted again, struggling for a grip on the man's slippery boots. She nearly fell on her buttocks as her heels lost their purchase in the mud.

Jamie staggered out of a billowing cloud. Coughing, his face flushed with heat, he gripped a rabbit cage in each fist. "They're gonna all burn!"

"We have to help Gunther!"

Somehow, she convinced him. Somehow, they dragged the body over the threshold. Blood oozed into the mud. Cinders sizzled on the wet ground.

She dropped Gunther's legs near the tree stump. "I can't find a pulse," she choked, pushing aside stringy gray hair with a trembling hand.

"Ain't he breathin'?" Jamie panted.

She couldn't bring herself to examine the wound below Gunther's shoulder blades. "I-I don't know."

"You made me touch a *dead man?*"

Jamie shrieked, retreating so hastily, he tripped over the stump. She squeezed her eyes closed. Somehow, she mustered the courage to roll the taxidermist. The shotgun had blown a hole clear through his other side. She might have retched if she hadn't been so desperate to find some sign of life in him. She squeezed his wrists, listened for his breath.

There was nothing.

"Miss Eden!" Jamie cried again from the direction of the shack. "Help me!"

Shaking nearly too hard to stand, Eden knotted her skirts above her knees; she forced her feet back past the blood-spattered ruts that the corpse had made in the mud. The shack's roof was a bonfire now. It was climbing dangerously close to the pine eaves.

"Open their cages!" Her eyes were watering as she

cleaved a path through the thick, roiling clouds. "They'll know what to do."

But lifting the metal doors wasn't easy. The heat had made the bars blistering hot. She shoved one of her riding gauntlets into Jamie's hand. "Hurry!"

"Where're my hounds?" he shouted at her.

"I don't know!"

The coons paced anxiously; the rabbits huddled wide-eyed and trembling in the rear of their cages. Eden swiped at smoke, at spider webs, at the pine-needle thatch that drooped from the roof. It smoldered into flames near her ears. Dear Lord, how many animals did Jamie have? She'd thought she'd convinced him that Collie couldn't save every whelp Gunther bred.

*Collie, Collie, where are you?*

Behind her, an ominous creaking all but obliterated the clang of a cage. Morgie and Rocky galloped for the door. Harriette chattered, her black eyes nearly red in the half-light. Eden gave up on the latch and grabbed for the handle, hauling the cage outside. When she stumbled, dropping it at her feet, the door sprang open, and Harriette charged after her brothers.

"How many more?" she panted as Jamie passed her, listing under the weight of another rabbit cage.

"Two! Maybe three!"

She gasped for air, halting just beyond the threshold. She didn't think the roof would last much longer.

"Come on!" Jamie dashed past her, fearless in his frenzy to rescue his wards. He'd bottle-fed most of them. He'd named every one. She suspected he'd have to be overcome by smoke to sacrifice a single coon or bunny.

Gritting her teeth, she forged inside. The ancient timbers were groaning. The door was consumed by the blaze. She snatched up a rabbit, kicking aside its cage. This would have to be their final trip.

"Come on, Jamie!"

"Where's Millie?"

"I don't know!" She grabbed the boy's collar.

"We have to find her!"

"There's no time."

"But she'll burn!"

Unable to battle both the squirming rabbit and the struggling boy, Eden lost her hold on the bunny. It thumped to the ground, loosing a spray of embers, before its long claws clattered on the floorboards and it scrambled for freedom.

"Millie, Millie, where are you?"

"Jamie, please! We have to leave *now*."

The sound of shredding wood made them both gasp and turn. The door toppled, belching cinders, smoke and flames. Jamie screamed. Eden spun him around, doing her best to shield his face and hair.

"Jamie! Are you all right?"

He coughed. Then he sobbed. "My arm got burned!"

Panic gnawed at her reason. The glowing red inferno that had once been the door was wedged diagonally across the exit. There was no other way out.

"You'll have to go outside. Put some water on it."

"But—"

"There aren't any more bunnies, Jamie. We're the only ones left." Her hands were shaking as she wrapped her coat around him. "You'll have to squeeze under the door. You can do that, can't you?"

He nodded tearfully.

"Run outside. As soon as you do, roll on the ground. Roll like a puppy would. Stop only when you're sure you're not burning. Okay?"

"Aren't you coming?"

"Yes, yes, now *go!*"

She shoved him, and he ran, wriggling into the triangular crevice like one of his rabbits. She heard a rip and his yike; the sickening smell of smoldering wool followed him over the threshold.

"Jamie!"

She heard him coughing on the other side.

"Jamie, I'm too big." With trembling fingers, she tore off her skirt and petticoat and tried to beat down the flames. "Get a bucket and wet down the door!"

"Okay. I'll be back!"

She barely heard his muffled cry above the roaring and crackling around her. Her sinuses burned; her throat felt like it had been scored by talons. She could hardly see the sky now—her sliver of freedom— through the boiling black haze. Wheezing, she tried to kick down the corner of the door that wasn't completely ablaze, but as the planks sagged lower, the walls crowded closer. She suspected that makeshift crossbeam was the only thing keeping the outer timbers from collapsing inward.

"Jamie!" Something crashed behind her—a shelf of watering bowls. She sobbed, slapping out the geyser of sparks that burned her sleeves and hair. The few feet left to her now weren't wide enough to swing her skirts. *Dear God, am I going to burn? Am I going to die before I can use my gifts—really use my gifts—and heal Michael?* "Jamie, hurry!"

"*Eden!*"

Michael galloped into the plumes of smoke, his heart wedged in his throat. Some sixth sense warned him she was in danger even before he saw the blood that led to Gunther's corpse.

"Doc!"

He recognized Jamie's voice, saw the boy struggling to haul a rusted water pail to the door.

"Miss Eden's stuck inside!"

*Merciful God.*

Instinct dissolved his next thought. Vaulting from the saddle, Michael grabbed Jamie's bucket, doused himself, and lunged for the hatchet that was jutting from the pine the boys had periodically hewn to thatch their roof. He could hear Eden's coughs above the roaring of the flames.

"Eden, stand back!"

"M-Michael?" Her throat sounded as raw as the fear that clawed his gut. "Michael, help me!"

He muttered a prayer and swung. The words came from nowhere, a catechism he'd long forgotten, a plea he'd stopped speaking, because every time he'd prayed, it had fallen on deaf ears.

"*. . . Deliver us from evil . . .*"

"Hurry!"

Her panic drove him harder, faster, hacking through flames and timbers to reach her on the other side. The heat scalded him through his damp clothes. Sweat stung his eyes; cinders sizzled on his flesh. He barely noticed. If she died, his life would be over, because she wasn't just the one true love of his heart. She was the bright, shining piece that was missing from his soul.

"Michael, the roof's caving in!"

"No!"

A lifetime—his own—flashed before his eyes. All the times he'd failed, all the times the Angel of Death had beaten him, paraded macabrely through his mind. In a flash of insight that made him sob, he realized the torment he'd caused himself had been misguided, even self-

ish. If Eden died this day, it was because God had called
her to Him with loving arms.

And nothing a husband or doctor might do could
keep her from that joyous reunion.

"Don't take her, God. Please, don't take her. I need
her more than you do. I want to start over, really start
over. She has so much to teach me . . ."

A shout rose behind him. Figures flitted like wraiths
through the hoary coil of clouds. From everywhere at
once, saddle blankets descended to smother the flames.
Dimly, he recognized Collie at his elbow, hammering a
gunstock against the door. A black-haired man with a
low-riding holster ran forward with a second hatchet,
while a man wearing a tin star shouted for water.

Iron bit into the blazing planks; wood chips and embers showered his shoulders. Between the combined
battering of hatchets and gun, the door split and finally
crashed, loosing a hail of sparks. Michael didn't wait
for Collie and Quaid to beat the flames to a less daunting height. He simply plunged over the threshold and
grabbed her.

A heartbeat later, the whole building collapsed, spitting tongues of flame like Chinese rockets.

She trembled against his wet length, coughing into
his shoulder. That she lived was an unquestionable miracle. He clutched her hard against his crashing heart—
hard enough to hold an indecisive spirit earthbound.
Blinking back the sting in his eyes, he carried her away
from the profane, away from the blood and sweat and
smoke that tainted the clearing. He took her as far as
the circle of trees would allow before he knelt to examine her, shrugging off his coat to shield her bloomers
from gawking deputies.

"Michael—"

"You're safe now," he choked, closing his ears to the shouts of the men who were struggling to keep the fire from spreading to the dogwoods and pines.

"But I have to tell you—"

The sight of tears streaking the ashes on her cheeks was his undoing. He kissed her hungrily, passionately, overwhelmed by the fierce, all-consuming need to make her want to live out her days as his one, his only, his wife.

He stopped only because she whimpered.

"Where are you hurt?" he rasped, running shaking hands over her arms, her spine, her legs.

"I'm not. Michael—"

"Your neck is burned," he muttered to himself, ignoring what was surely a brave but erroneous assessment. "And your hair is singed. I don't see any other damage to your head, thank God, although there appears to be a splinter in your—"

"*Michael!*"

He started.

"Listen to me."

The determination in her gaze made his gut clench. Fearing she would send him away, or worse, try to walk out of his life on her own, he mustered his best I'm-the-doctor glare. "We'll talk later. Right now, you're going to rest—"

"Doc!" Jamie ran up, panting. Soot smeared pink, raw patches of his skin where it peeked through shredded flannel and singed dungarees. "The sheriff's asking for you."

"The sheriff can wait. Your burns need to be salved. Get my valise. And the blanket in my saddlebags."

"Um . . . okay."

The boy ran off again, and Eden moistened her lips.

"I found Gunther. He's dead—"

"Sh. I saw."

"But he was shot. From behind."

*Murder.* Michael hardened his jaw.

"Do you think Collie—"

"God, I hope not."

Jamie dashed back with the valise and the blanket. To Michael's surprise, Eden struggled to her knees, knocking aside his hands while he tried to strip his wet coat away from her legs. She snatched the satchel from Jamie.

"Here." She shoved a tin of soft paraffin into Michael's hands as he tried to drape her with the blanket. "You salve Jamie. Then treat those blisters on your arms. I need to examine your head."

He frowned, refusing to believe he'd heard her correctly. "Let me worry about—"

"Turn around."

"Eden, you'll catch your death of—"

"Quit being a stubborn old billy goat!"

Jamie snickered. Goosebumps sprinkled Michael from his head to his toes. He didn't think the dampness of his clothing was to blame. The light in her eyes was a wonder to behold.

Stunned into silence, he bowed his head, kneeling meekly before her. A hundred questions circled, shrieking through his brain, as her nimble fingers probed and parted his hair. He wondered about Gunther. He wondered about the animals. He wondered what the devil Eden was doing pawing him at a time like this. The shack had dissolved into splinters. Distracted, he watched Quaid and Collie, Truitt and his men, beating the remains into a pile of smoldering ash. The leaves beneath Michael's knees were soggy; he suspected the only reason the trees hadn't lit like a bonfire was because they'd been thoroughly soaked the night before.

"So far so good," she muttered beside his ear. "I'm not finding anything."

"What—"

"*Shh!* Jamie, go find another blanket. Doc needs one, too."

The boy scampered into the clearing smoke, and Michael frowned.

"Would you mind telling me—"

"Michael Elijah Jones," she interrupted, "you are under *my* care now. And I'll ask the questions. Six months ago, after you were treating Jamie's crippled fawn, did you notice any insects crawling on you?"

He blinked at her. The avenging angel who'd faced down Claudia, Collie, and Sera on his behalf was now kneeling before him in all her charred and tattered glory. He couldn't remember her ever looking so beautiful. "I found a tick under my collar. But I assure you," he added hastily, "I took the proper precautions, and it's quite dead now ..." He frowned. Her eyes had grown positively luminous. "What?" he demanded again.

"And your illness mysteriously developed about a week later, didn't it?"

He stared hard into those triumphant jade pools before realization kicked him in the gut.

"Tick fever," he choked.

"Lucky for you, Talking Raven taught me how to cure it."

As hard as recognition hit him, understanding hit him harder. A tremor shook him to his bones.

"It's over now," she said softly, wrapping her arms around him. "You're not going to be an invalid. You haven't had the symptoms long enough for nerve damage to set in."

"But how did you—"

"Sera. When she found a tick on Vandy, I got the idea."

Michael squeezed his eyes closed. All this time, he'd never put two and two together. Nor had any of his university-educated colleagues. It had taken Eden, a woman who'd been trained by an Indian, a woman who studied nature instead of books, to trace his symptoms to their cause. And to think he'd been trying to convince her that her methods were outdated, inferior before new medical science. He hadn't been a goat, he'd been an ass!

*Gabriel, are you listening? If you are . . . thank you.*

"Jones!"

Michael tensed, recognizing Truitt's preemptive baritone.

"How's the missus?"

A barn-sized shadow fell across their bunker of leaves. Michael struggled for a semblance of professional courtesy. He and Eden had been on the verge of making peace; he wanted to capture the moment, not abandon it to play doctor. But a dead man was lying in the clearing. And God only knew how many others needed treatment for burns.

"I'm fine, sheriff," Eden said, her voice still hoarse. "Do your men need medical care?"

"She swallowed half a ton of smoke," he growled at his stubborn but adorable wife. "She needs bed rest."

"And you need to strip those wet clothes," she fired back.

Truitt's smile was fleeting. A large man, whose belly was exceeded only by his reputation as a deadeye, the lawman looked flushed, harried, and grim. "Sounds like you folks are back to normal. Jones, I need a word with you."

Michael muttered under his breath, but he rose, following Truitt to the center of the clearing, where two deputies, Collie, Jamie, Quaid, and Cassidy were gathered in a circle, staring at the blood-spattered blanket now draping Gunther. To Michael's consternation, Eden hugged her own blanket to her hips and followed.

"Now, Jamie's already told us," Truitt said, his spurs jingling as he walked, "that he and Mrs. Jones found the body sprawled across the doorstep when they were coming to feed the animals. Where were you?"

Michael resented the question. "Looking for Collie."

"You never found him, eh?"

Michael glanced uncertainly at the boy. Collie stood like a cornered wolf, his teeth bared, his shoulders tense and quaking. Arms akimbo, a deputy stood on either side of him. The man on Collie's left had confiscated his bowie knife and shotgun. Worry followed close on the heels of Michael's observation.

"I didn't shoot ol' Gunther," Collie snapped as the bull-necked sheriff halted before him.

"I'd like to believe you, son. But the truth is, you ain't been on good terms with Gunther."

"That don't mean I killed 'im."

Cassidy snorted. "Hell, sheriff. Gunther was madder than a wet hornet last night when I told him I found his stolen coons and hounds. I figure he rode up here and confronted the boy. When ol' Bert made like he was taking his rustled animals, MacAffee shot him in the back with that scattergun."

"That's Claudia's shotgun," Michael interceded.

"Where's Gunther's? He never rode anywhere without it."

"I never saw a shotgun," Eden said uneasily. "Or anyone in the clearing, for that matter."

"That's 'cause the boy had already hotfooted it down the mountain, ma'am," Cassidy said glibly. " 'Fore you rode up, he probably plugged ol' Bert, made that gun his own, then set the shack on fire to hide the evidence—"

"That's ridiculous," Eden flared. "Collie would never harm the animals. He was trying to *save* them from Gunther and the so-called gentlemen who liked to ride out to the compound each night and wager on which bunnies and coons the hounds would tear to shreds first."

Truitt cleared his throat. The deputies both fidgeted.

"No offense, ma'am," Cassidy said, spreading his hands in a placating gesture. "But it ain't any secret you've been trying to steer MacAffee down the straight and narrow. A fine lady like yourself can't be blamed if the boy turns plumb loco and sets out to sin."

Michael tossed a narrow glance at Cassidy's pinto, grazing near Brutus. The usual rifle jutted from the Texican's saddle boot. A battered shotgun was also strapped between his saddlebags. "And just what brings *you* to this clearing, Cassidy?"

Cassidy shrugged. "Same as you, I reckon. Saw the fire. Came to investigate."

"Yeah? You got here awfully fast. I don't suppose you have an alibi for your whereabouts this morning."

Cassidy arched a tawny brow. "Sorry to disappoint you, Doc. Me and Jesse were out yonder, fishing for breakfast." He smirked. "Shoot. You hurt my feelings tryin' to finger me that way. And here I thought we were almost family."

Michael might have lunged for the bastard's throat if three lawmen hadn't been standing in their circle.

"The fact is," Truitt said in dire tones, "it's the boy who's got motive." He addressed Collie again. "Claiming you didn't shoot Gunther ain't good enough. You need a witness. Where were you all morning?"

"I told you. In the cave by Yaller Ridge."

"Doin' what?"

"Sleepin'!"

A match hissed and flared to life. All eyes turned to Quaid. The Texican bent his head, puffing his cigarette against the flame he shielded in his hand. Unlike Cassidy, who looked like he'd recently scrubbed in the stream, Quaid's face was blackened by soot; the burns on his forearms were blistering. Parts of his shirt had been singed off; a gash trickled blood at his knee. Michael remembered how the outlaw had fought beside him, hacking at the door to free Eden. He remembered, too, that Quaid was sweet on his wife. The knowledge didn't make Michael any less suspicious. Whoever had started that fire had needed a matchsafe.

Quaid raised his head, his eyes squinting faintly from the smoke he'd exhaled. "You aren't thinking straight, MacAffee," he said casually. "You weren't sleeping all morning. Fact is, you were fishing earlier in that river below the ridge. Must've been about seven o'clock. I remember real clear, 'cause the smell of your campfire was making me hungry. Billy and me climbed the ridge and saw you filleting a trout bigger than my arm. Shoot. Don't you remember sharing a smoke with us 'round 'bout seven-thirty?"

Truitt's doubtful gaze darted between Collie and

Quaid. Michael noticed that Cassidy's neck had reddened.

"Is that true, son?" Truitt demanded.

Collie's chest heaved. For an unsettling moment, he scowled at his only alibi.

"I reckon," he said tersely.

"Michael, isn't Yellow Ridge about a half hour's ride from here?" Eden interjected hastily. "Jamie and I have been in this clearing since at least eight o'clock. And we heard the gun blast a good ten minutes before that."

Michael jumped on Eden's cue. "Collie travels on foot," he reminded the sheriff. "Even if he was smoking with Quaid as early as seven fifteen, he would have needed a horse to get here and kill Gunther before Eden arrived."

"*If* he was smoking with Quaid," Truitt repeated darkly. "I ain't convinced. Quaid, hand me your holster. You, too, Cassidy. I got more questions, but you're gonna want a lawyer before you answer 'em."

Cassidy shot Quaid a daggerlike glare.

"Collie, you're riding back to town with me and the deputies," Truitt continued. If he'd noticed the tension between the two Texicans, he didn't let on. "Jones, you, Jamie, and the missus are free to go."

A wide-eyed, shivering Jamie slid under Eden's arm. She glanced uneasily at Michael. "Sheriff, we want to come with Collie. We . . . well, we feel responsible for him."

Michael shook his head at her. "You, madam, are likely to collapse before you set foot in a stirrup. I'm taking you home. Jamie, too."

Her chin shot up, and her eyes flashed green fire, but he cut her off before she could assert her independence and insist, as she had in her letter, that she was leaving him. "The sooner I'm convinced you and Jamie are safe," he said in a fierce undertone, "the sooner I can get my attorney to speak Collie's case."

She hesitated, and he pressed his advantage. "Do me this favor, Eden. I would speak with you further but"—his gaze flickered to Collie—"this isn't the time."

She pressed her lips together. Reluctance was etched into every line of her face. As exhausted as she was, she still had the gumption to fight. He suspected he was going to have a devil of a time convincing her to come home to him again—unless he threw her over his shoulder and carried her there.

The prospect was appealingly primitive.

He caught her elbow and turned her toward Brutus.

"I'm perfectly capable of riding my own horse," she whispered hotly.

"As much as you like to contest the issue, I'm still your husband. Your doctor, too. Might we call a truce long enough to clear Collie of this murder charge?"

Impossibly long lashes fanned down over rebellious jade eyes. "He didn't do it, Michael."

"I know," he said more gently. He watched as a deputy removed the firearms from Cassidy's horse. "The trouble is, we have to prove it."

# Chapter 16

Three days had passed since the fire. Seventy-two hours of bed rest and pampering, as ordained by her husband.

Eden was going nuts.

Thank God for small miracles. With the echo of the doorbell still chiming through the hall, Eden threw back her quilt and eased a furtive foot off the bed. Much to her consternation, Stazzie woke up on the nightstand, sweeping her tail across the tray of medicines Michael had abandoned to greet their visitor. His bottle of horse-sized pills clattered to the floor.

"Shh!" Eden hissed as her furry jailor leaped to the creaking mattress. Stazzie had been Michael's ammunition for the bed-rest order. That he conveniently believed now, after weeks of skepticism, that Stazzie really did have the uncanny ability to sniff out sick people, annoyed Eden to no end. The pirate in him had all but marooned her on their four-poster bed. She'd been limited to ten-minute visits from relatives—to rest her voice, he'd claimed—and he'd insisted on preparing all her meals himself. She wouldn't have minded if his chicken broth weren't so bland. Michael, bless his heart, was a better doctor than a cook.

Fortunately Sera, her dearest, most loyal friend in the world, had stashed a box of saltwater taffy under the cushions of the windowseat. Claudia had brought it as a get-well gift; little had Auntie realized that Michael the Marshal would confiscate it at the door. Returning from the railroad ticket office with his one-way pass to Colorado, Rafe had overheard their argument, decided to join Sera in some sibling mischief, and had developed a make-believe pain. He'd distracted Michael with it while Sera sneaked the candy upstairs.

Eden smirked, tiptoeing to the windowseat to rummage behind its pillows.

If Michael ever found out, he would spin her horror stories about tooth decay. Honestly, the way he fussed over her health, one would have thought she was riddled with disease. He somehow had lost sight of the fact that *he* was the one in need of a cure. She'd had to threaten to lace Talking Raven's echinacea recipe with turnip juice just to make him crawl in bed and rest. But thanks to the blood-cleansing herbs, his symptoms had disappeared overnight. He'd confessed he felt more vigorous than he had in months. And he'd used this admission as his excuse to ignore her bed-rest order.

Maybe it was too much to hope that her triumphant tick-fever diagnosis would make Michael completely embrace her medical opinions.

Then again, while they'd hotly debated the cures for dyspepsia the previous night, he'd stopped himself, cleared his throat, and gruffly conceded that under certain conditions, peppermint or valerian might prove as effective as citrate of magnesia. Surprised by this about-face, she'd demanded to know what had made him change his position. To her amusement—and her complete mystification—he'd muttered something about billygoats and changed the subject.

Grinning at the memory, Eden unwrapped a piece of taffy. It was nice to know her husband no longer considered her a quack who tossed herbal salads.

It was even nicer to know that the use of her intuition didn't make her a medical menace, as she'd once thought.

Of course, adopting some of Michael's methods to complement her hunches and herbs hadn't hurt any. He'd taught her a thing or two about ointment rubbing that would go down in medical infamy. She was almost sorry his burns were healing—hers, too. Her husband could make the application of salve almost as erotic as . . . well, a certain memory she cherished about whipping cream.

A wistful sigh escaped her lips.

Vandy scrambled out of Michael's footlocker. Apparently the coon had spied a human playmate, one who was handling food, in neutral territory. Vandy had learned to suffer Stazzie's company, and vice versa, as long as they avoided each other's space. The coon had claimed the pantry. The cat had claimed the bed.

Now Vandy, reeking of pennyroyal, galloped across the carpet in a ripple of silvery brown. Eden didn't have long to slam down the lid of the taffy box and stuff a piece of candy into her mouth before the coon heaved himself onto the windowseat.

"Why don't you see who our visitor is?" she mumbled between chews.

Vandy whickered indignantly as she shoved him back to the carpet.

"Maybe it's Collie," she added as much for his benefit

as her own. It galled her that the boy still hadn't been released from jail. She, Michael, Claudia, Sera—all of them had been waiting anxiously for some development in the murder investigation. With the county judge riding the court circuit for another two weeks, no authority in town could keep Truitt from doing his inquiry the way he liked to do it: leisurely. He'd thrown his three suspects in a holding cell rather than risk loosing a murderer on the streets. Michael's attorney, along with Cassidy's and Quaid's, had screamed until they were blue in the face about their clients' Constitutional rights; Truitt had only threatened to lock up the lawyers, too.

Eden had to admit, Truitt the Tyrant, as Sera had publicly lambasted him, had impressed her with his concern for his constituents' safety. Silverton's sheriff hadn't been half as interested in justice.

Even so, Truitt had no right to act above the law. And he certainly had no right to act out his prejudices at Collie's expense. Eden and Michael both suspected that the sheriff had locked up Collie not because Truitt believed he'd committed murder, but because Truitt believed Collie would follow in his father's footsteps if some tinstar didn't put the fear of God in him. Rustling, Truitt had pointed out grimly, was a hanging offense in some states.

So Collie was being punished even though Gunther wasn't alive and had no heirs to press charges. Michael's lawyer had protested vociferously, pointing to Collie's sworn statement that he'd overheard Cassidy and Quaid plotting to beat him, use Sera, recover stolen bullion, and stop Gunther's card sharping days for good. Truitt hadn't been impressed.

Meanwhile, the Texicans had both denied Collie's accusations. Cassidy, as usual, had been the most vocal, accusing the boy of "cooking up some cock-and-bull tale" to pin the murder charge on him.

"A blind man can see that son of a weasel's got a hankering for my Sera," Cassidy had been quoted in Blue Thunder's newspaper. "Why, MacAffee's trying to get me hanged so I can't marry her!"

Needless to say, Sera was furious with Collie and beside herself with worry over Cassidy.

Eden just hoped Sera wouldn't do anything more foolish than carry picnic hampers to the jail twice a day. Rafe had said he wasn't concerned about Sera as long as Cassidy stayed behind bars. Even Michael had conceded that Sera had sense enough to realize that *someone* in that jail had killed Berthold Gunther.

Eden wondered. Was that someone Jesse Quaid?

Despite the rumors, she didn't want to believe that a man who'd touched her so tenderly, a man who'd appeared in the nick of time to help Michael and Collie chop her free of the shack, could be a cold-blooded killer.

And yet, she knew Collie hadn't murdered Gunther. And Sera knew Cassidy hadn't.

That didn't leave any more suspects.

Eden sighed, unwrapping another piece of candy. Was there anyone in the world who cared enough about Jesse Quaid to believe in his innocence?

*Uh-oh.* The front door slammed. Eden glimpsed a derbyed gentleman descending the porch steps and strolling back toward the street. Gulping, she plumped the windowseat's pillows and dashed on silent feet across the room. Unfortunately, she tripped over the hem of her bridal nightdress, dropping one of the taffy wrappers under Vandy's nose.

"No!" she whispered fiercely, lunging after the coon.

Undaunted, he snatched up the prize and dashed under the armoire.

Meanwhile, Michael's footfalls echoed in the stairwell.

She muttered an oath and dived into bed. She barely had time to smooth the coverlets and flip open the *Godey's Lady's Book* Rafe had so thoughtfully provided before the door swung open, and she was greeted by her husband.

He folded his muscular arms and propped his shoulder against the jamb. He was a breathtaking sight, the man she'd married. Her heart still did a dizzy little dance whenever she gazed on his ruggedly handsome face, on his powerful chest and corded thighs, and the perfectly flat abdomen that stretched between the two. He wore no coat or vest today, just the linen shirt, unbuttoned at the throat so that the coal-black hairs peeked through, his sleeves rolled to display his bunching biceps. She had to admit, she liked looking at her husband almost as much as she liked undressing him. But nothing, *nothing*, could compare to Michael's touch.

*I suppose convalescing does have that advantage.*

She tried to appear innocent. Nonchalant. He'd have none of it.

"I believe I heard tiptoeing up here," he drawled. "Those footsteps wouldn't have been coming from this room, would they?"

"Absolutely not."

"And the taffy wrapper Vandy's chewing?"

Her face warmed. "Good heavens. Wherever did he get that?"

Michael's dimples peeked, even though he tried to look stern as he closed the door and crossed to their bed. "You're supposed to ingest your medicine on an empty stomach."

"Have I told you you're a tyrant?"

"Quite regularly."

"Has it sunk in yet?"

His lips twitched. "You're a terrible patient."

"Now there's the pot calling the kettle black. Perhaps you should find some other poor, unsuspecting patient to bully."

"Oh no. You're all the torment I can handle."

"Michael Jones"—she rolled her magazine and smacked him on the knee—"that's a horrible thing to say to your wife!"

"Hmm." He sat beside her on the bed, displacing a disgruntled Stazzie. "Does that mean you plan to stay for a while?"

Her laughter died in her throat. He was serious. Beneath the playful manner, he was still deathly afraid she would walk out his door and never return. She'd tried to reassure him, of course, but he'd sensed she was hiding something and, unfortunately, he'd been right. Professional ethics and personal honor had kept her from confessing that on the day she'd walked out his door, her deepest fear had been that Michael had fathered Bonnie's child. Luckily, Jamie had leaked the news yesterday that Bonnie had finally agreed to marry Luke. Eden hoped that meant Bonnie had decided to bear her—their?—baby.

"Oh, Michael." She stroked his jaw, and evening stubble pricked her fingertips. "I told you I was home to stay."

He kissed her palm, pressing it fervently to his chest. "I hope so, Eden. We've been given a second chance. And this time, I want to do it right."

The sincerity in his voice tugged at her in a way no apology ever could. She knew he spoke from the heart. They'd taken the last seventy-two hours to rediscover one another, to understand each other's needs and feelings. Now that he was rested, without the burden of secrets and illness to weigh him down, she'd learned he was a bit of a chess sharper. That Ancient Greece and modern-day steam engines fascinated him. And that he was enormously gifted as a craftsman. He'd carved, from memory, a miniature wooden bust of her father, complete with stethoscope, spectacles, and thinning hair. When she'd unwrapped his gift, she'd cried, recognizing Papa's likeness instantly.

"My dearest love," she whispered. "I just want you to be happy. That's all I've ever wanted. To see you well and joyful."

"Then you know what's in my heart, Eden. Because that's all I want for you."

A tear slipped down her cheek. "I'm sorry I hurt you, Michael."

He caught the droplet on his thumb. For a moment, those sapphire-blue depths misted over. She couldn't bear to know her letter had caused him so much pain.

"I love you," he said huskily. "The rest is behind us."

He swam before her in a rainbow of tears. In the last three days, their marriage had been reborn. He'd become more than her hero, more than her husband; he'd become her friend. He'd encouraged her to tell him what she envisioned for their future. She'd spoken shyly of her newfound hope that they might travel beyond Blue Thunder, healing the sick and restoring their faith in medicine-show doctors. He'd conceded that with Claudia to watch over Sera—and Collie to watch over Claudia—such a lifestyle might be possible. But only, he'd added, until their first child was born. She'd been delighted to know that he wanted babies as much as she did; in truth, the way she pined for even his most innocent caress, she suspected their traveling days would be short-lived.

"Aren't you going to ask me who was at the door?" he murmured, that sensual, off-center smile she so loved flirting with his mouth.

"Well . . ." She couldn't quite hide her own smile. His manner suggested mischief. "Do I want to know?"

"Most definitely."

"Who, then?"

"Lydia Witherspoon's brother," he drawled, tugging gently on the ribbons that tied her bodice. "William's an alternate judge for the county court circuit. Lydia pulled a few sisterly strings, I'll wager, but Edward agreed to hear Collie's case. Once he listened to the testimonies, however . . ." Michael's smile turned Cheshire cat–like. "He released Collie from jail and reprimanded Truitt."

"Thank God," Eden whispered.

"There's more."

"Th-there is?" Her pulse quickened as the lace of her gown parted like petals beneath his fingers.

"Apparently Edward suffers from palpitations. He's eager to sample your heart tonic. So is my colleague, Dr. H. C. F. Meyer. No doubt you've heard of Lloyd Brothers of Cincinnati?"

Eden nodded, mystified. The Lloyds owned a well-respected pharmaceutical company.

"Well, I wrote Doc Meyer several weeks ago, because I respect his opinion. I asked for his advice about your father's remedies. Meyer frequented numerous Indian reservations in his early years, and he is rumored to use their recipes in his medical practice. While you were entertaining Sera earlier tonight, his response arrived. You know what he wrote?"

She shook her head, anticipation shortening her breaths as he peeled a panel of lace off her breast.

"He wrote that the Lloyd Brothers paid him a small fortune to distribute an echinacea recipe, one which he got from the Sioux. Apparently, it's not like typical nostrums. This patent medicine really works."

"You mean like Talking Raven's?" she teased him gently.

"Er . . . yes." His ears pinkened in the most endearing way. "I think we should mix a fresh batch of your father's heart tonic and visit the Lloyd Brothers in Cincinnati—by way of a certain Louisville hotel we know."

His smoky innuendo wasn't lost on her.

"A splendid idea," she said breathlessly. "When do we leave?"

"When you're feeling up to it."

She groaned inwardly, hard-pressed not to make a face. "Michael, I've *told* you. I'm perfectly well enough to leave this bed."

"Are you sure?" he purred.

"Quite sure."

His eyes slitted, gleaming twilight-blue as her gown at last fell away. "Perhaps I'm not being persuasive enough."

When his head lowered, a delicious shiver tiptoed down her spine. It was hard to think of protests, much less to speak them, when the moist heat of his mouth fastened on her breast. Sighing, she let her head drift back; she let his calloused hands stoke the hunger that only seemed to smolder, never bank, when he was near. She loved the way he kissed her, loved the way he touched, and when he pressed her down, she sank eagerly, reveling in the hardness of belted ribs and corded sinews against her softest places. His throaty growl of pleasure made her female parts yearn. Stripping off his clothes, she mapped his beloved ridges and contours with reverent hands, as if she were beholding him for the first time. She would never forget—could never forget—how casually death had knocked at their door.

"Promise me, Michael," she whispered against his lips. "Promise me no matter what we may face, you'll make each moment worth living."

He raised his head, and the love that poured from his eyes was like sunshine to her soul. "I can promise," he said huskily, "because you've taught me how."

He loved her until they knew the sweetest rapture, the tenderest bliss. She marveled that each joining could be better than the last. To know him so deeply, so intimately, had been her most cherished hope and yet, she had never dared to dream their romance could be as wonderful as this.

She snuggled against his chest as he tucked the quilt around her.

"Will you marry me?" he whispered against her hair.

She blinked, tilting her head back, surprised by his question in the most heart-stirring way. "I thought we already were."

"I never got to ask you. Not the way I always wanted to."

His confession almost made her cry again.

"Yes," she murmured, her chest swelling beyond the bounds of every feeling she'd every known. "I will marry you. For better or worse, for richer or poorer—"

"Till death parts us not."

"Oh, Michael. Can heaven really be better than this?"

Starlight feathered over his beloved features. Half man, half angel, and completely hers, he smiled.

"That's a tough question to answer when I'm holding Eden in my arms. Why don't you ask me again in a couple billion years?"

# Avon Romantic Treasures

*Unforgettable, enthralling love stories,*
*sparkling with passion and adventure*
*from Romance's bestselling authors*

# Nationally Bestselling Author
# CHRISTINA DODD

"Christina Dodd is everything
I'm looking for in an author."
Teresa Medeiros

## The Governess Bride series

## RULES OF ENGAGEMENT
0-380-81198-7/$6.99 US/$9.99 Can

## RULES OF SURRENDER
0-380-81197-9/$6.99 US/$9.99 Can

## And Don't Miss

RUNAWAY PRINCESS
SCOTTISH BRIDES
(with Stephanie Laurens,
Julia Quinn, and Karen Ranney)
SOMEDAY MY PRINCE
THAT SCANDALOUS EVENING
A WELL FAVORED GENTLEMAN
A WELL PLEASURED LADY
CANDLE IN THE WINDOW
CASTLES IN THE AIR
THE GREATEST LOVER IN ALL ENGLAND
A KNIGHT TO REMEMBER
MOVE HEAVEN AND EARTH
ONCE A KNIGHT
OUTRAGEOUS
TREASURE IN THE SUN

# America Loves Lindsey!
## The Timeless Romances
## of #1 Bestselling Author

| | |
|---|---|
| **KEEPER OF THE HEART** | 0-380-77493-3/$6.99 US/$8.99 Can |
| **THE MAGIC OF YOU** | 0-380-75629-3/$6.99 US/$8.99 Can |
| **ANGEL** | 0-380-75628-5/$6.99 US/$9.99 Can |
| **PRISONER OF MY DESIRE** | 0-380-75627-7/$6.99 US/$8.99 Can |
| **ONCE A PRINCESS** | 0-380-75625-0/$6.99 US/$8.99 Can |
| **WARRIOR'S WOMAN** | 0-380-75301-4/$6.99 US/$8.99 Can |
| **MAN OF MY DREAMS** | 0-380-75626-9/$6.99 US/$8.99 Can |
| **SURRENDER MY LOVE** | 0-380-76256-0/$6.50 US/$7.50 Can |
| **YOU BELONG TO ME** | 0-380-76258-7/$6.99 US/$8.99 Can |
| **UNTIL FOREVER** | 0-380-76259-5/$6.50 US/$8.50 Can |
| **LOVE ME FOREVER** | 0-380-72570-3/$6.99 US/$8.99 Can |
| **SAY YOU LOVE ME** | 0-380-72571-1/$6.99 US/$8.99 Can |
| **ALL I NEED IS YOU** | 0-380-76260-9/$6.99 US/$8.99 Can |
| **THE PRESENT** | 0-380-80438-7/$6.99 US/$9.99 Can |
| **JOINING** | 0-380-79333-4/$7.50 US/$9.99 Can |

## And in hardcover
### THE HEIR
0-380-97536-X/$24.00 US/$36.50 Can